Two New Family Members . . .

Pat had mixed some powdered milk in a bottle and fastened one of Skip's gloves over the top of the bottle with a rubber band. Now she was snipping off the end of one of the glove's fingers.

Jenny and Toby rolled over the floor with the cubs.

"They keep licking my face," Jenny giggled.

"That's 'cause you look like their mother," Toby said.

"And you look like their father," Jenny answered.

"What are you going to call them?" Skip asked.

"We already decided," Jenny said. "The black one is Blackie. The one with the ring around his neck is Ringo."

"Well," Pat shook the bottle, "let's see if this thing works. Blackie and Ringo will have to be the judges."

The Adventures of the Wilderness Family

Adapted by Martin Quinn

from a screenplay by
Stewart Rafill

Story by
Arthur R. Dubs

BALLANTINE BOOKS · NEW YORK

ISBN 0-345-25561-5-150

Manufactured in the United States of America

First Edition: September 1976

The Adventures
of the
Wilderness Family

Chapter One
The City

On high steel beams twenty stories above the streets of Los Angeles, Skip Robinson pushed up his welding mask and looked down at the streaming traffic below him. Even here he could smell the car fumes drifting upward and mixing with the smog that hung like a dome of doom over the city.

"Hey, Skip! You with me?"

Joe Bear, a Mohawk Indian, was, unlike his name, a thin, wiry man who moved nimbly among the open beams. He was foreman of the construction crew, and also Skip's friend.

"Thinking about that raise, huh?" Joe squatted beside Skip. "Well, you deserve it." The pounding of a jackhammer cut him off, and he waited until the racket subsided slightly. "You're the best man I have—even if you're not Indian!"

"No," Skip shook his head, "I wasn't thinking about that. I was"—a hint of embarrassment slipped into his voice—"remembering what we talked about."

"Camping? Sure, at the end of summer we can take a week off. We'll take our kids, too."

"Well, I was thinking about *more* than just camping . . ."

The jackhammer started up again; then a second hammer, two stories below. Overhead, a cement mixer

1

added to the racket. It was too much for Skip. He gave up trying to talk, and turned back to work.

"Later," Joe shouted, and moved on to check with other men of his crew.

The building they were putting up was thirty stories high. Construction was Skip Robinson's job and he was good at it. The pay raise said so, and he should have been happy. Thirty-three years old, with two children and a lovely wife, this curly-brown-haired, dark-eyed man had muscles and calluses from a lifetime of athletics and hard work. Other friends had gone on to desk jobs. Skip had always preferred work that used his body.

But when he pulled his welding mask over his face these days, Skip started thinking. Dreaming, to be honest. Dreaming that concrete gray could be forest green, and that the freon-cooled blast of an air conditioner could be a fresh mountain breeze. In the middle of a bus ride, or while seeing a movie, or when he was slamming one more rivet into steel, the dream would come! Skip would continue doing what he was supposed to be doing, but he would be seeing canyons of clean rock, water that reflected a pure sky, walls of high green pines . . . When the dream got too strong, he would force himself to return to the reality of noise, dust, car exhausts, and jackhammers—and tell himself to grow up.

The lunch horn sounded.

The men hastily opened their food boxes or collected at a sandwich truck that had been run up to the story now being completed. Skip ate an apple and rode the elevator down to the ground. He didn't have time for a sandwich or lunchtime banter. He was headed for the doctor's office, twelve blocks away.

Skip could have taken a bus, but he was too anxious and worried to sit for the ride. Besides, he liked to walk —even if it was through the litter of newspapers, gum wrappers, and beer cans that garnished the sidewalk. *Where does all the trash come from?* he asked himself.

There were recycling centers in town, but the city turned every box, wrapper, carton, or can into a tidal wave of waste.

When Skip reached Dr. Ian Miller's, he found his son, Toby, in the waiting room, thumbing and frowning his way through a medical report on air pollution. Toby was an eight-year-old miniature of his father, his hair a bit shaggier and his cheeks full of freckles.

"How you doin', Toby?" Skip patted his son's shoulder. His hand covered nearly half of Toby's back.

"I'm okay," Toby asserted. "Mom and Jenny are in there." He shot a glance toward a set of double doors.

Skip strode over to the examination room, knocked, and went in. He smiled at the doctor.

Pat, his wife, stood by the scale, anxiously watching her daughter. Pat had long blond hair, which glimmered even under the glare of the fluorescent lights, and blue eyes. But more than that, she possessed a simple, natural beauty—"the inner peace," as Joe Bear described it—that made people want to be around her. That inner peace was pretty well strained right now, Skip saw. He took her hand as he came up beside her.

Jenny sat on the white examining table. At eleven, she already had Pat's looks and gentle soul. Stripped to the waist, goose bumps on her arms, Jenny was little more than a frightened kid at the moment. From the other side of the table, Dr. Miller listened to her lungs through a stethoscope. *He wouldn't have needed a stethoscope last night,* Skip thought. Then her breathing had sounded like a rasping file.

"Breathe in. Hold it!" the doctor said mechanically.

Jenny inhaled, holding her breath with the ease of long practice. The doctor shifted the 'scope from one side of her back to the other. "Breathe out," Jenny mouthed silently.

"Breathe out," Dr. Miller said.

Skip smiled. *Thatta girl!* he thought.

"Hi, Dad!" Jenny chirped.

"Breathe in, don't talk."

Jenny wrinkled her nose at the doctor, but inhaled again. Skip noticed that Pat was biting on her lower lip. He lovingly squeezed her hand.

"Everything seems to be there." Dr. Miller removed the stethoscope from his ears.

"I *knew* it!" Jenny said victoriously.

"But"—the doctor stepped to his cabinet and selected a large syringe—"we should take some more blood samples."

The eleven-year-old's face fell. "Oh, no, not more! Dad, you said they wouldn't take any more."

Skip swore at himself for having been so optimistic.

"If Dr. Miller says so, Jenny . . ." His heart went out to her.

Jenny suffered the needle silently. She never cried or pouted once the operation began, and to Skip and Pat that always made it worse. *How many times,* he asked himself, *have we gone through the same scene? And how many times more?*

"Okay, Jenny." The doctor put the full syringe aside. "You get your shirt back on and go on out with Toby. I'm going to talk to your parents."

Pat kissed Jenny on the cheek. Jenny stared at the Band-Aid on her arm.

In his office, a few minutes later, Dr. Miller sorted wearily through laboratory reports. Skip and Pat sat tensely, facing the desk.

"Why more blood? What about all this medication and treatment she's been taking for the past year?" Skip began to protest.

Ian Miller sighed. "It only keeps it under control. It's—"

"Control!" Skip got mad. "She's been getting worse, Doc!"

"There must be *something* we can do," Pat suggested hopefully.

"All we can do is run more tests. Allergies are very frustrating problems. They can produce no more than a sniffle or a rash, or they can be very serious. They can be produced by any of a million things. Pollen. A particular fruit. Animal hair."

"We've gone through all the tests," said Skip.

"All the *standard* tests. Now we have to make up new ones for Jenny. It could be pollution in the air, chemicals in the water supply. There are half a dozen different chemicals in every item of food on the supermarket shelves. It could even be the pressure of living in the city. That's not unknown."

"This is where Skip works," Pat broke in. "This is our home."

"I know." Dr. Miller held up his hands. "And we'll keep working on this. She's a lovely girl . . . and we'll keep trying."

"What if she has another attack like last night?" Skip inquired.

"You have my home phone number. Call me."

Skip and Pat collected the kids on the way out. From a *National Geographic,* Jenny was making a good show of reading about pandas to Toby, but her parents did some reading of their own in the pallor of her skin.

"We're going to have to make a decision," Skip whispered to Pat.

"A decision about what?"

"Can you pick me up after work today? Bring the kids. We'll go out to eat."

"Sure, Skip." But Pat was a bit puzzled.

He had to jog back to the work site to beat the one o'clock horn. High on a scaffold minutes later, Skip connected acetylene and oxygen tanks to a welding gun, pulled his heavy mask over his head, and directed a blue-white flame against a girder. Sparks flew.

No afternoon ever passed more slowly.

What the doctor had been talking about, Skip thought, was poison. Something, somewhere in the city was poisoning Jenny. It could be what she breathed, or ate, or even felt in the pressure of growing up in the echoes of police sirens and shrieking automobile brakes. Even the medicine she took was a kind of poison. It stopped the attacks but left her listless and dull, the opposite of the girl she naturally was. His job? Their home? What were they for, if not to let Jenny grow up healthy and happy? Otherwise they were worth nothing.

And Toby . . . He suffered in a secondary way. At a time when the boy needed attention, all his parents' attention went to Jenny. Skip and Pat tried to be fair, but their concentration was always half on Jenny's breathing.

And Pat . . . Before marrying Skip, she'd had a successful career of her own, designing dresses for elegant shops in the Los Angeles area. Since the kids had come, she'd worked less and less; and since Jenny's condition became apparent, Pat was too worried to do any work at all except housekeeping and cooking. At the time of their marriage, Skip had promised her a chance to continue to do the creative designing she wanted, not because it was a pretty promise to make but because he had fully believed he could give her that opportunity.

Skip looked past whirling sparks to the gray dome of smog that sat on top of the city. There had to be something else. Someplace else. A city was supposed to exist for people. Instead, the city was choking them and stunting them—and what was *he* doing but adding one more tower to its already oppressive skyline?

"Hey, Skip!" Joe Bear yelled over the growling of a cement mixer. "You're off somewhere again."

Skip lifted his mask.

"You know, Joe, you're right. I am."

Chapter Two

"We're Getting Out!"

Pat moved over as Skip crawled behind the steering wheel of the pickup truck. Jenny and Toby were in the back with Crust, a yellow Labrador bigger than either kid but with an image of himself as an elite, bonbon-eating lapdog.

"You brought Crust? I wanted to take us to someplace *nice* to eat." He put the truck in gear.

"The kids wanted to bring Crust. He makes Jenny happy."

"He makes me happy, too. He just doesn't make restaurants happy."

Pat's smile broke into a laugh.

"All Crust asks is no pickle in his hamburgers."

"Two hamburgers again?"

"He's a growing dog."

"If he grows any more, we're going to have to get a bigger truck."

"No, he wants one for himself."

They both laughed. Skip put his arm around his wife, pulled her close, and kissed her. As always, he felt his tension draining away. She was half his strength—about the right proportion, it seemed to Skip.

They feasted on hamburgers, fries, and shakes at an

outdoor restaurant off the freeway. Skip had chosen the place because it had a garden for Toby and Jenny to play with Crust in while he and Pat talked.

"It's such a big move . . ." Pat studied her coffee.

"I know. But we always talked about it. It's what we always planned to do, Pat."

"Yes, but when the children were older. Or maybe for summers, when they were out of school. I mean, everyone *dreams* about doing that sort of thing. I guess I just took it *that* way."

"It doesn't have to be just a dream. If there's anything I'm good at, it's building things. And I've gone hunting all my life. We can do it!"

"The money, Skip." She looked up. "We don't have that much in savings. And we certainly aren't going to be making any out there! What about the cost of Jenny's treatments?"

"She won't need any out there. We won't need money for food or clothes. We'll grow what we need, and you'll make clothes that'll knock the squirrels' eyes out."

"But the cost of the land . . ."

"We'll use the savings, and sell our house and the truck. Pat, this is our chance to break away."

Pat brushed some of her blond hair back from her shoulder. Skip studied his wife, and her attractive sports blouse and skirt. She had the ability to make the most ordinary clothes seem beautiful.

"It's just such a big decision, Skip."

"Yes. But staying here is another kind of decision, and it's just as big. Should we stay here, locked into a filthy city, working for other people instead of ourselves, and waiting for the doctors to come up with a cure for Jenny? Or, do we take hold of our lives and make them the kind we want? I won't kid you. It won't be easy. We won't be able to depend on other people and there won't be any phone to call Dr. Miller on. It'll be uncomfortable as hell, to start with."

"That's putting it mildly," Pat made a wry smile.

"Right. And we'll miss our friends. And I know

we're going to be scared sometimes. What happens if one of us gets hurt? Or Jenny has worse attacks up there? I've thought of all of that and I can't make any promises. Maybe we *would* end up dragging ourselves back to the city, broke, without a home or a car. But the time comes when you have to try to take your life and make something of it to suit you. It's a chance."

"You mean, a challenge."

"Well, you can put it that way, too."

"I put it that way because I know you, Skip. As soon as you start thinking of something as a challenge, you think you have to accept it." Pat fell silent. Her eyes swung to the garden, where Jenny and Toby rolled over the artificial grass with Crust. "You want me to shut up, Skip?"

"No. It has to be half your decision, too. You have to want it as much as *I* do, or it'll never work. Not to mention the fact that I love you."

Skip paid the bill while the kids climbed back into the rear of the truck. Pat was smiling when Skip swung up into the seat beside her.

"You know what you are?" she teased. "You're nothing but an old romantic."

"Yeah?"

Skip eased out of the parking lot and accelerated into freeway traffic. Twenty miles of cars stretched in front and behind. Skip turned his head away from the cars when Pat kissed his ear.

"Let's take the chance," she said. "Let's do it!"

"You're serious . . . ?" He couldn't hold back the grin that started spreading across his face.

"It's worth a try," she said decisively.

"It's worth a try," he agreed.

Eight lanes of freeway rushed north. Skip took the first exit ramp he got to, coasted to a red light, and threw out his arms.

"We're getting out!" he shouted.

He hugged Pat. In the back of the truck, Crust barked and Jenny and Toby laughed.

"We're getting out!" Pat smiled and cried at the same time.

Jenny, and then Toby, echoed a call they still did not know the significance of. As the light changed to green, the cars behind started honking. For one family on the road, the horns could have been a thousand miles away.

"We're getting out!"

Chapter Three

The High Country

The peaks of the Rocky Mountains seemed to rise up and try to touch the aquaplane that skirted their crests. Here and there, deep valleys still held late-winter snow, but on the slopes wide stretches of green led to endless forests of spruce, aspen, and fir. There was not a sign of a house, not a single plume of smoke to smudge the clear blue of the sky, not a car or even a road. This was the high country. Wilderness.

For two months, the Robinsons had been preparing for this. Gradually they had given away, or sold, or thrown away all those possessions that had been necessary for life in the city: house, car, furniture, appliances, television, phone, toys, and a thousand other items. Dead weight, in Skip's opinion. Weight that never would have allowed them to soar over the mountains, as they were today, so light and free.

Pat was thinking of all her friends who had asked her to reconsider, and not to disappear into barren wilderness. But she had an eye for beauty and, looking down from the aquaplane, she felt sorry for her friends. *If they could only see!* she told herself.

Jenny and Toby pressed their faces against Plexiglas windows as if they could drink in the entire Rockies chain. As the plane banked, sunlight hit an eleven-thousand-foot peak and the mountain became

11

a dazzling cone of diamond ice set on a sloping green velvet rug.

The aquaplane pilot was a balding, friendly man called Jud. Skip sat beside him. Pat was in back with the kids, and in the very rear of the passenger compartment Crust lay groaning with anxiety on top of the supplies.

"Where you from?" Jud asked Skip.

"Los Angeles."

"What made you decide to leave?"

Skip glanced back at Jenny. "Lots of reasons."

Another glittering mountain swung under them, and then a dizzying new range. Skip felt Pat's hand on his shoulder.

"You like it?" Jud asked her.

"It's like living a dream . . ." she said.

"That's just what I was thinking," Skip nodded. His smile broadened.

Toby was busy mountain-watching, patting Crust, and keeping an eye on the copilot controls that turned in front of his father with each maneuver of Jud's wheel. From the start, he had been amazed with this plane that had pontoons as well as landing gear—and a pusher propeller mounted in back of the cabin!

"Have you ever seen so much fresh air?" Jenny beamed.

"Oh, we've got plenty of that up here!" Jud answered.

Amazing, Skip thought. On the high steel, in the middle of the city, he had always felt small, diminished. Above these mountains, each one great enough to cover downtown Los Angeles, he felt immense, as if he could walk in a giant's strides.

"Look, Dad!" Toby shouted all at once. "Look down there, you see 'em?"

Toby pointed. Up from a valley climbed a column of mountain sheep, their curled horns like dignified crowns.

"Bighorn sheep," Skip explained. "They're heading for the high country for the summer."

Jud banked the plane and flew low over the herd.
It scattered, the wild sheep racing with sure hooves
over ice and rock. As Jud pulled his wheel back, the
aquaplane cleared the mountain ridge, on which stood
one defiant, old ram. Ahead, the peaks were no less
starkly beautiful but more spread out.

Skip's eyes followed the reflecting ribbon of water
rushing by the base of the mountain.

"Not your everyday, commonplace creek," Jud
said.

Pat turned to Jenny. "A lot of open space down
there."

Jenny gazed back at the sheep. "You think the animals are friendly?"

"Most of them . . . I hope," her mother answered.

Jenny peeled herself away from the window long
enough to say, "It's going to be just wonderful, Mom."

By now, Toby was practically leaning on Jud's
shoulder.

"*I'm* going to catch a moose and my *Dad's* going
to milk it." Then his eyes narrowed. "You can do
that, can't you, Dad?"

"I've heard some old mountain men have done it,"
the pilot responded instead. "Of course, you'll hear
a lot of bosh from old mountain men," he added, to
Skip.

The former construction worker studied the map
on his knees. "How much farther is it?"

"Just a second and you'll see."

Skip and Pat had spent countless hours poring over
so many maps back in Los Angeles that they had become dizzy. Finally, they'd settled on a plot called
"the Taylor House"; but what it was, they admitted
they had no idea. Now those maps had become stu-
pefyingly real, right before their eyes, and they were
dizzier than ever. One more mountain wall approached
the plane. The wall slid under them and Jud pointed
to an oblong shimmer of light nestled among green
hills.

"See the lake up ahead?" Jud asked.

"That's it?" Pat asked, a hint of excitement in her voice.

"That is it!"

Skip folded his map.

The lake was about a mile across at its widest point, and ten miles long, fed by the same river Skip had noticed earlier. He and Pat looked down and saw nothing resembling a house, but they did see mile after mile of deep woods, and hills covered with wildflowers. As the aquaplane made its preliminary pass over the lake, a thicket of reeds exploded into a hundred ducks, honking and flapping in panic.

"Oh, look at them!" Jenny shouted.

"Do they belong to us, Mom?" Toby asked. "It's our lake."

"They're wild ducks, Toby. They don't belong to anyone."

As the plane wheeled around, a heavy-antlered moose swimming the lake gazed up. A series of V's in the water marked the passage of a beaver family. White-tailed deer broke from the trees, stopped to watch the course of the plane, and ran on again. The trees, Skip saw, were not just evergreens, but oak, maple, and birch.

"Nice-looking location!" Jud was nosing the plane toward the water.

"First real land we've ever owned."

"Beginner's luck, Skip."

Jud pulled the plane's nose up and let the engine go into a stall. Two pontoons slapped simultaneously on the surface of the water, spraying the fuselage. A mile away, the moose stepped out of the lake onto dry land, gave a look back, and continued his stately walk toward the trees. The aquaplane taxied to within fifty feet of a crescent-shaped, sandy beach. After a final roar, the engines shut off.

Skip pushed open his door. "Pat?" he said, with an "After you" wave of his hand.

"You go first."

He stepped out onto the plane's skirt.

The absence of the engine's hum made for a vacuum now, which all the quieter sounds of nature rushed to fill: the lapping of the water, the call of the jays, the sound of the breeze rustling the tree leaves.

Jud joined his customer on the skirt and took a deep breath of appreciation. "Feels good, huh?"

"Darn right it does," Skip grinned.

"Can't we get out?" Jenny interrupted.

"You bet!"

Skip helped his wife onto the skirt of the plane, and then Jenny and Toby. Crust took one look at the water, leapt into it, and started swimming for shore.

"What do you think?" Skip balanced his smile as he asked Pat.

"I think . . . it's beautiful," she reassured him.

"Hey, Dad!" Toby tugged on Skip's belt. "Carry me."

Skip hoisted the boy, gauged the depth of the water, and took a first step that dropped him into two feet of lake.

"Oooh, cold!"

"Crust didn't think it's cold," Toby remarked.

"That's why he's called a Labrador retriever, my boy."

Skip waded onto the beach, lowered Toby from his shoulders, removed his soaking boots, and went back for Pat. Jud was already carrying Jenny to shore. Skip put his hands up to Pat.

"Mmm, just like newlyweds!" She got comfortable in his arms.

From the beach, Jenny threw a stick far out into the water. Crust obliged by fetching it, coming back to land, and then shaking his water off on Jenny.

Toby had discovered an old, upside-down canoe under a maple tree. "Look, Dad, we can fish!" he shouted shrilly.

Skip set Pat down on the beach. "Don't let this become a habit," he warned her. But he was still smiling as he had been since the plane landed.

Pat, as soon as she was on her own feet again,

started some serious looking around. The lake lay nestled in the center of a big valley carved out of rock by, probably, an Ice Age glacier. The valley's meadows and shade trees would have graced any park, but there were sheer granite cliffs and impenetrable woods beyond that were truly raw wilderness. While Skip and Jud brought supplies in from the plane, all the anxieties that she had felt before returned to Pat in a flood.

"That's it!" Skip let two heavy sacks drop to the ground. "Tools, rifles, food—"

"How far is it to our nearest neighbors?" Pat asked Jud abruptly.

"Well, Twin Lakes is twenty miles southwest. There's three families there, at the ranger camp."

"Is there a road to Twin Lakes?"

Jud shook his head. "Cross-country all the way. You *could* follow that river at the end of the lake— the river you saw from the air—but *I* sure wouldn't advise trying it." The pilot added, to Skip, "You got your radio?"

"Right here." Skip lifted a watertight sack.

"You need any more supplies or anything at all, you can always reach me on that."

At that, Pat felt more at ease.

"What about the 'Rocky Mountain Review'?" she smiled.

Jud laughed and scratched his chin. "Every night, between 8:30 and 9:00, you can hear all the scandal in the Northwest."

"What's 'Rocky Mountain Review'?" Jenny inquired.

"A radio station," her father replied. "That's how people communicate out here in British Columbia."

Jud now shook hands with Pat and Skip. "Well, I'd better be on my way. Good luck!"

"Can't you stay for coffee?"

"Got two more stops to make today. I'll take a raincheck, okay? Bye, young lady." The pilot shook hands with Jenny. He waved to Toby. "Want to see your dad milk that moose!"

Skip walked Jud back to the edge of the water, where the bush pilot stopped and spoke in a low voice he had not used before.

"You know, I've brought a lot of young people out here in the last few years. Ninety percent of them I take back out in a couple of months. Carving out a home in a place like this isn't for most folks. It's no disgrace to face that. If things don't go right, I'm always on the other end of that radio." He gave Skip a firm handshake. "Sure hope you stay, though."

"Thanks for that. Thanks for everything!"

Skip rejoined Pat and the children. They watched Jud wade to the plane and start up the propeller. The aquaplane taxied into a slow turn to face the wind, almost came to a halt, and then picked up speed. Before it reached the middle of the lake, its pontoons left the water and it climbed to mountaintop level and banked into a turn as Jud waved from the cockpit. With a final waggle of its wings, the plane climbed for higher altitude, headed east, and was soon out of sight.

The Robinson family was now alone. Pat stood, her arms crossed, listening to the fading sound. Even Toby felt the sudden loneliness, and held on to Crust's neck.

"A nice man . . ." Pat said at last.

"That's the Code of the North." Skip put his arm around her. "Only nice folks allowed. That's us! Come on."

Chapter Four

A First Adventure

Skip and Pat shouldered their supplies and marched up from the lakeshore, walking faster when Jenny called that she could see their new house. It was close to the lake near a copse of spreading oak trees.

The sense of their abandonment was pushed aside by a growing excitement. Skip saw Pat's smile return. Jenny dashed ahead, her arms wide, followed by Toby.

"It's better than I ever thought it would be!" Pat said at fifty yards from the house.

At ten yards from the house, the whole family halted. Husband and wife let the supplies drop.

"The Taylor House," as it was called, was really nothing more than a tiny log cabin. Not only were its windows dirty and hanging open, but parts of the roof had fallen in. Skip and Pat saw gaping chinks in the walls where mortar had dropped from between the logs. The single door creaked on its hinges. In all, it presented the perfect picture of desertion and collapse.

"That's it?" Toby swallowed.

"Uh, that's it," Skip agreed. "Can't be so bad inside," he said as much for himself as for anyone else.

He moved warily up the steps to the cabin and

18

pushed open the door. It fell with an explosion of dust onto the floor inside.

"Is it a house or a death trap?" Toby asked, wide-eyed.

The others joined Skip and cautiously entered, stepping on the door. One steel cot frame without a mattress was squeezed against a wall. Shelves against another wall held nothing but a heap of nuts—and one bird's nest. Roof shingles lay on the floor. A small wood-burning stove and chimney completed the room.

"It's not as big as the *kitchen,* back home," Jenny's voice quavered.

"It's just temporary . . ." Skip glanced at Pat. "We'll build a bigger place next door!"

Pat had lifted the lid of the stove, and now took a quick step back when a furry face emerged.

"It's a raccoon!" Jenny was delighted.

Crust jumped forward, barking, and the coon ducked back inside. They heard a scuttling of small claws on metal.

Toby twisted his head to see inside the stove. "Where'd he go?"

"Up the chimney," Skip replied and went outside the cabin, followed by Pat and the kids.

Out of the chimney stack struggled the raccoon, who took one look at the welcoming committee and jumped onto the roof and from there to the branch of a tree nearby.

"I bet he lived in there," Toby said.

The raccoon sniffed at the Robinsons and made a final exit down the tree and into the woods. Everyone watched him but Jenny, whose mouth opened wide.

"Dad . . .!" She trembled, pointing.

Skip still watched where the raccoon had darted away. "The animals have had this place to themselves for some time. It'll take them a while to get used to humans again."

"Dad . . . !" Jenny said louder.

"What?"

Skip turned casually to where Jenny was jabbing

her finger and found himself face to face with a standing, five-hundred-pound black bear fifty feet away. The bear dropped to all fours and shoved its immense snout up at Skip. Its dark eyes seemed lost on a broad head trimmed with an ebony ruff. The bear's mouth showed two rows of inch-long canines.

For one heartbeat, Skip stared in surprise and then he pushed Jenny and the others back.

"Into the cabin!"

The Robinsons rushed up to the front of the house, where they saw, inside, the flattened front door. The cabin interior was not going to be any sanctuary.

"The roof!" Skip yelled.

The bear peered around the corner of the cabin at the family. Skip and Crust held their ground. *For all the good that's going to do,* Skip thought. Pat hoisted Toby and Jenny onto the low cabin roof and scampered up after them.

"Back!" Skip shouted at the bear, which merely advanced on him.

Skip picked up Crust, who was not too reluctant to gain the safety of the roof, and, as the bear was closing in, swung up onto the shingles himself. The bear clawed at the cabin wall, trying to climb after the family; but after a minute of having its paws thumped by Skip's boot, it gave up. With a tired yawn, the creature shuffled away from the cabin wall to the supplies, which it must have smelled, within.

"Where's the gun, Dad?" Toby asked.

"There!" Skip nodded down to the cabin's interior.

With more perseverance than skill, the black bear opened the supply sacks, discarded rifle, radio, and sewing kit, and bit into a sack of flour. Lifting the sack over its head, the animal poured the flour directly into its immense mouth.

"He's going to eat *everything!*" Jenny mourned.

"What are we going to do, Skip?" Pat asked.

"He's going to eat a little something and then he's going to leave."

An hour later, the bear had gorged on two flour sacks, a sack of dry milk, a jar of honey, and a smoked ham. Full, it rolled over the grass in luxuriant pleasure.

Overhead, the weather had by now changed. Gray thunderheads spilled over the mountains. Pat wiped a raindrop from her cheek.

"It's raining."

"A few drops," Skip said.

The next sound was a peal of thunder rolling down the valley. A few drops did fall, and then a few more, and, in a matter of less than a minute, buckets of rain.

Crust moaned and hung his head. On the ground, the bear lay on his back to let the rain fall in his mouth.

"*He* sure is having a good time," Toby growled.

"Unlike some people I could mention," his mother answered.

Soaked and miserable, the Robinsons huddled on the roof. Pat hugged Jenny, while Skip put his warm arms around Toby. Crust kept moaning—which was just what Skip felt like doing.

Chapter Five

Getting Started

Long after the rest of the valley's inhabitants had awakened to the new day, the Robinson family still slept. After the bear had finally gone, they'd spent the night salvaging what was left of their supplies, repairing the leaks in the cabin roof, and cleaning up the inside of their new lodging. Toby and Jenny curled up in their sleeping bags on the floor. Skip and Pat managed to get both their bags onto the cot.

Pat was the first to wake. She stretched, rose on one elbow, and broke into a smile. The window by the stove was open not only to sunlight and breeze but to something else: a blue jay that cocked its head at Pat in sharp-eyed study.

"Good morning," Pat said and reached out her finger.

The jay hopped from sill to stove, twisting its head at different angles to observe the cabin's new occupants.

"Skip," Pat whispered, and nudged her husband. "Skip, look."

"Mornin'," he mumbled with his eyes shut.

"Come here."

Pat put her finger near the bird's feet. The jay took

an offended hop into the air, pecked her finger, and flew out the window.

"Did you see it?" Pat punched Skip's shoulder.

"Wh-what?"

"A little bird was just here. He bit my finger."

"Did you bite him back?"

"I'm serious!"

"So am I." Skip reached over and pulled her close. "I want you to make this a double sleeping bag by tomorrow."

"Is that so?" she asked innocently With her left hand, she reached behind the cot and picked up an open canteen of water.

"Umm." Skip nuzzled her neck.

"Well, you'd better cool off, mister."

Pat held the canteen high and poured its contents over Skip. While he coughed and sputtered, she rolled off the cot and hopped away awkwardly in her sleeping bag. Skip grabbed the bag, while Crust's barking woke the kids.

"Get him, Mom!" Jenny shouted.

"Come on, Dad!" Toby answered.

With the kids as reinforcements, the tickling match turned into a free-for-all. Crust plunged into the middle of it.

"Oh, no!" Jenny yelled. "Look at that!"

Two raccoons stood half in and half out of the stove. From the animals' expression, they obviously found humans hard to believe.

After a breakfast of hot biscuits and jam—the raccoons had been evicted from the stove—Skip and Pat walked down along the edge of the lake. He carried a sack over his shoulder.

"There," Pat said, pointing up the easy slope. "That is where the Robinson house will be. And over there, the garden. We can use the old cabin as a larder. I can see it now."

"You're okay, you know that? Except for your

strange, neurotic impulse to throw water on the man you love."

"What's in that?" She nodded to the sack. "You've kept it tied up tight for weeks!"

Pleased that she asked, Skip finally unknotted the cords at the neck of the sack and took out an eight-inch wooden peg.

"My grandfather sent me these from Virginia when he heard we were moving up here. They're seasoned locust pegs—the best wood you can get for holding logs together. He made them himself. He said one generation of a family owed more to the generations that followed than just good wishes."

Pat examined the peg. It was round at one end and square at the other, and had been made with a lot of care.

"Skip, we're going to build the world's greatest cabin!"

"Like you said, we're going to try."

Building a new cabin was the first order of business for the Robinsons, and it was a business that occupied most of their daylight hours. Skip and Pat found, luckily, that the work never deteriorated into a chore; it was a creation, a growing part of themselves, their stake in the wilderness. More important, it was a creation made by all of them. For it was Jenny who found the slabs of rock that went into the foundation, and Toby who discovered the right kind of clay to mortar the rocks. Once the foundation pillars were eighteen inches high—high enough so that termites would be discouraged from attacking the logs (still to be added)—Skip and Toby went in search of maple trees.

Pat and Jenny, meanwhile, began planting their garden.

Before leaving Los Angeles, they had collected seeds of vegetables that could grow well in a cool climate, would supply a wide range of vitamins, and could be stored and preserved for eating in the wintertime. From the beginning, Pat had feared what would happen when the meager supplies they had brought ran out. Jud could bring some necessities, like flour, in by air, but not enough to keep four people well fed. The valley, however, was a green paradise among the mountains. Best of all, Jenny revealed that she had been reading up on what wild foods could be harvested directly from the woods whenever she and her mother made an expedition into the brush for food.

"Rose hips." Jenny would point to a wild rose. "Full of vitamin C."

Or:

"Chicory. We can use that for salads. Dad can use it for coffee."

Or:

"There's some plantain! And over there's some wild mustard for lettuce. And watercress! We couldn't starve out here if we tried!"

"Not with you around," Pat would say proudly. "By the way, how are you feeling?"

"Mom, I've never felt better."

And they would return, toting sacks heavy with nature's bounty. For fun, they would visit the "men," at work in the hills. To find them, all they had to do was follow the sound of the chopping.

One day . . .

"Timber!"

Skip stepped back from a falling maple tree.

Sixty feet of tree tilted, caught for a second on the branches of its neighbors, slipped free, and toppled to the ground. Pat and Jenny scrambled over the felled giant and started hacking off branches with hand axes.

"Only branches," Skip called. "No fingers, please!"

"Yeah," Toby chorused manfully.

He then picked up Skip's broadax and dragged it to the base of a fifteen-foot tree. After a preparatory spit on his hands, he lifted the ax. At least, he tried to. The heavy, double-faced head of the ax scarcely budged.

"Go ahead!" Jenny said.

"I am. Just checkin' this out, that's all."

His back to his sister, Toby gripped the ax by the middle of the handle.

"This is man's work," he shot back at Jenny.

Grunting, he lifted the ax, hoisted it over his shoulder and sat down under its weight. Immediately, he bounced onto his feet. "Don't say anything!" he warned.

"I'll just roll my eyes," Jenny squealed.

"Well, I can hear you gigglin'."

"Then all your muscles must be in your ears."

"Jenny." Pat shook her head, while she tried to stop her own laughing.

Toby got a stranglehold on the ax, right under its head. Carefully, he tapped the blade against the trunk.

"Man's work?" Jenny hooted. "A woodpecker could do better!"

"Dad!" Toby's face reddened.

"The problem here," Skip stepped in, "is that you're not taking a scientific approach. See, the weight of the ax has to be in the correct ratio to the size of the ax swinger."

"Yeah?"

"Sure," Skip said, straightfaced. "For a man of your size, a slightly smaller ax would better employ your physique. Like this hand ax." He handed the smaller tool to his son. "And you don't want to hit straight into the tree; you want to chop at an angle. No, not *that* much of an angle—because then you'll end up chopping your foot . . . That's it. Not too hard. Easy! You don't want to scare the sap out of the tree."

"Oh. Right, I mean," Toby nodded vigorously.

By noon, all but the last of the trees needed had been chopped and the Robinsons rested for lunch.

"Where's Crust?" Pat asked Skip. "I've never known him to miss out on food before."

"Maybe he went off on some private scouting. He was born to live in a place like this, you know."

"Like you, too."

"What I'm waiting for," Skip said softly so that the children wouldn't hear him, "is the day you say, 'like us.'"

"I know." She touched his hand.

"Sandwiches!" Jenny announced as she opened a sack. "With our very own local lettuce."

"Joe Bear told you all about how the Indians used to live, Dad. Did they have sandwiches, too?" Toby asked.

"No, but he told me a lot of other things. Did you know you can eat the inner bark of a birch tree? You can even cut it up and make spaghetti out of it."

"Yucky!" Toby made a face.

"And he said things about being a part of nature. How if you can fit yourself into harmony with the woods and the animals in it, you'll never be away from home—because home will always be around you."

"Look!" Jenny squealed.

A raccoon had crept onto the blanket beside her and was busy stuffing a sandwich into its mouth.

"Well, *these* animals certainly are at home around *us*," Pat complained.

After lunch, Pat took the broadax and started chopping down the last tree, a small birch.

"It makes me tired just to watch you." Skip was stretched out with a sprig of grass between his teeth.

"Watch out for flying chips." Pat raised an eyebrow.

Toby went back to work on his tree. He chopped away with a hand ax and, finally, a knife. "This is really the right . . . what's that word, Dad?"

"Ratio."

"That's what I meant."

"Timber!" Pat called out.

Skip opened his eyes to see the tree swaying toward

him. He hopped up and scrambled out of the way as it came down with a thud.

"That'll teach you to sleep on the job," Pat smirked.

Jenny walked over to Toby, who sat slumped in exhaustion. His tree showed a sizable dent, but it still stood upright.

"It's no use," he sighed. "This tree will never, ever fall."

Jenny studied her brother and studied the notch in the truck; she gave the tree a hard shove. With a snap, it broke and flopped to the ground.

"A woman's touch," she said simply, rolling her eyes up at the sky.

All the Robinsons now worked together trimming branches from the trees, changing them bit by bit into logs. Skip finally hitched the logs, in pairs, to ropes.

"Now, there are two ways of getting them back to the cabin," he explained. "There's dragging them uphill and over the rocks, and then there's the easy way. Which way should we take?"

"The easy way!" Toby yelled.

"You're learning fast."

The easy way was also the more exciting way: pulling twenty-foot logs downhill until they slid of their own accord, and then running and keeping ahead of them. Skip managed to do it, and once the logs were at the bottom of the hill and at the edge of the lake, Pat saw what was easy about the process: her husband tied all the logs together into a raft he could float lazily back to the cabin.

"Last one home is a rotten city slicker!" Skip began poling his raft.

"He looks just like Huckleberry Finn, Mom," Jenny said.

"A little over-age, but he's the only one we've got," Pat laughed.

Whimpering, Crust greeted them when they got back to the cabin. His muzzle was full of porcupine quills.

Jenny tended him like a nurse, gently removing the quills before they worked their way in deeper.

Later while Skip and Toby fished for supper, Pat and Jenny sat under a tree and watched the setting sun turn the sky more colors than there were in the rainbow.

"It's our sky," Jenny said. "Our lake, our mountains. Mom, have you noticed I haven't had one allergy attack since we came up here?"

"I do notice that sort of thing." Behind her back, however, Pat crossed her fingers.

Chapter Six

A Hunt

The cabin was dark. It was early morning. The only sound was the ticking of a clock, and the only one awake was Toby.

"Dad?" he whispered. "Dad . . . ?"

"What?" Skip muttered drowsily.

"Is it time yet?"

"Toby, I'll tell you when it's time. Go back to sleep."

Skip kept his eyes shut. He did not see the raccoon peeping inquisitively out of the stove, or Toby gesturing the animal closer.

An hour later, the alarm clock broke the silence. Skip awoke and quickly turned off the ringing. He rose and dressed for the day.

"What time is it?" Pat asked sleepily.

"Don't wake up," Skip told her.

"I put your . . . sandwiches on the shelf," she yawned.

"Thanks."

He moved as quietly as he could across the cabin and shook Toby's shoulder. Over Toby's shoulder popped a familiar masked and furry face.

"What's this?"

"He crawled in with me last night." Toby's face appeared beside the raccoon's.

Crust woke up, barking at the small intruder. Pat sat up an instant later.

"The raccoon." Skip picked up the animal and deposited it back in the stove. "He was sleeping with Toby. I never saw wild animals so tame before."

"Are you all right, Toby?" his mother asked.

"Yeah. He kept me warm last night."

"Get dressed, Toby," Skip said. "We'd better start out now."

Munching a breakfast of oatmeal cookies, father and son left the cabin as the first rays of the sun ran along the tops of the mountains. The valley itself was still dim in the blue light of pre-dawn. Crust ran ahead, sniffing the wind.

Their course took them on a wide curve along the foothills and then back to the lake. Rain had fallen during the night and spiderwebs glistened like necklaces strung between flowers. Skip carried his shotgun "broken" at the breach so that no accidental fall could discharge the shells in the double barrels.

"Look!" Toby pointed up.

Far overhead, the silhouette of a great bird soared in the sky.

"Golden eagle," Skip said.

"Is he hunting, too?"

"You bet he is. He's got sharper eyes than we do, but then he hasn't got Crust on his side."

"Crust's a hunting dog for real?"

"He's a retriever. As soon as we get a bird, you'll see all Crust's natural instincts come out." *I hope,* Skip added silently to himself.

By the time the hunters came down from the foothills to the lake, the first rays of the sun had touched the valley. Along the water's edge here was a swamp of reeds. Skip saw fresh deer and beaver tracks in the mud, but so far all Crust had flushed out was a chipmunk.

Suddenly, the dog bounded into the reeds. A flurry of feathers exploded from the swamp and a quail whirred into the air. Skip snapped the shotgun together, raised the barrel and fired. The bird plummeted into the lake, about thirty feet from shore.

"You got him! You got him, Dad!" Toby shouted, his hands still over his ears.

"Sure did," Skip chuckled with a sense of satisfaction. "Okay, Crust. Go ahead, go get 'im, boy! C'mon. Go get it!"

Crust barked, and wagged his tail furiously, but he didn't set one paw in the water.

"C'mon, Crust." Skip waved to the quail lying out in the water. "Go get it! Crust, what's the matter? Go get it!"

The Labrador put his paws on Skip's chest and licked his master's face.

"Crust . . . ? Oh, brother! Okay." Skip pushed Crust down. "Toby, you go get it."

"You shot it, Dad, not me."

"I don't *believe* this." Skip Robinson gave a long sigh, then removed his boots and socks and rolled up his pants legs. "Some team we have here!"

Gingerly, he entered the water, which was cold enough to send him up on his tiptoes. The quail looked farther and farther away. He could feel his legs turning blue.

"It's not *that* cold," Toby said from shore.

"*You* want to do it?"

"Nope."

The water came up to Skip's knees. After a last glare back at Crust, he dove into the liquid ice and swam toward the bird. He could not remember ever being in water so chill.

Toby watched his father getting closer to the quail. Crust barked with excitement.

"Go get it!" Toby urged Crust, and the retriever took a running leap into the water.

Skip was just reaching for the bird when Crust passed him and scooped it up in his mouth.

"Well, it's about time!" Skip was exasperated. And he could have sworn he saw a grin on the dog's face.

Sun and wind dried Skip's clothes as, quail in hand, the successful hunters started their hike back to the cabin.

"Guess you were right about Crust's natural instincts, Dad."

"I think *that* dog's most natural instinct is to eat, and he knows if we don't eat neither does he."

They had reached that part of the foothills where their path ran across a long slope of rocks and boulders leading down from a hill to the lake.

"Eating's what I do best, too," Toby said.

"Shh!"

Skip halted and looked around. He thought he had heard something as he stepped out onto the rocks at the top of the slope. He watched a pebble roll toward him. More pebbles and sand followed.

"Listen!" he told Toby softly.

From a slight trembling, the sound developed into a medium-sized roar, as if the hill were a jet taking off. The roar grew and became deafening. Rocks now rolled down behind the pebbles. Skip saw a boulder rocking, not far above them.

"Dad!" Toby screamed.

A rock the size of a football sailed between Toby and Crust. More rocks followed. Larger rocks.

"Toby! Crust!"

Skip picked his son up bodily, grabbed Crust's chain collar, and started running for a thick rock shelf that jutted out from the hill, thirty or forty yards to their left. He had to do broken-field running, dodging the rocks that flew and bounced about him. A wave of dust, stone, and boulders was sweeping down the entire hill and onto the slope. The ground danced under his feet. A pine tree was smashed in half by a huge rock. Almost blind from dust, and holding his arm around Toby's head, Skip stumbled as he ran, but he reached the rock shelf, pushed Toby and Crust under it, and spread himself protectively over them just as the whole brunt of the avalanche poured over the sturdy shelf.

Out of the corner of his eye, Skip saw boulders rolling like locomotives only a few feet away. One struck the rock shelf as it bounced, and ricocheted into the air. A tree branch cartwheeled by. Smaller rocks grazed Skip's shoulders and back. Skip feared that the shelf they were hiding under might collapse as well, but as abruptly as the rumbling had begun it subsided. A few loosened rocks skipped past, then some last pebbles—and it was over!

For safety, Skip waited a minute or two before raising his head. The slope below—as well as the hill above—was still. Sounds of birds and wind replaced the gruesome rumble of the rock slide.

"You okay, Toby?"

"Yeah." The boy stood and brushed dust out of his hair. "What caused it?"

"Probably the rain last night. The soil gets wet and shifts. Rocks start moving."

Crust, himself, slitedged cautiously out from under the rock shelf, took a couple of steps and sniffed. His ears rose. An instant later, he ran over to the slope, barking.

"Crust! Come back!" Skip shouted.

Ahead of the dog, Skip saw two small, dusty shapes trying to move backward.

"They're bear cubs!" Toby exclaimed.

They were black bear cubs. One was, beneath the dust that covered it, actually black; the other was grayer, with a white marking like a ring around its neck. Each was producing the best of cub growls at the larger dog.

"The mother could be around." Skip readied his shotgun. "Crust!"

He reached his dog and yanked him away from the cubs, who regarded Skip with mixed relief and fright. He had never seen such pathetic-looking animals, but he couldn't take any chances.

Toby looked around. "I don't see any other bears . . ."

The cubs sidled past Skip and began digging furiously at a pile of rocks. Puzzled, Skip helped them push some of the stones away. Soon enough, he saw the dusty paw of an adult black bear.

Toby's eyes went from the paw to his father's face. "What is it?"

"It's the mother, son," Skip said softly.

"She's dead?"

"Yeah." Skip patted Toby's arm.

The cubs sniffed at the paw and retreated, whining. They cowered together. Skip could see Toby trying to keep tears back.

"Still got that apple you brought, Toby . . . ?" Toby checked his knapsack and held the apple out toward his father. "Thanks. Now, *you* hold on to Crust. Hold him tight!"

The apple extended, Skip approached the cubs. They took one step back in unison, and then stretched out their noses to sniff the offering. Tentatively, one nipped at one side of the apple. The other cub nipped at the other side.

"Hey, you guys like apples," Skip said softly. "That's it . . . Good! Come here, Toby. Your turn."

Skip grabbed Crust's collar while Toby took the apple. The cubs had viewed Skip with some fear, but Toby was just their size.

"They're climbing all over me, Dad! They're going into my pockets. Get me another apple!"

Skip laughed, and put some facts together, at the same time. *The bear cubs aren't old enough to be weaned. Without their mother, they'll either starve to death or fall prey to some animal in the forest.* What he was going to do with two cubs he didn't know. He did know he could not just turn his back on them.

"Come on, Toby, time to go home."

"What about the cubs?"

"Oh, I suspect we'll have some company on the way."

Toby disentangled himself from the small bears. Crust still viewed them with less than complete amiability but kept his growls to himself. Skip swung the quail over his shoulder and started down the slope. Toby and Crust followed. The cubs sat bewildered for a moment, alternately casting sad eyes at where their mother lay and at the departing Toby.

"You sure they'll come?" Toby asked his father.

"Ask *them*."

Before Toby had the chance, he heard the two cubs falling in step on either side of him.

The hike home had all the aspects of a parade. Crust was in the lead, Skip carried his shotgun and quail, Toby marched like a young cadet, and the cubs brought up the rear—after a fashion. Half the time they were rolling on top of each other, or scrambling up Toby's back, or chasing squirrels, or tumbling off logs into a stream . . . Toby was never happier.

Crust turned his nose up in disapproval.

That evening in the cabin, Skip picked birdshot out of the quail. Pat had mixed some powdered milk in a bottle and fastened one of Skip's gloves over the top of the bottle with a rubber band. Now she was snipping off the end of one of the glove's fingers.

Jenny and Toby were rolling over the floor with the cubs.

"They keep licking my face," Jenny giggled.

"That's 'cause you look like their mother!" Toby teased.

One of the cubs turned and trailed a tongue over Toby's freckles.

"And *you* look like their father," Jenny retorted.

"What are you going to call them?" Skip asked from his corner of the room.

"We decided," Jenny said, "the black one is to be 'Blackie.' The one with the white ring around his neck is 'Ringo.' "

"Well"—Pat shook the bottle—"let's see if this thing works. Blackie and Ringo will have to be the judges."

She held the bottle upside down. A drop of milk hung from the glove finger that was cut. Blackie stood on his rear legs, sniffing the milk. Jenny held her breath.

"It works!"

Blackie sucked on the glove and almost pulled the bottle out of Pat's hand. Ringo clambered over Toby to join in.

"Wow!" Toby clapped his hands. "Is he hungry!"

"They're adorable, Mom." Jenny purred, helping with the bottle. "Do you think they'll always be as friendly as this?"

"I hope so."

"We'll have to let them go when they get big," Skip said. He looked at the clock. "Hey, we almost forgot about 'Rocky Mountain Review.'"

He turned on the transistor radio. A patchwork of static and voices filled the cabin as he manipulated the dial, until it came to rest on a strong signal.

". . . There's a note for Bill West. Your dog showed up at Smiley's again and he says you get first pick of the litter . . . There are packages at the ranger station for Joe Ballard. The dentist is going to be at the station tomorrow, too, so anyone who needs a tooth pulled, be sure an' be there . . . Now, attention everyone, 'cause I want to welcome some new folks into the area."

Skip turned up the volume of the radio, and tried to hide his pride.

". . . Skip Robinson an' his family have moved into the old Taylor house. I hear that his wife, Pat, is about pretty enough to charm a grizzly, an' that their two children, Jenny and Toby, are pitchin' in like grown-ups to build a new cabin. I wish them all the best in their new home . . . Well, that's it for tonight. The Green Hornet will not be heard again this week; it's still lost in the mail . . . This is the Voice of the Wilderness, Happy Jack Jackson, signing off!"

Pat smiled. Jenny and Toby looked as if they were about to burst with pleasure.

"That makes it official, doesn't it, Dad?" Toby said.

"Right. Now it's official."

Chapter Seven

Wilderness Mothers

With all the logs now at the site of the new cabin, the Robinsons could start putting up the walls.

Two long logs became the "sills," or bottom logs, of the walls. "Sleepers," the floor beams, were set four feet apart on the sills. Skip's locust pegs joined the sleepers fast to the sills. Wall logs followed. Each had to be hewed and notched so that it would dovetail with another at the corners of the cabin. Locked together, they made a single, solid unit as strong as the wood used; and Skip had chosen the best maple in the north country.

Each day ended with the satisfaction of visible progress—*and* aches and blisters. But somehow the aches and blisters were the gold medals of work. And the bear cubs were always on hand for comic relief.

As the walls rose, the task of lifting the new logs into place became more difficult. All the years Skip had spent in construction work came into play. So did the muscles of Pat and Jenny and Toby. With them pulling ropes from inside the cabin, and Skip pushing from outside, the heavy logs were slid up planks to the tops of the walls.

"Is this how the Egyptians built the pyramids, Pharaoh?" Pat called out one day.

"Same way. Slave power!"

"Plates," the top logs of the walls, were fixed with locust pegs and Pat and Skip then laid down the ceiling beams that would also serve as the floor of the children's sleeping loft. From there, they erected rafters with a forty-five-degree pitch to shed snow and water, and hammered home planks to hold the roof shingles.

Making shingles was a big task in itself. Each had to be wedged from a split maple trunk, drained of sap, and sanded. Skip was nailing them in overlapping rows on the ceiling when Jenny and Toby took a well-deserved break from work.

They hiked up the hills to some sloping meadows where Jenny had earlier seen dazzling fields of wildflowers. This time, she had brought along her guide to flowers.

"You think the kids in L.A. ever heard of Happy Jack Jackson?" Toby asked.

"They probably never even heard of the Rocky Mountains." Jenny shielded her eyes with her hand and gazed at the masses of spring flowers spread along the higher slopes.

"Let's go farther uphill."

"We already came farther than we were supposed to."

"Nothing's going to happen."

Jenny glanced back at the lake and cabin. Part of the reason she went on was simply because she could, now. In the city, just playing hopscotch would tire her. Here, she seemed to be able to run all day without panting once. And the flowers beckoned to her . . .

Bold red, pale blue, yellows brighter than the sun, flowers soon filled the text pages of her book, pressed between them for later identification. The best of the flowers they found was a delicate white blossom with graceful petals.

"I think it's a wild orchid, Toby. Let's take it home to Mom. I won't press it."

A faint sound, somewhere between the noise of

grating metal and a cat's meow, and above them, caught her ear. Toby looked uphill as well.

"What was that?" he asked a little nervously.

"I don't know . . ." Jenny answered. She carefully put the orchid stem in her book. "Let's see."

They picked their way through waist-high grass and over the graying trunk of a dead aspen tree. The intriguing sounds increased. They were like cat noises, but deeper and definitely wilder.

Jenny stopped Toby all at once. On a rocky knoll stood a rough pyramid of boulders. "Look, Toby," she said, almost in a whisper.

Staring down at the two children were two kittens bigger than any cats the kids had ever seen before. Of a soft slate color, gangly and with oversized paws, the kittens let out tiny screams.

"What are they?"

"They look like baby cougars!" Jenny's eyes widened. "We'd better get out of here."

"Where's the mother?" Toby thought of what had happened to the bear cubs' mother.

"I don't know, but we better scram."

They slipped back over the dead aspen. All flower plucking was at an end. Toby broke into a run.

"I think their mother would be mad if she saw us here," he yelled back.

A sound of thudding paws made him look back. The cougar kittens had come down from the knoll and were leaping across the dead aspen.

"Oh, no! They're following us!"

"Come on, Toby! Hurry up! Quick!"

Jenny and Toby raced through the meadow where she had picked the orchid, the thudding and screaming growing closer. Just six months old, the cougars could cover distance in half the time of human children, and their four soft paws gave them the agility of acrobats over the frequent scattered rocks.

"They getting closer," Toby yelled. *"Yeoww!"*

Suddenly he went down in a tangle of grass and cougar cubs. For all his kicking and punching, the cubs easily pinned him to the ground, licking his face and tugging at his shirt.

"They're killing me! They're killing me!"

Jenny had a better angle. "They're just playing."

"Yeah?" Toby sat up. The kittens rubbed against him, as much as asking to be petted. He scratched one on the forehead and it began to purr in a throaty rumble. "They scared me!"

Jenny petted the other kitten. It rolled on its back, feet up, to have its chest scratched.

"They're nothing more than babies," she laughed in delight. "I don't see their mother. Maybe they're on their own."

"Ouch! His tongue is rough."

"Let's go show them to Dad."

Jenny and Toby dashed down the hill. There was no need to carry the cubs: the kittens were not about to let new playmates escape easily. Between rocks, along the stream, across the meadows, the cubs romped beside the children. Lean, muscular, their long tails flying behind them, the baby cougars were marvels of coordination. One moment they would run from in back, and nip at Toby's sneakers; the next, they would race ahead to stage a mock attack on Jenny.

If only the whole world could be like this, she thought. *An adventure that people and animals could share together without fear . . .*

At the cabin, Skip was still hammering shingles, a leather hat on his head to shade him from the bright sun. Pat, mending clothes, stood as she saw Jenny racing downhill.

"Skip, look!" she said, worried.

"Mom! Dad!" Toby called.

The cougar cubs arrived at the cabin along with the kids. Pawing at Pat's sewing, and using the cabin logs as scratching posts, they showed every sign of settling in. Skip climbed down from the roof. Crust ran up from the lake and stopped short in his tracks.

"See what we got?" Toby put a hammerlock on one of the cubs.

"Where'd you find them?" Skip asked.

"We were up on the hill and they just followed us all the way home," Jenny explained.

"What about their mother?" Pat frowned.

"They don't have one—or we don't think so . . ." Toby answered.

Skip looked over the cubs. They were undoubtedly friendly, and they also looked pretty well fed. "Jenny, you show me where you found these," he said. "Toby, you stay here."

"What are you going to do, Dad?" his son asked.

"You just *never* take baby animals like these out of the forest. You should know better."

"But they did follow us," Jenny protested.

"And their mother's probably looking for them right now," Pat said.

Skip picked up the cubs, one under each arm.

"You just show me where you got them," he said firmly. "Crust, you come too!"

With a last concerned glance at his wife, Skip started up the hill. In his haste, he had not thought to take his gun.

Retracing the way Jenny and Toby had come with two big, squirming cougar kittens under his arms was hard work, but Skip's worry overrode his aching arms. A full-grown cougar was monarch of the Northwest, and an angry, *mother* cougar was one character he had no desire to tangle with. Keeping the kittens at the cabin would only bring her down into the Robinson living room. Killing the kittens and hunting the mother down was out of the question. He had come to the wilderness to live in peace, not start a war.

Shamefaced, Jenny trudged along with Crust. Her father's anxiety only made her feel the more guilty. She was the older sister, eleven years old. She should have known better.

It had seemed only minutes to come down from where they'd found the cubs. It took a wearisome hour to relocate the place. At last, they reached the dead aspen log and Jenny pointed up to the pyramid of boulders.

"They were by those rocks."

"That's their den up there, Jenny, you know that. You wait here with the dog."

Skip had swung one leg over the tree, when a large, tawny-brown form rose atop the boulders. It was the mother, her eyes fixed on Skip. Baring her fangs, she sent a full-throated roar over the hills.

"Run, Jenny!" Skip ordered. "Get out of here!"

Scared, Jenny tugged on Crust's collar and took off down the hill. Skip dropped the kittens. Crying, they ran quickly up to their mother.

Skip looked back and forth from Jenny to the cougars. He wanted to let Jenny gain some distance from him, and would not follow her yet, lest the cougar descend the hill. He stood stock still. Halfway between the den and the fallen aspen, the mother cat was examining her kittens. An angry swat sent them back to the den, and she turned to concentrate all her attention on the human "invader" of her domain.

Jenny and Crust had reached a stand of pines. Skip now ran at an angle down the hill, and away from Jenny. One look behind told him that the mother cougar was after him.

Seven feet long from her nose to the tip of her tail, the cougar shot down the slope like a gray bullet, clearing the aspen in one powerful leap. Skip ran as he had never run before, but each glance back revealed the cougar closing in. *He* hurled rocks; *the cougar* flew over them. Trees that he dodged she seemed to *flow* through.

Ahead, he saw a pile of logs. With a sharp log, he might be able to stand her off.

But he never got close.

Two paws landed on his shoulders and sent him rolling.

Before he could rise from his knees, the cougar was on him again. Man and cat weighed about the same, but she had fangs, razor-sharp claws, and a maternal fury. His vest and shirt ripped open, Skip felt the claws tearing into his back.

"Daddy! Daddy!" Jenny cried from the pine trees.

Skip swung his elbows and punched, but the cougar was quicker and twice as strong.

Cats kill with a bite through the skull, or rip open the stomach of their prey, Skip remembered.

His leather hat baffled her a little. Not much. Her claws sliced into his shoulder, her fangs tore through his shirt. She shook him like a rag doll. *Is this how it is all going to end?* he wondered.

A punch and a kick pushed the cougar back, but she only sprang again. Skip's blood marked her paws. Then a new growl entered the battle and the cougar swung around to face a new challenger.

His teeth bared, Crust darted at the big cat. Skip crawled aside and rose shakily. The mother cougar circled the Labrador, snarling and biting. Crust dodged each swat of the claws, attacking and barking. Dust shot into the air as the cougar sprung at Crust's throat. But the dog veered out of the way. He never took a step back, however. The cat screamed with frustration.

"Crust, get back!" Skip shouted. *"Back!"*

The cougar looked from dog to man. Dogs, she knew, were used by cougar hunters. Rifles might not be far behind. Besides, her kittens were safe.

"Get away, get out!" Skip threw his hat at her.

Like an empress, the mother cat turned and loped up the hill to her den. Using his last strength, Skip gripped Crust to keep the dog from going after her.

"All over, Crust. Good boy, good boy!"

Jenny came running. Her face was drenched with tears.

"Daddy, did she hurt you."

Skip wiped blood out of his eye.

"I'm all right. Now do you know not to take home wild babies?"

"You're bleeding, Daddy."

The blood streamed down Skip's forehead. His left arm was a scarlet red.

"It's okay, Jenny . . ." he gasped painfully.

The children stood silently and watched. Their father, stripped to the waist, sat on a wooden box while Pat bandaged his arm. Even the bear cubs had been quiet since Skip staggered down the mountain.

"Grrr!" Skip took a fake nip at Pat and made her jump.

The children laughed, but there was no amusement on Pat's face.

"Skip . . ."

"Come on, it's just scratches . . . You kids go and play with the bears. But stay close to the cabin!"

"We're sorry . . . Dad," Jenny offered.

"That's okay. Just remember what I told you."

"Okay," Toby brightened.

While the two younger Robinsons went off with Ringo and Blackie, Pat washed her hands. It had struck Skip more than once before that when Pat was angry, she could make a very loud silence.

"Hey, come on." He reached for her.

Pat drew away. "I don't know how you can take this so lightly, Skip."

"You want me to throw a tantrum?"

"You're making a joke out of it!" her voice rose. And there was real fury in it. "If anything had happened to the kids out there, I don't know what—"

"The only thing that happened to the kids," Skip interrupted, "is that they learned a valuable lesson."

"Lesson! This is some school!" Pat threw down her towel. "You risk your life to learn something. What if that had been Jenny out there with that mountain lion—or Toby?"

"But it wasn't, it was me!"

"You're not thinking about what could have happened."

"I'm thinking a lot about what could have happened! But it's over. It won't happen again."

"You're sure of that?" Pat crossed her arms.

"Look, in the city it might have been a car accident, or a robber . . ."

"Skip, all I know is that since we've been here you've been nearly flattened by an avalanche, and a mountain lion almost kills you. You can't promise that nothing more is going to happen."

He searched her eyes for a hint of compromise, but her blue eyes had turned to steel.

He snatched up his shirt. "I can't talk to you. I'm going for a walk."

Walking didn't make Skip feel any better. He soon went back to shingling the roof, even though he ached from the pain. Pat took some clothes and the washboard down to the lake—as much to put distance between herself and Skip as to do any laundering.

She knew that Skip had risked his life for Jenny and she loved him for it. The fact remained that neither Jenny nor Toby would have survived the cougar's attack, no matter how brave Crust had been. But her thoughts were conflicting. She had to agree with the points Skip had made. There was no lack of violence in the city. Every time they had driven out on the freeway, they'd accepted the likely chance of a car collision.

On the roof, Skip was replaying the argument from a different viewpoint. He understood Pat's anger. She was the same as the mother cougar when it came to her children. Mishaps in the city were something they had come to anticipate. The wilderness was new to them. Any violence here was stranger and more terrifying. And, he couldn't make any promises to her. Who knew what was going to happen . . . ?

Jenny was old enough to understand the tension between her parents. She left Toby with the cubs and walked over to the cabin.

"Dad, maybe you ought to cook dinner for Mom tonight."

"You know, that's a good idea."

At that moment, a buzz caught Skip's ear. Toby ran down along the beach, looking into the sky.

"You hear it?" Skip yelled, dropping from the roof.

"It's the plane!" Jenny grinned.

"What's he doing here?" Toby shouted to his mother.

Jud's aquaplane swooped over the treetops and banked out over the lake. Pat shouted in return to Jud's wave while Skip jumped into the canoe and pushed off from shore.

"It's the mail, it's the mail!" Jenny explained to Ringo and Blackie.

Jud made one more turn overhead as Skip paddled toward the center of the lake. In the middle of Jud's second pass, a package fell from the plane and splashed down into the water. Before the plane had passed from view, Skip was hauling the package into the canoe.

"Hey, big box for Jen and Toby!" he bellowed on the way back to shore.

They were jumping up and down on the sand as the canoe came in. Skip pulled a sealed box from the watertight package.

"Hooray!" Toby yelled.

"Who's it from?" Jenny asked.

"Board of Education." Skip handed her the box.

Jenny sagged under its weight. "How'd they ever find us up here?"

"I squealed," Skip admitted.

A box even from the Board of Education was an event. Jenny, Toby, and the bear cubs opened it and thumbed—or pawed—through the pages of the books.

"I want the books with pictures," Toby said.

Pat sat on the bank reading a letter.

"Your sister?" Skip asked gently. Pat nodded. "How is everything?"

"She sends you her love." Pat got to the bottom of the page. "And she says the smog is worse than ever."

A smile crossed her face. Skip knelt and put his arm around her.

Chapter Eight

A Housewarming

A cabin was not a home without a chimney. It meant a fireplace for cooking and heat. It also meant, for the Robinsons, work. Part of a side wall had to be sawed away and a new foundation laid. Flat rocks and clay had to be hauled to the cabin.

"Why can't we just use mud?" Toby wanted to know.

"Because bees will dig into mud," Skip explained. "It's very painful to share a cabin with bees."

"Well," Jenny said, "why does the foundation have to be so deep?"

"Because if you don't have a firm foundation, the chimney might fall over and take the wall with it. In the wintertime, a cabin without a wall can be very cold."

As the chimney grew, Skip explained some of the other fine points of construction. The opening directly above the fire was called the "throat," the space above the throat was the "scotchback." A chimney with a scotchback bigger than its throat, and a top about the same size as the throat, guaranteed a smoothly drawing fire.

"And that means that we won't have a cabin full of smoke."

"Smoke would keep the bees out," Toby ventured.

"Well, I hadn't thought of that." Skip scratched his chin.

The kids understood mortaring the chinks between logs of the walls better. Pat showed them how to push the clay in without leaving bulges that would catch rainwater, which might rot the logs. Toby thought Jenny looked improved with a clay mustache. Jenny thought Toby looked better with a clay nose.

The bear cubs were not a great help. If they were not wallowing in the clay, they were trying to push over the chimney. When Jenny and Toby took them out in the canoe, to spare the chimney construction, it was only a matter of minutes before all four were tipped into the lake and had to swim back.

Weeks went by, but at last the day came when the Robinsons walked out on the grass in front of their cabin and realized that the first big step was over. They had a home.

The walls were neat and trim. The chimney was straight and tall. The glass of the windows—Jud had flown it out to them soon after their arrival—reflected the flower boxes hung outside. Over the front door was a gable, in front was a porch, and hanging alongside by a log (left especially long) was a swing.

"I can't believe it," Pat sighed with awe, "I just can't believe it . . . "

"Look"—Skip hugged her—"for the work you did, *believe!*"

"Then what do we do today?" Toby's arms hung down.

"Today, Toby, we play." Skip swung him into the air.

That night, coals winked in the new fireplace. A soft glow spread over the stone mantel, over paneled walls and polished floor, new chairs and a new double bed. At the polished table of varnished birch, the Robinsons sat in their best clothes. Pat had done up her hair and put on earrings, which she hadn't had occasion to wear since they'd left the city. All the food had been dished out—except from one large covered dish in the center of the table.

"Thank You, dear Lord, for this beautiful day," Jenny said, lowering her head, "for home and work and happy play. Thank You for rest when the day is done, and love that takes care of everyone." She paused and added, "And, most of all, thank You for bringing us here!"

"Amen!" the rest chorused.

Toby cleared his throat and looked at his mother. "Okay?"

"Okay," Pat nodded.

He reached across the table and removed the plate cover from two golden roasted ducks.

"A duck! *Two* ducks!" Skip's mouth dropped. "Where did they come from?"

The kids looked proudly at Pat.

"She got them while you were fishing at the other end of the lake," Toby said proudly.

"First shot," Pat said casually.

"They were flying piggyback?" Skip raised his eyebrows.

Pat harrumphed, but she caught the pride Skip shared with Jenny and Toby. "Let's cut them," she suggested.

Toby sawed industriously at a duck leg. Jenny watched her brother with a critical eye.

"It smells fantastic," Skip said.

"It's cooked in wild onion," Jenny mentioned, as her own contribution.

"Everything here"—Pat spread her arms to take in the bounty on the table, and wider to take in the whole cabin—"we provided for ourselves!"

Skip and his wife looked at each other and spoke with their eyes. They had struggled and provided. Shared and survived. They were making it. And they loved each other.

"You're beautiful," he said, "—for a sharpshooter. Sure these ducks weren't sleeping?"

The light and the laughter from the new cabin filtered through the trees and out onto the lake.

A home was truly being born.

Chapter Nine

Timber Wolves

The days became warmer and longer.

Skip had fixed up the old cabin as a storehouse to keep dried meat and bulk supplies. What he was interested in for the summer, though, was a springhouse to keep fresh meat and butter cool. *The trapper who lived on the lake before must have had one,* Skip decided. The problem was finding it.

Accompanied by Ringo and Blackie, he searched the hills for traces of any overgrown path that might lead to a springhouse. He kept his ears open for sounds of a surfacing spring, and watched for those flowers—honeysuckles or arrowheads—that would grow best on moist earth. The bear cubs, meanwhile, insisted on getting teeth holds on Skip's trousers and trying to pull him toward any nearby stream. He had brought his rod and reel along on the expedition and to them that meant only one thing: fish. Logically enough.

"You might have a point, too," Skip conceded. The stream they were near now was fed by dozens of springs, any one of which could be the site of a springhouse.

After an hour's search, Skip was willing to admit defeat. *Maybe old man Taylor didn't like butter. Maybe the springhouse can never be found.*

"I give up. C'mon, cubs . . . Cubs . . . ? Ringo? Blackie?"

He couldn't see them, but he could hear the cubs' muffled whining.

"Darn it, Ringo, where are you?"

The whining grew louder but was still muffled. Skip followed the sound until he came to a double-door set nearly flush to the ground and hidden by bushes. The bar had fallen across the latch. The whines came from inside.

"You found it!"

Skip opened the doors, and was almost bowled over as the bears rushed out of their imprisonment. Then they tried to drag him away from what they considered a dungeon.

"Take it easy! Relax! I want to look this over. What do you think we've been searching for?"

Ringo shook his head.

The first thing Skip examined was the door. He was relieved to find that the bar could be turned from the inside of the door as well as the outside—a fine point that the cubs might miss, but Jenny and Toby would never accidentally lock themselves in.

Five wooden steps led down into a space about as big as a good-sized closet. The walls were stone and cement, Damp with the earth's moisture. The floor was actually a cement slab set down in an underground spring that ran along the bottom of the walls. Skip estimated the temperature of the springhouse at approximately 40 degrees. A perfect natural refrigerator.

"Mr. Taylor, you did good work," Skip said softly. As he emerged from the doors, he added, to the cubs: "You did, too."

Skip's favorite fishing spot was only fifty yards away, a stone shelf that jutted into a stream of fast-running, clear water and mountain trout. Blackie pushed his nose against a dry fly that Skip was tying to his leader.

"Hey, you don't want that. You want what it gets."

It didn't take long. Almost as soon as the fly hit the

surface of the water, a trout struck. Skip stripped in ten inches of game fish.

"Reward time!"

Skip unhooked the fish and tossed it on the stone shelf between the cubs. Ringo swatted at it. The trout wriggled and the cub jumped back. Blackie took his turn trying to subdue the fish. This was what their mother would be teaching them if she were alive, Skip knew. In a year, Blackie and Ringo would be wading right into the stream and getting their own supper.

He cast the fly back onto the water, into a pool in the middle of the stream where the big trout lurked.

Blackie's sharp ears caught the sound of a heavy paw on grass. The cub bumped into his brother, and both stared at the adult black bear that sashayed onto the stone shelf. The trout was forgotten. The cubs hustled away into the trees.

Abruptly, Skip's rod bent like a bow.

"Gotcha!" He watched a fat, glistening trout break water and run with the hook. "Come on!" Skip let the line drag out, and started to reel in his catch. "Fish fry tonight. You ought to watch this, cubs, see how the master does it."

The sound of a fish being eaten behind him reassured Skip. But the full-throated bear roar that followed made the hair on the back of his neck stand on end.

"Wha . . . ?"

It was the same black bear that had chased the family onto the cabin roof. Finished with the bones of the cubs' trout, the bear roared again and eyed Skip expectantly. The ex-hardhat dropped his rod and started running.

At the cabin, Pat was sewing patches onto worn dungarees. Jenny and Toby sat at the table, chins on hands, studying math. Crust filled the air from time to time with a yawn that expressed the ultimate in boredom.

"I just don't see how long division is going to improve my mind," Jenny complained. "My mind is fine as it is."

Pat looked up from her sewing. "You don't want to grow up ignorant."

"What's 'ignorant'?" Toby asked.

"Look it up," Jenny snapped.

Crust's yawning was contagious. Jenny put her hand over her mouth.

"How is math going to help us out here in the woods, Mom?"

"Maybe . . . " Pat said slowly, "you won't always live up here . . . "

"I always want to live here. I never want to go away," Toby asserted.

"Okay. What if you want to build a cabin?"

Toby thought it over. "Dad will help me."

"Oh, Mom, can't we play now and do our homework tonight?"

"You promise you'll do it? Really promise?"

"Yes!"

Two math books slapped shut.

"All right, you can go help your father fish. Tell him that lunch will be ready in twenty minutes."

"Hooray!"

Toby tore through the door. Jenny and Crust were right behind.

They knew about Skip's fishing spot. Cutting through the woods, they followed the stream. Crust made a foray into the woods to chase a badger.

"At least he doesn't go after porcupines anymore," Toby commented.

"That's because he's not dumb anymore."

When they came to the stone shelf and looked around, Skip's rod lay on the rock but their father was nowhere in sight. The cubs were gone, too.

"Gee, Toby, I wonder where they are. Dad would never just leave his rod."

"Yes, he would!"

Toby pointed to the big black bear returning to the

shelf from the trees nearby. Shuffling forward, the big animal blocked any exit for the kids.

"What do we do, Jenny?"

A growl turned the bear's head.

Racing out of the trees, Crust launched himself at the bear's back. Lazily, the bear wheeled and swatted the dog aside. Crust returned, snapping at the bear's paws. The children slipped nimbly around him and out into the meadow beyond the shelf.

"Crust, stay away!" Toby yelled.

Jenny held her brother. "Toby, you go and tell Mom. Do as I tell you!"

"What about you?"

"Do as I say!"

Toby bit his lip and started back to the cabin.

Crust and the bear were battling in the middle of the stream. Amid the splashing, the dog darted in with fast bites. The bear pushed him back as if to say, "Don't bother me." Soon it slapped Crust off and shuffled to the other side of the water. Undaunted, Crust ran after it.

"Crust," Jenny screamed, "you come back here!"

The dog suffered two more cuffs on the side of the head, and the bear broke into an easy run through the trees. Crust disappeared after it.

"Crust!"

Jenny's scream echoed through the woods.

Alone on the stone shelf now, Jenny hesitated. The other side of the stream had not really been explored yet. But what if Crust got hurt and needed help? *If I stay within sight of the lake,* she told herself, *I won't get lost.*

At the moment Jenny was wading the stream, Skip was rushing into the cabin. Two closed schoolbooks lay on the table.

"Where are the kids?" he asked Pat between deep breaths.

"What happened?"

"I just saw a bear. Where are they?"

"They went to get you."

Skip took his rifle from the rack above the fireplace. A sick feeling went through Pat as she watched him load bullets into the breech.

"Stay close to the cabin, Pat. I'll go and get them."

Pat followed her husband to the porch as Toby came running out of the woods.

"Dad! Dad!"

"Toby, where's Jenny?"

Toby got to the porch, panting.

"Crust went after the bear. She stayed with Crust."

"Stay here with your mother," Skip said, patting Toby's head.

From the porch, Pat and Toby watched Skip dashing back up the way Toby had come.

Far on the other side of the stream, Jenny staggered finally to a halt. The sound of Crust's barking had led her on and on, but she heard nothing now except the occasional rat-tat-tat of a woodpecker. All around her rose one-hundred-foot pine trees, almost blocking out the sky. She could not see the lake and she was totally lost.

"Crust . . . !"

The only answer was silence. This was the deep woods, a world of eerie quiets. Over the ground lay a thick carpet of pine needles. There were no bushes or flowers: not enough light came through the dense walls of trees. North? South? There were no directions here. Which way had she come? Needles covered her tracks. She thought of fairy tales, of Hansel and Gretel, and laughed. But not for long. This was serious and she was getting scared.

Downhill, she reminded herself. *Downhill has to lead to the lake . . .*

For an hour, Jenny pushed her way through the Her throat became hoarse. Eventually, she realized that she had lost all sense of direction. She was walking uphill!

For how long? she asked herself. She had to concentrate to hold back the tears.

"Crust, where are you?" she sang out.

No answer.

Should she stay where she was, or keep moving? Either way, she was lost. But maybe, just maybe, she would find her way out, or see the lake. Her mother would be angry when she got to the cabin, but Jenny was willing to face anything as long as she could see her mother again.

I have to think, she told herself.

Digging through the thick carpet of needles, she found a rock and began marking every fifth tree she passed. She didn't want to think of the odds against her father finding the marks among the thousands of pines, but at least it was something for her to do. She pushed on through the woods. In the city, she could have called home. Found a policeman. Read street signs. Here were only endless trees, so tall it hurt the neck to look up at them. The wilderness had seemed so friendly before. This was a different face, this was sheer fright.

Hunger and fatigue only made her fright worse.

"Am I going in circles?" she asked herself aloud. "What happens when night comes?"

Stumbling, she twisted her ankle and hopped painfully to a tree to rest against it.

"Hoooo!"

The great yellow eyes and sharp beak of an owl swung down from a branch at Jenny. Stumbling, she fell and rolled backward down a long slope, where she laid still . . . and hopeless. For a while, she did nothing but listen to the hush of the pine forest.

Then, suddenly, she heard a familiar husky breathing and felt a cold tongue on her neck.

"Crust!" Jenny sat up and hugged her dog. "Oh, Crust, where've you been? I'm so glad you came back!"

The Labrador went on licking her face until Jenny

got to her feet. The ankle was still sore, but Crust's presence dulled the pain a little.

Jenny brushed needles from her hair. "I hope you know your way out of here."

Together, they worked their way along the slope. In ten or fifteen minutes, Jenny could see more light through the trees. They were coming to the end of the pine forest.

Far behind them, Skip's trained eyes had followed Jenny's trail through the needles to the first marked tree.

"Good girl," he said, and then called out loudly: *"Jenny! Jenny!"*

He waited, and grimaced at the quiet. Raising his rifle high, he fired a shot into the air. As the blast dissolved into the forest, the quiet returned.

Skip slung the rifle over his shoulder and ran, his eyes constantly sweeping here and there for the marked trees.

Jenny and Crust had now escaped from the forest. Supporting herself with a long stick, she climbed a hill of boulders and aspen trees. The lake lay below. Somehow, she would have to go along it to get back to the cabin, because re-entering the pines would only get her lost again. How late it was she could not tell. A heavy mist was rolling in over the mountains and she felt a chill in the air.

"Dad . . . ! Toby . . . !"

No use.

She patted Crust, as much to reassure herself as him. "Up to us, Crust. We can do it, can't we?"

They started down the hill. The terrain was rugged, but Jenny knew the importance of getting to the lake before the mist did. When part of the mist shifted, she saw the pale outline of a full moon in the late-afternoon sky. Half hopping, half running, Jenny made her way down through the rocks and trees.

The mist was, visibly, spilling over the mountains toward the lake.

Now, from the hills behind Jenny, rose a wailing cry, a cry she had never heard before but recognized instantly.

A wolf!

Crust stopped to snarl.

"C'mon, Crust. We can't stop."

They ran over a meadow studded with rocks. Crust kept glancing back and showing his teeth. Jenny fell once and got up swiftly.

"Dad . . . !" Jenny cried as her weakened ankle gave way under her, dumping her to the damp sod.

Only a howl answered. Closer. She got up.

Jenny started running again, her wide eyes as much on the surrounding woods as on the ground in front of her. The howling increased, from one direction, and then from another. Always closer.

A stand of white birches loomed on Jenny's right. Through their slender trunks, she saw it. A brownish gray, slightly smaller than Crust, the wolf stood and watched her go by.

Crust growled abruptly toward the left. There Jenny saw a second wolf, padding the meadow silently, in pace with her. On the hill she had just left stood a third and a fourth wolf, howling, calling for the rest of the pack.

"Stay close, Crust!" Jenny held on to his collar.

She now dropped the stick. No more pain came from her ankle; now, she only wanted to run.

She did not want to look, but she could see more wolves falling into step around her, slipping through the trees, parallel with her, edging closer. The pack was gathering for the hunt, and it was hunting . . . *her*.

"DAD . . . !"

The wolves on each side were by this time no more than fifty feet away, the lake perhaps two hundred. Jenny glanced back at four of the animals closing in. They loped, their jaws open, their eyes fixed on her. As she stumbled and fell face forward, one of the pack dashed toward her and Crust chased it away.

"Crust," Jenny cried, "come back!"

In panic, she got to her feet and raced toward the water. She could hear the pack at her back. A wolf even larger than Crust ran by her side, its lips curled back from a double row of teeth.

Jenny reached the edge of the lake and dove in among the reeds. The wolves followed. Shrieking, she swung her arms at them.

"Get back! Get back!"

They drove her deeper into the water, their teeth snapping at her, their ears flattened on outstretched necks. They scrambled over each other to get at her. *"No!"*

A yellow form threw itself among the gray backs of the wolves. Crust knocked aside two of the smaller wolves. A third seized him by the neck and threw him down. Others dug their teeth into his legs and haunches. Then the dog amazingly struggled to his feet and drove some of his attackers back. In a moment, he was buried again under a pile of wolves.

Jenny could hardly follow the fight, but she could see the dog was losing. After each attack, it took longer for Crust to regain his feet. Strips of bloody fur hung from his side. He might have been able to stand off one wolf, face to face, but not a pack—not when jaws came from the front, sides, and rear. Tiring and wounded, he could only attempt to stand his ground to the last.

Reaching down into the water for a narrow branch floating there, Jenny tried to help Crust. Two of the wolves turned on her.

Then, as if they were frozen, the wolves suddenly stopped at the sound of a rifle.

"Jenny!"

Skip flew down the hill in long leaps. Firing a second time into the air, he then waded in among the wolves, swinging the rifle like a bat.

"Get out of here! *Get out!"*

One wolf went spinning off the rifle stock. The rest backed away. Except for the big lead wolf, who studied Skip with respect, and then slowly joined the remainder on the bank.

"Go!" Skip shouted.

The wolf pack gradually regrouped on the hill. In a minute, they vanished as silently and quickly as they had first appeared.

Jenny staggered out of the water and clutched her father's leg. "Daddy," she wept with relief, "I thought you'd never come."

"It's all right, Jenny." Skip hugged her. "Everything's all right."

"What about Crust?"

The retriever was licking his wounds and wagging his tail.

"He's okay, just got himself some scratches. Some old dog!" Skip picked Jenny up in his arms. "Let's go home."

At the cabin, Pat was staring out the door. She'd been there for more than an hour—as if by watching she could bring her daughter home.

From the table, Toby watched his mother. *This is a time,* he thought, *when it's up to me to help make her worry less.*

"You want to play checkers, Mom?"

Pat was about to say no when she realized what Toby was doing. "Sure." She shut the wooden door. "Why not?"

Toby got out the board and set up the pieces.

"Don't worry, Mom. Dad can handle anything."

"You get red?" Pat sat down and one of the bear cubs laid its head on her lap.

A beetle wandered across the playing board. Toby picked the insect up on the end of a pencil and became lost in thought. He was just as worried as his mother about his sister.

Then, suddenly, the bear cub sniffed, and lifted its

head to look at the door. Pat heard the sound of dancing paws and a scratch at the door.

"Crust!"

Opening the door, she found Crust—softly whining and spotted with dried blood. Out of the mist beyond the porch came Skip, carrying Jenny.

"What . . . happened?" Pat gasped.

"She's all right; she's sleeping." Skip entered the cabin and gently set Jenny on the bed. The girl awoke, groggy-eyed.

"Jenny," Pat cooed softly, sitting on the bed and running her hand over the eleven-year-old's forehead, "how are you?"

"I'm so . . . tired . . ." Jenny turned on her side and slipped back into sleep.

Pat glanced from Jenny to Crust, who had obviously been attacked by . . . something. Her hands curled into fists and finally her tears came.

"Skip, what happened?"

"Everything's all right, Jenny's okay. We have to get some water and alcohol for the dog. He's been hurt."

Later, when both children were asleep in their loft, Skip finished washing and bandaging Crust's wounds on the cabin porch. Pat stood beside him, gazing out on the mist that covered the lake like a down blanket. A full moon hung overhead, lending silver to the fog.

"You're done, Crust!" Skip set an alcohol-soaked rag aside. "Good dog. Go lie down."

Crust padded through the open door to lie by the fireplace.

Skip joined Pat in gazing toward the lake. Above the mist, mountaintops rose sharp and distinct in the moonlight. Ironically, their new home had never seemed more beautiful.

"You all right?" He touched Pat's arm.

"Yes." She blinked. "I knew something else like this would happen one day. If something had happened to you or Jenny . . ."

"I guess . . ." Skip sighed, "I guess we just bit off more than we could chew up here." He waited for her to reply, but knew she wouldn't until he asked the question she wanted. "Pat, okay. What do you want to do? You want to go back?"

She turned to him and her eyes searched his.

"Do you?"

"No," Skip answered.

"You want to stay here and go on risking the kids' lives."

"No!" He paused. "Pat, don't you think we were risking their lives in the city?"

"At least *there* we had some help!"

"Here we have to help ourselves. Look, those wolves scared me. But I don't want to walk away from everything . . . everything we *have* up here."

"It's not just *your* life, Skip."

"I know that. I understand the way you feel, but . . ."

"You don't." Pat shook her head. "I love this place as much as you do, but is it always going to be like this—like *today?*"

"I don't . . . know," Skip admitted. "I honestly don't know . . ."

Chapter Ten

Boomer

The next morning was bright and sunny. Breakfast was set on a newly constructed picnic table outside the cabin. After breakfast, as they sat relaxed and cheerful, Skip raised a subject for open discussion: Should the family stay in the wilderness, or pack up?

Toby played with a fishing pole. "I like it here."

"What about your friends?" Pat asked. "Don't you miss them?"

"Well, yeah, but I have new friends here. Ringo. Blackie. The raccoon. Gee, I hardly have a chance to get lonely."

"What about the things that frighten you?"

"I'm not scared of nothin'. Right, Dad?"

"Right, but you've got to have respect for things, Toby."

"Oh, sure, you gotta look out for things that can hurt you. And . . ." Toby pulled his ear and looked at the ground.

"And what?" Skip prompted him.

"Naw. It's corny, Dad."

"If you can't be corny with your own family, who can you be corny with?" Jenny put in.

"Well"—Toby went on pulling his ear—"the thing is, back in the city I was always in the way. I was just the baby, you know. Here, I'm important. I do real things and I can really help."

For Toby a statement that long was as grand as a speech. *And more intelligent than most speeches,* Skip thought. Pat was just as surprised and impressed.

"What about you, Jen?" she asked. "What do you think?"

"Oh, there're bad things . . ." Jenny thought of the wolves. Then her face lit up. "But there're a lot more good things."

"Like what?" Skip asked.

Jenny spread her arms. "Like having the best backyard in the world. And being together. In the city, you'd go off to work. We were in school. Mom was left alone at home. Now we do everything together. What could be better than that?"

Pat had no answer. She had never considered the opinions the children might have. Hearing them, it struck her that Jenny and Toby were developing in ways—good ways—that even a mother couldn't have predicted. Like strong young plants, brother and sister were growing fast under the wilderness sun. Pat had accused Skip of not taking the kids into consideration. Perhaps *she* was the one guilty of that particular error.

"Your turn, Pat," Skip offered.

"Looks like I'm outnumbered," she shrugged.

The children's clapping was interrupted by Crust's barking. Out of the woods came an unexpected sight: an old man in a battered hat, flannel shirt, suspended jeans, and boots. A white stubble covered his chin and more than one tooth was missing from his smile, but somehow that only made his friendliness all the more appealing. Moving along the trail, he pulled a rope attached to the hackamore on a mule loaded with supplies.

"Yer a *good* dog, eh? Lemme jus' tie up ol' Flora to this tree here." He hitched the mule to a branch before approaching the picnic table. Scratching Crust's head like a familiar acquaintance, he said,

"Call yuh Ol' Yeller, do they? Well, interduce me to yer folks, huh?"

"Hi there!" Skip shook the old man's hand.

"Howdy." He took in the Robinsons. "You folks are sure a surprise."

"We just moved in," Skip said, "—or we're trying to, anyway."

"Say"—a veteran eye surveyed the new cabin—"looks to me like yer doin' a good job. That's a fine set o' sticks yuh got there."

"Thanks. Uh, this is my wife, Pat."

Gallantly, the old man removed his hat to make a bow.

"Howdy, ma'am."

"Our daughter Jenny, son Toby."

Jenny got a bow and Toby a handshake and a grin. Skip and Pat looked at each other with amusement.

"Pleasure to meet yuh. Name's Willard Parks. 'Cept my friends—what's left of 'em, God bless 'em—call me Boomer. That's Flora, muh mule over there. Leastways, I call 'er Flora. Don't know what she calls me."

"Can I offer you some food, or something to drink?" Pat asked.

"That's mighty hospitable of yuh, lady."

"Some food" turned out to be two big helpings of pancakes and bacon, washed down with coffee. Between bites, Boomer managed to keep Jenny and Toby enthralled with a short history of his forty years' trapping and prospecting for gold in the north country. Finally, he burped politely and pushed his plate away.

"Eyes are gettin' bigger than muh tummy. Thank yuh, ma'am, that was a mighty nice spread for an ol' codger."

"You're very welcome, Boomer." Pat and Skip were as interested in Boomer's stories as the children, and it was a treat to have company. "Would you like just a little bit more coffee?"

"Don't mind if I do," Boomer confessed. "You folks plannin' on spendin' the winter up here?"

"We *were* . . ." Skip tilted the coffee pot. "But we might not, anymore."

"What happened?"

"Jenny was attacked by a pack of wolves yesterday," Pat explained.

Boomer frowned. "Wolves don't attack people. They're just inquisitive."

"No," Skip said. "I was there."

Boomer's frown deepened. In his shaggy way, he was a walking library of animal lore. He leaned toward Jenny.

"What happened, honey?"

"I was out chasing Crust, and——"

"Wait a second." Boomer held his hand up. "Who's Crust?"

"Our dog."

"Well, there yuh go." Boomer looked around the table. "Wolves'll go after a dog every time. No sir, only thing around here that'll attack a man is ol' Three Toes."

"Who's *that?*" Toby asked shrilly.

"Big ol' grizzly. Hated people ever since he got 'is foot caught 'n a trap. That's why he's called Three Toes. Real bad bear. Been known to bring down three, four cows in one night."

"He won't come around here, will he?" Anxiety filled Jenny's voice.

"Never has. Spends most of 'is time north of here." Boomer finished his cup and stood to stretch. "Mighty fine table you set, ma'am. Much appreciate it. Now I'll leave you folks alone an' get movin' on."

"Anytime, Boomer," Pat said.

The old trapper started back toward his mule, but his eye was caught by the weathered cabin Skip had renovated into a storehouse. The ex-construction worker caught the glance.

"You know anything about the man who built that little place?"

"Brings back a flood o' memories," Boomer nodded. "Yup, I knowed 'im. Knowed 'im an' buried 'im. It's been a long time since I sat up here with ol' Jake, swappin' lies."

"What sort of a man was he?"

"Sort o' man? Well, most folks didn't like 'im. But, then," Boomer chuckled, "Jake didn't like most folks! He sure did love his animals, though."

"What kind of animals?" Toby asked.

"Raccoons, otters, jays, an' magpies. You name it, he had it. Even had a flock o' wild geese."

"What did he do with them?" Jenny wanted to know.

"Raised 'em, raised 'em from babies. This place was a regular menagerie." Boomer whispered so that his mule wouldn't hear. "Ol' Flora used to hate it."

"Well, that explains why the animals around here are so tame," Skip said to Pat. An idea suddenly occurred to him. "Jake didn't by any chance have a black bear, did he?"

A smile started to creep across Boomer's lips.

"Why, yuh seen one?"

Toby was ready with the information. "One ate our supplies and tried to get Dad's fish."

"Sounds like ol' Samson," Boomer laughed. "Wait till he starts nibblin' on yer *ear!*"

"He's that tame?" Pat was amazed.

"Jus' like a ol' hound dog."

Toby remained skeptical. "How can you tell if it's him?"

"Well now, that's simple. Yuh jus' walk up an' interduce yerself . . . Right, Skip?"

"Right, Boomer," Skip agreed.

"Well, I'll be on muh way. Got fifteen miles to go today, an' . . ."

Boomer's voice trailed off as the two bear cubs made their first appearance of the day and made a beeline past Boomer to the mule.

"Dang blast it! Where'd *they* come from?"

"We're raising them," Toby said.

Flora, the mule, heehawed at Ringo and Blackie —which only made her all the more interesting to them. Bucking, she snapped her rope.

"Raisin' 'em? Flora, come back here!" Boomer started for his vanishing steed.

"Come on, Jen"—Toby joined Boomer—"we'll get her!"

Boomer turned down the help. "Don't *you* go chasin' after that mule! Yuh'll run 'er right outta the country."

"Toby, come back here!" Skip tried to keep from laughing.

"See yuh folks later." Boomer tried to run backward and make a polite exit at the same time. "Thanks fer the grub. Flora! Dang blast it, where're yuh goin'?"

"Bye, Boomer," Toby and Jenny called.

"Flora!!!"

After the old hunter's hasty departure, the family took a stroll through the woods. One object was pleasure: gathering wildflowers. The other object was serious business: if Jenny and Toby were going to have any more surprise mishaps in the wilderness, Skip wanted them to know what to do. As much as any classroom, the north country demanded education.

"What would you do if you're lost in the woods and your mom suddenly gets a terrible headache?" Skip asked his children.

"Give her an aspirin," Toby replied.

"You don't have any aspirin," Skip told them.

"Tell her to lie down and massage her head," Jenny said.

"That doesn't work either. Come on," Skip urged. "Oh-oh!" Skip jumped in fake horror. "Look out! There's a rattler!"

Pat joined in the game. "Where?"

"Too late." Skip smacked his forehead. "Jenny's already been bitten. What are you going to do, Toby?"

"Mom . . . ?"

"I'm not here," Pat said.

"Well, I know what to do, anyway."

"Hurry up," Jenny urged. "After all, I'm maybe dying," she wailed.

"The first thing you have to do is keep calm," Toby ordered her, "so your blood doesn't start racing. I'll put a tourniquet above the bite, and then"—he made a fiendish face—"suck out the poison. That's the best part!"

"Yuck!" Jenny wrinkled her nose.

Their walk soon brought them back to the lake. Sailing in over the trees and down to the surface of the water were great V's of Canadian geese. Big, handsome birds with black markings, they made the air whistle from the force of their wings. Without fear, they banked over the Robinsons' heads, dove towards the lake, stalled almost to a stop in mid-air above its surface, and then settled, splashing only very gently. More than any other animal, the geese symbolized to Skip the freedom of the wilderness. They were free to roam wherever they wanted, wherever there was a wind to catch . . .

"Maybe these are the geese Boomer was talking about," Pat suggested.

Jenny watched the birds with awe. "We should have brought something for them to eat."

"Maybe we *did*." Pat held up a bag of breadcrusts.

Excited, Jenny and Toby took the bag to the water's edge. Before the first crust was thrown, a goose, his head high with anticipation, waddled up out of the water.

"These *are* the tame geese!" Toby yelled.

More of the birds came onto the bank, until Jenny and Toby were literally surrounded by open bills.

Skip and Pat lay down on the grass to watch.

"Do you think I'm crazy," he asked her.

"Why do you ask that?"

"Oh, I was just thinking about how I'd try to explain all this place to some of my friends back in the city. I was thinking of their questions. Like, 'How are you going to make any money?' Or, 'When are you going to develop the lake? Put up some tourist cabins? Bring in some motor boats?' I mean, how do you explain to people that it's not necessary to devote your life to making money? That this place is developed now? Just the way it should be."

"Well"—Pat picked a flower and planted it in his hair—"there are two kinds of profits, aren't there?"

"What do you mean?"

"There's a profit you measure in money Then there's the profit you measure in happiness, health, and . . . becoming a better person. Overall, I think I can detect some signs of that profit already. *But,*" she smiled, "I have to tell you honestly that with flowers in your hair you *do* look a little crazy!"

"I love you, Pat." Skip pulled her face down for a kiss.

"Then you're not so crazy, after all," she murmured.

Chapter Eleven

Samson

The family returned from the lake with armfuls of flowers—enough, as Toby put it, "to drive a bumble-bee nuts." Skip led the way with the old French song "Alouette."

"Et la tête." He pointed to his head.

"Et la tête!" Pat, Jenny and Toby mimicked him.

"Et le nez." He pointed to his nose.

"Et le nez!"

"Et la bouche." He indicated his mouth.

"Et la bouche!"

And all together:

"Alouette, gentille alouette! Alouette, je te plumerai!!!"

The song ended as they reached the cabin. Skip held up both hands to make an announcement.

"And next spring, this will be the site of the greatest vegetable garden in the entire Rocky Mountains. Here, we will have rows of lettuce and tomatoes, he declared, pacing off some spaces of squares.

"Yeah!" Jenny and Toby shouted.

"Here, will be rows of peas and melons."

"Yeah!"

"And here, most important, will be row after row of . . . spinach!"

"Ugh!" Toby's face curdled.

"Who wants homemade bread and honey now?" Pat asked.

Jenny and Toby were first through the cabin door, whooping. Pat and Skip followed. The whoops died, and for two seconds there was absolute silence in the cabin. Then the whole family piled out the door even faster than they had gone in—and ran about twenty yards from the cabin before they stopped to look back. The flowers they'd picked were strewn like the debris of an explosion.

"That bear again!" Toby caught his breath. "Where'd he come from?"

"I nearly tripped over him," Jenny gasped.

"Skip," Pat asked, "what are you going to do?"

"I don't know, but I'm a little sick of him chasing us all the time."

"I bet it's the friendly one," Jenny exclaimed. "Samson."

"Yeah!" Toby liked the idea. "Go on, Dad."

"What do you mean, go on?"

"Go on and introduce yourself like Boomer said."

Skip rolled his eyes. In spite of herself, Pat began laughing.

"*Boomer* said it," Skip told Toby, "not me."

"You agreed with him."

Skip looked to his wife for her usual grasp on sanity, but all he saw in her face was a tightly compressed smile. The more he looked, the more her smile threatened to break into outright hilarity.

"It's not funny," he said. He stalled, hoping the bear might decide on his own to leave the cabin.

"Come on," Toby reassured his father. "I'll go with you."

"No, Toby, you stay here." Skip swallowed and took his first step back toward the cabin. "I'll go alone. Samson, huh?"

He gave Pat a glance to let her know he had been cornered into bravery and, as cautiously as a tightrope walker, walked up to the door and slipped inside.

The place was a mess. Honey seemed to have been

spread over the table, bed, chair, and floor with a paint roller, and scattered over all the honey was flour! It looked like an indoor snowfall.

Skip could not see the bear. He cleared his throat. "Ahem . . . Uh, Samson? You there, Samson?"

The head and eyes of a black bear covered with flour peered up from the other side of the big table.

"Hi, Samson. Having a good time? Boy, I *hope* it's you, Samson."

Skip edged around the table so that he could have a good look at his visitor. The bear dug its snout back into a big honey jar; its tongue lapped the bottom. Skip guessed the bear's weight at around five hundred pounds. A lot of bear. A lot of stomach.

"See what I've got here, Samson!" Skip picked up a loaf of bread from the table. "Want a little bread with your honey?"

With a grunt, the bear rose from the floor onto its hind feet, its eyes fixed on the bread. Skip was sure that this was the same bear that had chased him up on the roof and, later, away from the stream. He still was not sure it was Samson, but he intended to keep the relationship on a first-name basis, anyway, if possible.

"That's it, Samson. Come on . . ." Skip backed up toward the door, maneuvering around a chair and along the fireplace.

Standing erect, the bear was taller than Skip. It shuffled forward, its nose sniffing at the loaf.

"Good old homemade bread, Samson. Come on, we're almost there. Bet you can almost taste it now. That's"—Skip's foot caught on the logs beside the fireplace and he fell, tumbling, backward on the floor —"it!"

The bear dropped on top of him, pinning him to the floor. Skip turned his face as two big jaws gaped open. The jaws closed on the loaf of bread and lazily devoured it.

"Well, Samson, I guess it's you," Skip said through the falling crumbs.

Samson it was, and though Skip was able to disengage himself finally from the bear, he was unable to disengage the bear from the cabin. While the family cleaned honey and flour from the floor, Samson placidly watched—and ate. He would eat anything. He was, in the opinion of Jenny and Toby, the perfect garbage-disposal unit.

"Oh, boy," Toby yawned from his end of the table, "do you think he'll ever leave?"

Samson sat at the other end, beckoning with his paws to his mouth.

"I don't know," Skip answered.

"Maybe if we stop feeding him, he'll get tired," Jenny suggested.

Pat pulled a fresh pan of hot biscuits from the oven. "Or maybe he'll get angry!"

"Keep feeding him," Skip agreed. "But my arm's getting tired. Here, Toby, you take over."

Pat gave Toby the biscuits. He picked one up and gestured to Samson, who leaned over the table with his mouth open. Toby flipped the biscuit between the bear's teeth. With a gulp, it was gone.

"Remember, at the zoo, the signs that said 'Don't Feed the Animals'?" Toby picked up another biscuit. "I wonder if Samson can read."

"He'd eat the sign!" Jenny looked up from the wild-life book she had open. "It says here that bears gorge themselves before going into hibernation."

"It's not even autumn yet," Skip groaned.

"Maybe he's starting early this year," Pat grinned.

Samson grunted and nodded. He slapped his paws on the table and nudged Toby's hand with his nose.

Toby flipped another biscuit to him. "What are we going to do when we run out of food? Climb back on the roof?"

"Don't put your feet on the table," Pat told Samson. "Don't you know that's bad manners?"

By ten o'clock, the wick of the oil lamp had been turned down to a soft glow. Only Skip and Samson remained at the table. Everyone else was curled up in their beds.

"Good night, Jenny," Skip called up.

"Night, Dad."

"Good night, Toby."

"Night, Dad."

"Good night, Pat."

"Night, Skip." Pat turned over.

"Thanks a lot, guys," Skip added.

His eyelids were becoming as heavy as lead. Samson's eyes were still as bright as those of a man who has just stumbled upon a feast. Skip dug into the last sack of cookies. There were two cookies left.

"Don't you have a girlfriend someplace?" Skip asked the bear.

Samson shook his head and opened his mouth. Skip placed a cookie on the outstretched tongue.

"Maybe your phone is ringing. Maybe you're supposed to be at the Black Bear Social Club. You have a television? I bet you can still catch the Late Show."

Skip went to the bottom of the bag.

"Last one."

Samson took the cookie in both paws and gobbled it down. He held out his paws.

"No more." Skip folded his arms.

Man and bear watched each other. Skip still was not sure how tame Samson was, but he figured that even if the bear did eat him alive he'd be too tired to notice.

Samson burped suddenly, and licked his claws. Almost drunkenly, he slid away from the table and waddled over to the cabin door. Surprised, a weary Skip cautiously rose and went over to swing the door ajar.

"Good night, Samson." Yawning, he watched the bear sidle out into the dark. "Breakfast is at seven!"

Chapter Twelve

Samson Works for His Board

Toby sat on the grass. "What are you doing, Dad?"

Skip had laid out ten fifteen-foot logs along the lake bank. Using hemp rope, he'd lashed the logs together; and with a forked branch nailed to the end of a middle log, he had constructed a primitive oarlock.

He nailed a support onto the branch. "What does it look like?"

"It looks like a raft. But a raft floats."

"Well, this'll float."

"Float people?" Toby was dubious.

"That's what *he's* along for." Skip pointed the hammer at Samson. The black bear lay on the bank with an expression even more dubious than Toby's.

"Him?"

Skip tied an extra length of rope to the logs and trailed it up the bank. Then he stood over Samson with his hands on his hips.

"Okay, Samson, if you want to be a member of this family, there's one thing you have to learn. Those who eat, work. And I have just the work for you. Come on!"

Reluctantly, Samson got to his feet. His eyes narrowed as he took in the raft.

"No work, no food," Skip said firmly. "Let's go, moocher."

"You think he understands what you're saying?" Toby asked.

"Indians always said bears were cousins to men. This bear eats enough for five men, so I expect a lot of help. Come on!"

Skip started pushing the raft into the water. Samson shuffled to his side and he, too, gave the logs a shove. Toby joined in on Samson's other side.

On the bank Ringo and Blackie appeared.

"Don't wait for a special invitation," Skip shouted to them. "Come on!"

Inch by inch, the combined pushing of Skip, Toby, and the three bears moved the raft half into the water, where Skip called a halt.

"Okay, Samson." Skip bowed. "The honor's all yours. Hop in."

The big bear rose on his hind legs in dismay.

"Wow!" Toby roared. "The world's biggest guinea pig."

Ringo and Blackie looked from Samson to the raft.

"Come on, Samson," Skip urged him. "These cubs look up to you. Don't let them down. Be a man—I mean, be a bear. Think of Smokey, think of Gentle Ben."

Samson groaned.

"Okay, think of this."

Skip threw a fish on the middle of the raft. After a moment's hesitation, Samson lumbered out onto the raft. Before he could get back off, Skip and Toby gave the logs a final shove and the raft slid into the lake. Skip played out the rope.

Like a seasick passenger, Samson squatted on the raft, about twenty feet from shore. The water, Skip was pleased to see, didn't even come halfway up the logs.

"It works, it works!" Toby yelled. "If it'll hold *him*, it'll hold anything."

"Just what I was thinking," Skip said proudly.

"Once again, we see how Man's ingenuity enables him to travel over water as dry as on land."

Fish or no fish, however, Samson decided he did not like being the subject of someone else's experiments. Without warning, he dove back toward shore.

The power generated by an adult black bear's legs is better than half a ton of pressure. The raft shot away, across the surface of the water. With it went the rope, and with the rope—if he wanted to keep his raft—went Skip, up to his knees, up to his waist, and on up to his neck, sputtering in the icy water before he pulled the raft to a stop.

"Think of it this way, Dad," Toby called from the shore. "What if you'd built Samson a plane?"

In spite of such minor setbacks, and after a change of clothes for its builder, by noon the raft was ready for its first official voyage.

"Madame, your throne!" Skip sat Pat on a chair tied to the center of the raft.

"This will float?" she inquired uneasily.

"It's been tested, lady. Believe me, it's been tested!"

Jenny sat on the picnic basket, Toby on the coiled tow rope, and Crust and the cubs took uneasy positions aft. With his oar, Skip pushed off from shore.

A gentle current ran south through the lake, which became a river at its southern end. All Skip had to do for the downstream voyage was set the oar in its lock as a rudder, and steer.

"Look!" Jenny pointed to shore.

In a shambling lope, Samson was keeping pace with the drifting raft.

Pat raised an eyebrow.

"I thought you said Samson helped you with the raft. I wouldn't call where he is now exactly a vote of confidence."

"That bear," Skip muttered in return, "has no vision."

Like the raft, conversation drifted off. Not from boredom, but because floating over the crystal-pure water was a blissful experience. They felt no sense of real movement, yet Jenny and Toby could see the shore slowly passing in review. Birch trees, banks of flowers, reeds alive with geese and ducks seemed to sail past the eye. From underneath them, bass and trout rose to gulp and watch the strange craft floating above them.

"It's like a dream, Skip," Pat sighed.

"Better than a dream. It's real."

Samson was waiting for them when Skip steered the raft to shore.

Pat and Jenny carried a basket into a meadow of flowers and spread a cloth. Biscuits, salad, ham sandwiches, candied yams, and apple pie emerged from the basket. Ringo helped lift the honey jar out. Samson patiently waited in a sitting position until he was served.

"What I like about this place is that it's one big vacation," Toby remarked lazily.

"Hmmm." Pat paused in her preparations to glance at Skip.

All at once, the grass stirred by Jenny's knee and she picked up a small, squirming brown creature with pop-eyes and a stripe running from its nose to its shoulder.

"A toad!" she cried.

Toby looked up from his sandwich. "Nope."

"It is too a toad. It has bumpy skin."

"It's a tailed frog," Toby said authoritatively.

"Why, you're right." Pat examined the frog. "But who ever heard of a frog with bumps and a tail? Toby, how did you know what it was?"

"Ah, you know, I look at the books."

"He knows about all the amphibians and snakes in this area by now," Skip informed his wife. "We may have a zoologist in the family—while he's on vacation, you understand."

Samson grunted and looked so piteously at the food that Jenny let the frog go and tied an extra tablecloth around the bear's neck as a bib. Crust gave

Samson a cool but civil eye. Maybe the *Robinsons* had accepted the black bear as a member of the family, but their dog still considered that the big intruder was on probation.

There were times when Pat wished that memories could automatically be captured in slides. Then she would always have a picture of Toby's delight today in discovering that one of his raccoons had stowed away for a ride on the raft, or of Jenny feeding Ringo and Blackie honey now from a wooden spoon. Or of a family of deer that wandered, some distance away, on the meadow. Soon the cubs were awkwardly stalking them. Later, while Toby took on the cubs in a wrestling match, Jenny fed an apple to a fawn. The best picture of all, though, would have been the log seesaw, Jenny and Toby on one end and Samson on the other.

"You know, Skip," Pat whispered, "I've almost forgotten about Jenny's allergy attacks. It's been so long since she's had one."

"I don't miss them."

"Do you think Boomer was right, that the wolves really were after Crust instead of Jenny?"

"I can't say for sure. Boomer must know what he's talking about. I liked hearing about old man Taylor."

"And Samson?" Pat smiled.

"Yeah. Well, all the animals that the old man made friends with. *Now* the animals are Jenny's and Toby's friends. It's as if the kids got a gift from someone they never met. Sort of nice to know that you can pass love along like that."

There were other benefits, as well.

With all passengers except the black bear aboard the raft for the ride home, Skip found poling against the current heavier going than he'd expected.

"Dad, Jenny and I can walk back with Samson," Toby suggested.

"No, but that gives me a brainstorm. Hand me the rope, Tobe."

Skip took the curled rope, whirled the loose end over his head and flung it onto the bank at Samson's feet.

"I don't believe it, Skip," Pat said. "It's not going to work."

"Look, that bear will put anything in his mouth at least once."

Samson sniffed the rope. From sheer curiosity, he bit it.

Skip prompted the passengers. "Applause!"

"Good boy, Samson!"

"Yeay, Samson!"

The big bear tugged on the rope and the raft jerked forward over the surface of the water. Skip kept poling to help Samson and keep the raft away from the shore. Samson tugged again.

"He thinks it's a toy!" Toby shouted.

"And we've got four-paw traction working in our favor," Skip agreed.

Between Samson's towing and Skip's poling, the Robinson raft moved slowly home.

Chapter Thirteen

Skip's Plans —and Three Toes

Late spring slipped into summer and then summer began to wane. The first work of construction was done and the family moved full-time into the routine of providing food for themselves. The lake and valley supplied a steady bounty of fish and game and fruit. Pat picked the first harvest of her small garden. Summer squash, lettuce, tomatoes, and even corn ripened and overflowed the cabin table. Jud continued to airlift weekly the few goods—mainly flour and dry milk—the Robinsons could not produce.

Instead of simply dropping the package in a watertight bag, Jud surprised the family one day by landing his aquaplane and taxiing up to the beach. Skip helped the pilot bring some mysterious packages to shore.

"Take you up on that coffee now," Jud told Pat as he approached the cabin.

"It's about time!" she retorted.

Around the outdoor table, the men unwrapped the packages. One was a ten-gallon can of milk; the other was a big stoneware jar.

"That's wonderful!" Pat ran her hand over the jar's smooth side. "But who can they be from? I didn't order them."

"From me," Jud said. "Wife got a new jar and she

wanted to know who could use her old one. I didn't recollect you folks bringing in one of these and they can be awful handy."

Jenny examined the jar. "Looks pretty new to me."

"Well"—Jud blushed up to his bald spot—"let's say I've been keeping an eye on you from the air. I guess I'm just impressed enough by what you've done here to make an investment. Or maybe I just wanted some of your mother's coffee."

"Thank you, Jud." Pat kissed his cheek.

"And that coffee's just as good as Boomer said it was," Jud added, after a sip.

"Milk!" Toby ran up and peeked into the can. "Fresh milk."

"Well . . . not quite milk," Jud told Skip. "Buffalo milk."

"Buffalo?" Toby's eyes widened.

"There's a herd of them still running wild a hundred miles east. I apologize, it's not that great for straight drinking, but folks say it can't be beat for making cheese. Anyway, *I* love it."

"We'll have some cheese waiting for you next time you come by," Pat promised.

"Lady, I'm afraid you see clean through me," Jud laughed.

The creation of the buffalo cheese took place that evening. The addition of a natural coagulant by Pat had broken down the milk into cakelike curds that Jenny and Toby took great pleasure in crumbling between their fingers. Into the bowl of curds, Skip poured boiling water. Clouds of steam filled the cabin and sent the bear cubs scurrying under the bed.

Following Jud's directions, Pat stirred the water and curds until they blended into one rubbery mixture.

"That goo is cheese?" Toby inquired.

"You have no taste for the finer things in life," Jenny sniffed.

While the "goo" cooled, Pat made an apple butter

out of some wild apples Jenny and Toby had gathered from the woods. Once the apples were cooked until soft, she mashed them, added sugar and cinnamon, cooked them again, then put the apple butter in jars and sealed their tops with wax.

"Okay, chefs," she ordered Jenny and Toby, "now *I* rest and *you* work."

"Doing what?" Toby asked.

"The cheese is cool enough. I want you to make some softballs out of them."

That kind of work Toby enjoyed. He and Jenny formed balls of cheese and dropped them in a pail of salty water.

"Buffalo milk . . . curds . . . hot water . . . cold water," Jenny muttered to herself.

"What are you saying," Pat asked.

"Just trying to remember how we did this, so I could write it down in my diary."

"I didn't know you were keeping a diary, Jen."

"Every night, up in the loft, she's always writing," Toby said.

"Toby—!" Jenny glared at her brother.

"I think it's a good idea for one of us here to keep a journal," Pat said. "That way we can never forget about our adventures."

"Well," Jenny explained slowly as she patted together a ball, "that's why I *started* the diary. But now I'm doing it because I've decided to be a writer." The members of her family exchanged surprised glances, and Toby made a face at his sister. "Someday, I'm going to do a book about us and about the wilderness."

"I can tell you about the snakes," Toby offered.

"You're always telling me about the snakes." Jenny rolled her eyes. "You've got snakes on the brain!"

Skip picked a cooled piece of cheese out of the saltwater pail and cut off a slice.

"Let's find out about this buffalo cheese. Mrs. Robinson?"

Pat took a bite and rolled the soft, white cheese over her tongue. Toby and Jenny were next.

"Hey, that's not so bad," Toby nodded.

"Hey, that's really good!" Skip corrected him.

"A little like mozzarella," Pat decided, "but more taste. We can have lasagna à la buffalo!"

A while later, Skip took most of the cheese and apple butter to the springhouse. On the way back, he made a mental map of the expansions he would start the following spring. Pat's garden would be four times bigger. But the biggest development would be the addition of a cow—so that there would be a steady source of fresh milk. Chickens—for eggs. And another dog, so that Crust could begin a family of his own.

The main thing, he told himself, *is that there'll be another spring in the wilderness.*

Skip was convinced now. They were going to make it.

One hundred miles north, other plans were taking shape.

Along the bed of a mountain stream, a grizzly bear stood upright over the body of a dead elk and roared in triumph. The elk's head was twisted and limp, the neck broken from one swat of the bear's three-toed paw.

Hungrily, the bear sank on all fours and bit into its prey, its great teeth crushing flesh and bone. The sound of the feeding traveled through the evening air. Scavenger wolves slipped out of the trees to watch, but they came no closer. The bear had only to lift his eyes toward them to send them scampering in retreat. They could end as easily as the elk did.

In the American and Canadian wilderness there was but one animal with no fear of elk, cougar, wolf, or man. The largest land carnivore anywhere on earth, he was labeled by scientists *"Ursus horribilis."* "Grizzly" was shorter, and conveyed the terror of his presence just as well.

For an hour, Three Toes fed; and when he was sated he scraped rocks from the stream bed and fallen trees from the hill to cover the elk carcass. In a day or two, he might return to feed again; if he did the elk would still be there—beyond the reach of smaller predators. As he lumbered away, up the stream, wolves scattered before him.

Three Toes was an old bear. At twenty-five years, he had lived as long as any bear could hope to. The reasons for his long life were his immense size—at one thousand pounds, he was unusually large for a grizzly (and twice as large as a black bear)—and his experience. Scars marked the graying fur on his jowls and heavy neck and shoulders. There was hardly an animal in the forest he had not battled and defeated. He could be as silent as the wind when stalking an elk or a moose. During the mating season for bears, his bellows shook the trees. He reigned as a wary, intelligent king, challenged but never defeated.

His path took him away from the stream now, through a stand of timber and to the remains of a camp.

A cabin and a small corral sat in the middle of a clearing, but a tangle of brush had grown up in the clearing. Logs had fallen from the corral fence. The cabin, its windows and door broken in, was dark.

The bear paused by the corral and grunted. At this spot he had been attacked by two malamutes, and killed both. Halfway to the cabin, he'd been hit by .30-caliber rifle bullets fired by a trapper in the doorway. Three Toes hadn't slowed, however, no more than as if a bee had lit on his back. The man saved himself, barely, by riding away on a horse. The bear took out his frustration on the cabin, smashing in the windows and splintering the door into planks. He routinely visited the camp in hopes that the trapper would return, but the man never did. The camp remained deserted, the trapper had given up.

Three Toes moved on, upcountry from the camp, where some traps still remained—all of them expertly sprung and rendered harmless by the bear. He knew about traps. As a young cub, he had stepped on the pan of a trap, and iron teeth had snapped shut on his left front paw. For two days he'd struggled to free himself and during that agonizing time two emotions were printed forever on his mind: a wariness of all things metal and a hatred for the smell of man that was on that metal. He finally broke loose at the cost of half his paw. From then on, any man who crossed the path of a bear called Three Toes was in danger of his life.

The grizzly climbed a rocky outcropping up toward a moonlit crest of ponderosa pines. A rabbit dashed away from him respectfully. No bear's eyes were very clear beyond seventy yards, but few animals had keener senses of smell or hearing. And while a lumbering bear might seem slow, an angry one could charge over a short distance faster than most of its victims could draw a breath.

Three Toes ambled into the pines. Well fed now, his purpose was only to check the condition of the different lairs he had dug out in the forest. He rarely slept in the same lair two consecutive winters—another precaution that had allowed his reign to last as long as it had. A cool breeze ruffled his fur. Summer was coming to a close. In another two or three months it would be time to hibernate again.

Pushing aside a berry bush, he uncovered a hole three feet wide.

From instinct, Three Toes dug always his lairs on a slope. This cut down on the water runoff into his sleeping place during spring thaws. The hole also always faced north, so that the snow covering it would remain a deep, insulating blanket as long as possible.

Inside, this particular lair opened into a space ten feet deep and seven feet across. Roots of the giant pine above hung down like stalactites—a small inconvenience for the solidity the roots gave the roof of the den. He would sleep not on the den floor but on an earthen shelf, higher up the side of the den, where warm air would be trapped; and he would line the shelf with evergreen boughs.

Satisfied with his inspection, he emerged from the lair. This was where he would sleep until spring. He would wait until the first real snowfall before holing up. In that way the snow would cover his tracks.

Brushing past the bush, however, an image came to the bear's mind. The image—a memory—was brought on by his successful stalking of the elk and the visit to the abandoned camp. The year before, Three Toes had wandered far to the south of his accustomed territory. There, too, he had killed an elk. And there, too, he had come across an abandoned camp. The image was indistinct, but he could remember a small cabin, a lake, and the fading odor of man.

Before hibernating, before the long sleep, there was something he wanted to do . . .

Chapter Fourteen

The Grizzly's First Attack

Summer had come and gone. Gusts of wind moved clouds over the surface of lake, creating dark patches that shifted here and there over the surface of the water. The lake itself seemed to have changed color—blue had changed to gray. The hills were now gold and red with the drying leaves of maples and oaks; the evergreens, in contrast, still bristled with green.

One day, Skip and Jenny paddled the canoe across the water. The oars dipped, leaving a trail of whirls. Jenny had grown in six months. She was more a woman, less a girl. Toby, as well, had gained weight and muscles.

A honking caught Jenny's attention. From a far bank, geese rose into the sky, wings pumping. The V formation of birds wheeled over the lake, above the canoe, and turned to the mountains. Before they were gone, a second formation of geese was flying after them.

"Going south?" Jenny wondered aloud.

"Yes."

"Everything's leaving." Jenny rested her paddle on the canoe gunwales to watch the geese.

"Just the birds. They'll be back."

Jenny nodded and began paddling again. She and Skip now wore heavy flannel shirts, which provided a warm comfort against the chill of the breeze that blew across the lake.

"I'm going to miss them," she said. "I wish everything would always stay the same."

"Change is what life is all about. Nature's a cycle. You can't have spring without winter."

"What's winter going to be like, Dad? Are you going to teach Toby and me how to ski?"

"Winter's going to be a lot of fun. But it's going to be a lot of hard work, too. In late winter, we'll tap the maple trees and make some maple syrup. And I'm going to have to lay in a lot of extra meat this fall, Jen."

Jenny missed a stroke. She still had not accustomed herself to the idea of her father as a man who used a rifle.

"Do you have to?"

"If we're going to survive."

She gazed around the lake. The frost that capped the mountains all year long was descending to the hills. Jenny felt she could almost see its approach. Sometimes, when the canoe cut through a rough patch of water, wind would whip icy droplets across her face and she would shiver from a chill that had nothing to do with the cold.

"It's sad that some things have to die so that others can live, Dad . . ."

"Well, we *have* to kill—whether we like it or not. Or starve. In the city, meat packers took care of that for us. Here, we've got to do it ourselves."

The dawn of the following morning was a brilliant gold. *A good sun,* Skip thought. He hoisted his rifle on his shoulder while he waited on the cabin porch.

Toby came sleepily out of the cabin, rubbing his eyes. Crust was at the door, too, but Skip pushed him back. They were hunting more than birds today.

Skip closed the door. "You stay here, Crust."

Under his raccoon hat, Toby yawned.

"You awake, Tobe?"

"Uh-huh." Toby yawned again.

"Okay, then. Let's go!"

They took the path to the springhouse and across the stream into the pines. Months before, Skip had blazed trails through the dense forest, although by this time the kids knew it so well they could not have gotten lost in it if they'd tried.

"Look at that, Dad!" Toby was pointing to fresh scratches on a trunk.

"Oh, now you're *awake*." Skip smiled and glanced at the trunk. "That's just the mark a bear uses to lay out his territory, you know that. Probably Samson."

"Doesn't look like Samson's."

"Maybe another black bear. Samson can use some competition."

"He's getting too fat," Toby agreed.

Skip patted Toby's stomach. "Unlike anyone else, huh?"

They left the forest and crossed a sloping meadow of rocks and aspens. A pair of gray wolves slipped through the trees to watch them pass in peace. After the slope came a succession of small valleys and hills where streams ran past firs and birches down toward the lake. It was an area totally untouched by man, and usually left untraveled by Skip. If the north country was an animal sanctuary, this was a sanctuary within a sanctuary—a place Skip was resolved to leave alone unless his family absolutely needed to disturb it. That time had come.

Skip sank to one knee to examine a depression, carefully scooping away rotting leaves. *Moose,* he told himself. From the texture of mud in the track, it was no more than a few hours old.

Toby prodded his father's back.

In a stream, a bobcat was fishing for his breakfast. Poised on a flat rock in the middle of the water, it jabbed a paw at a trout. The fish escaped. The cat looked for another, its stubby tail and tufted ears erect in concentration. Nose nearly touching the water, it jabbed again. Missed. The third time the paw shot out—faster than Toby's eye could follow— a trout flipped up onto the rock. Before the fish could wriggle off, claws had landed on it.

Skip and Toby slipped away.

For two hours, they hunted among the streams, sometimes on the move and sometimes still-hunting under cover of branches. Skip found more tracks, even fresher. He guessed, at last, that he had missed the early morning visit of the moose to the streams and lake and that he would have to move to where the animal did its feeding.

"We haven't seen one all morning," Toby whispered. "You think they know we're hunting them?"

"They know."

Toby frowned. "You think we'll get one?"

"If we're a little patient. The Indians believed the moose has a spirit and that if you really need him, he'll be happy to give himself to you."

"Do you believe that?"

"After living out here, I believe a lot of things the Indians said."

"They were good people, weren't they, Dad?"

"Yes . . . they were good people."

Beyond the valleys, the land flattened, for a time, into a swamp of reeds and dead stumps. Skip and Toby saw in this seemingly dead landscape thriving communities of beaver, raccoons, and rabbits. But no moose.

Toby was, meanwhile, tiring. Mud rolled up into his socks, and once sucked his shoe off his foot.

While Toby retied his shoe, Skip's gaze wandered through the reeds. For a moment, his heart almost stopped. About fifty yards off, between the gnarled branches of a dead tree, was a telltale movement. Then stillness. Again, the movement; and this time Skip discerned the outline of wide antlers among the tree's bare branches. He put his finger to his mouth as Toby looked up.

The breeze was blowing toward them, carrying

their scent and the sounds of their movement away from the moose. Skip ducked silently through a cranberry bush. The moose was a big male, browsing among the reeds. Skip raised his rifle, aiming the open sights in back of the moose's shoulder at the heart.

The moose turned. Its head dipped down among the reeds.

Skip and Toby edged around for a clear shot. *If the wind holds,* Skip told himself, *I can still do it.*

The sound of a jay brought the moose's head up. Skip aimed again. For a moment, his finger rested on the rifle trigger.

The moose was a magnificent animal. In a zoo he might seem ridiculous, with his almost camel-like face. In the wild, his antlers spread nearly as wide as the branches of a young tree. His muscles stood out powerful and alive in the noon sun. His wise eyes now swung toward Skip.

Skip fired, and the moose dropped with a crash into the reeds. Another bullet went into the rifle breech and Skip aimed again, but there was no need. The reeds stilled, bent outward like a bower. The moose was dead.

Toby looked down at the mud and blinked.

"We did what we had to do, son," Skip said. "You understand?"

Toby swallowed and nodded.

The hardest work was yet to come. Skip would have to hang the moose up by the hind legs, bleed it, and then skin and dress it. To carry the meat back, they would have to rig a travois from two poles. But they'd have meat for the winter, thanks to themselves—and thanks to the wilderness.

In comparison to Skip and Toby, Pat and her daughter had set themselves a task that had immediate as well as future rewards: gathering wild berries. Pat in a long dress and Jenny in jeans took a casual stroll with empty buckets through a stand of delicate white birches. The bright sun and soft breeze made the leaves overhead shimmer like silver dollars.

Jenny paused to run her hand down the silky bark of one of the trees.

"Do you think trees have feelings, Mom?"

"Sure they do. They even like music; it helps them grow."

"Maybe we should sing to our vegetable garden every day."

"I said *music*," Pat laughed.

"You mean they're choosey?"

"They prefer *classical* music, I'm told."

Pat began dancing among the birches. Jenny joined her, swinging her pails. Crust ran around her in a circle, howling.

Pat shook her finger at the dog. "Music, maestro, please!"

They climbed past the birches to an area Pat had had her eye on since spring. Now the berries—blueberries, gooseberries, currants, and raspberries—were out in abundance, dappling the hillside with a thousand points of red, blue, and purple.

Blueberries could almost be reaped with a rake; raspberries had to be picked by hand. The tiny spikes of the bushes pricked the fingers, but not enough to dissuade two pickers with thoughts of raspberry sauce, pies, and cakes. The juicy fruit was soon filling their pails.

Crust got bored and wandered off in search of something worth chasing. But Jenny wasn't bored. She had worked out a system: one berry for the picker and two for the pail.

"You're not *eating* any?" Pat looked out of the corner of her eye.

"Toby's the one you'll have to watch," Jenny fibbed. "I bet he tries to eat it all when he gets back. He's a pig!"

"Jenny!"

"Well, he eats like one. If they do get a moose, there probably won't be anything but bones left by the time they get back. I bet if Toby really got hungry, he'd even eat his raccoon hat."

"Really, Jenny!"

About fifty feet of berry bushes separated Pat and Jenny now. The girl snuck behind a bush and scooped a whole handful of berries from her pail.

"You promise you aren't eating any?" Pat called to her.

"Me?" Jenny answered before bringing the berries to her mouth. Wild berries had a tang they never had in the supermarket.

Jenny paid no attention to the sound of the bushes stirring behind her. She scooped up more fruit, day-dreaming about snow and skiing. A pebble rolled past her.

"Crust? Is that you, Crust?" Jenny glanced back. "Come here!"

Three Toes pulled the bush aside and stood. His one-thousand-pound frame blocked the sun that had warmed Jenny's back.

For a moment, all air left Jenny's lungs and she could say nothing. The grizzly was immense, far larger than Samson. Ugly scars crossed his nose and face. He looked down on Jenny, spread his arms, and roared—a noise that was far more deafening than anything Jenny remembered ever hearing in Los Angeles.

"Mom!!!"

Jenny dove away, spilling the pails. Gained her wind, she screamed again.

"Jenny . . . ?"

Pat could not see her, only bushes waving. Then she spotted the bear walking, eight feet tall, and still roaring furiously.

"Mom!"

Jenny dove again as claws sliced the bushes she had reached. She stumbled and fell, crawled, gained her feet. She tried now to get to her mother, but the bear cut her off. She turned and ran down the slope, hearing the bushes being crushed a few steps behind her.

"Jenny!" At the sound of the heavy paws, Pat rushed after the girl. Brambles reached out and tore Pat's dress.

Three Toes's eyes were coals of hate. The very smell of people filled him with rage.

Hesitating in her plunge down the slope, Jenny saw a medium-sized pine tree and ran to hide behind it. Three Toes, in a mounting fury, pushed at the tree and it began to topple. Jenny could only duck away from the falling pine and continue her downhill race.

But the bear was nearly on top of her, the descent adding even more speed to his legs than usual.

Jenny looked back swiftly and saw that the great creature was moving much faster than she had imagined something so large could run. Slipping, in desperation, into a thick stand of new birches, she saw that the trees had slowed the bear. She could hear herself screaming and crying from fear; but part of her mind did not panic, and instead was working on how she would stay alive.

The bear roared in fury at the birches, which were like the bars of a cage keeping him out. Throwing himself at them, he broke through finally, bringing the girl within reach.

Jenny ran again. There were bigger trees down the slope toward the river. If she could climb one, she would be safe. A bear cub could climb a tree, but not a full-grown beast like the grizzly.

"Jenny, where are you?"

Pat staggered frantically through the birches and her eyes filled with horror at the sight of the huge animal. Three Toes was racing downhill in full pursuit of her daughter. The girl was just twenty feet ahead, jumping for the branch of an aspen. If she could reach it and climb up, she would get away. But the branch snapped, sending her rolling down the slope of rocks and shale.

At the bottom of the slope, Jenny stood dizzily. Her head rang. *"Jenny!"* she heard. *"Jenny!!!"*

Three Toes now lumbered less quickly down the

slope. The girl was tired, he could sense it. In a second it would be over.

But Jenny shook herself and ran among the rocks, balancing herself with her arms out. One slip on the loose shale would be fatal. Yet the bear was gaining. She even felt the thunder of his weight on the shale. Without glancing back, she threw herself suddenly to one side.

Pat reached the top of the slope of rocks and shale just in time to see the bear miss Jenny and continue, from his own momentum, down to the river bank. Roaring, he turned, puffing, and started back up the slope.

Pat waved. "Up here, Jenny! Up here!"

Jenny now saw her mother. She scrambled up the slope, but the loose shale slid away from her hands and feet. Every step up she took, she fell back half a step. Finally, a whole sheet of rocks slipped out from under her and carried her toward the waiting bear.

"No!" Pat screamed.

The falling rocks and dust blinded Three Toes momentarily. By the time his eyes cleared, the girl had ducked beyond his groping arms and was running again. But there was no place left to run . . .

Calling on reserves of strength she never knew she had, Jenny raced along the bank. She saw no trees to climb, or to hide among. She glanced across the river. On the opposite bank stood an old oak tree. If she could only reach its branches . . .

"Hurry, Jenny!" Pat shouted as she inched her way down the slope.

Jenny ran quickly into the river. Water came up her ankles, then to her knees, slowing her.

Three Toes pounded through the water, too. He had seen the tree. The bank below it had been cut away, sharp, by last year's floods, leaving no way to climb up to the tree.

Pat watched the bear closing in. "Jenny!"

Jenny sobbed on seeing the high bank. A dead end. She hid her face in her hands.

Three Toes was breaking the water into waves. His jaws were now open. The girl turned to face him hopelessly, and then—she was gone. She had slipped into the underside of the bank.

She pressed herself into the damp earth. Flood-waters had cut away considerable soil *beneath* the oak, as well, and small animals had burrowed into the soil, making the cavity even larger. The exposed roots of the oak tree hung down like a screen between her and the bear.

Claws reached in for her. She kicked back.

The bear raged at the bank. He could almost touch the girl, but he could not quite reach her. Furthermore, her crying only made him angrier.

Pat had reached the river bank. Across from her, she saw the grizzly push his head into the cavity beneath the oak, squeezing his jaws in between the tree roots.

Inside the burrow the teeth snapped shut. A fetid breath filled the small space. Jenny kicked out, and the teeth snapped again. She could even see the dark, obsessed eyes boring into hers. Then, abruptly, Three Toes pulled his head out, into the light. He knew he could not reach the girl while the overhanging shelf stood.

Rising to his full height, he roared, and brought down his heavy paws onto the lip of the bank, tearing apart the soil and grass there. The water in front of the bank began to turn brown.

Jenny had just dared to think herself safe when clots of dirt started to tumble down on her head.

He's ripping it apart, Pat told herself as she ran out into the river. *He's ripping the whole bank apart!*

The animal shook the bank, his claws slicing through the now-weakening dirt-and-rock shelf to expose more of the tree's roots—and the girl huddled beneath them. Large clots of soil and rock now fell, some of them into the water and some down inside the burrow. Maniacally, Three Toes flailed his claws against the bank again and again.

Jenny saw, all at once, the bear's complete arm sail down through the roof of her shelter.

"Mom, please!!"

The bear's body blocked the mouth of the burrow. Claws stretched in, groping for the girl and preventing any chance for escape.

"Stop!" Pat screamed at the bear, no more than ten feet away from him. She threw a rock, attempting to distract him.

Three Toes hesitated only for a moment. *First the girl.* Then *the woman,* he must have thought. With a final thrust, he tore the entire roof of the bank apart.

Pat's eye had fallen on a tree branch floating down the river. It was a branch that Skip would have found heavy. Nevertheless, she managed to pick the branch up and shift all of its weight onto her shoulder.

"I said stop!"

She ran at the bear and threw the branch at him like a spear. One sharp, broken fork dug into the grizzly's back and he wheeled from the bank, bellowing.

"Run, Mom!" Jenny shouted.

Pat raced back across to the far bank. Infuriated, the bear lunged after her, gaining on her with every step. He was only a step or two behind Pat when teeth dug into his rear leg.

Three Toes halted, roaring. A yellow dog was snapping at his feet. Three Toes slapped it back, raking yellow hair and blood. The bear had killed so many dogs, Crust seemed to him no different. Then he would attend to the dog's owners.

But Crust was no ordinary dog anymore. Since coming to the wilderness, he had fought a cougar and a wolf pack. He ducked a second sweep of the claws and leaped up for the bear's eyes. Dog and bear went down in the water. Crust was up first and bounded to the shore. Snarling, the bear lumbered after him.

Pat had recrossed the stream again to the destroyed bank.

"Are you okay, Jenny?" she gasped, reaching into

the burrow and pulling her daughter out, into her arms.

Covered with dirt, Jenny was sobbing hysterically. She couldn't talk, but with her mother's help she was able to stumble out into the water.

Three Toes now angled around toward the woman and girl; but Crust cut him off, herding him in the other direction. The dog had learned a great deal from his sparring with Samson. He would not be faked into a rush at the grizzly. Instead, he ducked and feinted, always an inch ahead of the bear's claws. Almost always. Crust was losing blood from three different wounds. Sooner or later, he would slow—or fall. Until then, nevertheless, the dog would fight.

The uneven battle moved from the shore to the trees and up the slope. Jenny and Pat made their escape.

Chapter Fifteen

Skip's Search

"Is he coming back? Do you think the bear will come here?" Jenny asked from her bed.

Every time Pat thought the girl had recovered from the experience, Jenny would start shivering and crying uncontrollably. Then she would ball the sheet up in her fists to the neck of her nightgown, and stare at the window.

"No-o-o." Pat poured hot water from a kettle into a cup. She took it to the bed. "Here, try and drink this."

Jenny sat up and took a sip. Just the aroma of sassafras tea could be comforting most of the time. This was not most of the time. This time it would take more to calm her.

"How do you feel?" Pat ran her fingers over Jenny's forehead.

"You really don't think he'll come here?"

Pat put as much conviction in her voice as she was able. "No. He's miles away by now!"

"What—what about Crust?" Tears formed in Jenny's eyes.

"I . . . don't know, dear."

Jenny lay rigid under the blanket, her eyes staring blankly at the ceiling or at the window, her hands cupped around the tea for warmth. Her mother sat beside her, gently rubbing her brow.

Pat's eyes traveled over the interior of the cabin. Over the cups and dishes in the cupboard; the chairs drawn neatly up to the table; the half-finished hooked rug hung on the wall. All the touches that made a home. But what kind of a home was it? What kind of a place was it where a child's life was constantly in danger? *Why did we come here, why did we stay?* she constantly asked herself.

She jumped in fear as the door swung open.

When Skip and Toby entered, Pat could not restrain herself anymore, and tears filled her eyes. Skip had come in with a smile of triumph—which collapsed as he saw Pat and Jenny.

"What happened?" He rushed over to them.

"Skip . . ." Pat fell into his arms. "A bear!"

"Are you *all right?*" Skip held her close and looked over at Jenny's tear-stained face. "Jen, you all right?"

Jenny reached out for him. "Daddy . . ."

"Toby, shut the door, please," Skip ordered.

"But the moose."

"Forget about the moose! Shut the door."

Skip guided Pat to the bed and they sat there with Jenny. The more he learned of what had happened, the more angry and sick he felt inside.

"A grizzly bear, you're sure?"

"I can't be sure of anything anymore," Pat said. "We were supposed to be safe here, we were so sure about that. Now this! That bear was crazy, Skip. He deliberately tried to kill us. For no reason!"

The hike back from the swamp dragging a two-hundred-pound travois had caked Skip's face with dirt and sweat. He wiped his eyes.

"This was at the river, below the berry patches?"

Pat took a deep breath. "Yes."

"And Crust . . . ?"

"I think he would have been home by now," Toby answered in a strangely adult tone.

"I guess so," Skip nodded. "Well, there are still a couple of hours left before dark. I'm going after that bear."

He strode to the mantel, filled his hand with .30-caliber bullets, and stuffed them in his parka. Then he took the shotgun off the rifle rack, broke it, fed it two shells, and laid it in Pat's hands.

"You know how to use this?"

Pat nodded with dry eyes.

"Let's go, Dad." Toby started for the door.

"No. No, you stay here with your Mom."

"I'm ready," Toby persisted.

"Stay here," Skip said from the door.

"Find *Crust*," Jenny begged.

"Don't worry, sweetheart. Be back soon."

"Skip"—Pat touched his arm—"Skip, please . . . watch yourself."

"Sure."

The door shut and Pat dropped the bar across the latch. Toby stared at his sister and mother.

"I wouldn't want to be that bear right now!"

Outside, Skip pulled the travois into the old cabin. He emerged, surveying the sky. The clouds of early evening were already starting to gather around the mountaintops as he struck out through the woods.

Pat had said the bear acted crazy. It was weird enough for a grizzly to be in this part of the country: usually they stayed in higher country. Crazy or not, from the description of the attack Skip recognized the signs of a primitive intelligence. Indians had said bears were the closest animals to men. Cousins. Which made this sort of killer all the more dangerous.

Skip reached the berry patch.

The bear could be waiting anywhere in the bushes. *They knock down their victims with their claws*, Skip remembered. *They finish off their victims with their fangs*. He held his rifle tight to be able to get off at least one good shot, and stepped among the bushes.

An upended pail displayed a skirt of red berries. A rag of cloth from Pat's dress flew from a bramble. Cautiously, Skip descended the hill. A small tree was ripped out by its roots. Farther down, he passed a birch tree snapped in two.

How big is this monster? he asked himself.

From the top of the shale slope, he looked down on the small river that flowed out of his lake. A twig cracked behind him and he whipped around to fire. A jay was hopping along the ground. Nothing more.

Sliding down the shale on his seat, he kept the rifle ready. What filled his eyes now was the sight of the opposite bank. Under a huge oak tree gaped a tremendous hole, almost as if that part of the river bank had been destroyed by explosives. Perhaps a ton of earth had literally been ripped out, leaving nothing but broken and mutilated tree roots. Could any animal be that strong—and have that much hate?!

Skip found his answer when he reached the nearer bank. Here, he noticed the tracks of a dog, and of a bear headed back toward the slope. He knew Crust's pawprints. The prints of the bear were gigantic, and one of the paws had only three toes . . .

Pat stayed near the bed, soothing Jenny while Toby carried over a cup of tea for his mother. She had noticed that in this crisis, Toby seemed to stand taller. More and more he was starting to resemble Skip.

Jenny had fallen into an uneasy sleep. A cold sweat beaded her forehead. When she did awake, she would stare at the window without a word.

Toby looked at his sister, worried and anxious. He gave Pat the cup.

"Did it really scare you, Mom?"

"Yes."

"How big was it?"

"Huge."

"Was it the bear Boomer told us about? Was it Three Toes?"

"I don't . . . know." Pat sipped her tea.

"Did you do anything?"

"Well, we ran, Toby," she answered, brushing brown curls from his eyes.

"You should've hit him in the stomach. That always works!"

"I'll remember that for the next time." *There'll be no next time,* Pat hoped. *The memory of one encounter is enough.* With a conscious effort, she turned her concern into a smile. "You didn't tell me about your hunt, Toby."

"It was great," he began enthusiastically. "We went really far. We saw a bobcat fishing, and lots of beavers—and then we finally found the moose in a swamp. Dad had to shoot him so we could have meat for the winter." Toby shook his head. "What I don't understand is why Three Toes tried to hurt you and Jenny. He didn't need to hurt you. Why did he try to do that?"

"I wish I could answer that." Pat ran the back of her hand down Jenny's cheek. "I really wish I could."

Skip followed the tracks of the bear and the dog up to the higher slopes of the hill. Along the way, he had found trampled bushes and spots of blood. Once he was near the top of the hill, the tracks faded among the boulders and rocks.

He climbed the sheerest outcropping of rock. Daylight was fading fast, but from this vantage point he could see for miles in every direction. He turned slowly, scanning rocks, wind-bent fir trees, and dusky-colored bushes. He estimated the limit of his accuracy with a rifle at three hundred yards. But if he could just hit the bear and slow him down . . .

"Come out, wherever you are," Skip said to himself.

On the north side of a not-so-distant slope, he saw something moving.

He came down the outcrop running. Despite his fatigue, he had never run faster, looking neither to his left nor right, breaking directly through brambles. A striped fence lizard dodged away. Skip heard his lungs straining; his legs felt like wood, but adrenaline kept them moving.

The slope, he saw when he reached it, still wore a sheen of ice from last winter's snows. The movement he had seen was gone, but the bear could be lurking behind any of a dozen house-sized boulders balanced on the hillside.

Skip had just gone by a smaller boulder when he heard a paw step behind him. He spun with his rifle barrel out.

Crust limped from behind the boulder, his tongue hanging and his tail wagging weakly. Deep cuts marked the dog's ribs and head.

"Crust!" Skip knelt and hugged him. "You crazy dog, you great old dog you!"

The Labrador stood to lick his master's face.

Skip couldn't contain his laughs of relief. "You nut! No broken bones, huh? You okay? You're something else, you know that?"

He patted Crust and stood. Again, his eyes were sweeping the slope. "Where's that grizzly, Crust? Where do you think that bear has gone?"

Together, Skip and Crust searched for the giant bear's tracks.

As still as stone, Three Toes waited. From the high timber stand he could see neither the man nor the dog, but he could smell and hear them. As long as the wind blew toward him, he had the advantage. It would be night soon and they would leave.

The dog had been a problem. Other dogs had made the mistake of pitting their strength directly against his; this one hadn't. Now the grizzly had a decision to make. Already headed north to his usual territory, he could keep on going. Or he could backtrack to the lakeshore.

He sniffed the wind, and the odor of the hunters brought on the old rage. This was *his* country, *his* wilderness . . .

" . . . See anything, Crust? . . . Careful, boy! . . . Getting dark . . ." The faint words blew through the air.

Three Toes was too smart to growl, but his lips curled up from his teeth.

". . . Let's look up in those trees, Crust . . ." he heard.

Then steps approaching the timber.

He slipped away through the forest, heading north. When the man and dog gave up, then he could backtrack and take the easier route, maybe find a moose or elk, too . . .

Chapter Sixteen

One Thousand Pounds of Hate

Morning sunlight poured through the cabin windows. Skip was at the table having an early-breakfast coffee with Pat. The kids were still asleep, Toby in the loft and Jenny in the big bed.

"Are you *sure* it was Three Toes?" Pat asked.

"I followed his tracks for at least five miles. They just kept heading north. It was Three Toes."

Pat glanced over at Jenny. "Do you think he'll come back here?"

"No. Anyway, I'm going to go out after him. How's Jenny?"

"Still tossing and turning. I don't understand it. I was sure she'd get over her fright by now. Skip . . . Skip, we have to talk about this."

"Yeah," he nodded. "You mean about leaving here. But first, I'm going to get Three Toes. I'm going to get him, Pat. Everything'll be all right. I'm going to take care of it."

He kissed her. Then he slipped on his parka and took his rifle off the rack. At the door, he had to push Crust back inside.

"Thanks for everything, but you stay here, boy. Stay here!"

From the porch, Skip went across to the storehouse cabin, where he cut off slabs of moose meat and put them in a medium-sized cloth bag. He made a backpack out of the sack, with cord. *Got to get me a regular backpack,* he reminded himself. Finally, rifle in hand, and extra cartridges in his parka pockets, as well as an ax and some rope through his belt, he set out alone up into the woods.

Jenny was not the only one who'd had a bad night. Skip had spent the dark hours dreaming and thinking about the grizzly. The more he'd thought about it, the more he was sure that Three Toes had stayed only barely ahead of him and Crust the day before. Which meant the bear was not really lighting out north. Not running. Waiting. For what?

So far as Skip knew, the bear had never come across to the camp by the lake, so there was little danger for Pat and the kids as long as they stayed in the cabin. Three Toes would still be in the general area of the high timber stand where his last track was discovered. And after yesterday's activity, the bear would be hungry as well.

Skip planned to give him plenty to eat.

He had dressed in clean clothes. Now, at the first stream he came to, he stripped and bathed, and then daubed himself and his clothes with mud. He took a particularly fatty piece of meat and rubbed it over his rifle, sack, ax, and ropes. As much as possible, he wanted to erase the human scent that would give him away. He picked up a dry leaf and let it fall. A light wind pushed the leaf against his chest. Good! The wind was against him.

When he reached the timber stand, Skip immediately set to work felling four young trees and trimming them to slender logs of equal length. He didn't worry about the sounds of activity chasing the bear. With Three Toes, it would only be part of the bait. Through the woods came the return hammering of woodpeckers and the raucous call of jays.

He lashed the poles together and dragged them deeper into the stand. *This,* he thought, *is the most dangerous. With both hands hauling the poles, the rifle slung across my back, I'd be an easy mark for ambush. But it has to be done.*

An hour passed before he found the spot he wanted: a small clearing about ten feet across. A circle of dense ponderosa pines crowded together overhead to block out the sky. A leaning maple, hollow and rotting, stood among the pines; it had enough leaves left for cover.

Expertly, Skip now constructed a pyramid-shaped cage out of the four poles, lashing them together at the peak and at two-foot intervals down the sides, where he notched the wood. He tied the end of his longest stretch of rope in a second knot around the top of the pyramid. Holding the other end of this rope, he climbed the maple to where its branches met the pines'—about forty feet above the ground. Looping the rope over a stout pine branch, he climbed about ten feet back down the maple, where he began pulling. Slowly swaying, the pyramid of wood and rope rose until it blended in with the overhanging branches of the pines.

A steel trap or a net would have been better. This makeshift cage would do, though. The nylon rope had a tensile strength of three thousand pounds. The wood was green, flexible, and tough. Not even Three Toes could escape in time.

On the ground, Skip set out the meat directly in the center of where the cage would fall. Then he climbed back up the maple and retied the cage rope on the branch in a half-hitch, so that the rope could be quickly loosened with a tug. Skip settled on a branch just below, with a last length of rope he had reserved for himself. His rifle slung over his shoulder and neck, he lashed himself, back against bark, to the tree. His feet rested on branches; his arms were free to aim and fire.

Pat tried to maintain a semblance of ordinary life that morning. Since Jenny remained in bed and refused food, Pat thought of the one spectacle that might bring a smile to the girl. She winked at her son.

"A bath?" Toby asked.

"That's right." Pat poured hot water into the tub.

"Why me?"

"Because we go by order of dirt around here, buster. You've got enough dirt on you from yesterday's hunt to plant potatoes. Get your clothes off."

"What if I don't want to?"

Pat picked up a towel and snapped it against the seat of Toby's pants.

Toby jumped. "Okay, I want to!"

He got undressed and tested the water with his toe. "Hot! My foot's turning red!"

"The water's already turning brown," Pat shot back. "Go on!"

Inch by inch, the boy sank into the tub, maintaining a steady stream of complaints. "Grow potatoes? I feel like a *boiled* potato. Ouch! Doesn't anybody ever take a *cold* bath? If I cook, you'll be sorry! You oughtta put some carrots in her. You'd have soup. Toby soup . . . What's this?"

"What does it look like?"

"Soap. This soup is going to taste awful."

Pat looked toward the bed. Jenny was trying to laugh, but the effort was too much.

The bear cubs, Ringo and Blackie, were definitely interested, however. They half tumbled down the loft ladder and waddled over to the tub, where they stared at Toby's misery.

"You guys are lucky, you never have to take a bath," he said. "No one could even force you to, not even— Hey, what are you guys doing?"

Ringo was climbing into the tub, and Blackie followed. Overflowing water ran across the cabin floor while Toby's squawks filled the room. Normally, Pat would have chased the cubs out the door. This time, she stood by and prayed for as much as a giggle from Jenny, but her daughter was staring at the window once more.

Three Toes had smelled the meat for hours, and he'd circled around the origin of that smell sniffing for the scent of a man. The scent he hated so much was in the air, yes, but so faintly that he could not tell from where or how old it was. What's more, he was hungry. He had had a long trek south from his home territory and the fight of the day before had only sharpened his appetite.

Finally, he approached the bait.

From long experience, he had the habit of caution. As soon as he saw the clearing, he stopped. Slabs of pink meat covered with flies lay in the center of the clearing. He lifted his nose, trying for the giveaway scents of man or of metal. The more he smelled, the more the aroma of decaying meat stimulated the saliva of his mouth.

Skip had heard and seen nothing, except for the sawlike buzzing of the flies. Cramps had stiffened his legs. Now he counted off a minute to shift his weight without making a sound.

Most of all, Skip was afraid. Afraid that the trap had failed and that even now the bear had found the cabin. Waiting had brought on depression. Skip was the one who had wanted to come to the wilderness. He was the one responsible for the safety of the family. They could be in the city right now. Not as healthy. Not as happy, perhaps. Safer, though, that was for sure. All they'd achieved at the lake could be wiped out by the swipe of a paw.

Skip held his breath. Every thought left his mind. He heard Three Toes.

On the perimeter of the clearing, partly hidden by the low branches of a pine, the bear studied the bait. He looked for broken boughs on the ground that would indicate a covered pit. Or a stake, for a hidden chain. His eyes kept returning to the meat.

Bigger than Samson. Much bigger than Samson, Skip realized as the grizzly stepped into the clearing. He could not help glancing up at the hanging cage. Could it hold anything so big?

His fingers crawled along the branch to the cage rope. The bear stopped about five feet from the bait. Skip could not swing his rifle around without scaring the bear off, but his hand reached for the knot, nevertheless.

The bear took another step to the meat.

And another.

Skip pulled the knot open. The cage hurtled down from the branches and trapped the huge creature, which roared and threw itself against the cage ropes.

Skip aimed and fired. Chips flew from a pole. The bear smashed the cage from one side of the clearing to the other. Skip fired again, then reloaded. The ropes of the cage burst and the bear ran into the trees. The shattered cage collapsed.

Impossible, Skip thought. *The ropes are new!*

Skip worked a bullet into the rifle breech. But the woods were silent. There was no sign of the bear. Sweat rolled down Skip's forehead. Even the birds were quiet.

Suddenly the maple tree lurched. Only the rope binding his waist to the trunk kept Skip from toppling. The tree shook again. Three Toes was knocking it down. Rotten roots popped out of the ground.

Skip twisted. He could see the bear standing and heaving from the other side of the tree, but he couldn't get a clear shot at the animal.

As more roots snapped, the leaning tree tilted closer and closer to the ground. Skip was soon twenty feet from the earth, then fifteen feet . . . The rifle fell from his grasp. The bear heaved again methodically. Skip tried to undo the rope pinning him to the tree, but the shaking of the tree had moved the knot out of reach. Three Toes was now the trapper and Skip the imprisoned animal!

A long string of old, grayish roots pulled out of the earth.

The grizzly roared. One more push and the man would be dangling within reach.

Skip pulled out his hunting knife and sawed at the

rope around his waist. The nylon threads turned the blade aside.

Over the sound of the bear's roars grew the bass vibrations of the entire maple lifting out of the earth. Skip continued to hack at the rope as the bear put all his immense strength into a final push. Creaking, the maple swung. Its upper branches tangled with the pines, delaying for a moment the crash of its fall.

Skip hacked furiously at the rope. It finally ripped apart and he fell on his hands and knees to the ground —the maple after him, first slowly and then with gathering speed, until it sheared through the lowest branches of the pines. Pine needles rose in a cloud. Three Toes jumped over the still trembling maple.

Skip reached his rifle—not far from where he had fallen—twisted onto his back and fired. The bullet passed over Three Toes's head. Loading quickly, he fired again; but by then the grizzly had veered to the side and vanished among the pines.

Shaking, Skip got to his knees.

The big bear had disappeared; he might be ten feet away, or a hundred. The cage had been destroyed, first by the grizzly and then by the upended maple. Skip had fired four times. Four misses. It wasn't a draw: Three Toes had won. Easily. Skip's task now was not to find the bear, but to get home alive.

Everything he knew about grizzlies told Skip the bear was sure to attack him on his way home. In the timber stand? Among the tangle of scrub and brambles? The boulders?

Three Toes watched from a nearby glade, below the clearing and on the way the man must have come. The bear now dug up earth and lay down inconspicuously near Skip's probable path. When the man came by, he could be brought down with one swipe of claws.

The man, however, was not returning by the same route. The bear watched him climb a tree to scan the woods. For ten minutes, the man remained in the tree, and when he came down he avoided the glade.

Skip had chosen a route that took him through an area of the timber stand where younger trees grew. The thinner firs and pines couldn't hide anything with the grizzly's bulk. From there, Skip moved downhill through a thick carpet of ferns, where only a mouse could slip toward him undetected. As he walked, he put a full load of bullets into the rifle.

In frustration, Three Toes watched his enemy's retreat.

"Mom?"

Worn out by looking after Jenny, Pat was sleeping, her arms around her daughter. Toby pulled his raccoon hat snugly on his head.

"Mom, I'm going out now. Okay?"

Toby closed the door on Crust, picked up a hatchet from the porch, and set out for the springhouse. *What Jenny needs,* Toby thought, *is some cheese. Besides, sitting inside the cabin all day is boring. The hatchet'll protect me.*

Toby whistled while he walked. The springhouse was only a couple of hundred yards from the cabin. He had barely entered the woods when a raccoon dropped from a tree branch onto his shoulder.

"You can come, but only if you promise not to try to steal anything from the springhouse. Right?"

The raccoon jibbered and sniffed Toby's raccoon hat.

"Hope it wasn't anyone you knew," Toby apologized. "Don't worry, you're safe with me. Everything happens to Jenny—not me. I wish *I'd* run into old Three Toes."

Toby dragged the hatchet. *Next spring,* he told himself, *I may just be big enough to handle the broadax.*

"Almost there. Now, you be good," he told the raccoon.

The coon stopped jibbering. As it sniffed the air, its ears rose to sharp points. Toby could just see the doors of the springhouse when the raccoon dove from his shoulder and ran.

"Some company!"

Toby lifted the double-doors and let them flop shut behind him as he descended. A candle and a box of wooden matches were always left in the corner. Toby lit the candle and looked toward the shelf where the cheese was kept.

"Darn!" He snapped his fingers. "The hatchet."

The hatchet lay on the ground where Toby had dropped it when he'd opened the doors. Standing over the hatchet was Three Toes, waiting for the boy to emerge.

Toby was halfway up the steps when he saw two orange pinpoints of light in the springwater that ran along the edge of the floor.

"What's this?" He scooped a brown salamander out of the water. "I'm going to look you up in the book when I get back to the cabin."

The doors of the springhouse swung open. Toby looked up at his father, who was out of breath and holding his rifle.

"Hi, Dad. See what I found!"

Skip's face was pale and dripping perspiration.

"Never mind that," Skip gasped, short of breath. "Let's go."

"Okay."

Toby stuffed a cheese into his shirt and blew out the candle, then came out of the springhouse and shut the doors. He had barely picked up the hatchet before Skip lifted him onto his shoulders.

Instead of taking the path directly down to the cabin, Skip went toward the stream.

"This isn't the way home, Dad!"

"We're going by way of the stream and the lake."

"Great!"

Toby wondered idly why his father was not more angry about the trip to the springhouse, but he was too delighted with the ride to wonder for long. Furthermore, Skip was too preoccupied with trying to pick the most open country to walk through to be angry with Toby.

The boy hadn't noticed the pawprints around the hatchet. Skip had.

Chapter Seventeen

Death Trap

The wind rose during the night, tossing sudden squalls of rain against the cabin. Skip, determined to go out again for the bear as soon as possible, slept in a chair beside the fireplace.

Pat shook his arm. "Skip?"

He opened his eyes blearily. "Time to go?"

"It's Jenny. She's very sick. Her temperature's been going up all night."

"Why didn't you wake me before?"

"You were so tired out I wanted you to sleep. But now her fever's over 104."

By the time he reached the bed, Skip was wide awake with fear and concern. Jenny's face was flushed and dry. Worst of all was the wheezing, the old wheezing that had kept them up so many nights in the city. He put his hand on her forehead and winced.

"Sounds like one of her allergy attacks."

"That's what *I* thought." Pat bit her lip.

"We'd better get the doctor here quick."

Their conversation woke the bear cubs. Rubbing his eyes, Toby, too, climbed partway down the loft ladder.

Skip turned on the radio. Holding the microphone in one hand, he dialed with the other. The radio speaker was silent. He turned the radio off and on a second time. There were no station voices, not even static. He lifted the radio and tilted it, and heard loose tubes roll about inside.

"It's broken!"

"Oh, no!" Pat held her head in her hands.

"How did it get broken?" Skip asked.

"Uh . . ." Toby began, "the bear cubs did it. It was an accident. I tried to fix it."

"But you should have told us, Toby." Skip put the radio back.

"Skip, what are we going to do? She needs a doctor."

"Yeah." He listened to the gasping sound of Jenny struggling for air. "Yeah, she sure does. I'm going for help."

"How?"

"The river. The ranger station's about twenty miles downstream. Twin Lakes. I should make it there before noon." Skip slipped on his parka. "Just try to keep her temperature down."

"Skip, Jud said you shouldn't try the river. It's too rough."

"The faster the better." He took the shotgun from the rack, loaded it, and gave it to Pat. "Don't go outside for *any* reason! Not until I get back!"

"Skip . . ."

"I'll make it. That's not just a promise, Pat. We'll *all* make it."

Before she could answer, he was out the door.

As he ran to the canoe, Skip's eyes were on the sky. The rain had, fortunately, stopped; and now he saw why. Wind was literally chasing the clouds away, breaking them up and scattering them. The surface of the lake was choppy and dark.

Skip turned the canoe right side up, threw in a paddle and slid the boat into the water, stepping in as the stern cleared dry land. As soon as his knees hit the canoe floor he was paddling. The paddle sliced through the water in slightly angular strokes, so that he could maintain a straight line towards the southern outlet of the lake. He was lucky; the wind was behind him, adding a stiff, invisible push.

A duck trying to take off into the wind swerved into a long turn and dove back down to the water. Skip estimated the wind's strength. *About thirty m.p.h. And rising!* Moving with the wind and waves, the canoe was almost flying.

The southern tip of the lake was a swampy maze of tiny islands and half-submerged logs. While Skip maneuvered around them, he saw a family of beavers hurriedly gathering twigs to bolster their home. The real blow was yet to come.

Where it ran out of the lake, the river was wide and shallow. The hardest part would come when it narrowed and rushed down through the mountains. Skip remembered the white water he'd seen from the plane when he and his family had first come to the wilderness. He remembered, also, what he had just said to Pat: "We'll *all* make it." Skip firmly believed this. Not because everything depended on *him*. Things depended on *all of them* now.

He checked his watch. Only an hour gone and he was making good time.

The wind had increased, throwing the tops of trees together. On the high mountains, wild sheep huddled close to one another. A boulder, tipped by the wind, hurtled down a slope. At the edge of the lake, behind Skip now, surf whipped onto the shore.

Three Toes stood in the swamp. The bear had followed the canoe, hoping the man would be driven in from the lake. Instead, Skip had gone down the river. The grizzly watched a water snake wriggling onto an island. A small pine tree growing on the island was bowed by the wind until its top nearly touched the water.

The river, Three Toes must have decided, *will take care of the man!*

So the bear turned back toward the old Taylor camp.

The wind raged through Jenny's feverish dreams. In her mind she saw herself, Toby, her mother, and her father sitting around the table. She, herself, was saying grace: ". . . And love that takes care of everyone. And, most of all, thank You for bringing us here." Then the wooden table would turn to dirt, the dirt would turn to claws, and the sleeping Jenny bunched up the blanket in her fists.

Toby handed his mother a wet cloth. "She's not going to die, is she?"

Pat mopped Jenny's brow.

"No, Toby. A fever is the way the body fights things. There's a big battle going on in Jenny right now."

"What can we do about it?"

"We try to help her win. That's all we can do."

In spite of closed windows and door, some wind forced its way into the cabin and made the flame of the oil lamp dance. Pat looked at the clock on the mantel. Three hours had passed since her husband left.

Water was at least two inches deep in the canoe, but Skip was within five miles of the ranger camp. He was no longer paddling so much as merely trying to control the canoe. The river current carried him with the force and speed of a train.

Ahead, the mountains closed in to form a steep, narrow gorge through which the choked river fell in giant leaps. Not even the howling of the wind could cover the roar of white water smashing through its rapids. Even if Skip wanted to turn aside now, he couldn't, for the current sucked him wildly forward.

Desperately, he steered into a tree snagged between some rocks. From there he had a view that took away his breath.

In the space of a thousand yards, the river dropped a probable thousand feet, cascading in torrents among mammoth boulders. Uprooted trees and brush spewed along with the river and were sometimes lost in clouds of mist that billowed up the walls of the gorge. He watched one tree splinter against the boulders and cartwheel through the air before disappearing again in clouds of water vapor.

As best he could, Skip plotted a twisting course through the rapids, a zigzag that crossed possibly sinister whirlpools and circled jagged stones and banks of spray he could not see through. He was convinced that he wouldn't come out of the rapids—not alive. But he had to try.

Pushing off from the tree, at once he and the canoe shot forward. It dove between two rocks, landing bottom down ten feet below and spinning full circle. Skip straightened out in time to ride a solid spume of water. In a sense, there was no "water" anymore—only jets of white spray, mammoth rocks, and dizzying gulps of air. The canoe pitched forward on another spume of blinding spray, landed fifteen feet below this time to carom off a boulder and leap again. Skip steered around the toothlike edge of a jutting rock. The canoe swung around, falling backward. He held on to the gunwales and, in a pool, he got the bow forward. Immediately, he and the canoe were lifted and thrown into a second pool, which poured into a roaring stairway of rapids.

A boulder now crushed the canoe's bow. The craft edged free and dropped, bouncing like a toy as one rock and then another struck its sides. Water in the canoe was up to Skip's thighs. He had no time to think anymore—only to react. When, through the mist, loomed a sharp-edged boulder, Skip pushed away from it with the paddle—and the paddle snapped in his hands.

The roaring of water grew. Skip could see nothing but mist until, as the canoe shot through the white curtain, he was wrenched by a thirty-foot drop onto seething stones. The canoe had slammed down sideways, and broke. Skip was not aware of falling from the craft, only of fighting his way to the surface of the water. A log pushed him under. He rose again. The current swung him around, sucking him down and forward.

Reaching out, he clutched at a boulder, but the river peeled his fingers loose and whipped him toward the final, enormous steps of the rapids.

The log that had hit Skip was whirling, trying to bore its way between two rocks. He reached with both hands and grasped the log, tearing skin from his fingers and palms. But the log stopped. One arm around it, Skip stretched for one of the rock shelves that ran like a serrated edge across the river to a low-hanging branch.

If he could only get to that branch . . .

Back at the lake, the wind was no longer a blow. It was a gale. Throughout the forest, dead trees fell with the sound of a giant's footsteps.

In the cabin, Pat studied a thermometer. It read: 105 degrees.

Toby watched his mother's face. "The battle's still going on, isn't it?"

"Yes." Pat shook the mercury down.

"You want me to go get some cold water from the lake?"

"Thanks, Toby. No, we'll stay here."

Her last word was lost in an explosion of fire and ash from the fireplace. She ran from the bed and shut the chimney flue.

"It's just the wind, Toby."

She swept embers back onto the hearth while whines came from under the bed, where Ringo and Blackie had taken refuge.

"Scared me, too, for a second," Toby admitted.

"Don't worry. As long as we're in here, we're safe."

Toby was about to nod when he heard a strange sound overhead.

"What's that?"

Three Toes stood beside the storehouse. No creature but a bear could have held his ground against the gale, and the grizzly leaned with all his weight into the wind. Waves rolled up the beach into the vegetable garden. Not only dead trees but live ones as well sprawled in the cleared area around the Robinsons' cabin.

The big bear squinted through the dust. The swing on the front of the cabin porch jumped wildly. Shingles chattered on the cabin roof. One shingle tore off and flew away. Another followed, and then two and three at a time, revealing the bare ribs of ceiling beams.

Skip rested on the tree branch.

Soaked and weary, he craned his neck back to look up the vertical stone walls of the gorge. The top of the chasm was at least two hundred feet above the water. And there was no path. The wall was almost sheer, with hardly any brush growing on it.

His eyes were drawn back to the river. He tried to find some place along the base of this or the opposite wall, some rocks where he could climb along over the spray. But where the rapids were worst, there the walls plunged directly into the water.

Skip's body ached for warmth and rest. His hands were raw. He made himself think about Jenny, and Pat and Toby, in order to forget the pain. And he started climbing.

From the start, he knew it was impossible. Spray leapt up and tried to pull him from the rocks. His fingers, dug into tiny handholds, could not wipe the water from his face—so he was blinded from time to time. Skip found, however, that the constant freezing and thawing of the seasons had cracked even the flat granite face of the cliff.

About twenty feet above the water, he reached a rock "chimney," a fissure about three feet wide running almost to the top of the cliff. With his forearms and the soles of his boots pressed against the sides of the chimney, he was able to gain a squatting position in the fissure. Now, keeping himself steadied with his boots, he shifted his forearms up the walls, brought his boots up to new footholds, and then shifted his arms upward again. In this manner, he managed to climb about five inches at a time. He could not be quick or careless, for the rock was slick from water vapor.

Chapter Eighteen

To the Clifftop

A cabin window flew open. Pat ran to pull it shut and lock it.

"I hope Dad's okay," Toby worried.

"He'll make it."

Pat looked out the window blankly at her now-"underwater" garden. *Even if Skip made it to the ranger station,* she thought, *no plane will be able to land on the lake in this windstorm.* It would have been so easy to cry from frustration. They had left the city for Jenny's health. Now the girl was fighting for her life and they couldn't even reach a doctor. They'd come to the wilderness for freedom, and it was as if they were prisoners inside their cabin.

She sat back down on the bed. Jenny's fever had reached the top of the thermometer. Pat removed a warm, damp cloth from her daughter's forehead and replaced it a fresh, cool one.

Toby sat on the floor consoling the bear cubs, who stared nervously up the loft stairway at the gaps in the roof where shingles had been stripped off.

"This is the first time I ever saw them when they weren't hungry. I guess they're really scared. You scared, Mom?"

"Very."

"You don't look it."

"No?" Pat was surprised.

"Well, Dad said not to worry if anything ever did happen to him, because you could take care of everything. Maybe even better than him, he said."

"He *did,* did he?"

"Uh-huh. He said the cabin, and everything, depended on you—like you were the heart of it. Nothing really bad could happen if you were here. I guess he thinks a lot of you."

Pat assumed Skip did, but she had never heard it expressed this way before, and she smiled despite her concern. Toby had said just the right thing to buck her up.

"I guess he does," she agreed.

Between his legs, Skip could see the rapids a hundred feet below. He tried not to think about that, however, and concentrated on the danger at hand. Beginning at his eye level and running about ten foot up the chimney was a collar of damp moss. The moss had come off on his fingers when he touched it experimentally. He dreaded to think about resting his elbows and feet on the moss. But the booming of the rapids reminded him: he had no choice.

As cautiously as a man trying to ice-skate on water, Skip propped his forearms on the moss and shifted his feet. Already, the moss began to slip. Feet in place, he cautiously shifted his elbows' position again. By inches, he rose. The muscles of his legs and back stiffened with cramps.

Finally, his feet reached the moss.

The moss was soft—a pleasant relief from the hardness and friction of the rock. Skip found his concentration relaxing—and the moss slipped. As he started falling, all of the moss crumpled and peeled off the slick rocks. He hurtled down the chimney, still trying to dig in his elbows and boots. One leg dangled free. He pulled it up and jammed it desperately into one chimney wall as he twisted his back against the other. And he stopped.

Skip had lost twenty feet of hard-won climbing. One arm was bloody and maybe broken. The rapids roared below, inviting him to fall the rest of the way.

He twisted back into climbing position and tested his bad arm on the rock. Pain shot through his elbow right up into his brain. It was a pain he would take. Not ignore, but take. The thing he feared more was dullness—not being able to feel when his arm was touching rock. He inched his way back up.

When he reached the place where his fall started, Skip found that his plummeting had scraped off the treacherous moss. Bad arm and all, the climb was easier.

It took him an hour, nevertheless, to climb to the top of the chimney. The top of the cliff itself was only ten feet above. But it could have been a thousand: the rock between him and the cliff's edge was nothing but smooth granite, without so much as a hairline crack to hold on to, only a strip of moss from here on up on one side of the chimney and the dangling roots of a gnarled aspen growing on the lip of the chasm.

If only I had a rope. Skip told himself. *It would be so simple to throw a loop over the aspen and hoist myself up!*

Or would it?

He leaned to one side of the chimney wall and tried unbending an arm. It was as stiff as wood. The other arm was the same, and he had to assume his legs were as cramped and useless.

From far down, the river continued to send puffs of vapor up to him. He twisted inside the chimney to put the pressure on his back and legs, forcing one arm straight and then the other. There would only be one chance and he was determined to make it the best he could. Patiently, he kneaded his arms—a procedure that accentuated the agony of battered and tired muscles. He noticed for the first time that one sleeve and most of the back of his shirt had been torn off during the fall. Slowly, however, pain and sensation returned. His arms were not limber, but at least they could move. He did the same for his legs, pinching and kneading them until their dull ache became as sharp as needles.

He couldn't take any more time. Not only because of Jenny, but because the longer he stayed in the chimney the sooner his arms and legs would turn stiff again. He took a last, long look at the river below.

"Well, I'll make some splash."

He twisted so that he faced the chimney's inside surface and his back was to the gorge. He sighted along the moss, which ran for eight feet above him. Then a foot of bare rock. Then the roots. With his right foot, he searched for the best possible grip to push off from. He rocked from side to side to create some momentum. He counted from "ten" down, and took a deep breath at "one."

He swung out of the chimney, his fingers clawing at the moss.

Drier, the moss was firmer than the moss farther down. Clots of it fell from his hand and he had to keep moving up constantly: as soon as he stopped, he would have fallen.

Moss rolled over his shoulders and face. Four feet left to go and his momentum was slowing. His fingernails dug through the moss into the tiny crevices the moss grew from. His left arm, the bad one, slapped against bare rock on the other side. With the last swing of his right arm, he stretched and clutched the aspen root. Dirt poured over his head as he got both hands on the root and pulled. Then his fingers touched bark! He wrapped them around the tree's narrow trunk and hauled himself to the lip of the cliff.

As he got both elbows over the lip, the aspen ripped away roots and toppled, falling end over end until it faded into the mist of the rapids.

On top of the cliff, Skip tried to stand. He sank to his knees as his muscles started shaking uncontrollably. Then, gradually the tremors passed. About a mile off, where the river widened again into a placid stream, he could see the fire tower of a ranger station.

Skip did not have to walk all the way. As soon as he came down from the cliff and had wandered through a copse of trees, he found himself beside a horse corral. The very man he had come for was in front of a two-story cabin, sheltered from the wind, working on a motorcycle.

Jud dropped a wrench. "Where'd *you* come from?"

"River!" was all Skip could say.

The pilot gave a long whistle while he looked at Skip's cuts and torn clothes.

"I'd've sworn that any man who ever tried to tell me it could be done was a liar or crazy. You're neither of those, Skip!" The whole shock of belief hit Jud. "You did it! You came down that blasted river! Son of a gun. By why?"

When Skip told him, Jud raced into his house. Five minutes later, he was back out with a spare leather jacket and helping Skip onto the rear seat of the cycle.

"Called the dock and they're already gassing up the plane. Old Doc Evans is at Swan Lake. We'll pick him up there and go on to your place. Take us about an hour, all told. You feel up to riding?"

Skip slapped Jud's back. "Let's go!"

Chapter Nineteen

Grizzly in the Cabin

Pat sat on the bed holding Jenny and Toby. Overhead, the roof shingles had stopped chattering. For the past thirty minutes, the howling of the gale had decreased a bit in volume. From time to time a blast of wind would rattle the windows, but each time less violently than before. Now it seemed that the wind was puffing with exhaustion.

"It's just about over . . ." Pat said wearily.

"It nearly blew the whole house down!" Toby commented.

"It only *sounded* like that . . . I think Jenny's fever has gone down, too."

Jenny's forehead felt cool. She awoke in her mother's hug. "What happened, Mom . . . ?"

"Nothing."

"Nothing?" Toby asked. "We were almost blown back to California. You missed everything, Jenny. You should see outside. It's like a flood!"

"Toby, instead of getting your sister excited, why don't you get her some tea from the stove? Nothing much happened, Jen. Just a little storm and you slept right through it."

"Where's Daddy?"

"He went for the doctor, dear."

"He went down the river," Toby called back from

135

the stove. "I bet he just set a record. We'll be able to see the plane come back through the window."

Jenny did not want to look through the window. She managed a game smile and whispered to Pat, "Daddy . . . went down the river?"

"He'll be okay. Right now, we're concerned about you. How do you feel?"

"A little weak . . . but a lot better. Gee, I kept having nightmares and . . ." As Jenny sat up, the color left her face again. "Did Daddy get the bear?"

"We told you." Toby served her a mug of tea. "Dad went for the doctor. Those dumb cubs broke our radio . . . Well, you *did!*" he repeated for Ringo and Blackie.

"Don't worry about that . . . bear," Pat told Jenny. "I'm sure he's forgotten about you, so you might as well forget about him."

"And Crust?" Jenny asked. She heard a familiar scuffling from under the bed and the retriever stuck his head up on the blanket. "Oh, Crust!"

The dog jumped on the bed and licked Jenny's face. She kissed him on the nose.

"Take it easy, Jenny. You're still a sick girl. Have some of that tea," her mother advised her.

"We really had a big storm here, Mom?" Jenny sipped. "I *am* sorry I missed it!"

"We missed 'The Green Hornet' on the radio, too." Toby frowned. "And it was just getting excit—"

Crust's growl interrupted the boy. The hair on the retriever's back stood up. Everyone silently followed Crust's stare at the door.

The bar of the door was moving slowly up and down on the latch.

"Someone's there. Maybe it's Dad!" Toby jumped from the bed.

Crust's low growl became a snarl. His teeth showed and he dug his claws into the blanket.

"Mommy!" Jenny cried.

"Toby, don't open it!" Pat ordered.

"I'm not. I'm just checking."

While the door bar edged up and down, Toby got flat on his stomach and peeked through the crack at the bottom of the door. He looked back with a grin.

"Mom, it's just Samson. Can't I let him in?"

Pat bent and saw what Toby had seen: the claws of a bear standing on the porch. But she knew what Crust knew, as he stood glaring and barking, his usually friendly face a mask of hate.

"No, Toby."

"But what if he's hurt? Please?"

"No!!"

Pat picked up the shotgun and checked to see that it was loaded. She tried to remain calm but her fingers seemed to have turned to rubber. Jenny had squeezed herself into the corner of the bed, sobbing. A contagious fear was in the cabin. Whining, the cubs had climbed the ladder to the loft. A moment later, the bar came free of the latch, but then fell into it again. Pat could hear the boards of the porch groaning as the thing outside shifted its weight. The boards had never groaned under Samson.

"Wh-what is it, Mom?" Jenny asked.

"I don't know, Jen. Toby, now get up." Pat moved to the center of the cabin, facing the door. She cocked the twin hammers of the shotgun. "Toby, get over to the *side* of the door. Good. Now, when . . . when I tell you to, I want you to open the door and jump as far back out of the way as fast as you can. Do you understand?"

The eight-year-old understood. With a dry mouth, he stood by the entrance to the cabin, inches from the still-moving bar.

"Ready, Toby?" Pat aimed the shotgun at the center of the door.

"Ready."

Pat took two deep breaths.

"Open it!"

Toby lifted the bar, swung the door open and dove toward the corner of the room.

Pat faced Three Toes.

The grizzly, even bigger than the door, roared with surprise. His eyes seemed to burn through Pat straight at Jenny. As the door swung back, he slapped it open again and started into the cabin, walking upright.

The staggered triggers of the shotgun were stiffer than Pat had remembered. Her first shot was high and boomed into the wall above the door. Her second was level and straight, aimed straight at the grizzly's head.

But the bear was gone. Her second shot had been too late.

She ran to the door, locked the bolt shut, and stepped back, her arms shaking.

"Mommy, what are we going to do?" Jenny cried.

Pat laid the shotgun across the table and gripped the back of a chair until her trembling ceased. *I have to keep hold of myself, have to think.*

"Mommy . . . ?"

"Okay, Jen." Pat controlled her voice. "We kept him out."

"It was Three Toes, wasn't it?"

"I think so."

Pat took a box of shotgun shells from the mantel and tore it open. The shells rolled over the table. She picked up two and reloaded the gun.

Toby examined the floor. "I don't see any blood. You missed him."

"I guess so," Pat tried to joke, "or we'd have a bearskin rug."

The other shells . . . Pat told herself. *I'll maybe need those that fell.* She slipped on her cooking apron and poured the spare shells in its pocket.

"Is he going to come back?" Jenny asked.

"We'll be ready, honey, if he does," Pat reassured her.

"I never heard of bears going after people in their cabin," Toby said. "I didn't think even grizzlies did that."

Holding the shotgun ready, Pat looked out the

various windows and saw no sign of the bear by the lake. Nothing by the storehouse.

"I wish—I wish Daddy was here," Jenny sobbed.

"Well get along," Pat said soothingly. "The bear can't get in a locked door. There are three of us and we have a shotgun. He's a dumb bear to stick around here and he's going to be a dead one if he bothers us again. So, you take it easy, Jenny, because this is our home and we're just as tough as he is!"

She stopped talking for a moment, amazed. She was sounding just like Skip, and the kids were listening—a lot less panic-stricken than they'd been a minute before.

"You two climb up on the bed behind Crust . . . Who wants toast?"

"You're going to make toast *now?*" Jenny inquired.

"Well, we don't plan to starve to death either, do we? Do we, kids?"

Toby shook his head. "No!"

"Right," Pat said.

As if they were having nothing more than a late breakfast, Pat made a tray of toast and tea, which she carried to the bed. There, with the shotgun across her lap, she began telling Jenny and Toby a fairy tale. Part of it was from *Hansel and Gretel,* part from *Tom Sawyer,* and part from *Alice in Wonderland.* She was determined to tell the world's longest story—to tell it all day and all night if necessary. While she told it, her eyes kept stealing to the clock on the mantel. And she kept silently asking herself, *Skip, where are you?*

Minutes had stretched into an hour. Pat was beginning to hope the bear was gone when Crust slipped from the bed to the center of the floor. He stared at the door.

Pat went on with the fairy tale. Crust turned his stare toward a wall. His ears rose. Pat kept talking.

"Maybe Crust hears the plane," Toby interrupted.

"Maybe," Pat said. She didn't think so. "Let's finish the story."

Crust shifted again, to stare at the back wall of the cabin. Pat's voice faded. The dog's eyes slowly swung to the wall by the bed. Then they swung back to the door.

The cabin became as quiet as a tomb.

Pat, Jenny, and Toby sat and watched the Labrador, whose whole being was directed now at the door, then at the far wall, and then went from one corner to the other; then, again, he stared in a slow sweep of the back wall. The bear was circling the cabin.

"Mom?" Jenny said weakly.

The window by the bed was smashed into shards of glass. A giant paw reached in, the claws knocking Pat off the mattress.

Three Toes then reached it farther, his whole arm sweeping over the blanket. Jenny and Toby screamed and squirmed swiftly away from the groping paw. Window curtains fell on the floor. Three Toes squeezed his head in the window, forcing the sash to snap.

Pat sat up on the floor, blinking. The kids were in the far corner of the bed; the grizzly was reaching for them. She found the shotgun behind her and swung the double barrels toward the window. Three Toes saw the twin 12-gauge mouths of the shotgun and heaved himself back out of the window as the woman aimed. Pat pulled both triggers and all that remained of the sash and curtain rods exploded out the window. The whole area around the window was scarred and blackened.

"Mommy! Mommy!" Jenny screamed, holding a pillow over her chest.

"Did you get him?" Toby asked breathlessly.

The wall began shaking with heavy pounding. The bear was hitting the outside of the cabin in rage, as if he would tear the wall apart if he could.

Pat picked out the hulls of the spent shells from the shotgun and replaced them with two new ones from her apron pocket, then snapped the barrel back to the stock. More than words, her crisp action halted the kids' hysteria. She knew that the slightest indecision on her part could have panicked the two into running out of the cabin, where Three Toes would have had them at his mercy.

The pounding stopped. All Pat could hear now was Jenny's sobbing—and the racing of her own heart. After the earlier attack, at the river, she had wondered what was wrong with the bear, what could fill any animal with so much hate. She wondered no longer. Her instinct for the protection of her children left no room for doubt or fear.

"Crust," she asked in a low voice, "where is he, boy?"

"You're cut, Mom!" Toby broke in.

"Shh!"

Pat brushed a trickle of blood from her temple. Crust's stare had slid along the back wall to the far wall. Pat rested her finger on the trigger.

Three Toes's paw smashed ear-shatteringly through the cabin's other window.

In the same second, Pat fired. Glass, curtains, and sash blew out of the window. Most of Pat's china, flower vases, and clay pots lay shattered on the floor. But specks of red dotted the debris.

"You got him, Mom!" Toby shouted.

Just barely, she knew.

The bear now pounded on the walls as if he could turn the cabin over.

"Quiet, kids!"

Pat pulled the bed into the center of the back wall, out of reach of either of the windows. She didn't see Crust's attention move to the door.

"Mom, look!" Jenny yelled.

The pounding had ceased. The bar of the door was lifting up again. A shoulder pressed against the strength of the bolt. The iron whined, but held. The bear's roars grew, pain added to his hate.

"No!!!" Jenny and Toby shouted together.

The center of the door planking suddenly flew

across the cabin. Three Toes's bloody paw came through and ripped out the whole bottom of the center plank.

Pat reloaded the shotgun feverishly. However, as she snapped the barrel up it would not shut. One of the plastic shells was snagged at the base. She couldn't get the shotgun either open or shut.

"Mommy!!!"

Three Toes was turning the center of the door into splinters. With each scoop of his paws, he ripped out more planking. As he smashed in the top of the center plank, the children could see his dark eyes.

Pat quickly hit the shotgun barrel against the floor. The barrel came open. She fished out the bad shell and took another shell from her apron. The shell rolled out of her fingers.

With two final, tremendous blows the sides of the door caved in. Mouth gaping, Three Toes entered the cabin. Crust threw himself at the bear, stopping him at the door.

The screaming and roaring had confused Pat. Another shell slipped out her fingers. Finally, she held on to one but then couldn't hold the barrel still enough to load it.

Jenny covered her eyes. "Mommy, look out!"

A slash of claws sent Crust into the stove. The dog collapsed, stunned and helpless. The grizzly roared with triumph and rose to his full height inside the cabin.

Pat dropped the shell once more. Nevertheless, she stood her ground, placing herself between the bear and her children.

Then, all at once, Three Toes wheeled around where he stood.

Surprising Pat, Jenny, and Toby, the grizzly roared out through the smashed door. A roar answered him, and the grizzly lunged back out of the cabin.

"Samson!" Toby shouted gleefully.

From the front lawn came the sound, now, of two

bears meeting. Pat slipped a shell into the shotgun and steadily snapped it shut.

No black bear would ordinarily clash with a grizzly, especially one of Three Toes's proportions. Yet Samson's first charge bowled the grizzly over and his fangs slashed at the bigger carnivore's neck. Three Toes kicked free a moment later and rolled to his feet. Samson's second charge was met with a swipe that sent the black bear nosedown into the dirt.

Samson was brave, but he was fighting a king. Three Toes had weight and muscle and a savagery that had defeated grizzlies twice as strong as Samson. As the black bear attacked again, Three Toes knocked him aside and pinned him to the ground. The grizzly's long fangs tore into black fur and flesh.

Pat stood on the porch. A cloud of uprooted and flying grass and dust partly obscured the fight, but she could see that Samson was getting the worst of it.

Samson jolted the grizzly's head with a slap upward. Another of the black bear's thrusts raked the grizzly's stomach. But Three Toes matched Samson swing for swing, knowing how much more he was hurting the smaller bear. As Samson staggered, Three Toes closed his jaws on the black bear's neck and shook him like a stuffed pillow.

Pat could not shoot; she feared she would hit Samson as well as Three Toes. Nevertheless, she lifted the barrel high and fired—once.

Three Toes rose from his victim. The black bear was still alive, but helpless now. The danger was the woman and the gun. Moreover, Three Toes's fear of the weapon had temporarily vanished. He charged toward the porch, gathering speed with every step. At last, he would rid the woods of people—they were his woods.

Pat had a single shell left. She waited until the charging grizzly was just yards away. Then she took one step toward him and pulled the trigger.

Chapter Twenty

Pat Makes Her Decision

"There it is!" Skip pointed through the windscreen of the aquaplane toward his cabin.

"Do me a favor." Doc Evans called from the plane's rear seat. "I just bandaged that arm. Don't use it for a while—not even to comb your hair!"

Jud banked the plane into a long approach to the lake. He agreed with the doctor. Trying to restrain Skip Robinson's anxiety was like trying to hold on to a lighted firecracker.

The aquaplane descended over the trees, its shadow slipping finally beyond the branches and flickering over the lake's surface, becoming smaller and more distinct. Aimed directly at the camp, its fuselage skirt and pontoons at length touched water. By the time the plane was taxiing close to shore, Skip opened the door and stood outside, one leg dangling over the wave spewed up by the skirt.

Doc Evans was a stout mountain man himself, but he couldn't help looking at Skip's arm and shaking his head.

Jud shrugged. "Sometimes good men make lousy patients."

As soon as the pilot shut the engine off, Skip was in the water and wading to shore. What he saw when he got there almost dropped him to his knees.

"Wow . . . !" Jud said slowly as he caught up.

The devastation accomplished by the storm would have been bad enough. Half a dozen trees lay scattered over the ground. The vegetable garden was a swamp of mud and planting sticks. But what shocked the three men more was the cabin. Singles were ripped from the roof; windows were smashed; the walls looked as if they'd been beaten in with an ax; glass and splinters were everywhere; the door no longer existed. But most shocking of all, lying in front of the cabin, one paw on the porch, was the gray hulk that had been Three Toes.

Skip ran across the lawn. Jumping over the dead grizzly, he ducked through the shattered doorway.

Pat was sitting up in bed, her arms around Jenny and Toby, who were asleep.

"Everything's all right . . ." she said calmly.

Skip got to the bed in one giant step and gathered her into his arms.

Jenny leaned on an elbow while the cold disk of Doc Evans's stethoscope moved about her back. Skip and Pat stood by the bed. Toby was outside helping Jud drag and roll the grizzly down to the beach.

"Breathe again . . . Again . . . Once more . . . That's fine!" Evans pulled the stethoscope plugs from his ears. "All done."

Jenny sat up. "What's the verdict?"

"You have the lungs of an eleven-year-old," he answered with mock gravity. "And you're going to spend the next two days in bed."

"Oh, no!" she protested. "Not two more days!"

"Either that, or another shot."

"I'll take the two days," Jenny moaned after a moment's consideration.

"I thought you'd say that." The doctor grinned as he closed up his bag.

Toby ran in with a pair of young raccoons. "Look

what *we* found!" He dumped them on the bed and the tiny creatures climbed up on Jenny's head.

"You take those back outside!" Pat told Toby. "Jenny's sick."

"Oh, she can have *some* company," Dr. Evans laughed.

The raccoons snuggled into Jenny's neck, making her giggle.

"We have to give them names," Toby said.

"Like what?" Jenny was trying to protect her ticklish areas from the raccoons' wet noses.

"Goo Goo," was Toby's suggestion.

"Goo Goo?" Jenny wrinkled her nose.

The doctor stepped out on the porch now and grinned reassuringly at Skip and Pat. He saw the concern still on their faces. "Well, the only thing that I could find wrong with her was a severe virus infection. It's good you got me up here. Those shots I gave her should take care of it."

"That's all?" Skip was surprised.

"What about her allergy? Her lungs?" Pat asked.

"Nothing wrong with her lungs. Clear as a bell. Just give her the medicine I gave you and she'll be good as new in a couple days." The old mountain doctor took a long second look at the exhaustion in Pat's eyes. "How are *you* coping? You're a brave lady, but that was quite some experience."

"I'm . . . fine," Pat said.

"Well"—the doctor turned to Skip—"you keep an eye on her. And you keep that new radio in a safe place, hear?"

"Sure," Skip agreed.

While Pat and Doc discussed the medicine, Skip strode down to the shore to help Jud float Three Toes, on an improvised raft of three logs tied together with rope, to the aquaplane.

"You're crazy!" the pilot said to Skip. "There's no better treat than bear steak. Or bear stew. You and Pat sure earned this one."

"I think . . . it's better just to get him out of here."

"Well, don't think of him as a killer bear anymore. He's only meat now, and there's a long winter coming."

Paddling and poling slowly across the now-calm water, they got the bear to the back of the plane, where Jud—used to bulky and sometimes heavy deliveries—had created a drop-door under the end of the fuselage. Hitching a stout rope around the grizzly, he looped it through two handles inside the wide hold and he and Skip both pulled on the rope and pushed upward.

"I'm not worried about the winter anymore," Skip said, and explained why.

It took some time to get the heavy grizzly loaded, but all too soon the aquaplane was gathering takeoff speed across the surface of the lake. The Robinsons—Jenny, wrapped in a heavy coat, included—plus Crust, the bear cubs, two raccoons, and Samson, who had returned to the camp, nursing his wounds, all stood on the shore and waved good-bye. The plane climbed above the pines, waggled its wings, and headed south.

"I wish they could've stayed longer—even if Doc did give me shots," Jenny said.

Skip cleared his throat. "Well, I asked Jud to come back in the morning. He'll fly us all out."

Toby and Jenny looked at each other dumb-founded.

"What do you mean?" the boy asked.

"I mean, we're going back home to the city."

"This is our home, right here. I love it. I don't want to go," Toby pleaded.

Jenny joined Toby. "What about all our friends?" She put her arm around Samson. "How could we abandon them?"

"What about Three Toes?" Skip asked her softly.

"He's gone now," she answered bravely. "I don't want to leave now, just when everything is perfect. Mom, tell Dad we don't want to go!"

Pat sighed. Just watching Jud take off, a good part of her had wished she were on the plane.

"You really *want* to stay, in spite of what you say, don't you?" she asked Skip pointedly.

"Only if *you* do. Pat, I'm not going to be happy here unless you are. I asked you a long time ago for the chance to come up here and try this. We've tried. *You've* tried harder and faced more than *me*. When I got here this afternoon and saw what a mess the camp was, all I could think of was you and the kids. I couldn't have cared if this whole place was picked up and dropped in the ocean—as long as you were safe. *You're* all I care about. If you want to go . . . I'll understand."

His wife reached out to take his hand.

"Give me a chance to . . . think about it. Okay, Skip?"

"Sure."

While Skip and the children stayed by the cabin, Pat walked alone up into the hills.

She felt dishonest about taking time to come to a decision she had already made. They had tried to make a life in the British Columbian wilderness and it hadn't worked out. No one was to blame, least of all Skip. The place was still too strange and too dangerous. A city family didn't fit in.

One moment it was tranquil, and the next a storm was tearing trees out of the ground. She only had to look at the woods around her to see the terrible effects of the gale. *Most animals are friendly, true,* she admitted. *The ones that aren't friendly can kill you, though . . .*

They could move back to the city. Maybe the suburbs. Have a backyard. Get used to television again and the smell of car exhaust, and the wails of police-car sirens. The kids could go back to a real school. She might be able to get a job part-time, designing again. None of them would like it at first, but in time they'd get used to it and the wilderness would turn back into a dream.

She climbed past the trees to the slopes where

Jenny always went in search of wildflowers and was surprised to find any flowers left after the storm. But there they were, bright and colorful beds of them lifting their heads to the late-afternoon rays of the sun. *It's incredible,* she thought, *that I'm still living out a day that started so long ago, when Skip set out for the river.*

She sat down among the flowers. The cabin was hidden from view, but she could see the quiet lake, the mountains glinting crystal and green under a vast, azure-blue sky. A soft wind tugged at her hair. She listened to a late bee zooming among some autumn flowers.

Through the buzzing, all at once she became conscious of another sound.

"Come on, Flora, don't be like that! Come on!"

Pat looked behind her.

"Boomer! Hi!"

"Why, Miz Robinson, we was jus' comin' down to yer place."

Boomer Parks took his beaten hat off his head. He grinned with more gum than teeth as he led his mule down the hill toward her.

"It's good to see you and Flora."

"Well, I 'membered that meal yuh gave me. This windstorm come up an' I know what it can do to shingles. Thought mebbe I could pitch in an' pay yuh back fer that good eatin'. I split a mean shingle!" The mule nudged his back. "Don't pay no mind to Flora. She thinks I'm just comin' round fer the food. A mule, ma'am, is a suspicious animal. Not one o' yer good biscuits'll pass muh lips till I got yer cabin lookin' like a model home. That's a promise."

"That's very kind of you, Boomer, but it won't be necessary. We're . . . going to be leaving here tomorrow. We're giving up the camp . . ."

Boomer's grin shrank. "Oh. I confess that comes as a surprise. I hadn't figured on that. Yuh mind if an ol' fool like me asks yuh why?" The mule jerked on her rope and Boomer turned sternly. "Yoo hush up, Flora. Lady an' I want to talk."

He settled into the grass beside Pat.

Haltingly at first, she related to the trapper why she and Skip had left Los Angeles. The more she told him, the easier the telling was. And Boomer, like most mountain people, was a good listener. She told him about the cougar, the wolves, and—as his concentration sharpened to a sympathetic frown—the ordeal of Three Toes.

"Well . . ." Boomer shook his head. "Can't say that I blame yuh. In a few months, you folks've gone through more'n most people do in a lifetime. An' yuh done us all a favor by puttin' an end to Three Toes. Anyway, I knew yuh wouldn' be packin' without a mighty good reason. Say, lookit that over there!"

On a rock about thirty yards to Pat's left sat the mother cougar.

The big cat gazed idly at Pat, and then its yellow eyes swung proudly to follow her two cubs, who were stalking a butterfly. The cubs had grown a lot since Pat had last seen them. They were nearly as large as their mother, but there was still a lot of kitten left in their romping.

"Ol' Jake never had a pet *cougar,* that I can recollect," Boomer scratched the stubble on his chin. "You tame those cats?"

"No. That's the one that attacked Skip."

"Well now, she was doin' her motherly duty as she saw it. Same as you with Three Toes! But these cats here, they seem to think yer part o' the natural scenery now."

Pat watched the mother cat stretch out on the rock. Boomer glanced slyly at the woman.

"Yuh see, most families that come out here an' then pack it in, they're goin' 'cause they failed. *Yoo* folks didn't fail. Don't yuh ever for a minute think yuh did. Yoo did yer bit. Built yer cabin. Cleared up that grizzly for the rest o' us. Yer gon ter leave a lot o' four-legged an' two-legged friends out there. Matter o'

fact, scenery's gonna be a sight unnatural without yuh."
He put out a callused hand. "Been proud to know
yuh."

They shook hands.

"Thank you, Boomer. Thanks for everything."

"Pleasure's mine."

"Well . . ." Pat stood. "I think it's time I went back
to the cabin."

"Be right along. Wanta give Flora a chance at that
clover."

Pat ran down the hill. Boomer scratched his chin
as he watched her go. He turned crossly on the mule.

"Now, don't yuh go thinkin' I said all that jest to
have a free meal goin' here! It was all true!"

Flora lowered her head as if in shame.

Pat ran until she was in sight of the cabin—and
then she slowed down to a walk, a serious expression
on her face. When she came around the corner of the
cabin, Skip and the kids were sitting dejected on the
grass. As they looked up, she put her fists on her hips.

"Look, gang, if this is going to be our home, we'd
better clean it up!"

Three surprised faces almost split with grins. Pat's
made a fourth.

"We're *staying!!!*" Toby leaped into the air.

"*Staying!!!*" Jenny hugged Crust.

Skip hugged Pat and swung her around. "Seriously?" he asked.

"Seriously. But this place is a mess!" After a fervent kiss, she added, "I just found out where we belong. If we belong here, it's got to be our home."

Boomer now appeared with Flora. From Pat's wink
he could tell which way the decision had gone, and he
punched the air.

"I told yuh those shingles'd need fixin'!"

Ringo and Blackie ran circles of excitement around
Toby. When he got dizzy and fell, the cubs raced toward the mule. Flora took one startled look at them
and bolted. The rope jumped from Boomer's hand.

As the mule galloped past the storehouse, Boomer took out after her.

"Flora! Dad-blast it, Flora, come back here! Dangdest mule I ever saw!"

Toby started to race along with Boomer, then stopped and looked back at his mother and father.

Boomer waved him on. "Come on, Toby! You help me!"

Skip, Pat, and Jenny watched the race and rocked with laughter—not so much with amusement as with pure joy.

toba, in colors of lilac and tangerine and bubblegum-pink, the Northwest Territories rising above them in mint-green. On this map, Nunavut did not yet exist. On this map, the teenage Hayden had printed a series of runes that ran up the length of the Tuktoyaktuk Peninsula and marched through the Beaufort Sea to Sachs Harbour.

Miles had the image of Hayden wrapped in an Eskimo coat with a fur-lined hood, traveling across the plain of a frozen sea on a dogsled, and behind him the sheet of ice was breaking into jagged jigsaw pieces. The pallid seabirds skated circles overhead, screeching: *Tekeli-li! Tekeli-li!*

It had already occurred to him that this was just another dead end—

Another Kulm, North Dakota—

Another Rolla, Missouri—

Another humiliation like the one at the JPMorgan Chase Tower in Houston—the security guard escorting Miles out of the Sky Lobby and depositing him onto the plaza. *Mister, you've been warned before,* the guard said—

All of those times when he'd been convinced he was on the verge of catching Hayden at last.

He had taken caffeine pills during the last part of his drive on the Dempster Highway, and now his heart didn't want to slow down. He could feel his pulse in the membranes of his eyeballs, in the soles of his feet, in the roots of his hair. And though he was so tired—unbelievably tired—though he stretched out on the thin motel room mattress and pressed his head onto the pillow, he didn't know whether he would be able to go to sleep.

He tried to meditate. He imagined he was back in his apartment in Cleveland, the sheer white curtains were moving in a morning breeze, and his face was pressed against the nice extra-heavy pillow he'd purchased for himself at Bed Bath & Beyond, and he was going to wake up and go to his job at Matalov Novelties, and he had given up on detective work forever.

He was twenty-nine years old when he moved back to Cleveland—this was after his last expedition, his trip to North Dakota—and he had decided that going home, returning to the city of his childhood, would give him a sense of stability and equilibrium. Months had gone by and he hadn't heard from Hayden, and he felt as if his mind were clearing. He was going to enter a new phase of his life.

Cleveland was not in great shape. At first glance, it appeared that Cleveland was in the midst of its final death throes: infrastructure collapsing, stores closed and boarded up, Euclid Avenue—the great central street—dismantled, the asphalt torn off and piled along the sidewalk, the left lane a muddy trench lined with orange construction barrels, the beautiful old buildings—May Company, Higbee's—hollowed out, belts of empty lots and haunted-looking warehouses.

This had been ongoing for as long as he could remember—for years and years the city had been sliding into ruin and despair, people always spoke with nostalgia about the former glory of the city's past, and he had never taken such talk particularly seriously.

But now it looked like a place that had been bombed and then abandoned. Driving downtown for the first time, he had an apocalyptic feeling, a last-man-on-earth feeling, even though other cars were driving a few blocks ahead, even though he saw a dark figure disappearing into the doorway of a ramshackle tavern. It was the feeling you got when you woke up and everyone you loved was dead. Everyone was dead, and yet the world was continuing on, austere and thoughtless, the sky stirred full with gulls and starlings. A blimp floated lethargically in the haze above the baseball field like an old balloon that had been discarded in a muddy lake.

But he needed to try to think more positively! Not everything had to be so morbid, as his mom always said.

He had rented an apartment on Euclid Heights Boulevard, not far from the University Circle area, not far, actually, from the street where he and Hayden had grown up.

But he wasn't going to think about that.

His apartment was in an old brownstone called the Hyde Arms. Third floor, one-bedroom suite, hardwood floors and refurbished kitchen, heat and water inclusive, cats welcome.

He thought about getting a cat, since he was settling down after all. A big, friendly black-and-white tuxedo cat, a mouser, he thought, a companion—and the idea pleased him, not least because Hayden had always had a horror of cats, various superstitions about their "powers."

He had found one of his old friends from high school in the phone book—John Russell—and he had been surprised and actually moved at how happy John Russell was to hear from him. They used to play clarinet together in the marching band and they used to hang out together all the time and John Russell said, "Why don't we go out for a drink? I'd love to catch up!"

Which was exactly what Miles had hoped for when he'd returned to Cleveland. A night out with an old buddy, renewed friendships, familiar places, easy but not unserious conversations. A couple of nights later, the two of them sat in Parnell's Pub, a nice corner bar near the art-house movie theater, and there was a real Irish bartender—"What can I get for you, gents?" he brogued in his pleasant accent—and two televisions mounted unobtrusively in the alcoves above the liquor bottles played a baseball game that people were periodically noticing, as meanwhile the jukebox was emitting rock music that seemed vaguely college-educated, the clientele both reserved and relaxed, not too boisterous, not too aloof.

This could be *my* bar, Miles thought—imagining a scenario in which he and his group of friends met regularly for drinks, and their lives had the fixed rhythms and amusing complications of a well-written ensemble television show. He'd be the funny, slightly neurotic one, the one who might get involved with a smart, edgy younger girl—possibly with tattoos and piercings—who stirs up his life in interesting and comical ways.

"It's fantastic to see you, Miles," John Russell said, as Miles was eking his way through this reverie. "Honestly. I can't believe it's been ten years! Good Lord! More than ten years!" And John Russell put his palms against his cheeks, comically miming surprise. Miles had forgotten about John Russell's odd, nerdy gestures, as if he had learned about emotions from the anime cartoons and video games he used to love.

"So what have you been doing with yourself?" John Russell said, and he raised his eyes as if he were prepared for Miles to reveal a remarkable story. "Homunculus!" as he used to say, back in their teenage years—by which he meant: "Incredible!"

"Miles," he said, "Where have you *been* all these years?"

"A good question," Miles said. "I wonder that myself sometimes."

He was indecisive. He didn't want to get into all of the stuff about Hayden—which would have, he supposed, come across as ridiculous and exaggerated in any case. What would he say? *I've basically been wasting the past decade of my life pursuing my insane twin brother. You remember Hayden, don't you?*

Even mentioning Hayden's name was probably bad luck.

"I don't know," he told John Russell. "I've been somewhat—nomadic, actually. Involved in a lot of different stuff. It took me about six years to finish college, you know. There were . . . some issues. . . ."

"I heard," John Russell said, and he made what Miles assumed was a commiserating expression. "My condolences about your parents."

"Well," Miles said. "Thank you." But what was there to say? How do you respond to expressions of sympathy, so long after the fact? "I'm better now." That was a good answer, he decided. "It was difficult, but—I've gotten myself together, it's been awhile and—and I guess I'm just thinking about settling down for a while. Looking for a job, you know, whatever."

"Most definitely," John Russell said, and nodded as if Miles had been articulate. What a relief! For as long as they'd been friends,

John Russell had always been a blithely, blissfully accepting kid—the perfect friend when you had a crazy brother and a troubled home life and limited social skills—and in personality he was essentially unchanged, though he'd aged radically in other ways: his hairline had receded, and the bare dome of his head now looked more oblong, and his chin had grown weaker, and he'd gotten heavy in the stomach and hips and bottom, so that he was shaped a little like a bowling pin. He was a tax attorney.

"I'm not necessarily looking for anything specific at this point," Miles was saying. He still felt vaguely embarrassed and—he couldn't help it—defensive. "Some job . . . and, I don't know, go back to school? I need to get more focused in my life, I guess. I've wasted a lot of time."

But John Russell only tilted his head sympathetically. "Who knows?" he said. "I actually sometimes wish I'd done more traveling and maybe a little *less* settling." And he patted his round belly wryly.

"I think probably most people waste their lives in one way or another," John Russell said. "You know—one time I tried to figure out how much time I'd spent in my life playing video games and watching TV. My rough estimate is, like, ninety-one thousand hours. Which is actually probably conservative, but that amounts to just over ten years. Which I have to say, I found a little scary—though, it hasn't stopped me from watching TV and playing video games, but—it's sad, I guess."

"Well," Miles said. "It seems like it would be hard to calculate something like that."

"I've actually put together a spreadsheet," John Russell said. "I'll show it to you sometime."

Miles nodded. "That would be cool," he said—and he couldn't help but think how the idea of John Russell's "spreadsheet" would have delighted Hayden.

"That kid is a bigger freak than we are, Miles," Hayden used to say.

And Miles would protest. "We're not freaks," Miles would say. "And he isn't, either."

"Oh, please," Hayden would say.

He remembered how amused Hayden had been by the fact that John Russell went by both his first and last name. "What a ridiculous affectation," Hayden had said. "But I actually kind of like it." And then Hayden had performed a small parody of John Russell's delicate hen-like way of walking. Which, despite himself, Miles had found hilarious, and even now it was hard not to think of John Russell as a humorous character.

But he was not going to think about Hayden.

"Anyway," he said.

He and John Russell had pints of beer, and both of them lifted their glasses to their lips and took a sip. They smiled at each other, and Miles was aware of how urgently he wanted them to be friends, to be normal friends, but instead there was an awkward silence that he didn't know how to fill. John Russell cleared his throat.

"In any case," John Russell said, "people take different paths. Like—for example—did you hear about Clayton Combe? You remember him, don't you?"

"Sure," Miles said, though he hadn't thought of Clayton Combe in years.

He was a boy at Hawken School that both he and John Russell had disliked: a bright, popular student, beloved by nearly everyone, athletic, good-looking, but also, they thought, a condescending ass. He had the most hideously self-satisfied grin Miles had ever seen on a human being.

"You won't believe this," John Russell said, confidentially. "Everybody thought he was going to do so well? As it turns out, he killed himself. He was an investment banker at ING, and there was an embezzlement scandal of some sort. He claimed he wasn't guilty, but he got convicted and he was supposed to get about fifteen years in prison but then he—"

John Russell raised his eyebrows significantly. "*Hung* himself."

"That's awful," Miles said.

And it was, though he didn't necessarily feel that badly about it. He remembered how Hayden had disliked Clayton Combe intensely—how he used to mimic Clayton's way of tilting his head back when he smiled, as if he were being applauded. Hayden would raise his hand and wave to an imaginary, appreciative crowd, like a beauty queen on a float, and Miles and John Russell used to find this parody uproarious.

And then, Miles couldn't help it, the detective part of him woke up and blinked.

Wasn't ING one of those companies, Miles thought, one of the many entities that Hayden bore some grudge against?

Hadn't he mentioned it in one of his emails? One of his various rants?

But he didn't have to let himself go in that direction.

"Poor Clayton," he heard himself murmur. "That's so . . . ," he said. "So strange."

But was it? Was it strange?

He reflected on this, in the week after that conversation with John Russell. Why did it always have to circle back to Hayden? Why couldn't he just sit there and have a pleasant conversation with an old friend? Why couldn't the story of Clayton Combe just be a bit of gossip? And he refused to research it. He was not going to look up news articles about Clayton Combe; he was not going to turn it into some paranoid fantasy.

But then, ultimately, he wrote it down in his notebook anyway:

Did Hayden destroy the life of Clayton Combe and drive him to suicide?

Unknown.

He was feeling very vulnerable at that point. Very vulnerable and unsettled and depressed, and he kept thinking about what John Russell had said. *Most people waste their lives in one way or another.*

I have to change directions, Miles thought. A person can use his life wisely, if he just thinks about it. If he just makes a plan, and sticks to it!

Yet, despite his best intentions, he'd find himself going through his files once again.

He'd find himself staring out the window of his apartment, looking out toward the northeast, out over the suburban treetops. A few blocks away was the street where his family used to live, and he could feel their old house sending out uninterpretable signals, telegraphing its absence, since of course it wasn't there any longer.

He thought about going over to look at the site.

What was left? he wondered. Was it just a grassy lot? Was there a new house where the old one once stood? Was there anything left that he would recognize?

The house had burned down during his sophomore year at Ohio University. Hayden had been missing for more than two years by then, and Miles had never been able to bring himself to come back. What reason was there? His father, his mother, even his stepfather, Mr. Spady, were all dead, nothing to return for except morbid curiosity, which he ultimately resisted. He didn't want to see the remains of the structure, burnt timbers and caved roof, charred pieces of furniture; he didn't want to imagine the windows lit with fire, the neighbors gathering on the lawn as the fire truck and ambulance arrived.

He didn't want to envisage the possibility of Hayden standing there, shadowed in the copse of lilacs at the edge of the yard, perhaps with his arsonist's tools still in a backpack on his shoulder.

There was no real evidence of this—nothing beyond a vivid snapshot in his imagination, a picture so sharp that sometimes he couldn't help but add the house to the tally of Hayden's crimes. The house, and his mother and Mr. Spady.

And now, he thought, there was poor Clayton Combe, hanging himself in a jail cell. He thought of Hayden's Clayton Combe impression: chin up, eyes rolled back, mouth stretched into a rictus of self-regard.

Down below his third-story window, he could see the roof of the building next door; a mummified newspaper, still rolled and rubber-banded but slowly decaying; and a smattering of leaves came running down the alleyway in a formation like birds or football players; and then a helicopter appeared, gliding heavily, passing close to the treetops, its thick propellers chopping the air up. On its way to the hospital, no doubt, though Miles watched it sternly. For years, Hayden had believed that helicopters were spying on him.

A few days later, Miles had found a job. Or rather (he sometimes thought) the job had found him.

He was downtown, had managed to put together a few interviews, low-level programming and IT support, an "associate" position at the public library, nothing spectacular, but who knew? He was settling down, he thought, he had to be persistent and optimistic—though optimism wasn't easy to come by walking down Prospect Avenue. So many empty storefronts with their long-faded SPACE AVAILABLE signs, so many soundless blocks. Probably, he thought again, it was a mistake to come back.

He was thinking this when he saw the old novelty shop, Matalov Novelties, just around the corner on 4th Street, nested among the ancient jewelry stores and pawnshops.

He was amazed it was still there. It was the last place he would have thought of surviving the economic spiral that had overcome most of these downtown establishments. Matalov Novelties hadn't crossed his mind in years—certainly not since his father had died, back when they were thirteen.

When they were children, their father used to take Miles and Hayden with him when he went to the novelty store. A treat—to go with their father to this peculiar run-down establishment. *The magic shop*, he called it.

They had never been allowed to see their father perform—not as a clown, not as a magician, certainly not as a hypnotist. At home, he was reserved, untheatrical, which had made their visits to Matalov Novelties all the more impressive in their minds. Their father holding their hands: "Don't touch anything, boys. Just look with your eyes." Which was very difficult, since it was, after all, a magic store—rows and rows of shelves, floor to ceiling, a clutter of antiques and odd devices, wooden figurines like chess pieces in the shapes of gargoyles, Chinese finger traps, feather boas, top hats and capes, an elderly rhesus monkey in a silver cage—

—and then the old woman would emerge. Mrs. Matalov. Aged but not doddering, though her spine was curving into a question mark, a hump raising her bright silky blouse. Her hair was like dandelion fluff, dyed a peach color, and her lips were red with the waxy, glistening lipstick that old silent-movie actresses wore.

"Larry," she said, her voice accented. Russian. "So good to see you!" Their father made a small bow.

When Mrs. Matalov saw Miles and Hayden, she performed a brief dramaturgical double take, drawing a slow gasp through her teeth, her eyes widening.

"Oh, Larry!" she said. "Such lovely boys. They break my heart."

As Miles thought back to this, it felt more like a memory of a children's storybook than an event that had actually happened. Like a lie Hayden would make up. And so he was hardly surprised to find that Matalov Novelties appeared to be closed. A folding metal grate was pulled across the entranceway, and the narrow shop window was covered with paper.

But still—beyond the grate, through the frosted glass of the door, he could see that the place wasn't empty. He could make out shelves, and when he reached through the grate to tap on the glass, he thought he saw movement. He stood there, hesitantly, and soon, enough time had passed that he began to feel foolish he was still waiting.

Then, abruptly, the old woman jerked the door open and peered out at him through the bars.

"No retail!" she shrilled. "No Indians, no Browns, no Cleveland memorabilia. This is not a retail establishment." Her accent was muddy, even thicker than he remembered. He stood gaping as she waved a hand at him: *go, go.*

"Mrs. Matalov?" he said.

Needless to say, she had aged in the seventeen years since he had last seen her. Even when he was a child, she had been an old woman; now she was practically a skeleton. She had grown shorter, smaller. The curve of her spine was so pronounced that her vertebrae stood out in ridges along her stooped back, and her head was tilted toward the ground so that she had to peer up like a turtle to see him. Her hair was very thin, just a few sparse tufts, though still dyed the color of a peach. It was impossible that she was still alive, Miles thought. She must be well into her nineties.

"Mrs. Matalov?" he said again. He tried to speak loudly and clearly, and he put on what he hoped was a winning smile. "I don't know whether you would remember me. I'm Miles Cheshire? Larry Cheshire's son? I'm in Cleveland and . . ."

"One moment," she said crossly. "You're babbling, I can't hear what you're saying. One moment please."

It took more than a moment for her to unlock the metal grate and pull it back, but once it was open, she appeared to be willing to let him inside.

"I'm really sorry to bother you," Miles said, gazing around, the rows of shelves the same as he recalled, the junk-store smell of cigarettes and dust and sandalwood and wet cardboard. "I," he said sheepishly, "—don't mean to intrude. I haven't been in Cleveland in many years and I was just passing by. Nostalgia, I guess. My dad was an old customer of yours."

"Larry Cheshire, yes. I heard you already," Mrs. Matalov said sternly. "I remember. I myself am not a nostalgic person, but come in, come in. Tell me what I can do for you. You, too, are a magician? Like your father?"

"Oh," Miles said. "No, no." As his eyes adjusted to the dimness, he saw that the shop was not, after all, unchanged since his childhood.

It was more like an old garage or attic, and the shelves extended back where the dark aisles were clogged with a disorder of stacks of partially opened boxes. Clustered at the front of the shelves were a number of desks and tables, each one bearing a number of old personal computers of various antiquated generations; and monitors, and tangled birds' nests of electrical cords and connection wires. At one of the desks sat a dark-haired girl—perhaps twenty or twenty-one years old?—wearing black clothes and black lipstick and pointed silver earrings, like the teeth of some prehistoric carnivore. She glanced up at him, expressionless and emanating irony.

"No, no," Miles said. "Definitely not a magician. I never exactly pursued—" And he felt himself blushing, he didn't know why. "I'm not anything, really," he said, and watched as Mrs. Matalov stalked through the maze of desks—a wobbling but unexpectedly swift gait, like someone hurrying over thin ice.

"What a shame," Mrs. Matalov said. She sank into a wheeled office chair, where several ornamental pillows cushioned her back. She motioned for him to come and sit as well. "Your father, I liked him very much. Such a kind and gracious spirit."

"He was," Miles said. She was right: but how much time had passed since he'd remembered his father? An old bit of grief awakened and turned over in his chest.

"Poor man!" she said. "He was a very talented performer; you knew that. If he had lived in a different time, he might have made a lot of money, instead of playing at children's parties." She clucked her tongue at this, a series of soft exclamation points, and Miles felt as if she were going to reproach him, a young man who was squandering his life. But she merely eyed him shrewdly.

"And what of your brother?" she said. "He is not a magician, either, I take it?"

"No," Miles said. "He—"

But what was Hayden? A magician of sorts, perhaps.

"I remember the two of you," Mrs. Matalov said. "Twins. Very pretty. You were the timid one, I think," she said. "Miles. A little mouse name. But your brother—" And here she raised a finger and wagged it, unspecifically. "He was a very naughty one. A thief! I saw him stealing from me, many times, and I would have caught him by his neck! But." She shrugged. "I did not want to embarrass your father."

Miles nodded uncomfortably, glancing over to the dark-haired young woman who was watching him with a look of almost imperceptible amusement.

"Yes," Miles said. "He could be—mischievous."

"Hmm," Mrs. Matalov said. "Mischievous? No. Worse than that, I think." And she regarded Miles for what felt like a long time. "I pitied you," she said. "So shy, and with a brother such as that!"

Miles said nothing. He hadn't expected to find himself in this situation—in this gray fluorescent-lit windowless place, the old woman and the dark-haired girl both observing him closely. He had not expected to find his father—or himself—so closely remembered. What should he say?

Mrs. Matalov took a cigarette from a pocket of her thin cardigan, and Miles watched as she toyed with, but did not light, it. "I had a sister," Mrs. Matalov said. "Not a twin, but very close in age. A terrible show-off. If she had not died, I would never have escaped her shadow." She shrugged, raising her thin eyebrows mildly. "So—I was lucky."

She rummaged again in the pocket of her cardigan, and drew out a clear plastic lighter, which she, trembling, tried to operate. Miles gestured uncertainly. Should he help her?

But before he could decide, the dark-haired girl spoke suddenly. "Grandma!" she said sharply. "Don't smoke!" And Miles sat back.

"Ah," Mrs. Matalov said. She looked at Miles darkly. "This one," she said—referring to the girl, he guessed. "Another naughty one. She doesn't approve of smoking—but drugs! Drugs she likes. She likes them so much that the police come and put an electronic monitor upon her ankle. An electric bracelet. What do you think of that? And now, poor thing, she is my prisoner. I keep her trapped here, and she should be less nosy or I will put a cloth over her cage like a parrot."

Miles was speechless. Too many things, too many odd revelations were revolving in his head, though he did exchange glances with the girl, her curtain of black hair and complicated eyes communicating a series of impenetrable messages.

Mrs. Matalov, meanwhile, had managed to strike the flint of her lighter, and she put her cigarette to her mouth, impressing a tattoo of lipstick onto the filter.

"So—" she said, appraising him. "Miles Cheshire. What brings you here to Cleveland? What is it that you do, if you are not a magician?"

Miles mulled over this question. What was he? He regarded the wall, tiled with framed black-and-white photos, various costumed performers from the thirties and forties, wearing tuxedos and capes, turbans and goatees, expressions of theatrical intensity. There was Mrs. Matalov herself—Mrs. Matalov, age perhaps twenty, not unlike her granddaughter in her dark-eyed beauty, wearing spangled circus-performer's tights and a headdress made of peacock feathers. A magician's assistant, performing at the fabulous Hippodrome Theater, capacity of thirty-five hundred, a beautiful stage, now nothing but a parking lot on East 9th.

And here was a photograph of his father as well. His father, tall and magisterial in a cape, a thin mustache of greasepaint sketched beneath his nose, a wand held aloft in his right hand, bouquets of roses and lilies at his feet. His eyes kind and sad—as if he knew that, years and years later, Miles would look at this picture and miss him once again.

"Do you know about computers?" Mrs. Matalov was saying. "We have very large Web presence. We rarely do business anymore outside of the Internet. I don't open my doors anymore, to tell you the truth. Twenty years now, and I can count on my hands the number of paying customers who have walked into my store off the street. It is nothing out there now but homeless and shoplifters and tourists with their horrible children.

"I have always hated children," Mrs. Matalov said, and her grand-daughter, Aviva, raised her eyebrow and stared at Miles.

"That's true," Aviva said.

And Miles said: "I do know about computers. Actually. I mean, I'm kind of looking for a job."

Later, he found it difficult to explain that this encounter seemed extraordinary without sounding as if he were trying to be melodramatic, without acting as if he believed that something—what?—*supernatural?*—had happened.

"It freaked me out, kind of," he told John Russell later. They were sitting once again in Parnell's, and Miles was thinking of some of the things that Mrs. Matalov had said to him.

I pitied you, Mrs. Matalov had said. And: *If she had not died, I would never have escaped her shadow.* And: *He was a very naughty one! A thief!* And: *He will come to a bad end, your brother. I can assure you of that.*

"I think it's great," John Russell said. "So you're carrying on the family tradition. That's very cool, in a way."

"Yes," Miles said. "I guess so."

And now, sitting in another bar, four thousand miles from Parnell's Pub, these were the things that skated across the surface of his consciousness. These were the images that came to him as he sat at the bar in Inuvik with the cell phone pressed to his ear: The burning house. The helicopter. The knotted sheets around Clayton Combe's neck. John Russell lifting his glass of beer, Mrs. Matalov putting her cigarette to her waxy red lips.

Each image distinct and capsulized, like tarot cards laid down one by one.

"Certainly," he said to the American woman. "Yes, absolutely. I'd like to meet with you. I'd like to speak about this matter in more detail. Could we possibly . . ."

———

He had spent a good part of the day wandering around Inuvik. It was daylight, still daylight, when he woke up, and when he went outside, the sky was dark blue, fading into white at the lip of the skyline. The clouds were stacked up against the horizon like mountains. Or maybe they were mountains that look like clouds, he wasn't sure. Some concrete slabs had been laid down into a sidewalk that ran between the road and the parking lots of the multiple boxy buildings—all of which had the cheap, hastily constructed look of a strip mall, corrugated siding, satellite dishes bending their heavy heads over the roofs. He had his sheaf of posters, and he paused to staple one to a bare telephone pole, and the paper rippled uncertainly, impermanently, in the wind.

He would blanket the city, Miles thought. He stood there leafing through the glossy *Inuvik Attraction and Service Guide,* which had been available for free at the hotel desk. Where would Hayden have been spotted? Boreal Bookstore? The famed Igloo Church, Our Lady of Victory? The extension campus of Aurora College? He had looked over their list of courses, and he felt a light spark of suspicion. Microsoft Excel: Level 1, with George Doolittle; Foot Reflexology Certification, with Allain St. Cyr; Advanced Wilderness First Aid, with Phoebe Punch. Did those sound like invented names?

Or what about the Inuvik liquor store? The bars—Mad Trapper Pub, perhaps, or Nanook Lounge? Perhaps Hayden would have rented a car at Arctic Chalet, or spent some time in the library, perhaps he'd hired a guide of some kind and headed out toward— what?

God! This was what always happened to him. He would begin in a state of urgent determination, but by the time he reached his destination, his confidence would dissipate.

What did he even know about Hayden anymore? After ten years, Hayden was hardly more than conjecture—a collection of postulations and projections, letters and emails full of paranoia and innuendo, phone calls in the middle of the night in which Hayden ranted about his current fixations. There were a few possessions Hayden had left behind in various apartments across the country, a few strangers who had seen or known some version of Hayden.

In Los Angeles, for example, Miles had found the abandoned apartment of Hayden Nash, whom neighbors described as dark-haired, "possibly Hispanic," a "reclusive guy" that apparently no one ever spoke with, and whose filthy apartment was cluttered with stacks of tabloid newspapers and indecipherable dot matrix printouts, and two dozen computers, all of the hard drives degaussed and irrecoverable. In Rolla, Missouri, professors described Miles Spady as a very bright young mathematician, a thin blond-haired Englishman who claimed to have done his undergraduate work at the Computer Laboratory of the University of Cambridge. There were some fellow students, acquaintances, to whom Hayden had told assorted lies and so forth, which Miles had recorded diligently:

His father was a well-known stage magician back in England, one of these acquaintances told Miles.

His father was an archaeologist who had been studying some Native American ruins in North Dakota, said another.

His parents had been killed in a house fire when he was a small child, said a third.

He was very eccentric, they told Miles. But it was fun to listen to him.

"He had this theory about ley lines. Geodesy, you know? We used to go out to the Stonehenge model on the north campus, and he would take out this old map of the world that he had drawn all over. . . ."

"I think he might have been crazy. He was a good mathematician, but . . ."

"He told me this peculiar story about being hypnotized, and he suddenly remembered all his past lives, a ridiculous story about pirates, or ancient kings or some sort of fantasy world. . . ."

"He said he had a nervous breakdown when he was a teenager, and his mother made him stay in the attic, and she used to tie him to the bed when he went to sleep and he'd lie awake all night thinking that there was a fire downstairs, thinking he smelled smoke. It was hard not to feel sorry for him, he was such a sweet-tempered person. You didn't know what to think when he would tell you these horrible things about his past. . . ."

"He had a twin brother who died in an ice-skating accident when they were twelve. And I gathered that he still blamed himself. I felt bad for the guy, actually. . . . There was a lot of . . . you know . . . deepness . . . under the surface. . . ."

There had also apparently been a girlfriend, an undergraduate student named Rachel, but she had refused to speak to Miles, she wouldn't even open the door when he stood on the porch of her ramshackle student house, she merely peered out at him through the door-chain crack, a single blue eye and sliver of face.

"Please," she said. "Go away. I don't want to have to call the police."

"I'm sorry," Miles said. "I'm just trying to find out some information about. Um. Miles Spady. I was told that you might be able to help me."

"I know who you are," she said. Her eye, framed and disembodied in the slice of door frame, blinked rapidly. "I *will* call the police."

He didn't have the nerve—the aggressiveness, the imposing persuasiveness—of a true detective. He had left as she'd instructed, and walked for a ways, and he could feel his determination lifting up off him, trailing away in the late October drizzle.

There actually was a scale model of Stonehenge on the campus. A half-size replica, the granite stones carved in the university's high-pressure water-jet lab. He stood there looking at it, the four pi-shaped archways facing away from one another, north, south, east, west.

Oh, what was the point, he thought, what was the point in hounding the poor girl? Why was he even doing this? He should just get on with his own life!

It wasn't until a few weeks later, long after he'd left Rolla, that it occurred to him: *Maybe Hayden had been there.*

What if Hayden was there, in Rachel Barrie's house, when Miles came that day? Was that why she wouldn't let him in? Was that why she wouldn't open the door more than a crack? He could picture Hayden, the shape of him, somewhere beyond the foyer, Hayden listening, probably no more than a few feet away from where Miles was standing on the porch.

Too late, he felt the realization settle into him. A shudder. A sickness.

"Hello?" said the voice at the end of the phone. "Hello? Are you still there?"

And Miles straightened. Back in the bar. Back in Inuvik. His memories had been pulling past him in a train of hieroglyphs, and it took him a breath or two to settle back into his physical body.

"Yes," he said. "Yes, absolutely."

He was trying to recover the detective part of himself.

"I . . . ," he said. "We . . . ," he said. "I'm very eager to speak with you. Can we set up a time to talk in person?"

"How about now?" the woman said. "Tell me where to meet you."

14

The message arrived on his computer his first night in Las Vegas, and once again Ryan couldn't help but feel a bit antsy.

This was the third or fourth time a stranger had contacted him out of the blue, writing to him in Russian or some other Eastern European language. In this case, it was someone named "новый друг" and Ryan's Instant Messenger window made its knock-knock sound.

новый друг: добро пожаповать в лас-вегасе

—and Ryan immediately closed the window and shut down the computer and sat there as a creeping feeling dappled its way up his arms and down his back. Why did he let this stuff get to him?

"Shit," he said, and folded his hands over the glass-topped hotel room desk, staring at the blank black screen of his laptop.

He had been doing so well. He had learned the ins and outs of Jay's schemes fairly quickly, had taken to it, Jay said, "like a duck to quack," and it was hardly any time at all before he was juggling nearly a hundred different personas.

"I can tell that you're my son," Jay said. "You've got the talent."

And he had been having fun, for the most part. He loved traveling—driving, flying, riding the Amtrak train—a different city every week, a new name, a new personality that he could try out, a new *role*, as if each new trip were a movie he was starring in. Floating through, that was what he thought sometimes. Floating. There was a great relief of freedom, swashbuckling, becoming a smooth con man criminal thief, the idea of adventure and rule-breaking and shifty, vaguely alluring danger.

And yet, there were times when his calm began to abandon him, brief moments—an unexplained IM, a suspicious clerk at the DMV, a credit card charge abruptly denied—and suddenly he'd feel that old panic crackling across the back of his neck, a shadow had been trailing after him all along, and suddenly he knew that if he turned to look over his shoulder, there it would be.

At times such as this, he wondered if he had the nerve for this lifestyle after all.

Maybe he was just being paranoid.

He had reported this anomaly before, these unexplained messages in Cyrillic letters, and Jay hadn't been concerned at all.

"Oh, don't be such a pussy," Jay told him.

"Doesn't it seem—suspicious?" he'd asked Jay, but Jay wasn't concerned.

"It's just spam," Jay had told him. "Just block it and change your user name, man. There's all kinds of random crap out there."

Jay explained that he had been using Internet servers in Omsk and Nizhniy Novgorod to scramble their IP addresses, and so, he said, it wasn't a surprise that they got occasional Russian junk mail. "It's probably about cheap prescription drugs, or penis enlargement, or hot teenage lesbians."

"Right," Ryan said. "Ha."

"Don't be so uptight, Son," Jay said. And Jay was basically a very cautious person, Ryan thought. If Jay wasn't worried, then why should he be?

Still, he didn't turn the computer back on.

He stood there, holding his cell phone, waiting for Jay to answer, staring from the window on the thirty-third floor of the Mandalay Bay hotel.

Here was Las Vegas spreading out before him: the pyramid of the Luxor, the castle turrets of the Excalibur, the blue glow of the MGM Grand. The Mandalay Bay itself was a big shining gold brick on the edge of the strip. From the outside, at least, the windows were shimmering golden reflective glass, so that no one could see him standing there, peering out. It was a cityscape that looked as if it had been invented, architectural shapes that might appear as the cover illustration for one of those fantasy novels he used to read back in high school, or digital imagery from a big budget SF movie. It would be easy to believe he'd landed on a different planet, or traveled into the future, and he put a hand to the glass, letting these pleasant, calming whimsies settle over him.

The outward wall of his hotel room was a single window, and with the drapes pulled open he could stand there at the very lip of the building like a swimmer on a diving board.

"Hello?" Jay said, and Ryan paused.

"Hey," Ryan said.

"Hey," Jay said. And then there was an expectant pause. Ryan wasn't supposed to call unless it was urgent, but it seemed like Jay was too mellow—probably too stoned—to take Ryan's concerns seriously. Sometimes it was strange to think that Jay was actually his father, strange to think that Jay was only fifteen when he was born, and even now he didn't look like he could be old enough to have a twenty-year-old son. He didn't look much older than thirty. It made more sense, Ryan often thought, to think of him as an uncle.

"So . . . ," Jay said. "What's up?"

"I was just calling to check in," Ryan said. He shifted the phone to his other ear. "Listen," he said, "did you just IM me?"

"Um," Jay said. "I don't think so."

"Oh," Ryan said.

He could hear the gurgling sound of a bong as Jay drew in smoke, and then the arrhythmic clicking percussion of Jay's keyboard as he typed.

"So what do you think of Las Vegas?" Jay said after a pause.

"Good," Ryan said. "Good, so far."

"It's pretty magnificent, isn't it?" said Jay.

"It is," Ryan said, and he looked down into the dusky expanse of the city. Below him a line of taxis was slowly nudging its bovine way up toward the front entrance, the pylon sign that flanked the building with its giant LED screen playing images of singers and comedians flickering above the necklace of headlights along Las Vegas Boulevard—

"It's—" he said.

—and in the other direction, if you faced away from the strip, there was the airport just beyond an old boarded-up courtyard motel across the street; there was a tract of bare desert earth and some strip malls and houses that ran in sheer planes toward the mountains.

"It's great," he said.

"Can you see the Statue of Liberty?" Jay said. "Can you see the Stratosphere tower?"

"Yeah," Ryan said. He was aware of his reflection standing just beyond the edge of the window, hovering in the air.

"I love Vegas," Jay said, and then he paused, reflectively. Perhaps he was thinking of the instructions he and Ryan had gone over together, perhaps wondering if he needed to repeat them—but he just cleared his throat.

"The main thing," Jay said. "I want you to have a good time. Get laid a couple of times, okay?"

"Okay," Ryan said.

Behind him, on the bed, he had laid out his stacks of plastic ATM cards, rubber-banded together in groups of ten.

"I mean it," Jay said. "You could use some—"

"Yeah," he said. "I hear you."

It was April. Months had passed since Ryan's death, and he was doing okay with that. He had basically worked through his Kübler-Ross stages, he guessed. There actually hadn't been much denial or bargaining involved, and the anger he experienced felt kind of good. There was a pleasure in stealing, a warm flush as he moved money from one fake bank account to another, as another credit card arrived in the mail.

In the bathroom, he applied adhesive to his bare scalp and arranged his shaggy blond Kasimir Czernewski wig. He shaved and dried his upper lip and then brushed on some spirit gum so that he could attach his mustache. He had to admit that it was fun to put on a disguise, that instant in the mirror when a new face looked back at him.

He had been traveling away from himself for a long time now, he thought—for years and years, maybe, he had been trying to imagine ways to escape—and now he was actually doing it. It even felt glamorous, in a bathroom such as this: the wall-length mirror and beautiful porcelain sinks, the sunken Jacuzzi tub, the standing shower with its frosted glass door, the commode separate in its own little room, with a telephone on the wall next to the toilet paper dispenser. It was all very sophisticated, he thought, and he adjusted his black Kasimir Czernewski glasses and brushed his teeth.

Get laid a couple of times, Jay had said.

And he thought: *Okay. Maybe I will.*

———

The last time Ryan had sex, he was a junior in high school, and it had turned out to be very problematic.

The girl's name was Pixie—that was what she went by—and she had moved from Chicago to Council Bluffs with her father, and even though she was fifteen, two years younger than he, she was a real city girl—a lot more worldly than Ryan.

She had a lip piercing and an eyebrow piercing and dyed white-blond hair with some strands of pink, and her eyes were traced with black liner. She was just barely five feet tall—thus "Pixie" instead of her real name, Penelope—and she had a body like a cherub or a curvaceous teddy bear, smooth perfect olive skin and large breasts and a full mouth, and even before the end of the first week of school people were referring to her as Goth Hobbit, and Ryan had laughed with everyone else.

So he'd never exactly known what she'd seen in him, except that she sat behind him in period six band. He was a trombonist and she was a drummer, and if he turned his head, he could watch her out of the corner of his eye, and the first thing he noticed about her was this expression, a focused and blissful attention to her page of music, the way her lips parted, the way the sticks moved in her hands as if she weren't even thinking of them, the graceful loose-ness of her wrists and forearms. And, yes, the slight vibration of her breasts when she gave the drumhead a decisive stroke.

And so he couldn't keep from glancing at her from time to time surreptitiously until one day as he was breaking down his trombone after class and lubricating the hand slide, and she stood there star-ing at him with her head cocked to one side. He had arranged the pieces in the velvet indentations of his instrument case, and at last he looked up at her.

"Can I help you?" he said, and she raised one eyebrow—the one with the thin metal ring in it.

"I doubt it," she said. "I was just trying to figure out if there was some reason you keep staring at me, or if you're just autistic or whatever."

He was not that popular; he was used to being made fun of by various people, and so he tightened his lips and inserted his cleaning brush into the mouth of his slide. "I don't know what you're talking about," he said.

And she shrugged. "Okay, then, Archie," she said.

Archie. He didn't know what that was supposed to mean, but he didn't like it. "My name is Ryan," he said.

"Okay, Thurston," she said, and appraised him once more, dubiously. "Can I ask you a question?" she said, and when he continued to pack up his instrument, she smiled, puckering her lips out in a wry, challenging way. "Does your mom buy your clothes for you, or do you honestly intend to dress like that?"

Ryan looked up from his trombone case, fixing her with a look that he thought of as particularly icy. "May I help you?" he said.

And Pixie evaluated this, as if it were a real offer. "Maybe," she said. "I just wanted to tell you that if you did something with yourself, you could probably actually be fuckable." And then she gave him that smile again, lopsided, a gangster smirk.

"I just thought you'd want to know," she said.

He thought about this as he rode down the elevator, and then he pushed it into the back of his mind again, back to the nearly subconscious place where Pixie had been lingering for the past few years.

In the elevator, a miniature LED screen was blaring scenes of some Broadway-style musical entertainment, and the girl standing in front of him shifted her weight from foot to foot as she watched the video. She had a very short skirt and incredibly long bare legs—they seemed to go all the way up to her rib cage, beautiful downy brown legs—and Ryan observed them silently. The skirt ended just slightly below the slope of her buttocks, and he let his eyes run down the back of her thighs to her calves and ankles and sandaled pink-soled feet. He watched as she got off the elevator, and the man beside him made a low sound in his throat.

"Mm, mm," the man said. "Did you see that?" He was a black man, perhaps fifty years old, wearing a pink polo shirt and kelly green pants and carrying a bag of golf clubs. "That was a sight to see."

"Yes," Ryan said, and the man shook his head in exaggerated wonder.

"*Damn,*" the man said. "Are you single?"

"Yeah," Ryan said, "I guess I am." And the man shook his head again.

"I sure do envy you," the man said—and then, before he could say more, the elevator doors opened and three more beautiful teenage girls entered their enclosure.

What if he *did* meet a girl, he thought. That was what people did in Vegas, that was what a lot of people came here for. All over town, he supposed, they were hooking up, seducing their way into one-night stands or stumbling drunkenly into liaisons with strangers. He himself had never picked up someone at a bar, or a casino, though obviously it was possible. You saw it on TV all the time: a man approached an attractive woman; there was some flirtation or suggestive small talk; and shortly thereafter, the couple was having sex. It should be fairly simple to accomplish. If he could get a 2200 on the SAT, he should be able to get laid in Vegas.

But standing there on the main floor of the casino, the very idea of "meeting someone" seemed heartbreakingly complex. How would you even talk to another person in such a place? He peered out at what appeared to be an enormous video arcade, rows upon rows of glowing neon games and slot machines, stretching as far as he could see, hundreds and hundreds of people feeding their individual screens, which showed playing cards or rolling numbers or animated cartoon characters, and he found himself thinking of the photographs he'd seen of sweatshops—cavernous factory lofts, columns of workers sewing seams into blouses or riveting eyelets into shoes, a hive in which each worker was submerged in a constant, lonely activity. Meanwhile, all around him people wandered the aisles and walkways, with that peculiar blankness tourists had as they moved through the paces of being entertained, an aimless shuffle that people took on in shopping malls and national monuments and so forth.

At last, Ryan fell into the flow of foot traffic around the circumference of the main gaming area. In front of him, a pair of blond women in matching capri pants spoke to each other in Dutch or Norwegian or some other language. Up ahead, a mild bottleneck was forming as people paused to watch an elderly man in a cowboy hat and flowered Western shirt performing a card trick. The man held up the ten of spades to show the crowd, and there was a spatter of applause. The magician gave a small, gracious bow, and the blond women stopped and craned to see what was going on.

But Ryan moved past, feeling again in his pockets for his stack of ATM cards, which was almost as thick as a deck of playing cards.

There was a lot of cash that needed to be withdrawn before the night was over.

It was annoying to find himself thinking of Pixie again.

In the past few years, he had been pretty successful at keeping her out of his conscious thoughts, and it was disturbing to find her lingering there now. There was a certain way she would press her nose and lips to his neck, just under the line of his jaw; a way she would slide her hand down on his arm, as if she were trying to make his skin adhere to her palm.

It was not as if he had been in love with her. That was what his mother said later.

"It's just ordinary lust, but at your age you can't tell the difference."

And probably his mother was right. Pixie was not what he had thought of when he'd imagined "falling in love"—and in fact, he couldn't remember if the word "love" had ever been mentioned. It wasn't the type of thing Pixie would have said.

"Fucking"—that was more in line with Pixie's vocabulary, and that was what they were doing within a few weeks of that first conversation in the band room, fucking first in a motel on a band trip to Des Moines, and then fucking after school at Pixie's house while her dad was at work, and then fucking in the school building, in a storage closet in the basement near the boiler room, fucking on top of boxes of industrial paper towels.

"You know what's funny?" Pixie said. "My dad totally thinks I'm this innocent virgin. He's like a zombie since my mom died, poor guy. I don't think he realizes that I'm not twelve anymore."

"Geez," Ryan said. "Your mom died?" He had never known anyone who had experienced that kind of tragedy, and it made him feel even more awkward to be naked in her room, with her girly pink bedspread and her collection of Beanie Babies staring down at them from their shelf.

"She had some deal with her lungs," Pixie said, and she uncovered a pack of Marlboros from a hiding space behind a Harry Potter novel on her bookcase. "Bronchiolitis obliterans, it's called. They don't know how she got it. They thought she could have been exposed to toxic fumes of some sort, or it could have been brought on by a virus. But no one knew what she had. The doctors thought she had asthma or whatever." She looked at him, cryptically, and he watched as she withdrew a cigarette and lit it. She put her face near the open window and exhaled.

"That's awful," Ryan said. Uncertain. What was he supposed to say? "I'm really sorry," he said.

But she only shrugged. "I used to think about killing myself," she said. And she blew a stream of gray-blue smoke through the screen, into the backyard. She peered at him, matter-of-factly. "But then I decided that it wasn't worth it. It's too angsty and whiny, I think. Or maybe . . . ," she said. "Maybe I'm just too beyond caring to bother." She leaned back, kneading the crumple of sheet and blanket with her bare foot, and he watched her toes as they clenched and unclenched. He was a little stunned by such talk.

"Listen," he said. "You shouldn't think about killing yourself. There are a lot of people who—care about you, and . . ."

"Shut up," she said, but not unkindly. "Don't be a nerd, Ryan."

And so he didn't say anything more.

Instead of going back to school after lunch that day, they stayed at her house and watched movies that Pixie was obsessed with. Fourth period: here was *The Killers,* with Lee Marvin and Angie Dickinson. Fifth period: *Something Wild,* with Jeff Daniels and Melanie Griffith. Sixth period: fucking again.

I am actually doing this, he thought. *I am really, really, really doing this—*

The hotels were interconnected. He passed through one casino cavern and boarded an escalator and a series of moving walkways that rivered past mall-like hallways lined with souvenir shops, and then he found himself in a replica of an Egyptian tomb, and then inside another warehouse-size casino floor, and there were a few more ATM machines to attend to, and then there was the Excalibur, which was themed to look like a medieval castle, and people were lined up to dine at the Round Table buffet, and he made a couple more withdrawals.

And then, at last, after winding his way through the corridors of the Luxor and the Excalibur, he emerged into the outdoors, into the open air, and he had about ten grand in his backpack. That was the thing about Vegas—you could withdraw five hundred dollars, one thousand, three thousand from an ATM and it was not that unusual, though he knew that he would have to retire Kasimir Czernewski after this trip. Which was sad, in a way. He had spent a lot of time building up Kasimir's life in his mind, trying to conceptualize what it would be like to be a foreigner, a young man starting with nothing and working his way toward the American dream. Kasimir: essentially easygoing, but also crafty in some ways, determined, taking night school classes and struggling to establish his little private investigator business. You could make a television series about Kasimir Czernewski, a kind of comedy-drama, he imagined.

Outside, people were moving down the sidewalk in groups of five or ten or twenty, and the flow had grown more purposeful, more like the movement of big-city people down a street. On one side, car traffic was dragging slowly past, and on the other, hawkers stood and handed out cards to passersby. They were primarily Mexican men, and they would draw attention by slapping their handouts against their forearms—*clap, clap, clap*—and then flicking out a single card and extending it.

"Thank you," Ryan said, and he had gathered about twenty of them before he began to say, "I'm set." "No thanks." "Sorry."

The cards were advertisements for various escort services, pictures of girls, naked, airbrushed, with colorful stars printed over their nipples. Sometimes the letters of their names covered their privates. Fantasie, Roxan, Natasha. *Beautiful Exotic Dancer in the privacy of your own room!* the card said. *Only $39!* And there was the phone number to call.

He was lingering on the street, looking at his collection of escort girls—imagining what it might be like to actually call one of them—when he heard the Russian men approaching.

At least he thought they were Russian. Or they were speaking in some other Eastern European language. Lithuanian? Serbian? Czech? But in any case, they were talking loudly in their native tongue—*Zatruxa* something something. *Baruxa! Ha, ha, ha*—and Ryan looked up, startled, as they approached. There was a bald one, and one with his blond hair moussed into stiff hedgehog-like spikes, and another with a checkered cabbie golf cap. All of them wearing colorful Hawaiian shirts.

They were all three carrying those enormous souvenir drink

glasses that were so popular on the strip, containers that looked like vases, or bongs—round, bulbous bases with long, piped necks that eventually opened into a tuliped rim. He assumed that these glasses had been engineered so that they were hard to spill, and yet held the maximum amount of alcoholic beverage allowed.

They came toward him, noisily joking in whatever Slavic language they were speaking, and he couldn't help it. He froze there, staring at them.

Back when he was a freshman at Northwestern, his roommate, Walcott, used to scold him.

"Why do you always stare at people?" Walcott said, one night, when they were walking down Rush Street in Chicago, looking for bars that might take their cheap fake IDs. "Is that, like, an Iowa thing?" Walcott said critically. "Because you know, in cities, it's not cool to gape at people."

Walcott was actually from Cape Cod, Massachusetts, which wasn't a city, but he had spent a lot of time in Boston and New York, and so believed himself an expert on such things. He also had a lot of opinions about what people from Iowa were like, though he had never been there, either.

"Look," Walcott said, "let me give you some advice. Don't look at people directly in the face. Never—let me reiterate—Never, *never, NEVER* make eye contact with a homeless person, or a drunk, or anyone who looks like they are a tourist. It's a super-easy rule to remember: do not look at them."

"Hmm," Ryan said, and Walcott patted him on the back.

"What would you do without me?" Walcott said.

"I don't know," Ryan said. He looked down at his feet, which were weaving along the dirty sidewalk as if by remote control.

He never would have chosen Walcott as a friend, but they had been thrown together by fate, by the administrative offices, and they'd spent an enormous amount of time together that first year, so Walcott's voice was still ingrained in his head.

But now it was too late. He stood, making eye contact, staring, and the bald Russian had noticed him. The bald man's eyes lit up, as if Ryan were holding up a sign with his name on it.

"Hey there, my main man," the bald Russian said, in a thick but surprisingly slangy English—as if he'd learned the language by listening to rap music. "Hey, how you doing?"

And this was the thing Walcott had warned him about. This was the problem with being from Iowa, because he had been trained, for years and years, to be polite and friendly, and he couldn't help himself.

"Hello," Ryan said, as the three men came toward him, grinning as they clustered around him. A bit *too* close, and he stiffened uncomfortably, though he found himself putting on his pleasant, welcoming Midwestern expression.

The man with the spiked hair let out a burst of unrecognizable Russian syllables, and the men all laughed.

"We . . . ," said the spike-haired man, and struggled a moment, trying to think of words. "We—tree—alkonauts! We—" he said. "We come with peace!"

They all found this uproarious, and Ryan smiled uncertainly. He shifted his shoulder, the backpack with his heavy laptop and about ten thousand dollars in cash tucked into one of the pockets. Stay calm. He was at the edge of the curb, and tourists and partygoers and other walkers were moving around them with glazed, bedazzled expressions. Not making eye contact.

He was trying to decide how nervous he should be. They were out in the open, he thought. They couldn't do anything to him right here in the middle of the street—

Though, he remembered a movie he'd seen where an assassin

had expertly severed the saphenous vein in his victim's thigh, and the victim had bled to death right there on a busy street.

The men had formed a circle around him, and he could feel the flow of traffic on Las Vegas Boulevard at his back. He took a step, but the men just gathered closer, as if following his lead.

"You like the cards?" said the bald one. "You like the cards, my main man?"

And Ryan was certain he'd been caught. His hand went automatically to his pocket, where he had his stack of ATM cards. He rested his palm against his thigh, thinking again of the saphenous vein.

"Cards?" Ryan said weakly, and he tried to glance over his shoulder. If he dashed into the four lanes of Las Vegas Boulevard, what were the chances that he would be hit by a car? Fairly high, he guessed. He shook his head at the bald man, as if he didn't understand. "I . . . I don't have any cards," he said. "I don't know what you mean."

"You don't understand?" the man said, and he laughed with good-natured surprise, a bit taken aback. "Cards!" he pronounced, slowly, and he gestured at Ryan's hand. "Cards!"

"Cards!" the spike-haired man repeated, and he grinned, showing his gold-tipped front teeth. He held up a dozen or so of the cards from the escort services, fanned out like a hand of poker, a full house of Fantasie and Britt and Kamchana and Cheyenne and Natasha and Ebony.

And then Ryan realized what they were talking about. He glanced down at the stack of pictures he himself had collected as he walked down the strip. "Oh," he said. "Yeah, anyway, I . . ."

"Yes, yes!" said the bald one, and the men all burst into laughter again. "Cards! Beautiful girls, my main man!"

"Thirty-nine United State dollars! Incredible!" said the man in the golf cap, who had so far been only observing. And then he let out an extended comment in Russian, which was met with more hilarity. The man held out one of his own cards for Ryan to take, offering it.

"You like Natasha. Big titty Russian girl. Very nice."

"Yes," Ryan said, and nodded. "Yes, very nice," he said, and he gazed down the block—Bally's, Flamingo, Imperial Palace, Harrah's, Casino Royale, the Venetian, the Palazzo—all the places he had been planning to visit, all the ATMs he still had to withdraw from before he came at last to the Riviera, where he would check in to the hotel under the name Tom Knott, a young accountant who was attending a convention.

"My name is Shurik," said the bald Russian, and held out his hand to be shook.

"Vasya," said the one with the spiked hair.

"Pavel," said the one in the cap.

"Ryan," Ryan said, and he felt his face growing hot almost immediately as he pressed palms with the three men, one after the other. It was the most basic mistake—his own real name, given thoughtlessly, and he felt more flustered than ever. *Mr. J so good to find,* he thought. Was it significant? Or not?

"Ryan, my main man," said Shurik. "We come with us, yes? Together. Come. We find the best girls. Right?"

"Right," Ryan said. And then, as the three of them parted for him, as they prepared to fall in behind him, following with their giant tulip cups and their cards and their hopeful, friendly expressions, he made an abrupt feint, a zigzag, pushing himself into the flow of tourists on the sidewalk.

And then he took off running.

It was a stupid thing to do, he told himself later.

He stood in the queue at the check-in desk of the Riviera Hotel, his heart still quickened in his chest.

The poor guys. How startled they'd been when he broke off and dashed away. They hadn't made any attempt to pursue. Thinking of their stunned expressions as they watched him flee, he couldn't believe they'd ever been anything more than innocent foreign tourists. A bunch of drunken guys, looking for a native to befriend.

Jay was right: he needed to calm down.

Still, it was hard to shake the adrenaline once it set, that tight, jittery tension, and he sat in his room in the Riviera—Tom Knott, age twenty-two, of Topeka, Kansas—looking again at the escort girls. *Natasha. Ebony.*

This was the thing he hated most about himself, about his old self—that nervousness, worry knitting inside of him. By the time he got to his sophomore year at Northwestern, he spent so much time fretting about all the work he wasn't doing that he didn't have time to actually work.

He guessed that was why he found himself thinking about Pixie again. Despite what had happened, despite the aftermath, the six weeks he had spent with Pixie had probably been the best time of his life. They were skipping classes fairly regularly, and he had been getting home in time to destroy the letters the school was sending about his absences and tardies, and erase the messages on the answering machine from the attendance secretary, and his parents had continued obliviously without noticing anything out of the ordinary. He was, he realized, a pretty good actor. A pretty decent liar. He had not done any homework of significance for a while by that point, and for the first time in his life he had taken a test and he had absolutely no idea what they were asking him. It was his chemistry midterm, and he circled multiple choice questions at random and invented calculations that he had no idea how to perform, and he had a wonderful thought.

I don't care about anything.

It was like the fundamentalist kids when they talked about being born again. "Jesus came into my heart and emptied me of my sin," a girl named Lynette had told him once, and in some ways that was what had happened to him. All his burdens were lifted, and he felt light and transparent, as if the sunlight could shine right through his body.

I don't care about anything, he thought, *I don't care about the future, I don't care what happens to me, I don't care what my family thinks, I don't care, I don't care.* And each time he said it in his mind, it was as if a weight detached and flickered away like a butterfly.

And then one day he came home and his mother was in the kitchen, waiting.

As it turned out, it was not the attendance secretary or one of his teachers who had contacted Stacey; it was Pixie's father. He had apparently intercepted some of the emails they had exchanged, and had found Pixie's journal, and then—this was the aspect that Ryan hadn't expected or understood—Pixie had confessed everything to her father.

Who was enraged. Who wanted to kill Ryan.

"Do you have a daughter, Mrs. Schuyler?" Pixie's father had asked, and Ryan's mother was sitting there at work, at her desk, in the office of Morgan Stanley in Omaha, where she was a CPA, and Mr. Pixie said, "If you had a daughter, you would know how I feel.

"I feel violated. I feel defiled by your pervert son," he told Stacey. "And I want you to know," he said, "I want you to know that if it turns out my daughter is pregnant, I am going to come to your house and I am going to take your son and knock his teeth through the back of his fucking skull."

By the time Ryan came home, Stacey had already called the police, who had charged Pixie's father with aggravated menacing, and she was talking to a lawyer friend who was getting a restraining order, but she didn't tell him this when he came into the kitchen and opened the refrigerator and peered into it. He didn't pay much attention to her. She was often in a bad mood, as far as he could tell. She would situate herself in the kitchen or the TV room or some other area where they could see her being silent, and then she would emanate dense radioactive waves of negativity. He knew better than to look at her when she was in this mode.

And so he got out some milk as she sat there at the kitchen table. He shook some cereal into a bowl and poured milk over it, and he was about to take his snack into the TV room when Stacey looked up at him.

"Who are you?" she said.

Ryan lifted his head, reluctantly. This was also her method, these soft-spoken inscrutable questions. "Um," he said. "Excuse me?"

"I said: who are you?" she murmured in a sadly musing voice. "Because I don't think I know you, Ryan."

He had his first glimmer of nervousness then. He knew that she had found out—what? How much? He felt the expression on his face tightening and growing blanker. "I don't know what you're talking about," he said.

"I thought you were a trustworthy person," Stacey said. "I thought you were responsible, mature, you had a plan for yourself. That's what I used to think. Now I can't fathom what's going on inside of you. I have no idea."

He was still holding his bowl of cereal, which was making almost inaudible whispering noises as the puffed kernels soaked up the milk.

He couldn't think of anything to say.

He didn't want his adventure with Pixie to be over, and he imagined if he just said nothing, it would last for a while longer. He could still be happy, he could still not care about anything, he could still meet up with Pixie in the morning on the north side of school and watch her smoking a cigarette and toying with her lip ring, threading it back and forth through the flesh of her mouth.

"Do you want to ruin your life?" Stacey was saying to him. "Do you want to end up like your uncle Jay? Because that is the way you are headed. He screwed up his life when he was just about your age, and he has never recovered. Never. He turned himself into a loser, and that's where you're headed, Ryan."

———

It wasn't until years later that he understood what she was talking about.

You are going to end up like your father, that was what she actually meant. His father: Jay, getting a girl pregnant at age fifteen, running away from home, floating from shady job to shady job, never to settle down, never to have a normal life. In retrospect, he could see why she had come down so hard on him, he could even sympathize somewhat. She knew what kind of person he would become, even before he did.

And she was not going to let him end up like Jay. For two weeks, Ryan had been sent to a wilderness camp for rebellious teens, while his mother put the pieces of his life back in order. One of those hiking and team-building and group therapy isolation camps, full of military-esque counselors doling out "tough love" and diagnosing their psychological sicknesses. They had lost their way; they were suffering from unhealthy misperceptions about themselves; they needed to change if they ever wanted to become productive members of society, if they ever wanted to see their friends and family again. . . .

Even when he returned, he was under what basically amounted to house arrest for the rest of the school year. She had taken away his cell phone and Internet privileges, and then she had contacted all his teachers to make arrangements for him to make up all the work that he had missed, and she had him seeing a therapist once a week, and she enrolled him in an SAT prep course, and in a community service program called the Optimist Club, which met three days a week to clean up parks and give toys to poor children and conduct recycling drives and so forth. She switched him out of band, which was the only class he had shared with Pixie, though it actually didn't matter because Pixie herself had been transferred by her father over to St. Albert High. He never saw her again. Her father was found guilty of aggravated menacing and sentenced to probation.

As for Ryan's father, Owen, he was mostly uninvolved during this period, taciturn and glum as he always was in the face of Stacey's stubborn organization. Owen did manage to talk her into letting Ryan take guitar lessons, and that was one nice thing about his last year and a half of high school. He and Pixie had talked about forming a band, in which she would be the drummer and he would be the lead singer, and he used to like to fantasize about that. He liked to sit in his room and make up songs on the Takamine that Owen had bought for him. Ryan wrote a song called "Oh, Pixie." Very sad. He wrote another called "Aggravated Menace," and one called "Soon I'll Be Gone," and "Echopraxia," which, if he ever made an album, might end up being the single.

It was pathetic, he thought, to be thinking about those lame old songs.

It was depressing because he had spent the whole night thinking about Pixie, remembering her, wondering where she was now. What had happened to her? And he was nowhere close to getting laid.

It was even sad that his paranoia about the Russians had turned out to be nothing, after all. Despite his encounter on the street, there hadn't actually been any intrigue, there hadn't been any adventure with gangsters, nothing but the herds of tourists and the workers who went about the job of fleecing them with the grim nonchalance of a clerk at a late-night convenience store.

Maybe he would always be lonely, he thought, and he spread out the escort service cards on the desk and looked at them. Fantasie. Roxan. Natasha.

He sat there at his hotel room desk, contemplating. He typed in his name and room number, and there was a breath as the cyberspace made its connection.

He opened up the Instant Message window, and

No, there wasn't any new greeting in Cyrillic.

And so he just typed a note to Jay. "Mission accomplished," he wrote, and then, he decided, he might as well go to bed.

They could be leaving soon. That was one thing. On their way to New York, and then to international destinations.

And they could be rich, too, if everything went according to plan. *If* she was the type of person who would do this sort of thing.

The documents were spread out between them on the kitchen table, and George Orson adjusted and aligned papers in front of him, as if parallel lines could make their conversation easier. She saw him glance up, surreptitiously, and it almost embarrassed her to see his eyes so earnest and guilty—though it was also a relief to have him wordless. Not trying to assure her or convince her or teach her, but just waiting for her decision. It was the first time in a while that a choice of hers had mattered, the first time in months she didn't feel as if she were walking in some dreamscape, amnesia-scape, everything glowing with an aura of déjà vu—

But now it had solidified. His schemes. His evasions. The money.

She lifted a single sheet off of the sheaf that he'd laid in front of her. Here was a copy of the wire transfer. *BICICI,* it said at the top.

Banque Internationale pour le Commerce et l'Industrie de Côte d'Ivoire. And there was a date and a code and stamp and several signatures and a total. *US$4,300,000.00.* Here was the letter confirming the deposit. "Dear Mr. Kozelek, your fund was deposited here in our bank by your partner Mr. Oliver Akubueze. Your partner further instructed us to execute transfer of the fund to your bank account by completing the bank's transfer application form, and he also endorsed other vital documents to that effect. . . ."

"Mr. Kozelek," Lucy said. "That's you."

"Yes," George Orson said. "A pseudonym."

"I see," Lucy said. She looked at him, briefly, then down at the paper: *US$4,300,000.00.*

"I see," she breathed. She was trying to make her voice cool and disinterested and official. She thought of the social worker she and Patricia had to visit after their parents had died, the two of them watching as the woman paged through the papers on her cluttered desk. *I wonder what experience the two of you have with taking care of yourselves?* the social worker said.

Lucy held the paper between her thumbs and forefingers in the way the social worker had. She glanced up to look at George Orson, who was sitting patiently across the table, holding his cup of coffee loosely, as if warming his fingers, even though it must have been eighty degrees outside already.

"Who is Oliver Aku—?" she said, stumbling over the pronunciation, in the way she'd once clumped ungracefully through French sentences in Mme Fournier's class. "Akubueze," she tried again, and George Orson smiled wanly.

"He's nobody," George Orson said, and then after a brief hesitation, he tilted his head regretfully. He had promised to answer any question she asked. "He's—just a middleman. A contact. I had to pay him off, of course. But that wasn't a problem."

Their gazes met, and she remembered what George Orson had once told her about how he used to take classes in hypnosis: those bright green eyes were perfect for it, she thought. He peered at her, and his eyes said: *You must relax.* His eyes said: *Can you trust me?* His eyes said: *Aren't we still in love?*

Perhaps. Perhaps he did love her.

Perhaps he was only trying to take care of her, as he said.

But it was frustrating, because even with all these documents in front of her, he was still vague with the truth. He was a thief, that much he had admitted, but she still didn't understand where the money had come from, or how he had managed to acquire it, or who, exactly, was looking for him.

"I didn't steal from a *person,* Lucy—that's what you have to understand. I didn't take money from a sweet old rich lady, or a gangster, or a small-town credit union in Pompey, Ohio. I've taken money—embezzled, let's say—from an *entity.* A very large, global entity. Which makes things a bit more complicated. I mean," he said, "I remember that you used to be interested in someday working for an international investment firm. Like Goldman Sachs. Right?

"And if, for example, you were able to figure out a way to skim money from the treasury of Goldman Sachs, you would soon come to understand that they would do everything in their power to find you and bring you to justice. They would utilize law enforcement, certainly, but they would probably also resort to other means. Private detectives. Bounty hunters. Would they employ assassins? Torturers? Probably not. But you understand what I'm saying."

"No, I don't, actually," Lucy said. "Are you saying you stole money from Goldman Sachs?"

"No, no," George Orson said. "That was just an example. I was just trying to . . ." And then he sighed, resignedly. A sound unlike George Orson, she thought, almost the opposite of the conspiratorial chuckle she'd first found so attractive and charming. "Look," he said. "I wish things hadn't come to this. I kept thinking I could just sort this out on my own and you wouldn't even have to know about—any of this. I thought I could work everything out so you wouldn't have to be involved."

And he was quiet then, brooding, tapping the edge of his fingernail against his coffee cup. *Tink, tink, tink.* Both of them self-conscious and anxious. It was depressing, Lucy thought—and perhaps it actually had been better when she didn't know anything, back when she was trusting him to take care of things, trusting that they were on their way somewhere wonderful, a shy but witty young woman and her urbane, mysterious older lover, maybe on a cruise ship on their way to Monaco or Playa del Carmen.

She reflected, letting this old fantasy brush briefly over her. Then, at last, she lowered her head to peruse the other documents George Orson had presented to her.

Here was the travel itinerary. From Denver to New York. From New York to Felix Houphouet Boigny airport in Abidjan, Ivory Coast.

Here were the social security cards and birth certificates they would use: David Fremden, age thirty-five, and his daughter, Brooke Fremden, age fifteen.

"I can get the passports expedited; that won't be a big problem," George Orson was telling her. "We can have a rush passport in two to five days. But we would need to act right away. We'd have to go to a courthouse or a post office to put in the application tomorrow—"

But he stopped talking when she looked up at him. She was not going to be rushed. She was going to think about this scrupulously, and he needed to understand that.

"Who are they?" she said. "David and Brooke?"

George Orson gave her another reproachful frown. Still, even now, recalcitrant with his information. But he had promised to answer.

"They aren't anybody in particular," he said wearily. "They're just people." And he passed the palm of his hand across his hair. "They *died,*" he said. "A father and daughter, killed in an apartment fire in Chicago about a week ago. Which is why these documents are quite useful to us, *right now*. There's a window of time, before the deaths have been officially processed through the system."

"I see," she said again. It was about all she was able to think of to say, and she shut her eyes briefly. She didn't want to picture them—David and Brooke, in their burning apartment building, gasping in the smoke and heat—and so instead she stared hard down at the birth certificate as if it were a list of test questions she was studying.

Certificate of Live Birth	*112-89-0053*
Brooke Catherine Fremden	*March 15, 1993*
4:22 A. *Female*	*Swedish Covenant Hospital*
Chicago	*Cook County*

Here was the maiden name of the mother: Robin Meredith Crowley, born in the state of Wisconsin, age thirty-one at the time of Brooke's birth.

"So," Lucy said after she had perused this document mutely for a while. "What about the mom? Robin. Won't they ask about her?"

"She actually died some time ago," George Orson said, and made a small, shrugging gesture. "When Brooke was ten, I think. Killed in a, hmmm." And then he grew reticent, as if to spare Lucy's feelings—or Brooke's. "In any case," he said. "The mother's death certificate is there somewhere, too, if you want to . . ."

But Lucy just shook her head.

A car accident. She supposed that was what it was, but maybe she didn't want to know.

"This girl is only fifteen," Lucy said. "I don't look like a fifteen-year-old."

"True," George Orson said. "I hope that I don't look like I'm thirty-five, either, but we can work on that. Believe me, in my experience, people are not good at judging age."

"Hmm," Lucy said, still staring down at the document. Still

thinking about the mom. Robin. About David and Brooke. Had they tried to escape the fire, had they died in their sleep?

The poor Fremdens. The whole family, gone from the face of the earth.

Outside, in the backyard, the late morning sun was burning brightly over the Japanese garden. The weeds were tall and thick, and there was no sign of the little bridge or the Kotoji lantern statue. The top of the weeping cherry rose up out of the weeds as if gasping for breath, the drooping branches like long wet hair.

There were so many, many things that were troubling about this situation, but she found that the one that actually bothered her the most was the idea of pretending to be George Orson's daughter.

Why couldn't they just be traveling companions? Boyfriend and girlfriend? Husband and wife? Even uncle and niece?

"I know, I know," George Orson said.

It was uncomfortable because he was such a subdued George Orson, a diminished version of the George Orson she knew. He shifted in his chair as she turned from staring out at the backyard. "It's regrettable," he said. "To be honest, I'm not particularly happy about it, either. It's more than a little creepy for me, as well. Not to mention that I've never had to think of myself as someone who's old enough to have a teenage child!" He tried out a small laugh, as if she might find this amusing, but she didn't. She wasn't sure exactly how she was feeling, but she wasn't in the mood to appreciate his clever remarks. He reached out to touch her leg, and then thought better of it, drew his hand back, and she watched his proffered smile shrink into a wince.

This wasn't what she wanted, either: the tense discomfort that had developed between them ever since he had begun to tell her the truth. She had loved the way that they used to joke together. *Repartee*, George Orson called it, and it would be terrible if that was gone, if somehow things had changed so much between them, if their old relationship was now lost, irretrievable. She had loved being Lucy and George Orson—"Lucy" and "George Orson"—and maybe it was just an act that they were doing for each other, but it had felt easy and natural and fun. It was her real self she had discovered when she met him.

"Believe me, Lucy," he was saying now, very solemn and not like George Orson at all. "Believe me," he said. "This wasn't my first choice. But I didn't have much recourse. In our current situation, it wasn't particularly easy to acquire the documents we needed. I didn't have a whole variety of choices."

"Okay," Lucy said. "I get it."

"It's just pretending," George Orson said. "A game we're playing."

"I get it," Lucy said again. "I understand what you're saying."

Though that didn't necessarily make it any easier.

George Orson had "some things to take care of" in the afternoon.

Which was almost reassuring, at some level. Ever since they had come here, he had been disappearing for hours at a time—vanishing into the study and locking the door, or driving off without a word in the old pickup, off to town—and today was no different. After their talk, he'd been in a hurry to get back to his computer and she'd stood there in the entrance of his study looking at the big desk and the old painting with the safe behind it, like a prop in a bad murder mystery.

He put his hand on the doorknob. She could tell he wanted to close the door—though not in her face, of course—and he hesitated there, his smile first reassuring, then tightening.

"You probably need some time to yourself, in any case," George Orson said.

"Yes," she said. She watched as his fingertips twitched against the clear cut glass of the doorknob, and he followed her eyes, looked down at his impatient hand, as if it had disappointed him.

"You know that you don't have to do this," he said. "I wouldn't blame you if you wanted to leave. I realize that it's a lot to ask of you."

She wasn't sure how to respond. She thought:

She thought:

Then he shut the door.

For a time, she paced outside of the study, and then she sat at the table in the dining room with a diet soda—it was a hot afternoon—and she pressed the cool damp can against her forehead.

She had been left to her own devices in this way for weeks now, left to watch TV endlessly, adjusting the ancient satellite dish that turned its head with a slow metallic hum, like the sound of an electric wheelchair; laying down hand after hand of solitaire with an old pack of her dad's playing cards that she had brought with her for sentimental reasons; browsing through the bookshelves in the living room, a dreadful collection of old tomes that you might find in a box at an old lady's yard sale. *The Death of the Heart. From Here to Eternity. Marjorie Morningstar.* Nothing anybody had ever heard of.

She was trying to think. Trying to imagine what to do, which was exactly the same thing she'd been doing for almost an entire year, ever since her parents had died. Scoping through the future in her mind, trying to draw a map for herself, looking out into a great expanse like a pilot over an ocean, looking for a place to land. And still no clear plan emerged.

But at least now she had more information.

4.3 million dollars.

Which was a significant and helpful detail, if in fact it could be believed. There were aspects to his story—to this whole thing—that felt exaggerated, or embellished, or distorted. Some aspect of the truth was concealed within what he'd told her, in the manner of those old picture puzzles she used to love as a child, drawings of ordinary landscapes in which simple pictographic figures—five seashells, or eight cowboy hats, or thirteen birds—had been hidden.

She selected an old hardcover from the shelf, and once again she riffled through the pages. Over the past few weeks, she had been through every book on the shelf, thinking that perhaps a note would drop out from between the pages. She had been through every cabinet in the kitchen, every dresser in every bedroom; she had tapped the walls as if there might be a secret door or compartment. She'd even been down to the lighthouse-shaped office of the motel, where she'd looked through the dusty rack of brochures for local amusements that had long ago closed down, where she'd opened boxes to find elderly rolls of toilet paper, still wrapped in plastic, cabinets full of moldering towels; she'd even been into the motel rooms themselves. She'd taken the keys from the hooks behind the counter and opened the rooms one by one—cleared out, all of them, no beds, no furniture, nothing but bare walls and bare floors, nothing but an unremarkable coating of dust.

In all that time, the only clue she'd found was a single golden coin. It was in a cigar box on a high shelf in a closet in one of the empty bedrooms on the second floor of the house, along with some oddly shaped rocks and a tiny horseshoe magnet and some thumbtacks and a plastic dinosaur. The coin was heavy, and appeared to be an old gold doubloon, very worn, though it was most likely just a child's souvenir of some sort.

Still, she had taken it, she had hidden it in her suitcase, and it was this coin that she thought of when she had first seen the deposit slip. *4.3 million dollars,* and childishly she'd had a brief image of chests full of these golden coins.

Of course she was aware that greed was part of her decision. Yes, she knew that. But she did also love him, she thought. She loved the way it felt to be with him, that easy, teasing camaraderie, that sense he gave her that the two of them, only them, had their own country and language, as if, as George Orson used to tell her, they'd known each other in another life—and she guessed that she could even stand to be Brooke Fremden for a while if he were David. . . .

And it could even be fun.

It could be one of those confidential adventures that they shared. One of the stories that made up a private history that only they knew about. They would be at a dinner party in some place like Morocco and someone would ask how they had met and the two of them would exchange private looks.

It was almost three-thirty in the afternoon when he finally emerged from the study. Lucy was sitting in the living room in one of the high wingback chairs that had been draped in a tarp, staring again at Brooke Fremden's birth certificate.

Here were the scrawled signatures at the bottom:

I certify that the personal information provided on this certificate is correct to the best of my knowledge and belief. That was the father.

I certify that the above named child was born alive at the place and time and on the date stated above. That was the doctor—Albert Gerbie, M.D.

And when she looked up, George Orson was standing at the edge of the room. He had been combing his hands through his hair, and now it stood up in tufts, and he had the look of someone who had been reading scientific formulas or columns of numbers for too long, an expression both tense and vacant, as if he were surprised to find her sitting there.

"I have to go out for some supplies," he said. "A few things that we need."

"Okay," she said, and he appeared to relax a little.

"I want to try to buy a few things that make you look younger," he said. "What about something pink? Something a bit girly?"

She looked at him skeptically. "Maybe I should come with you," she said.

But he shook his head emphatically. "Not a good idea," he said. "We shouldn't be seen together in town. Especially not now."

"Okay," she said, and he glanced at her gratefully as he put on the baseball cap he always wore when he was making an excursion. He was thankful, she supposed, that she wasn't arguing with him—and he touched her hand, running his fingers distractedly along her knuckles. She gave him a hesitant smile.

He hadn't locked the door to the study.

She stood at the door of the house watching the old pickup as it turned onto the county highway that led away from the motel. The sky was scalloped with layers of pale gray cumulus clouds, and she folded her arms across her chest as the pickup went up over a hill and vanished.

Even before she turned back to the door, she knew that she would go straight to the study, and in fact she even quickened her pace. That locked study had been a point of contention between them, ever since they'd arrived. His *privacy*—though didn't that contradict all his talk, all the things he'd said about sharing their own secret world, *sub rosa,* he said.

But when she brought this up, he only shrugged. "We all need our personal caves," he'd told her. "Even people as close as we are. Don't you think?"

And Lucy had rolled her eyes. "I don't see what the big deal is," she said. "What, are you looking at porn in there?"

"Don't be ridiculous," George Orson had said. "It's just part of having an adult relationship, Lucy. Giving people their space."

"I just want to check my email," she said—though in fact, there wasn't anyone who would have sent her a message, and naturally he knew that.

"Lucy, please," he said. "Just give me a few more days. I'll get you a computer of your own, and you can email to your heart's content. Just be patient a bit longer."

The study was much messier than she expected. Very unlike George Orson—who was a folder of clothes and a maker of lists, a man who hated to see clutter or dirty dishes in the sink.

So this was a side of George Orson she'd never seen, and she stood, uneasily, on the threshold. There was a sense of feverishness, chaos, panic. In any case, there was no doubt that all of those hours and hours he had spent holed up in this room had not been spent idly. He had been working, just as he'd claimed.

There was a jumble of different machines in the room—several laptop computers, a printer, a scanning bed, other things she didn't recognize—all of them connected in a tangle of cords and plugged into a strip of electrical sockets. The lips of his bookshelves were lined with empty soda cans, energy drinks, and there was a smattering of discarded clothes on the floor—a pair of boxer shorts, some T-shirts, a single sock curled up—along with many, many chocolate bar wrappers, though she had never seen George Orson eat candy. Some books were also spread out here and there—their pages tagged and bulging with bookmarks. *The Sacred Pentagram of Sedona. Fibonacci and the Financial Revolution. The Thing on the Doorstep. A Practical Guide to Mentalism.*

And there were papers strewn everywhere—some in piles, some crumpled into balls and discarded, some documents taped to the walls in a haphazard collage. The drawers to the file cabinet—the one he said he couldn't find the key to—had all been taken out, and the overstuffed hanging folders were stacked into various towers around the room.

It could easily be mistaken for the room of a crazy person, she thought, and a nervous feeling settled in her chest, a smooth, vibrating stone forming just below her breastbone as she stepped into the room.

"Oh, George," she breathed, and she couldn't decide if it was scary, or sad, or touching to imagine him emerging day after day from this room as his normal, cheerful self. Coming out of this tsunami with his hair combed and his smile straightened, to make her dinner and reassure her, to watch a movie with his arm draped gently over her shoulder, the day's frenzied activity closed and locked behind the study door.

She knew well enough that she shouldn't move anything. There was no way to tell what organizational principal was at work here, though it might not appear as if there were any. She stepped attentively, as if it were a lake covered with new ice, or a crime scene. It was okay, she told herself. He had promised to tell her everything, and if he hadn't, it was her right to find out. It was only fair, she thought, though she was also uncomfortably aware of those fairy tales that had scared her when she was a child. *Bluebeard. The Robber Bridegroom.* All those horror movies in which girls went into rooms they weren't supposed to.

Which was paranoid, she knew. She didn't believe that George Orson would hurt her. He would lie, yes, but she was sure—she was positive he wasn't dangerous.

Still, she crept forward like a trespasser, and she could feel her pulse ticking in her wrist as she laid one soundless foot in front of the other, picking a slow pathway through the clutter, treading with deliberate steps along the edge of the room.

The papers taped to the walls were mostly maps, she saw—road maps, topography, close-ups of street grids and intricately detailed coastlines—not places recognizable to her. Scattered throughout these maps were some news items George Orson had printed from the Internet: "U.S. Prosecutors Indict 11 in Massive Identity Fraud Case," "No Developments in Case of Missing College Student," "Attempted Theft of Biological Agent Thwarted." She glanced at these headlines, but didn't pause to read the articles. There were so many; every wall of the whole room was papered with 8½ x 11 sheets of paper. Maybe he *had* lost his mind.

And then she noticed the safe. The wall safe he had shown her the first day they had arrived, back when this room was just another one of the dusty curiosities he was touring her through. Back when he blithely told her he didn't have the combination.

But now the safe was open. The painting that had hidden it, the portrait of George Orson's grandparents, was swung back, and the thick metal door of the safe was ajar.

In a horror movie, this would be the moment in which George Orson would appear in the doorway behind her. "What do you think you're doing?" he would purr in a low voice, and she felt her neck prickle even though the doorway was empty behind her, even though George Orson was long gone, on his way to town.

But still she walked toward the safe, because it was full of money.

The bills were in bundles, just like you saw on TV in gangster movies, each stack about half an inch thick, rubber-banded and piled into neat columns, and she reached and took one. One-hundred-dollar bills. She guessed that there must be about fifty bills in each rubber-banded little bale, and she balanced one in the palm of her hand. It was light, no heavier than a pack of cards, and she riffled through the stack, not breathing for a second. There were thirty of these little parcels: about a hundred and fifty thousand dollars, she calculated, and she closed her eyes.

They really were rich, she thought. At least there was that. Despite her doubts, despite the chaos of papers and garbage and the books and maps and news stories, at least there was that. Up until then, she realized, she had almost convinced herself that she was going to have to leave.

Without thinking, she touched the cash to her face, as if it were a bouquet. "Thank you," she whispered. "Thank you, God."

16

They had arranged to meet in the lobby of the Mackenzie Hotel, which was where the woman said she was staying. "My name is Lydia Barrie," she had told him over the phone, and when he gave her his name, there was a moment of hesitance.

"*Miles Cheshire*," she repeated, a skeptical edge to her voice—as if he had given her some stage name. As if he had told her his name was Mr. Breeze.

"Hello?" he said. "Are you still there?"

"I can meet you in fifteen minutes," she said—a bit stiffly, he thought. "I have red hair, and I'm wearing a black overcoat. We shouldn't have trouble finding each other."

"Oh," he said. "Okay."

Her voice was so curiously clipped, so strange and abrupt, that he felt a pang of uncertainty. When he went around putting up his flyers, he had imagined that—at the very best—he would get a few responses from some local teenagers, perhaps a clerk at the liquor store, or a waitress, or a curious and watchful retiree, or some derelict interested in the reward. That was the type of caller he usually got.

So this woman's eagerness made him uncomfortable.

He probably should have been more cautious, he thought. He probably should have deliberated more before arranging a meeting, he should have prepared a cover story.

All of which came to him too late. Too late he remembered the letter that Hayden had sent him: *someone may be watching you, and I hate to say this but I think you may actually be in danger,* and now he thought perhaps he shouldn't have been so quick to dismiss Hayden's warning.

But the woman had already come into the lobby. She was already peering around, and he was the only person standing there. He glanced over his shoulder, to where the girl at the front desk was talking avidly on the phone, utterly oblivious as the woman came toward him.

"Miles Cheshire?" she said, once again pronouncing his name with a faint touch of skepticism, and what could he do? He nodded, and tried to smile in a way that would seem honest and disarming.

"Yes," he said. He shifted uncertainly. "Thank you for coming," he said.

She was, Miles guessed, a bit older than he was—somewhere between thirty-five and forty, he imagined, a thin, striking woman with high cheekbones and a sharp nose and smooth red hair. Her eyes were large and gray and intense, not bulging, exactly, but prominent in a way that he found unnerving.

He was also aware of how dumpy he looked, in cheap jeans and an untucked, un-ironed button-down shirt, more than a little disheveled, he realized, probably smelling of beer and the cheap barroom fish he'd eaten for dinner. Lydia Barrie, on the other hand, was wearing a light, glossy black trench coat, and emitted a faint scent of some mildly floral businesslike perfume. She fixed her gaze on him, and her eyebrows arched as she looked him up and down.

She removed a thin cloth glove to shake his hand, and her palms were soft and lotioned, very cold. But it was she who shuddered when Miles's fingers touched her palm. She was staring at his face, her big eyes round with suspicious hostility.

"It's striking," she said. "The person in your poster is also named Miles." He watched as her lips pursed: an unpleasant memory. "His name is Miles Spady."

He stood there, blankly. "Well," he said.

Obviously, he should have been prepared for this. He had encountered this particular alias before, back in Missouri—it was an unpleasantly pointed invention on Hayden's part, a secret jab, marrying Miles with the last name of their hated stepfather—and there had even been the time in North Dakota when Hayden had checked into a motel using the name Miles Cheshire.

It was foolish of him to give this woman his real name, a stupid mistake, and he tried to think. Should he show her his driver's license, to prove his own honesty?

"Well," he said again.

Why hadn't he done more preparation? Why hadn't he dressed up a bit, why hadn't he memorized a simple explanation, instead of thinking he could extemporize?

"That's not actually his real name," Miles said at last. It was the only thing that he could think of, and—oh, why not? Why not just tell the truth? Why was he still playing a game that had long ago grown stale? "Miles Spady—" he said. "That's just a pseudonym; he does that all the time. Frequently, he'll use the names of people he knows. Miles is my name, and Spady is the name of our stepfather. It's a joke, I guess."

"A joke," she said. Her eyes rested on his face, and her expression flickered as her thoughts settled into place.

"You're related to him," she said. "I can see the resemblance."

Well.

It took him aback. It was a peculiar feeling, after all this time.

In all the years he had been showing this old photo of Hayden, no one had ever made the connection. For a while, it had dumb-founded him, and then eventually it was just another small, nagging doubt.

They were identical twins—obviously there was a similarity—so why had it been so many years since anyone had remarked on it? Miles guessed that he'd aged differently than Hayden had—he'd gained weight, his face had hardened and grown thicker—but still, he had always felt a little hurt that no one ever seemed to connect his own face with the boy in the poster.

So it was a relief, even a consolation, to hear her say the word "re-semblance." It was as if his body solidified for the first time in—he couldn't remember how long.

Miles let out a breath.

"He's my brother," he said at last, and it was such a liberation to say it, such a release. "I've been looking for him for a long time now."

"I see," Lydia Barrie said. She regarded him, and her hostility de-flated slightly. She pushed a strand of hair behind her ear, and he watched as she closed her eyes, as if she were meditating.

"Then I guess we have something in common, Miles," she said. "I've also been looking for him for a long time."

He was lonely: that's what he told himself later, when he began to worry that he should have been more cautious, more circumspect. He was lonely and tired and disoriented and sick of playing games, and what did it matter? What did it matter?

They sat at the bar of the Mackenzie Hotel, and he had another few beers, and Lydia Barrie drank gin and tonics, and he told her everything.

Well—almost everything.

It was disconcerting, he found, once he began to put the whole story into words. Their unbelievable childhood—which, even in the blandest summary, sounded like a comic book. Their magician/clown/hypnotist father. The atlas. Hayden's breakdowns, the past lives and spirit cities, the various identities he inhabited, the emails and letters and clues that mapped out a treasure hunt Miles had been pursuing for years now. Perhaps that was the most embarrassing thing to admit, that he had been following this trail for more than a decade now, and hadn't gotten any closer.

How did you explain that? Was it enough to say that they were brothers—that Hayden was the last person alive in the world who shared the same memories, the last person who could remember how happy they were at one point, the last person who knew that things could have been different? Was it enough to say that Hayden was a conduit through which he could pass back in time, the last thread that connected him to what he still thought of as his "real" life?

Was it enough to say that, even now, even after everything, he still loved Hayden more than anyone else? He still longed for the old Hayden every day, the brother he had known as a kid, even though he knew that would sound crazy. Desperate. Pathological.

"I'm honestly not sure what I'm doing at this point," he said, and he folded his hands on the surface of the bar. "Why am I here? I don't actually know."

Over the years, he had imagined himself telling his tale to someone—a wise therapist, perhaps; or a friend he'd become close to—John Russell, maybe, given time and proximity; or a girlfriend, once they'd gotten to know each other and he was sure she wouldn't immediately run away. The girl at Matalov Novelties, Aviva, Mrs. Matalov's granddaughter, with her dyed black hair and skeleton earrings and sharp, sympathetic, knowing eyes—

But he never would have imagined that the person he'd finally reveal himself to would be someone like Lydia Barrie. There were, he thought, few people more unlikely than this owlishly watchful, tightly wound woman, with her gloves and her trench coat and her pale, elegant skin.

But it was, nevertheless, easy to talk to her. She listened intently, but didn't seem to doubt what he was telling her. None of this surprised her, she told him finally.

Lydia Barrie had been looking for Hayden for more than three years—or, to be exact, she had been looking for her younger sister, Rachel.

Hayden was Rachel's fiancé. Or had been.

"This was back in Missouri," Lydia Barrie said. "My sister was attending the University of Missouri at Rolla, and your brother was her teacher. He called himself Miles Spady—he was a graduate student in math. He was supposedly British. He said he'd gone to Cambridge, and his father was a professor of anthropology there, and I think we were a little dazzled by him when he came home with her that December.

"We were five women. It was Rachel and me and our middle sister, Emily, and my aunt Charlotte, and our mother. Our father died when we were young, and so there was that: it was a novelty to have a man in the house.

"And it was also that my mother was so ill. She had ALS, and she was in a wheelchair by that time. We all knew that she was going to die soon, and so—I don't know—everyone wanted it to be a wonderful Christmas, and I'm sure he realized that. He was very charming, and kind to our mother. She wasn't able to talk anymore, but he would sit with her and converse, and tell her about his life back in England, and—

"I believed him. He was convincing enough, at least. In retrospect, I realize that his accent struck me as slightly put-on, but I didn't think too much about it at the time. He seemed very smart, very nice. A little eccentric, I thought, a little *affected*, but nothing that made me feel especially suspicious of him.

"Undeniably, I wasn't paying an enormous amount of attention. I was living in New York, just home for a few days for the holiday, and I was involved in my own life, and I wasn't terribly close to Rachel. We're eight years apart, and she was—always a very quiet girl, secretive, you know? And in any case, I thought it was silly for them to be saying they were *engaged,* since they weren't planning to get married until after she graduated from college, and that was well over a year away. She was a junior at the time.

"And then, in October of the following year—about five months after my mother died—the two of them disappeared."

Lydia Barrie was reticent for a moment. Staring into her drink. Miles wondered whether he ought to tell her about how obsessed Hayden used to be with orphans. How they used to play pretend games when they were children in which they were orphans in danger, runaway orphans, how he used to love this children's book, *The Secret Garden,* about a little orphan girl . . .

But perhaps this wasn't the best time to mention it.

"I was so angry with her," Lydia Barrie said, at last, softly. "We hadn't been talking. I was upset with her, because she hadn't come to our mother's funeral, and so we were out of contact, and it was actually some time before I realized that she was not in school anymore. And there was no way to reach her.

"They left town together, apparently, but no one knew where they were going, and they effectively . . . Well, it probably doesn't sound ridiculous to you if I say that they vanished."

And she looked at Miles with her large, prominent eyes, and he was aware of how pale her skin was, almost transparent, like onion paper through which he could discern her delicate veins. He watched as she reached up and pushed a strand of hair behind her ear.

"My family hasn't seen Rachel since," Lydia Barrie said.

Rachel, he thought. He recalled her name, the name he had been given by Hayden's friends from the math department.

That girl, peering out of the door of the crumbling rental house, the screen door with the torn flap in its mesh, the dusty sofa parked underneath the front bay windows.

It came to him with a shudder. His own appearance in the story that Lydia Barrie had been telling. He had been following it, almost abstractly, picturing that December scene, Hayden in the living room with the mute quivering mother, the two of them staring into the fire, under the shadow of a blinking Christmas tree; Hayden at the breakfast table with these women, buttering toast and talking in his stagy British accent, which, Miles remembered, was one of his favorites; Hayden placing his arm across Rachel Barrie's shoulder as gift-wrapped packages were being distributed, a carol playing from the stereo.

He saw all of this in his mind as he listened, as if he were watching the grainy, sweetly sad home videos of some strangers, and then abruptly Rachel Barrie's eye appeared in a door crack and gazed out at him.

I know who you are, she said. *I'll call the police if you don't leave.*

The two of them, Miles and Lydia, sat there at the bar, both of them quiescent. She lifted her glass, and even though there were other people in the bar, talking and laughing, and there was music playing, he was aware of the faint xylophone rattle of ice in her glass.

"I think I saw your sister, once," he said. And then, seeing her expression brighten, he amended quickly.

"In Rolla," he said. "It was about five years ago. It must have been right before they . . ."

"I see," she said.

He shrugged regretfully—he was familiar with the way those sparks of information could light up and then extinguish. The repeated letdowns, the discouragement.

"I'm sorry," he said.

"No, no," she said. "I didn't mean to seem—disappointed." She looked down at her glass, touched the condensation along the rim.

"It's been ages since I've met anyone who's actually seen her. So: tell me everything you remember. It's important, and useful, even the small things. Did she speak with you at all?"

"Well," he said.

It felt as if there were an intimacy in the way that her eyes had settled on him, waiting, damp and sadly hopeful. What could he tell her? He had talked with some people, other graduate students whom, no doubt, she had also talked to; he had gone to that house, where Rachel was living, and she had come to the door briefly, but she hadn't said much, had she? Just threatened to call the police— which had scared him, he guessed. He was a coward about authority, he had always felt that the cops would side against him, how could you explain a person like Hayden, after all, without sounding crazy? *I know who you are*, Rachel said. *I will call the police.*

And why hadn't he been more persistent? Why hadn't he pushed his way inside, sat down with the poor girl and told her exactly who he was, and who Hayden was?

He could have helped her, he thought. He could have *saved* her.

He looked back down at his hand. Even in identical twins, the fingerprints, the creases of the palm, were distinct, and for a moment he imagined telling Lydia this random fact, he didn't know why.

In the beginning, Lydia had tried to contact the authorities. But they hadn't been particularly concerned or helpful.

After that, there had been a series of private detectives.

"But that was very expensive," she said. "I'm not a wealthy person, and in any case, I never managed to hire anyone who was especially bright. They just followed one dead end after the other, charging me hourly plus per diems all the way through, and getting nowhere. Not with your brother.

"These detectives would spend, I don't know—hundreds and thousands of dollars—and then they would come back to me with these ridiculous things. A post office box in Sedona, Arizona. An Internet polling company in Manada Gap, Pennsylvania. An abandoned motel in Nebraska. And then one of them wanted money to pursue some *international leads,* as he called them. Ecuador. Russia. Africa.

"And for a while, I suppose I convinced myself that I was getting somewhere. That I was getting closer, even though—"

She smiled tightly, wearily, and Miles nodded.

"Yes," he said.

He knew the exhaustion that a person began to feel after a few years. Trying to find Hayden required a particular stamina, a patience for small details that might lead nowhere, the perseverance of a cartographer who was mapping a shoreline that wound and raveled into the horizon, that you'd never reach the end of.

He sometimes thought about the autumn after their father died. That was when Hayden had been fascinated with irrational numbers, with the Fibonacci numbers and the golden ratio, making drawings of rectangles and nautilus shells and meticulously filling pages and pages of a notebook with the infinite decimal extension of the ratio.

Miles, meanwhile, found his first semester of algebra almost unbearable. He would look at the equations and he couldn't make them *mean* anything, nothing but a spidery scuttling behind his forehead, as if the numbers had turned into insects inside his brain. He would sit there and glare at the problems—or, worse, he would begin to do them and his own solutions would somehow detour onto an unexplainably wrong track, so that for a time he'd believe that he'd finally figured out a method—only to discover that, in fact, x did not equal 41.7. No, x equaled -1, though he had no idea how that was possible. Sitting before a work sheet of these equations, night after night, was the worst fatigue he'd ever experienced, so eventually his mind felt like it had been eaten away into a lace of thin, almost weightless threads.

"Oh, *please,*" Hayden used to say, and he would gently take the paper from Miles and show him, once again, how easy it was. "You're such a baby, Miles," Hayden said. "Just pay attention. It's simple if you just take it in steps."

But Miles was frequently near tears by that point. "I can't do it," he would say. "I can't think the right way!"

It was that frustration, that sense of futility he would later remember when he began looking for Hayden. He could see the same thing in Lydia Barrie's expression.

Lydia combed her fingers gently through her hair, and looked down critically at her highball glass, which was empty, save for a lime slice that was curled into the fetal position at the bottom. She was, Miles thought, a little drunk, and she looked less refined and dignified. Her hair hadn't fallen back into its previously sculpted form, and a few strands were awry. When the noncommittal ponytailed bartender came over to see if she wanted another drink, she nodded. Miles was still working on his beer.

The bar was dark and windowless, and replicated the pleasant feeling of night, though outside the sun was still shining.

"It's funny," Lydia said, and she watched gloomily as first a napkin, and then the refilled glass, was placed on the bar in front of her. "Honestly, I suppose I must have spent thirty thousand dollars on these detectives, and after a while I think I just kept pressing forward because I didn't want to believe that the whole thing was a waste.

"I don't know," she said, and drew a breath. "I suppose I can understand why Rachel would leave and never contact me again. I can understand why she wouldn't want to speak with me. I said some very unkind things to her, when she didn't come to our mother's funeral. I said some things that I regret.

"But she hasn't contacted our sister Emily, either. Or Aunt Charlotte. I understand that she was very unhappy, and maybe she was so devastated by our mother's death that she couldn't stand to face it.

"But who just abandons their family in that way? What kind of person decides that they can throw everything away and—*reinvent* themselves. As if you could just discard the parts of your life that you didn't want anymore.

"Sometimes I think, well, that's where we are now, as a society. That's just what people have become, these days. We don't value connection."

She peered at him, and the composure she'd had when they first met had dissipated. There was a precarious aura in the air, an unnerving weight.

"I've done some things," she said. "I've slept with people that I never talked to afterward. I left a job once. I left on a Friday and I didn't call or tell my boss that I quit, or anything. I just never went back. I once told a man I worked with that I went to Wellesley— I guess that I was trying to impress him, and when he asked me about people he knew who had graduated from Wellesley, I pretended I knew them. Because I wanted him to like me.

"But I never *disappeared*," she said. Her hand closed around her drink, her manicured nails, and her fingertips flattened and blanched against the glass. "I never vanished, so that no one could find me. That's a bit extreme, isn't it? That's not normal, is it?"

"No," Miles said. "I don't think it's normal."

"Thank you," she said. She gathered herself, straightened, ran the flat of her palms against the front of her blouse. "Thank you."

Perhaps she was as crazy as he was, Miles thought, though he wasn't sure if that was a comforting thought. Perhaps there were people all over the world whose lives Hayden had ruined, they were a club, a matrix that crisscrossed over the map, who knew how many there were? Hayden's influence expanding outward like the Fibonacci numbers he used to recite—1, 1, 2, 3, 5, 8, 13, 21, 34, 55, 89 . . . and so on.

Meanwhile, Lydia Barrie had pressed the heel of her palm

against her forehead and closed her eyes. Miles thought that perhaps she'd fallen asleep, and he thought about sleep himself. He
was so tired—so tired—so many hours of driving, so many hours of
daylight and thinking, thinking.

But then Lydia lifted her head.

"Do you think she's still alive?" she whispered.

It took Miles a moment to realize what she was asking.

"Well," he said. "I don't know what you mean."

"I think he might have killed her," Lydia Barrie said. "That's
what I mean. I think she might be buried somewhere, anyplace, any
one of the places that I've traced them to, or someplace I don't
know about. That's why—"

But she didn't finish. She didn't necessarily want to continue
with this line of thinking, and so she only sat there, her palm
pressed against her face.

"Of course not," Miles said. "I don't think he's—"

Though in fact he *did* think so. He imagined, once again, their
old house on fire, he could picture his mother and Mr. Spady in
their bed on the second floor, perhaps waking up too late, the room
filled with smoke—or perhaps not waking up at all, perhaps only a
few seconds of struggle, their eyelids fluttering awake and then closing again as the oxygen vanished and the wallpaper lit up with trick-
les of flame.

Was it so far-fetched to imagine that Hayden had done something to Rachel Barrie?

"I have some papers upstairs in my room," Lydia Barrie said
thickly. "I have some—documents." He observed her as she
brought her gin and tonic into the air. As she touched the edge of
the glass to her lips.

"I think they are authentic," she said, and took a long sip from
her drink. "I think they'll be of interest to you."

Sometimes Ryan imagined that he saw people from his past. Ever since his death, this had become a regular occurrence, these minor hallucinations, tricks of perception.

Here, for example, was his mother, standing on a busy street corner on Hennepin Avenue in Minneapolis, her back to him, opening an umbrella as she hurried into a crowd.

Here was Walcott, sitting in the window of a bus full of rowdily singing fraternity brothers. This was in Philadelphia, not far from Penn, and Ryan stood there staring as they were borne past, all of them tunelessly caroling along with Bob Marley.

Their eyes met, his and Walcott's, and for a second Ryan could have sworn that it truly *was* him, though the Walcott on the bus just peered out at him, his mouth moving, "Every little thing gonna be all right," they were singing, and Ryan was aware of motion passing over him, a shadow of a bird or a cloud.

This is what it would be like to see a ghost, he thought, even though he was the one who was dead.

He knew it wasn't really them. He was aware that it was just a trailing cobweb of subconscious, a misfiring synapse of memory, an undigested bit of the past playing games with him. He had been letting his mind wander too much, he thought; that was all it meant. He needed to focus. He needed to meditate, as Jay suggested. "You need to find the silence inside yourself," Jay advised, and one day when he was back from a particularly stressful trip, they listened together to one of Jay's relaxation CDs. "Picture a circle of energy near the base of your spine," the CD told them, while they sat in chairs in the darkened back bedroom, their bare feet on the floor. "Inhale . . . exhale . . . letting your breathing become deep and even . . ."

And it *was* relaxing, actually, though it didn't really help. The next week, in Houston, he thought he saw Pixie—her hair longer and darker but still recognizable—the very image of Pixie, in fact, smoking a cigarette on the curb outside the downtown Marriott, looking bored and wistful as she toyed with the thin ring in her eyebrow.

No.

It wasn't her, he realized, he could see as soon as he stepped out of the taxi that this woman was probably in her thirties or even forties. Why had he even thought there was a resemblance? It was as if she had only been Pixie for a second, appearing just for a few shuttering snapshots out of the corner of his eye. Another little con game his brain had played on him.

Still.

Still, he thought, it was not entirely impossible—even in a country of three hundred million—it was not beyond the realm of possibility that he might eventually encounter someone he once knew.

In fact, he was pretty certain he had actually seen his old psychology professor, Ms. Gill, in an airport bar in Nashville. His connecting flight had been late, and he had been lingering in the terminal of Nashville International, pulling his wheeled carry-on past newsstands and fast-food booths and souvenir shops, looking for some way to distract himself, and there, suddenly, she had been. Sitting in the Gibson Café underneath some guitar memorabilia, she had regarded him casually as he walked by. And then their eyes had connected, and he saw her expression tighten, a startle of attentiveness crossing her face.

It appeared as if she recognized him from somewhere; he saw her puzzling. His head was shaved, and he was wearing aviator sunglasses, and a short-sleeved security guard's uniform, so it was surprising that she would even look twice. But she did. Wasn't he one of her former students? Didn't he look like that boy who had died—who had committed suicide—the one who had been failing her class, who had come to her office to see if there was any way he could do work for extra credit?

No. She wouldn't have made that connection. It was only that he looked vaguely familiar, and she scrutinized him for a second, a sad, single professor lady with a bad haircut and an overbite, she had perhaps contemplated suicide herself, she had thought about that kid, drowning himself in the lake, and she had wondered what that would feel like, she herself had always thought that carbon monoxide would be the way to go, carbon monoxide and sleeping pills, no struggle . . .

And he walked by and she put her vodka and cranberry juice to her lips and he thought about Jay's meditation audios.

"The next energy level is near your forehead," the woman narrator said, in her soothing, dreamy monotone. "Here is the chakra of time, the circle of daylight and nighttime in their eternal passages, which will guide you to awareness of your soul. Let yourself free your mind, and as you accept the power and awe of your own soul, so will you realize the soul within everyone and everything."

He thought of this as he queued himself into the line at the airline check-in desk, and he placed his fingers lightly to his brow.

"That's where the pineal gland is," Jay had told him. "That's where your melatonin comes from, and it regulates your sleep cycle. That's cool, isn't it?"

"Yeah," Ryan had said. "Interesting!"

Though now he wondered what Ms. Gill would have had to say about it all. She had been skeptical, as he remembered, with no patience for New Agey nonsense, and he looked over his shoulder.

Despite his talk of meditation and relaxation and so forth, Jay had been feeling anxious lately, too.

"God damn it, Ryan," he said. "Your jitters are starting to rub off on me. I've got the fucking fantods, man."

Ryan was sitting at one of the laptops, opening a bank account for one of his new acquisitions—Max Wimberley, age twenty-three, of Corvallis, Oregon—and he glanced up, still typing, filling in the blocks of information on the application.

"What's a fantod?" he said.

"I don't know," Jay said. He was at a computer of his own, tapping on the escape key with his index finger, and he shook his head at the screen, irritably. "It's just some old-timey Iowa word that my dad used to use. It's like, when a goose walks over your grave. Do you know that saying?"

"Not exactly," Ryan said, and Jay let out an abrupt, particularly foul set of curses.

"I can't believe this," Jay said, and he smacked the palm of his hand down onto his keyboard, hard enough that two of the letter keys popped out and bounced onto the floor with a small rattle, like a pair of dice. "God damn it!" Jay said. "I've got a bug on this computer! That's the third time this week!"

Jay pushed his hair back from his face, tucked it behind his ears, combing the sides of his head nervously with his fingers.

"Something is going on here," he said. "I've got a bad feeling, Ryan. I don't like it."

Ryan wasn't sure what to think. Jay could get temperamental sometimes. He liked to act as if he were the mellow, easygoing philo-
sophical type, but he had his own superstitions, his own fears and
illogics.

For example, there was that argument they'd had about the driver's licenses. This was back when Ryan had first left college and
started working for Jay, back when he was going to the DMVs, traveling to various states.

Back then, Ryan didn't truly understand what he was doing. He
figured that it was illegal somehow, but then again a lot of things
were illegal and they didn't necessarily hurt anybody. He was still
trying to get his mind around what was happening to him. His decision to leave college. His failure to call his parents, the "search"
for him that he had somehow managed to lose control of. He was
still trying to adjust to the idea that Jay was his real father, that
Stacey and Owen had been lying to him for his whole life.

Participating in a little shady activity fit in with the general murk-
iness of his thought process at the time.

Besides which, it wasn't as if he were robbing a bank. It wasn't as
if he were mugging old ladies or cheating orphans. Instead, he'd
spent a lot of time waiting. Standing in line. Sitting in plastic chairs
against the wall across from the Department of Motor Vehicles
counter. Reading Wanted posters that had been taped to the wall,
various public service things about drunken driving and wearing
seat belts and so on.

He watched the other people as they took their tests and made
their applications, paying attention to the questions they were
asked, the snags they ran into—no social security card, no birth certificate, no proof of residency.

After a while, he had come to be particularly interested in the
issue of organ donation. For the clerks, it was a rote question.
"Would you like to be an organ donor?" the clerks would ask, mon-

otone, reciting: "Joining the donor registry is a way to legally give consent to the donation of your organs, tissues, and eyes upon your death, for any purposes authorized by law. You could save up to seven lives through organ donation and enhance the quality of life for over fifty others through tissue and eye donation. May I take this opportunity to sign you into the registry?"

Ryan was surprised by how many people were taken aback by this question. In Knoxville, for example, there was one old hippie man, gray ponytail and cutoff jean shorts, who had laughed aloud. He looked over his shoulder at the rest of them, as if a joke were being played on him. Ryan watched as the man's grin wavered, as the man thought briefly about his own death. Being cut up and taken apart. "Heh, heh," the man said, and then he shrugged, making an expansive motion of his hand. "Why . . . sure!" he said. "Sure, by God, why not?" As if this were an act of bravado that the rest of them would be impressed by.

In Indianapolis, there was the old woman in her lemon-yellow jacket and pants, who paused for a long time to think about it. She became very grave, folding her hands over each other. "I'm sorry," she said. "We don't believe in that."

In Baltimore, there was the tough-looking hip-hop guy, muscle T-shirt pulled tight over his chest, jeans sagging down to show his boxer shorts. But he drew back from the clerk in genuine—almost childlike—horror. "No, ma'am," he said. "Uh-uh." As if someone might be waiting in the back room with a saw and a scalpel.

As for Ryan, he didn't have any qualms. It was a basic social good, like giving blood or whatever. Just the right thing to do, he thought, until he had come home that weekend with his cache of fake IDs.

"What the fuck?" Jay said. He had been in a good mood until he had started to look at the licenses that Ryan had given him. "Ryan, dude, you signed up as an organ donor on every goddamn one of these things."

"Uh . . . ," Ryan said. "Yeah?"

"What the hell," Jay said—and his face reddened in a way that Ryan had not yet seen. Jay cultivated a slacker look, his straight black hair down to his shoulders, vintage thrift store clothes. But his expression became impressively hard and threatening. "What the hell were you thinking, man?" Jay said, and gritted his teeth abruptly. "Are you out of your mind? These are ruined!"

"But—" Ryan said. "I'm sorry, I don't get what you're saying."

"Jesus Christ," Jay said. "Ryan, what happens when you add your name to a state organ donor registry?" His voice had grown lower, and he spoke slowly and rhetorically, enunciating Organ. Donor. Registry. Each word a balloon he was poking with a pin.

"I don't know," Ryan said. He was flabbergasted, and he tried to speak lightly, a cautious, apologetic shrug. But Jay didn't stop glaring at him.

"Do you realize that you consented to give the federal and state government access to your private medical and social history? Any confidentiality between you and a doctor is now moot. They are now legally allowed to examine current and past medical records, laboratory tests, blood donations—"

"I didn't know that," Ryan said, and he looked at Jay uncertainly. Was he joking? "Are you sure? That doesn't sound—"

"Doesn't sound what?" said Jay fiercely.

"I don't know," Ryan said again. He thought: *It doesn't sound true.* But he didn't say that.

"You don't know," Jay said. "Did you read the contract you signed?"

"I didn't sign a contract."

"Of course you signed a fucking contract," Jay said, and now his voice was hot with disgust. Controlled contempt. "You just didn't read it, dude. Did you? They told you to sign on the line and you signed, isn't that right? Isn't that what you did?"

"Jay," Ryan said, "it wasn't even my own name."

"Do you think that matters?" Jay said. "The names on these cards are *our* names. We worked hard to harvest these names. They're like *gold* to us. And now they are open to government surveillance. Totally useless!" He shook one of the laminated cards between his thumb and forefinger, repulsed by it, and then flipped it across the room, where it hit the wall with a tick. "Completely. Ruined. Shit! Do you get that?"

There were things about Jay that he still hadn't figured out—the unpredictable bursts of temper, the oddities of philosophy, the supposed facts that sounded made-up, which Ryan guessed were mostly gleaned from conspiracy theory websites.

Did Jay really believe in the stuff about chakras, for example? Was he serious when he consulted the Ouija board on the coffee table, or when he began to hold forth on various "shadow government" organizations such as the Omega Agency and secret societies such as the Bilderberg Group and the Order of Skull and Bones at Yale, and the global surveillance network, Echelon—

"We have no idea what our government is up to," Jay said, and Ryan nodded uncertainly.

"That's why I've never felt like I'm a criminal," Jay said. "The people who control this country are the real gangsters. You know that, right? And if you play by their rules, you're nothing but their slave."

"Uh-huh," Ryan said, and tried to read Jay's expression.

Was he kidding? Was he a bit crazy?

There were times when Ryan was aware that the choices he'd made would come across as incredibly reckless to an outside observer. Why would he leave behind a pair of stable, loving parents, and throw his lot in with someone like Jay? Why would he abandon a good college education to become a petty con man, a professional liar and thief? Why was he so relieved that he would never have to be part of his nice family again, that he would never have to take another class, that he would never have to put together a résumé and go out on a job interview, that he would never have to try to get married and have a family of his own and participate in the various cyclical joys of middle-class life that Owen had been so attached to?

The truth was, he was actually more like Jay than he was like them; that was what they didn't ever realize.

Stacey and Owen's life, he thought, was no more real than the dozens that he had created in the last year, the virtual lives of Matthew Blurton or Kasimir Czernewski or Max Wimberley. Most people, he thought, had identities that were so shallow that you could easily manage a hundred of them at once. Their existence barely grazed the surface of the world.

Of course, if you wanted to, you could inhabit one or two personas that accumulated more weight. If you wanted, Jay said, you could have wives, families even. He said he knew of a guy who was on a city council in Arizona, and who also ran a real estate business in Illinois, and who was also a traveling salesman with a wife and three children in North Dakota.

And then there were the people who could actually be a single, significant individual. You would have to start work on such a persona from very early on, Ryan thought, maybe from childhood. You'd need a certain precise confidence and focus, and all the abstract elements of luck and circumstance would have to arrange themselves around you. Like, for example, becoming a rock star, building a talent and a name for yourself, working your way into the public eye. He had thought about that a lot, he had liked the idea of turning into a well-known, respected singer-songwriter, but he was also aware that he was never going to be quite good enough. He could sense his own limitations, he could intuit the road blocks that were just a ways down the path of that particular ambition, and truthfully, if you knew you were going to probably fail, then what was the point? Why bother? If you could have dozens of lesser lives, didn't that add up to one big one?

He thought of this again as he maneuvered his way through the airport in Portland, Oregon. The rental car safely abandoned, the prepaid wireless phone crushed under the heel of his shoe and dropped into a trash can, the brand new Max Wimberley driver's license and plane ticket produced for the security officer at the front of the passenger security line, his backpack and laptop and shoes and belt and wallet placed in plastic tubs and sent along their way through the X-ray machine on the conveyor belt, and then he himself, Max Wimberley, motioned forward, passing through the doorway-shaped metal detector. All without incident. All simple, no problem, nothing to worry about at all. Max Wimberley could move through the world with much more ease and grace than Ryan Schuyler could have ever managed.

"Okay," he murmured to himself. "Okay."

He sat there in the boarding area, with a chocolate frozen yogurt shake and a copy of *Guitar* magazine, his backpack in the seat beside him. He made a quick, surreptitious scan of the other people in the seats around him. Youngish, tightly wound businesswoman with a palm pilot. Elderly hand-holding couple. Jocky Asian guy in a Red Sox cap. Etc.

No one who looked at all familiar.

There hadn't been any hallucinations on this trip, and he supposed that was a sign. The last vestiges of his old life were finally fading away. The transformation was almost complete, he thought, and he remembered those long-ago days when he drove around trying to compose a letter to his parents in his head.

Dear Mom and Dad, he thought. *I am not the person you thought I was.*

I am not that person, he thought, and he remembered those Kübler-Ross stages Jay had told him about. This was what acceptance felt like. It wasn't just that Ryan Schuyler was dead; Ryan Schuyler had never existed in the first place. Ryan Schuyler was just a shell he had been using, maybe even less real than Max Wimberley was.

He looked down at his boarding pass, and he could almost feel the residue of Ryan Schuyler exhaling out of him, a little ghostly bat with a human face, which dissolved into a shower of tiny gnats and dispersed.

"Okay," he whispered, and closed his eyes briefly. "Okay."

It was late and warm when he arrived in Detroit Metro, 1:44 A.M. after a connection in Phoenix, and he walked purposefully through the hushed terminal toward the long-term parking garage, where Jay's old Econoline van was waiting for him. He stopped at a gas station to buy an energy drink, and then he was on the interstate, feeling very calm, he thought, listening to music. He rolled the windows down and sang for a while.

North of Saginaw, he turned west onto a highway, and then onto a county two-lane, over some railroad tracks, the houses farther and farther apart, his headlights illuminating the tunnels of woods, some trees beginning to bud with spring leaves, some dead bare skeleton branches mummified in a gauze of old tent caterpillar webs, with only occasional squares of human habitation cut out alongside the road. Back in the 1920s, according to Jay, the Purple Gang from Detroit had one of their hideouts up this way.

At last, he turned onto the narrow asphalt lane that would eventually turn into a dirt road that led up to the cabin, deeper into the forest. It was about four in the morning. He saw the lights of the porch shining and as he pulled up he could hear that Jay had his music going, a thump of old-school hip-hop, and he noticed that a couple of Jay's computers had been tossed out into the gravel driveway. They looked like someone had taken a baseball bat to them.

And in fact, just as Ryan turned off the ignition, Jay came out onto the porch carrying a silver aluminum bat in one hand and a Glock revolver in the other.

"Fucking hell, Ryan," Jay said, and he tucked his revolver into the waistband of his pants as Ryan stepped out of the car. "What took you so long?"

In general, Jay didn't tend to carry guns around, although there were a number of them in the cabin, and Ryan wasn't sure how to react. He could see that Jay was fairly drunk, fairly stoned, in a mood, and so he took vigilant steps across the gravel as he approached the house.

"Jay?" he said. "What's wrong?"

He followed Jay onto the screened porch, past the cast-iron woodstove and the cheap lawn furniture, and into the living room of the cabin, where Jay was in the process of dismantling another computer. He was unplugging various wires and USB cords from the back panel of the machine, and when Ryan came in, he paused, running his fingers through his long hair.

"You're not going to believe this," Jay said. "I think some asshole has stolen my identity!"

"You're kidding," Ryan said. He stood there uncertainly in the doorway, and watched as Jay lugged the disconnected computer off the table and let it fall heavily, like a cement block, to the floor.

"What do you mean, 'stolen' your identity?" Ryan said. "Which one?"

Jay looked up, blankly, holding a limp cord as if it were a snake he had just strangled. "Christ," he said. "I'm not sure. I'm starting to feel concerned that they all might be contaminated."

"Contaminated?" Ryan said. Despite the fact that Jay was carrying around a revolver and dismantling computers, he still looked relatively calm. He wasn't as intoxicated as Ryan had thought at first, either, which made things seem more serious. "What do you mean, contaminated?" he said.

"I lost two people today," Jay said, and he bent down and pulled an old laptop out of a cardboard box that had been shoved under one of the tables at the back of the living room. "All of my Dave Deagle credit cards have been canceled, so somebody must have gotten into him a few days ago. And I started to get nervous and I started to go through everybody, and it turned out that someone had cleaned out Warren Dixon's money market account, some fishy electronic transfer—and this happened, like, this morning!"

"You're joking," Ryan said. He observed as Jay began to attach the old laptop to various plugs, watched the machine begin to quiver as it booted up.

"I wish I *was* joking," Jay said, and he stared hard at his screen as it sang out its tiny melody of start-up music. "You better get your ass online and start checking your people. I think we might be under attack."

Under attack. It might have sounded silly and melodramatic, out here in the woods, in this room that looked like a cross between a college dorm room and a computer repair store, the thrift store couch surrounded by tables that were cluttered with dozens of computers, beer cans, candy wrappers, printers, fax machines, dirty plates, ashtrays. But Jay had tucked the revolver into the waistband of his jeans, and his mouth pulled back in a grimace as he typed, and so Ryan didn't say anything.

"You know what?" Jay said. "Why don't you buy us some plane tickets? See if you can get us some reservations for someplace out of the country. Anyplace that's third world is fine. Pakistan. Ecuador. Tonga. See what deals you can get."

"Jay . . . ," Ryan said, but he sat down at the computer as he had been instructed.

"Don't worry," Jay said. "We're going to be fine. We have to pull together, here, but I think we're going to be totally fine."

18

Lucy and George Orson were in the old pickup together, on their
way to a post office in Crawford, Nebraska. It was the perfect place
to submit their passport applications, according to George Orson,
though Lucy wasn't sure why this town was better than another, why
they had to drive three hours when there were surely a lot of cruddy
post offices closer to home. But she didn't bother to pursue the
matter further. She had a lot on her mind at the moment.

The sense of relief she'd felt when she'd discovered the stacks of
cash had begun to dissipate, and now she was aware again of a flutter in her stomach. She had a memory of that roller coaster at the
Cedar Point amusement park, back in Ohio. Millennium Force,
with its three-hundred-ten-foot drop, the way you would wait there,
once you were strapped in, the heavy ticking of the chain as you
were pulled slowly up the slope to the top of the hill. That terrible
anticipation.

But she was trying to appear calm. She sat subdued in the passenger seat of the old pickup, watching as George Orson shifted

gears, wearing the hideous pink shirt George Orson had bought for her, with its cloud of smiley-faced butterflies printed down the front. This was his idea of what a fifteen-year-old girl might wear—

"It makes you look younger," he said. "That's the point."

"It makes me look retarded," she said. "Maybe I should act like I'm mentally handicapped?" And she extended her tongue, making a thick cave girl grunt. "Because I can't think of any fifteen-year-old who would wear this shirt, unless she was in some kind of special education group home situation."

"Oh, Lucy," George Orson said. "You look fine. You look the part, that's all that matters. Once we're out of the country, you can wear whatever you want."

And Lucy hadn't argued any further. She just looked balefully at her reflection in the bedroom mirror: a stranger she'd taken an instant dislike to.

She was particularly upset about the hair. She hadn't realized that she'd been attached to her original hair color—which was auburn, with some highlights of red—until she had seen what it looked like when she dyed it.

George Orson had been insistent about this—their hair, he said, should be approximately the same color, since they were supposed to be father and daughter—and he came home from his trip to the store with not only the horrible pink butterfly shirt but also a bag full of hair dye.

"I bought six of them," he said. He put a grocery bag on the kitchen table and drew out a glossy box with a female model on the front of it. "I couldn't decide which one of them was right."

The color they'd eventually chosen was called brown umber, and to Lucy it looked like someone had painted her hair with shoe polish.

"You just have to wash it a few times," George Orson said. "It looks fine now, but it will look completely natural once you've worn it for a couple of days."

"My scalp hurts," Lucy said. "In a couple of days, I'll probably be bald."

And George Orson had put his arm around her shoulder. "Don't be ridiculous," he murmured. "You look terrific."

"Mm," she said, and regarded herself in the mirror.

She did not look *terrific,* that was certain. But perhaps she looked like a fifteen-year-old girl.

Brooke Catherine Fremden. A dull, friendless girl, probably pathologically shy. Probably a little like her sister, Patricia.

Patricia used to have anxiety attacks. That was what Lucy was thinking about as she sat in the pickup on the way to Crawford, her heart vibrating oddly in her chest. Patricia would exhibit all kinds of bizarre symptoms when she was having an "attack": her forehead and arms would feel numb, she would have the sensation of bugs in her hair, she would think her throat was closing up. Very melodramatic, Lucy had thought then, unsympathetically. She remembered standing in the bedroom doorway, impatiently eating a piece of toast, with her book bag over her shoulder as their mother urged Patricia to breathe into a lunch sack. "I'm suffocating!" Patricia gasped, her voice muffled by brown paper. "Please don't make me go to school!"

It all looked very fake to Lucy, though she wouldn't have wanted to go to school, either, if she were Patricia. This was during a period when a group of especially mean seventh-grade boys had singled Patricia out for some reason, they had developed a whole elaborate series of comic routines and sketches that involved Patricia as a character, "Miss Patty Stinkbooty," who they pretended was the host of a children's program with puppets that they also had a series of goofy voices for. All kinds of idiotic gross boy humor that had to do with Patricia farting, or menstruating, or having cockroaches crawling in her pubic hair. Lucy could remember the three of them during lunch, Josh and Aaron and Elliot—she still even remembered their stupid names, three nasty, skinny boys doing their routine at their cafeteria table, laughing and chortling until the milk they were drinking came out of their noses.

And Lucy herself had done nothing. Had merely observed stoically as if she were watching some particularly gruesome TV nature program in which jackals killed a baby hippopotamus.

Poor Patricia! she thought now, and placed her hand to her throat, which felt a bit tight, and her face felt a little numb and tingly.

But she was not going to have an anxiety attack, she told herself.

She was in control of her body, and she refused to let it panic. She placed her hands on her thighs, and let out an even breath, staring fixedly at the glove compartment.

She imagined that all of the money from the safe were there inside that glove compartment. And they weren't in a pickup. They were in the Maserati, and they weren't driving through the sand hills of Nebraska, which, as far as she could see, weren't even sandy, but just an endless lake of rolling hills, covered with thin gray grass and rocks.

They were in the Maserati and they were driving on a road that overlooked the ocean, a Mediterranean blue ocean with some sailboats and yachts floating in it. She closed her eyes and slowly began to fill her lungs with air.

And when she opened her eyes, she felt better, though she was still in a pickup truck, and she was still in Nebraska, where some freaky rock formations were cluttered along the horizon. Were they called mesas? Buttes? They looked like they were from Mars.

"George," she said, after she had gathered herself for a minute or so. "I was just thinking about the Maserati. What are we going to do with the Maserati?"

He didn't say anything. He had been mute for an unusually long time, and she thought that was what had brought on her nervousness, the lack of his conversation, which, despite everything, still might have buoyed her. She wished he would rest his hand on her leg, like he used to do.

"George?" she said. "Are you still alive? Are you receiving transmissions?" And at last he turned to glance at her.

"You need to get out of the habit of calling me George," George Orson said at last, and his voice wasn't as soothing as she'd hoped. It was, in fact, a bit austere, which was disappointing.

"I suppose," she said, "that you want me to call you 'Dad.' "

"That's right," George Orson said. "I guess you could call me 'Father' if you prefer."

"Gross," Lucy said. "That's even weirder than calling you 'Dad.' Why can't I just call you David, or whatever?"

And George Orson had looked at her sternly—as if she really were just an impertinent fifteen-year-old. "*Because*," he said. "Because you are supposed to be my daughter. It's not respectful. People notice it when a child calls a parent by their first name, especially in a conservative state such as this. And we don't want people to notice us. We don't want them to remember us when we leave. Does that make sense?"

"Yes," she said. She kept her hands in her lap, and when she felt her heart palpitate, she let out a breath. "Yes, Dad," she said. "That makes sense. But I sincerely hope, Dad, that you're not going to talk to me in that condescending tone all the way to Africa."

He glanced at her again, and there was a glint of an edge in his eyes, a hint of fury that made her flinch inwardly. She had not seen him truly angry before, and she realized now that she didn't want to. He would not be a very nice father, she realized. She didn't even know why, but she intuited it suddenly. He would be cold and demanding and impatient with his children, if he ever had them.

She thought this, even though his expression softened almost immediately.

"Listen," he said. "Sweetheart, I'm just a touch nervous about this. This is very serious business, now. You have to remember to answer to 'Brooke,' and you have to be sure that you never, ever call me George. It's very important. I know it's hard to get used to, but it's only temporary."

"I understand," she said, and she nodded, gazing again at the glove box. Out the window, she could see a rock formation that looked like a volcano, or a giant funnel.

"Do you see that up ahead?" George Orson said—David Fremden said. "That's called Chimney Rock. It's a national historic site."

"Yes," said Brooke.

It was weird to be a daughter again. Even a pretend one. A long time had passed since she'd thought about her own real father, for months and months she had been valiantly containing those memories, setting up walls and screens, pushing them back when they threatened to materialize in her daily consciousness.

But when she said the word "Dad," it was more difficult. Her father seemed to genie into her mind's eye as if decanted, his mild, round earnest face, his thick shoulders and bald head. In life, he had never seemed disappointed by her, and though she didn't believe in spirits, in an afterlife, she didn't believe, as Patricia did, that their dead parents hovered over them as angels—

Nevertheless, she felt a twinge when she called George Orson "Dad." A small stab of guilt, as if her father could know that she'd betrayed him, and for the first time since his death, he seemed to lean over her, palpable, not angry but just sort of hurt, and she was sorry.

She had truly loved him, she guessed.

She knew that, but it wasn't something she had allowed herself to think about, and so it came as a surprise.

He'd been a low-key presence in their house, without much of an opinion about the raising of girl children, though Lucy believed he was more temperamentally suited to her than her mother was.

He was a private person, like Lucy, with the same cynical sense of humor, and Lucy remembered how they used to sneak off together to see horror movies, which her mother would have forbidden— Patricia was the type of girl who had nightmares over a Halloween mask, or even a movie poster, let alone the actual film.

But Lucy wasn't scared. She and her father didn't go to such movies for thrills. Watching horror movies was oddly relaxing, for both Lucy and her father, it was like a kind of music that confirmed the way they felt about the world. A shared understanding, and Lucy never got frightened, not exactly. Occasionally when a monster or killer would pop out, she would put her hand on her father's arm, she would lean closer to him, and they would exchange a glance. A smile.

They understood each other.

All of this came to her as she and George Orson drove without a word, and she pressed her cheek against the glass of the passenger seat window, watching as a cloud of birds lifted up from a field, pulling up in a plume as they went past. Her thoughts were not clearly articulated in her mind, but she could feel them moving swiftly, gathering.

"What are you thinking about?" George Orson said, and when he spoke, her thoughts scattered, broke up into fragments of memories, the way that the birds separated out of their formation and back into individual birds. "You look as if you're deep in thought," George Orson said.

Dad said.

And she shrugged. "I don't know," she said. "I guess I'm feeling anxious."

"Ah," he said. He turned his eyes back to the road, touching his index finger lightly to the bridge of his sunglasses. "That's completely natural."

He reached over and patted his hand against her thigh, and she accepted this little gesture, though she wasn't sure if the hand belonged to George Orson or David Fremden.

"It's difficult at first," he said. "Making the switch. There's a bump you have to get past. You get used to one mode and one persona and there can be some cognitive dissonance, when you transfer over. I know exactly what you're talking about." He ran his hand along the circumference of the steering wheel, as if he were shaping it, molding it out of clay.

"Anxiety!" he said. "I've been there, plenty of times! And, you know, it's particularly hard during the first one, especially, because you're so invested in that idea of self. You grew up with that concept—you think there's a *real you*—and you have some long-standing attachments, people you've known, and you start to think about them. People you have to leave behind—"

He sighed, and even grew slightly wistful, maybe thinking about his late mother, or his brother who had drowned, some long-ago family outing on the pontoon when the lake was still full of water.

Or not.

It suddenly seemed so obvious.

What had George Orson said to her? *I've been a lot of people. Dozens.*

She had been in an alternate universe for a long time now, she thought, and she had been floating behind George Orson as if in a trance. And then abruptly, as they drove along toward the distant post office, she felt herself awaken. There was a flutter, a lifting, and then her thoughts began to fall into place.

He didn't have a brother, she thought.

He hadn't really grown up here, in Nebraska. He had never been a student at Yale; nothing he'd told her had been true.

"God," she said, and shook her head. "I'm so stupid."

And he glanced over at her, his eyes attentive and affectionate. "No, no," he said. "You're not stupid, honey. What's the matter?"

"I just realized something," Lucy said, and she glanced down to where his hand was still resting on her leg. His hand, she would recognize it anywhere, a hand that she had held, that she had put to her lips, a palm that she had traced her fingertips across.

"Your name isn't really George Orson, is it?" she said, and—

He was motionless. Still driving. Still wearing those sunglasses, which reflected the road and the rolling horizon, still the same man she had known.

"George Orson," she said. "That's not your real name," she said.

"No," he said.

He spoke gently, as if he were telling her bad news, and she thought of the way the policemen had come to their door on the day their parents were killed, the way they delivered the news in cautious intervals. *There had been a terrible accident. Their parents were severely injured. The paramedics had arrived at the scene. There wasn't anything the paramedics were able to do.*

She nodded, and she and George Orson looked at each other. There was a silent, tender embarrassment. Hadn't this been understood yesterday, when he showed the Ivory Coast bank account, when he'd produced their fake birth certificates? Hadn't it been obvious?

It should have been clear, she guessed, but only now did it begin to sink in.

She looked down at her pink T-shirt, her breasts pressed flat by a sports bra.

"That isn't really the house that you grew up in, is it?" she said, and her voice felt pressed flat as well. "The Lighthouse. All of the stuff you told me. That painting. That wasn't your grandmother."

"Hmm," he said, and he lifted his fingers from her thigh to gesture vaguely, an apologetic fluttering movement. "This is complicated," he said ruefully.

"It always comes to this," he said. "Everyone gets so hung up on what's real and not real."

"Yeah," Lucy said. "People are funny that way."

But George Orson only shook his head, as if she didn't get it.

"This may sound unbelievable to you," he said, "but the truth is, a part of me truly did grow up there. There isn't just *one* version of the past, you know. Maybe that seems crazy, but eventually, after we've done this for a while, I think you'll see. We can be anybody we want. Do you realize that?

"And that's all it comes down to," he said. "I loved being George Orson. I put a lot of thought and energy into it, and it wasn't *fake*. I wasn't trying to fool you. I did it because I liked it. Because it made me happy."

And Lucy let out a small, uncertain breath, thinking: a host of thoughts.

"Why would you want to be a high school teacher?" she said at last. It was the only thing that came to her clearly, the only one of the thoughts that could be articulated. "That doesn't sound fun at all."

"No, no," George Orson said, and he smiled at her hopefully, as if this were the exact right question—as if they were back in the classroom, discussing the difference between existentialism and nihilism—as if she'd raised her hand and she was his beloved student and he was excited to explain.

"It was one of the best things I've ever done," he said. "That year in Pompey. I always wanted to be a teacher, ever since I was a kid. And it was great. It was a fantastic experience."

He shook his head, as if he were still entranced by it. As if high school had been some exotic foreign land.

"And," he said, "I met you. I met you, and we fell in love, didn't we? Don't you understand, honey? You're the only person in the world I've ever been able to talk to. You're the only person in the world who loves me."

Had they fallen in love? She guessed they had, though now it felt like a weird idea, since it turned out that "George Orson" wasn't even a real person.

Thinking about it made her feel dizzy and squeamish. If you took away all of the pieces that made up George Orson—his Lighthouse Motel childhood and his Ivy League education, his funny anecdotes and subtly ironic teaching style and the tender, attentive concern he'd had for Lucy as his student—if all of that was just an invention, what was left? There was, presumably, someone inside the George Orson disguise, a personality, a pair of eyes peering out: a soul, she supposed you might call it, though she still didn't know the soul's real name.

Which one did she have feelings for—the character of George Orson, or the person who had created him? Which one had she been having sex with?

It was a bit like one of those word games George Orson had been so fond of offering up to their class—"Strange loops," he called them. *Moderation in all things, including moderation,* he said. *Is the answer to this question no? I never tell the truth.*

She could picture the way he had grinned when he said that. This was before she ever had an idea that she would become his girlfriend, long before she could have imagined that she would be driving to a post office in Nebraska with a fake birth certificate and reservations for a trip to Africa. "I never tell the truth," he told the class, was a version of the famous Epimenides paradox, and then he explained what a paradox was, and Lucy had written it down, thinking that it might be on a test, possibly she could get extra credit.

They had come now almost to the edge of Crawford, and George Orson—David Fremden—pulled over to consult the map he had downloaded from the Internet.

They had parked in front of a historical marker, and after he was finished examining his papers, George Orson sat there for a while, regarding the sign's metal tablet with interest.

Named for Army Captain Emmet Crawford, a Fort Robinson soldier, the city lies in the White River Valley in Pine Ridge country and serves an extensive cattle ranching and farming area. The Fort Laramie–Fort Pierre Fur Trail of 1840 and the Sidney–Black Hills Trail active during the Black Hills gold rush of the 1870s both passed through this site. Crawford has been host or home to such personages as Sioux Chief Red Cloud; former desperado David (Doc) Middleton; poet-scout John Wallace Crawford; frontierswoman Calamity Jane; Army scout Baptiste (Little Bat) Garnier, shot down in a saloon; military surgeon Walter Reed, conqueror of yellow fever; and President Theodore Roosevelt.

It was a sad piece of work, she thought.

Or at least she found it sad, at this juncture in her life. What had George Orson told their class once? "People like to contextualize themselves," he told them. "They like to feel they are connected to the larger forces of the world in some small way." And she recalled how he had tilted his head, as if to say: *Isn't that pathetic?*

"People like to think that what they do actually matters," he'd said, dreamy, bemused, passing his gaze over their faces, and she remembered how his eyes rested in particular upon her, and she'd straightened in her chair, a little flattered, a little flustered. And she'd gazed back at him and nodded.

Thinking of this, Lucy put her hand to her throat, which continued to have that constricted feeling, that anxiety attack feeling.

People like to think that what they do actually matters.

It had occurred to her that, in fact, her own proof of identity— Lucy Lattimore's birth certificate and social security card and so forth—were back in Pompey, Ohio, still in a plastic Ziploc bag in the top drawer of her mother's bureau, along with the ink prints of Lucy's baby feet, and her immunization history, and any other paperwork that her mother had deemed important.

She hadn't bothered to bring any of this stuff with her when she and George Orson had left town, and now, she realized, she probably had more documentation for Brooke Fremden than there was for her real self.

What would happen to Lucy Lattimore now, she wondered. If she no longer entered the public record, if she never held a job or applied for a driver's license or paid taxes or got married or had children, if she never died, would she still exist two hundred years from now, free-floating and unresolved in some record bank in some government dead-letter office computer? At some point, would they decide to expunge her from the official roster?

What if she could call someone? What if she could talk to her parents, for one last time, and tell them that she was alone and broke and about to fly to Africa under an assumed name? What advice would they give her? What would she even ask?

Mom, I'm thinking about not existing anymore, and I was just calling to ask your opinion.

The thought was almost enough to make her laugh, and David Fremden looked over to her as if he had noticed movement. Attentive and dad-like.

"In any case," he said. "I suppose we should get going."

Jay Kozelek was standing on the curb outside Denver International when a black Lexus cruised up alongside him and came to a stop. He watched as the tinted window on the driver's side slid down with a faint pneumatic hiss, and a thin, dapper blond dude peered out at him. A young guy, about twenty-four or twenty-five. Preppy: was that the right term?

"Mr. Kozelek, I presume?" this person said, and Jay stood there blinking.

Jay didn't know what he had been expecting, but it certainly wasn't this—this slick-looking character with his designer horn-rim glasses and his natty sports coat and turtleneck and his movie-star teeth. Meanwhile, here was Jay with his old hiker's backpack and army surplus jacket, wearing sweatpants, his hair pulled back and rubber-banded. Not washed in a while.

"Uh," he said, and the guy grinned, pleased with himself, as if he'd pulled off a good practical joke. Which, Jay guessed, he had—and so he tried out a sheepish smile, though he actually felt vaguely nervous. "Hey, Mike," he said, very mellow. "Where we headed? Out to your yacht?"

Mike Hayden regarded him. No reaction.

"Get in," Mike said, and there was a click as the rear door unlocked, and Jay balked just for a second before he climbed into the backseat, pulling his raggedy backpack behind him.

Was this a trap, maybe?

It was a brand-new car, with that leathery sweet chemical smell, spotless, and as Jay adjusted his knees, Mike Hayden turned around and offered his hand. "A pleasure," he said.

"Likewise," Jay said, and when he took Mike Hayden's hand, it was cool and dry. He was apparently not going to be asked to sit in the front seat, which was heaped with papers and a crumpled fast-food bag and a closed laptop and a smattering of cell phones—five of them, clustered in the debris like eggs in a nest.

Their eyes met, and though he didn't know what Mike Hayden's lingering look was meant to convey, there was this expectation in it, and he sat back in his seat as if he had been given a warning.

"It's wonderful to finally meet you in person, Jay," Mike Hayden said. "I'm so pleased that you decided to come."

"Yeah," Jay said, and then sat back as the car accelerated smoothly away from the curb, picking up speed as they slid in and out of the traffic that was nosing its way toward the airport exit, as they pulled onto the interstate and the rain clouds towered above them in the wide sky.

Jay and Mike Hayden had first met in an online chat room, one of those hidden, private spaces where hackers and trolls tended to gather, and they had hit it off right away.

This was back when Jay was living in a house in Atlanta with a bunch of computer nerds who thought of themselves as revolutionaries. The Association, they called themselves, which Jay tried to point out was the name of a horrible band from the 1960s. "You know those stupid songs. Like 'Windy.' Like 'Cherish.' " And he sang a line or two, but they just looked at him skeptically.

And so he was beginning to realize that he was a little too old to be living with them. They had some good ideas about moneymaking schemes, but they were just kids, very juvenile a lot of the time, sitting around watching bad horror movies or arguing about pop-culture crap, pop music and TV and comic books and various websites and memes that the housemates briefly became excited about. They were too stoned and lazy to manage much follow-through, but for Jay it was different. He was thirty years old! He had an actual child out there somewhere, even if the child didn't know that he was its dad. A son, fifteen years of age. Ryan. He figured it was about time to get into more serious business.

"I know what you mean," Mike Hayden had said, as they typed to each other in the chat room. "I'm interested in serious business as well."

At the time, Jay didn't know that the guy's name was Mike Hayden. The guy went by the user name "Breez," and he was well-known among certain circles of the Internet community. All the hackers in Jay's house were in awe of him. It was said that he had been personally involved in a huge national blackout, that he had managed to shut down power grids all across the Northeast and Midwest; it was said that he had stolen millions of dollars from several major banking firms, and that he had engineered the conviction of a Yale University professor on charges of trafficking in pedophilic photos.

"I wouldn't fuck around with that guy if I were you," said Dylan—one of Jay's housemates, a plump, bearded twenty-one-year-old kid from Colorado, with a face the shape of a yam. "That dude is, like, the Destroyer, man," Dylan said earnestly. "He'll trash your life just for the fun of it."

"Hmm," said Jay. It was an odd thing for Dylan to say, he thought, since Dylan and his buddies spent a good portion of their time playing mean, stupid practical jokes on the Internet—posting bestiality porn videos on some lady's bichon frise website, The Wonderful Fluffy World, and uploading graphic accident photos to message boards meant for children; terrorizing some poor girl who maintained a tribute site for a dead pop star they all loathed, sending hundreds of delivery pizzas to her house and getting her power turned off; hacking into the website for the National Epilepsy Foundation with a strobe-like animation they'd decided might send the epileptics into seizures. They sat around doing imitations of convulsions, and chortling wildly as Jay stood by watching with uneasy disapproval. It could get tiresome, he told Breez.

" 'Tiresome,' " said Breez. "That's a polite word for it."

It was about three in the morning, and Jay and Breez had been chatting companionably for a few hours. It was a nice change of pace, Jay thought, to talk to someone his own age, though also intimidating. Breez wrote in complete sentences, in paragraphs rather than long blocks of text, and he never misspelled words or used abbreviations or jargon.

"I do get a bit tired of all of these little trolls," Breez said. "All the antics and the middle school sense of humor. I'm beginning to think there should be a eugenics program for the Internet. Don't you think?"

Jay wasn't sure what the word 'eugenics' meant, and so he waited. Then he typed: "Yeah. Absolutely."

"It's nice to meet someone with some common sense," Breez said. "Most people just can't accept the truth. You know what I mean. Do they think we can just continue on like this, all this babble and bullshit, as if we're not on the edge of ruin? Do they not see it? The Arctic ice cap is melting. We've got dead zones in the oceans that are expanding astronomically. The bees are dying, and the frogs, and the supply of fresh water is drying up. The global food system is headed toward collapse. We're like Fibonacci's rabbits, right? One more generation—ten, fifteen more years, and we'll have reached the tipping point. Basic population-projection matrices. Right?"

"Right," Jay said, and then he watched the small, blinking heart-beat of the cursor.

"I'll tell you a secret, Jay," Breez said. "I believe in the ruin lifestyle. Straight-up anarchy is not that far away. Very soon, we're going to have to start making some difficult choices. There are too many of us, and I'm afraid that before long the question will have to be asked: how quickly can you eliminate three or four of the world's six billion people? Do you get rid of them in the most just and equitable way possible? That's the question humanity should start pondering."

Jay considered. *The ruin lifestyle?*

"There are certainly portions of the herd that deserve to be thinned, that's all I'm saying," Breez said. "Is there still room on earth for people like your loathsome nose-picking roommates? Would the world be better off without the type of people who become investment bankers? Can you think of a lower form of life? These people are supposedly so smart and talented. They go to Princeton, or Harvard, or Yale, and then they become 'investment bankers'? Can you think of a more repulsive waste?"

And Jay didn't say anything. Was the guy kidding? Was he a nut-case?

But still, he was impressed by the things Dylan had told him. "That dude is the Destroyer," Dylan said. "He's stolen probably fucking millions of dollars—" And Jay could feel these thoughts slowly tilting and turning slow Ferris wheels in his head. He was pretty stoned.

And, actually, he had to wonder—a guy like this, did he know things that Jay didn't know? Was he simply paying more attention, while most of the rest of the world was just cruising along, not thinking things through to their logical conclusion?

The ruin lifestyle.

"I'm not sure what to say," Jay responded at last. "There's a lot of things I haven't thought about too deeply, either, to tell the truth." He paused. "It sounds like you're a lot smarter than I am," Jay said.

It was a kiss-ass move, no doubt, but he was curious. What did this guy have besides talk?

"Why don't you call me on my cell?" Breez typed. "I have terrible insomnia. Nightmares. I like the sound of a human voice, every once in a while."

And that was how they had become friends.

That was how he learned that the famed "Breez" was actually a guy named Mike Hayden, an ordinary person who had grown up in the suburbs of Cleveland, and—whatever else he had accomplished, however rich and infamous he was—he still felt lonely. He was looking for someone he could trust, he said. "Which is not so easy to find, in our business," he said.

"No doubt," Jay said, and he chuckled moodily. He and his roommates were living in a bungalow in the Westview neighborhood, southwest Atlanta, and he had to admit, he said, that he was thinking about moving on. They had been involved in mostly amateur crap, he said—sitting in the parking lot outside BJ's Wholesale Club or Macy's or OfficeMax, searching for holes in the wireless networks of the stores, collecting credit and debit card numbers as they were entered into the registers. It didn't seem to be going anywhere.

"It's actually not a bad idea," Mike Hayden said. "I know a guy in Latvia who has a computer where you could store the data—and he knows a guy in China who can imprint blank cards with the numbers. People are doing it. You can get a pretty decent harvest from it, if you're smart and aggressive about it."

"Yeah, well," Jay said, "smart and aggressive is not the name of the game around here. I don't think any of these kids know what they're doing."

And Mike Hayden was thoughtful. "Hmm," he said.

"Yeah," Jay said.

"So what are you going to do about it?" Mike Hayden said. "Are you just going to sit there?"

"I don't know," said Jay.

"If I had access to all of those numbers that you collected," Mike said, "I could really do something with them. That's all I'm saying. We could work together."

"Hmm," Jay said. It was dark in the house, though through one of the doorways Jay could see Dylan, his face lit by computer light, his fingers moving over the keyboard, and Jay lowered his voice, cupping his hand over the mouthpiece of the cell phone he was talking into.

"I have to tell you the truth," Jay said. "I'm in a different situation from these guys. I need to start thinking about the future, if you know what I mean. I'm thirty years old. I've got a kid out there somewhere—a kid, fifteen years old, can you believe it? I'm not in the daydream age of youth anymore, frankly."

This revelation had given Mike Hayden pause.

"Why, Jay," he said at last, "I didn't know you had a child! That's so awesome."

"Yeah," Jay said, and he shifted. "A son. But it's complicated. I gave him up, like, for adoption, in a way. To my sister. He doesn't know that I. That I'm his dad."

"Wow," Mike Hayden said. "That must be intense."

"His name is Ryan," said Jay—and it was nice, actually, to tell someone this, he felt a warm, paternal glow briefly opening up. "He's a teenager. Can you believe that? It seems unbelievable to me."

"That's so cool," Mike Hayden said. "It must be such a great feeling—to have an actual son!"

"I guess," Jay said. "It's not like he knows or anything. It's more like this awful secret thing between me and my sister. Most of the time it doesn't even feel real to me, to be honest. Like it's an alternate universe or something."

"Hmm," said Mike Hayden. "You know what, Jay? I like the way you think. I'd enjoy meeting you. Do you want me to get you a plane ticket?"

Jay didn't say anything. In the living room, he could hear the roommates cackling about some new joke they'd recently come up with, a prank to do with doctored photos of a female celebrity. They hadn't made money in weeks.

Meanwhile, Mike Hayden was still talking about Ryan. "Geez, I wish I had a son!" he was saying. "That would make me so happy. All I've got left is my twin brother, and he's been so disappointing lately."

"That's too bad," Jay said, and he shrugged his shoulders, though he realized that Mike Hayden couldn't see such a gesture through the phone. "I suppose you have to work on these kinds of relationships, right? You can't take anything for granted."

"True," Mike Hayden said. "Very true."

And now here Jay was. A week later, and he and Mike Hayden drove east from Denver, he and Breez, he and the Destroyer, traveling through Colorado, and Jay was basically prepared to betray his former roommates.

He didn't feel that bad about it. They were truly assholes, he thought, though he couldn't help but feel nervous as the sky darkened over Interstate 76, and they passed through the thick plumes of steam that billowed out of the sugar beet factory just beyond Fort Morgan, and a flock of grackles lifted up out of the field, a long, streaming formation. It was as if the world had conspired to seem ominous.

He shifted, picked up his backpack, and moved it a little to the right. It was awkward to be in the backseat, like Mike Hayden was a taxi driver or a chauffeur, though Mike himself acted perfectly at ease with the situation.

"So how's your son doing?" Mike Hayden said, and when Jay looked up, he could see Mike's eyes in the rearview mirror.

He shrugged. "Fine," Jay said. "I guess."

It was awkward. Though at the same time, there wasn't anyone else in the world he'd ever talked to about this stuff.

"I don't know," he said at last. "We— Actually, to be honest, Mike, I've never actually spoken with the kid. You know, after my sister adopted him . . . I had some problems. I was in jail for a short while. And my sister, Stacey. We had a falling out, a lot of it having to do with—her not wanting him to know. She didn't see the point in getting him confused, which I understand, I guess, although— it's a difficult thing to get my mind around."

"So—he's actually never met you?" Mike Hayden said.

"Not exactly," Jay said. "My sister and I haven't spoken since he was about one year old. I doubt if he's even seen a picture of me, except of when I was a kid. My sister has been a real hard-ass about this stuff. When she cuts you off, she cuts you off, and that's it. I did try calling her once. You know, I was curious. I just thought I could say 'hi' to the kid, but she wasn't having any of it. As far as the kid is concerned, I barely exist."

"Wow," Mike Hayden said, and again Jay saw the eye, reflected in the rearview mirror, glancing back at him. A surprisingly sad, com- passionate eye, Jay thought, though also unnerving. "Wow," Mike said. "That's an incredible story."

"I guess so," Jay said.

"Tragic."

"I don't know about that," Jay said, and he shrugged. To tell the truth, he didn't know how to feel, exactly—here in the lush, ex- pensive chamber of the Lexus; here with this unexpected Mike Hayden, with his sports coat and trimmed fingernails and formal manner, asking him about all this private stuff.

When they had started talking together on the phone, they'd had some very long, personal conversations—not just about busi- ness ideas, but also about their lives. He had learned about Mike's childhood, the father who was a hypnotherapist, who had commit- ted suicide when Mike was thirteen; the abusive stepfather; the twin brother who had been everybody's favorite, who could do no wrong, while Mike was basically invisible.

"I was very close to my dad, and after he was gone, I just felt like a stranger in my own family," Mike told him. "It seemed like they would have been happier without me, and so I left. I never saw them again, and I guess I probably never will."

"I know what you mean," Jay said. "That was what it was like in my family, too. Stacey was ten years older than me, and she was, like, this star student. They were so proud that she became a CPA. A fucking accountant! And I was supposed to be, like, 'Oooooh: worship. So impressive.' "

Mike Hayden found this hilarious. "Ooooh, worship! So impressive!" he repeated, imitating Jay's tone of voice. "Dude, you slay me."

It was Mike Hayden's opinion that Jay should contact his son. That Ryan should be told the truth about his adoption, and all the rest.

"I think he deserves to know the truth," Mike Hayden had said. "That is not a cool situation with that sister of yours. She's controlling, don't you think? And think of poor Ryan! If the people that you think you love are hiding something that important, it's a major betrayal. That's one of those things that screws up the karma of the entire world."

"I don't know," Jay said. "He's probably better off."

But in some ways Jay had taken this advice to heart. Jay was actually thinking a lot about this situation, ever since he turned thirty, and Mike Hayden's friendship and counsel had been important to him.

But at the same time, it felt funny to be talking about it now, with this—stranger. With this young, fussy-looking Mike Hayden. It was always the problem with virtual relationships, Internet friendships, whatever you wanted to call them. There was always a shock, in which you realized that the person you had been building in your mind—the simulacrum, the avatar—didn't resemble the actual flesh and blood in the slightest.

He wondered if it had been such a good idea to leave Atlanta. Perhaps, he thought, he shouldn't have been so forthcoming about the schemes the Association was involved in; perhaps he shouldn't have ever mentioned his son—and he felt a pinprick of unease, imagining the boy, his son, sitting peaceful and unaware back at Stacey's house, "doing so well," Stacey had written, back when Jay was in jail that first time, back when Ryan was just a toddler. "You've done a good thing for him, Jay. Don't you forget that."

And now Mike Hayden—Breez—knew about him. He remembered again what Dylan had said about Breez: *He'll trash your life just for the fun of it.*

He wiped his damp palms on his pant legs, then combed his fingers through his hair as they passed from Colorado into western Nebraska. They were listening to some awful, repetitive classical music, dreadful stuff that sounded like scales being played over and over on a piano.

It was coming on dusk when they pulled into the motel. The Lighthouse Motel, it said, but the neon wasn't lit, and it looked abandoned.

"Home at last!" Mike Hayden said, and he moved the gear stick into park with a flourish. He turned to look over his shoulder, grinning as Jay looked up from his mumbling backseat thoughts.

"This is my place," Mike Hayden said. "I own it."

"Oh," Jay said, and he peered out. It was just an old courtyard motel, with a big replica of a lighthouse at the entrance, a cement cone painted in red and white stripes like a barber pole. "Huh," he said, and tried to nod appreciatively. "Cool."

They walked, Jay and Mike, up the path that led from the motel to the old house on the hill, not saying anything. It was drizzling, late October, and it didn't seem to know whether it planned to rain or snow. The wind pitched the dry high weeds back and forth.

The house that stood above the motel was one of those places you would see in Halloween illustrations, the classic "haunted mansion" sort of deal, Jay thought, though Mike acted as if it were an architectural wonder.

"Doesn't it blow your mind?" he said. "It's called Queen Anne style. Asymmetrical façade. Cantilevered gables. And the turret! Don't you love the turret?"

"Sure," Jay said, and Mike Hayden leaned toward him.

"I managed some extremely interesting things with this estate," Mike said. "The former owner actually died three years ago, but her social security number is still in play. As far as the official record goes, she's still alive."

"Oh, okay," Jay said. "That's cool."

"Wait—it gets better," Mike said. "Because as it turns out, she had two sons. Both of whom died young, but I think they are resurrectable. The best thing is, if they were alive, they would be just about our age! George. And Brandon. They both drowned—when they were teenagers. They were out swimming in the lake, and Brandon was trying to save George. I guess it didn't work out."

Mike Hayden let out a stiff laugh, as if there were something bitterly funny about this fact that Jay didn't quite understand.

"Listen," Mike said. "How do you feel about becoming brothers?"

"Um," Jay said. He glanced at the place that Mike's hand was resting: the ball of his shoulder, and he didn't tighten or flinch. It was one of the advantages that he'd learned from his year in Vegas: a decent poker face.

He was being offered an opportunity. He had dead-ended in Atlanta, and here was a chance to move on.

Did it matter that he himself had been played a little bit? Did it matter that, for a short time, he had actually felt closer to Mike Hayden—Breez—than was probably wise? Did it matter that he'd revealed personal information, did it matter that this guy, whatever his name was, now knew personal details about his life? About his son. His secrets.

Yes, of course it mattered, dumb shit. He had been a fool, and

Mike Hayden—or whoever—was smiling gently. As if Jay were a puppy in a glass case at a pet store.

"One of the things I can show you," Mike Hayden said. "There are some phenomenal things you can do with dead people. Do you have any idea how many unclaimed estates there are in this country? It's like Risk or Monopoly or whatever. You can just land on a property, and basically it's yours, if you know what you're doing."

Mike laughed, and Jay laughed a little, too, though he wasn't exactly sure what was funny. They had come to the porch of the old haunted house, and Jay watched as Mike Hayden withdrew a key ring from his pocket, a thick, jingling wind chime of keys. How many? Twenty? Forty?

But he had no difficulty finding the right one. He inserted a key into the keyhole just below the doorknob and then made another flourish with his hands, like a stage magician: abracadabra.

"Just wait until you see the interior," Mike Hayden said. "There's a library. With an actual wall safe behind a painting! Doesn't that kill you?"

And then Mike Hayden stiffened—as if he were suddenly embarrassed by this burst of goofy enthusiasm, as if he thought Jay might make fun of it.

"I'm so glad that we're going to be working together," he said. "I've always missed having a true brother, you know? When you're born a twin, there's always this part of you that wants that other person in your life. That other—soul mate. Does that make any sense?"

He opened the door and an odd, musty scent poured out. Jay could see, just beyond the foyer, beyond an expanse of faded oriental carpet, some furniture that was covered in sheets, and a large staircase with a coiling banister.

"I've taken care of your associates back in Atlanta for you, by the way," said Mike Hayden. "I suspect that the Feds have already begun to round the little buggers up, so—we're free of that interference, at least."

And with that, he and Jay stepped into the house.

PART THREE

✦⟩⟨✦

First say to yourself what you would be; and then do what
you have to do.

—EPICTETUS

In the photograph, the young man and the girl are sitting on a sofa together. Both of them have gift-wrapped packages in their laps, and they are holding hands. The young man is blond and slender and pleasantly at ease. He is looking at the girl, and you can see in his expression that he is making some gently teasing joke, and the girl is just beginning to laugh. She has auburn hair and mournful eyes, but she is looking at him now with open affection. It's obvious that they are in love.

Miles sat there, staring at the picture, and he wasn't sure what to say.

It was Hayden, all right.

It was his brother, though you wouldn't have ever believed that he and Miles were twins. It was as if this Hayden had been raised from birth in a different life, as if their father had never died, as if their mother had never grown angry and distant and desperate with him, as if Hayden had never lain ranting in an attic room, his hands cuffed to the bed with cloth ties, calling out, his hoarse, hysterical voice through the closed door, muffled but insistent: "Miles! Help me! Miles, cover my neck. Please, please, someone has to cover my neck!"

As if through all that time, some other, normal Hayden were growing up, going to college, falling in love with Rachel Barrie. Slipping into the world of ordinary happiness—the life, Miles thought, they both should have been granted, good suburban middle-class boys that they were.

"Yes," Miles said. He swallowed. "Yes. That's my brother."

They were sitting in Lydia Barrie's room in the Mackenzie Hotel, in Inuvik, but for a moment it didn't feel like they were anywhere. This place, this town, the boxy, flimsy buildings with their corrugated sheet-metal siding, as impermanent as a hastily erected movie set; this room with the rim of steady, implausible sunlight glowing through the edges of the shades on the window—it all felt so much less real than the young people in the picture that it wouldn't have surprised him to learn that, in fact, it was he and Lydia who were nothing but figments.

He let the pad of his fingertip rest lightly on the glossy surface of the photo, as if he could touch his brother's face, and then he watched as Lydia reached down and gently lifted the photograph out of his hands.

"Listen," he said. "Is there a way I can get a copy of that picture? I'd very much like a copy."

There was no way to explain the sense of sadness that he felt, the sense that this photo she was tucking away was almost supernatural: a picture of what might have been. For himself. For Hayden. For their family.

But that wouldn't make sense to Lydia Barrie, he thought. To her, Hayden was merely a fake, a scam artist, an imposter in her family photo. She didn't realize that the person she had known as Miles Spady was a real possibility. An actual existence that might have been.

———

"I imagine that you're hoping to save him," Lydia Barrie said, and she gave Miles a long, searching look he didn't quite understand.

She'd had a lot to drink that night, but she didn't act drunk, exactly. She wasn't stumbling or anything, though her movements seemed more premeditated, as if she had to deliberate before she executed them. Still, there was something very precise about the way she carried herself. She was a lawyer, with a lawyerly sort of grace—a flourish in her wrist when she filed the folder back in its place in her leather portfolio, a sharply choreographed *click* as she opened the matching attaché, an elegant *swiff* of paper as she laid her documents down on the bed between them. You could see that she was drunk only when you looked in her eyes, which had a damp unfocused intensity.

"You think if only you can find him, you can somehow convince him to—what?" She paused, long enough so they could both note how illogical he was.

"What exactly are you thinking, Miles?" she said mildly. "Do you think you can talk him into giving himself up to the authorities? Or perhaps you can talk him into coming back to the U.S. with you, and get some therapy or something? Do you think it's possible that he'll voluntarily allow himself to be committed to an institution?"

"I don't know," Miles said.

It was unnerving to be so transparent. He wasn't sure how she had so accurately articulated his own line of thinking, the doubtful ideas he'd entertained over the years, but hearing them spoken aloud made him aware of how lame and flimsy they sounded.

He didn't exactly have a plan, to tell the truth. He had always thought that when—if—he finally caught up to Hayden, he would have to improvise.

"I don't know," he said again, and Lydia Barrie fixed him with her bright, slurry gaze. Even drunk as she was, he could tell that she had been a terrific prosecutor—deadly, no doubt, during cross-examination.

He looked down with an abashed, rueful smile. He'd had a bit to drink himself, and perhaps that was why it was so easy for her to read him. But, he thought, it was also true that he was not particularly cagey. That had always been his problem—even from the womb, some amniotic chemical must have been washing over him, he had been primed from birth to be the credulous one, the mild twin, easily manipulated.

"He's not who you think he is, Miles," she said. "You know that, don't you?"

She had already told him her various theories concerning Hayden.

Some of them, he basically agreed with.

He knew, without question, that Hayden was a thief, that he had defrauded numerous individuals and corporations, that he had focused particularly on several investment banking firms, from which he had possibly stolen millions of dollars.

Miles doubted that such a large sum was actually involved.

As for Lydia Barrie's other accusations, he wasn't so sure. Was Hayden involved in setting loose various Internet worms—including one that had shut down Diebold Corporation's computers for more than forty-five minutes? Had Hayden hijacked the cell phone of a hotel heiress and for a brief time convinced her father she'd been kidnapped? Had Hayden ruined the career of a Yale University political science professor by planting pedophilic photographs onto his computer? Was he a supporter of and financial contributor to terrorist organizations, including one environmental group that advocated the spread of biological weapons as a means of slowing overpopulation?

Had Hayden orchestrated the suspicions of embezzlement that had forced Lydia Barrie to leave the law firm of Oglesby and Rosenberg under a cloud of unverified accusations, which had marred and perhaps ruined her career?

It was far-fetched, Miles thought, to suggest that Hayden was involved in all of this. So many different things.

"You make him sound like some kind of supervillain," Miles said, and he let out a small chuckle, to show her how silly it sounded. But she merely raised one eyebrow, expectantly.

"My sister has been missing for three years," she said. "That's not a comic book story, for me. I take it very seriously."

And Miles found himself blushing. Flustered. "Well," he said. "I understand. I didn't mean to—belittle—your situation."

He looked down at his hands, down at the meticulous stacks of papers she had arranged for him to examine, staring at the head-line of a newspaper article she had photocopied: "U.S. Prosecutors Indict 11 in Massive Identity Fraud Case," he read. What to say?

"I'm not trying to make excuses for him," Miles said. "I'm just saying—it strains credulity, you know? He's only one person. And he's actually— I grew up with him, and he's actually not that much of a genius. I mean, if he's done all the stuff you think he's done, wouldn't someone have caught him already?"

Lydia Barrie tilted her head, and once he met her gaze, she didn't break eye contact. "Miles," she said, "you haven't looked at all the information I've got here yet, have you? We—you and I— might be in a unique position to bring your brother to justice. To try to help him, cure him if you will. To hold him accountable for his actions. He may not be a 'supervillain,' as you put it, but I think we can both agree that he's a danger to himself. And to other peo-ple. We can agree on that point, can't we, Miles?"

"I don't think he's evil," Miles said. "He's—troubled, you know? I honestly think a lot of this is just like a game. We used to do all these kinds of games when we were kids, and in a lot of ways it's still the same thing. It's, like, role-playing for him. Do you see what I'm saying?"

"I do," Lydia Barrie said, and she leaned forward, and her ex-pression looked almost sad, almost sympathetic. "You're a very sen-timental person," she said, and then she smiled, very briefly and mildly, and rested the cool, smooth palm of her hand against his wrist. "And very loyal. I admire that enormously."

He was aware that there was a possibility that she was going to kiss him.

He wasn't sure what he thought about it, but he could sense that odd, heavy feeling in the air, like a barometric drop before a thunderstorm descended. She didn't understand what he was trying to tell her, he thought. She wasn't exactly his ally, he thought, but nevertheless he felt his eyes closing as she leaned toward him. That uncanny sunlight was still glowing around the edges of the window shade as her hand slid up his forearm to his biceps, and okay, yes, their lips were touching.

When Miles woke up in the morning, Lydia Barrie was still asleep, and he lay there for a time with his eyes open, staring at the red numbers on the old digital alarm clock at the bedside. At last, he began to discreetly grope around under the blankets for his underwear, and once he found them, he carefully put his feet into the leg holes and pulled them up over his thighs. Lydia Barrie did not stir as he padded his way toward the bathroom.

Well. This was unexpected.

And he couldn't help but feel a tiny bit pleased with himself. A bit—uplifted. He was not used to this: falling into bed with women, even very drunk women, was not a usual occurrence. He looked at himself critically in the bathroom mirror. He was not double-chinned, but he almost was, unless he kept his jaw lifted. And he was fat enough in the middle that he had man boobs and a round toddler-like gut. How embarrassing! There was a miniature traveler's bottle of mouthwash on the ledge of the sink, and he poured a finger of it into a glass and swished it around in his mouth.

She was deeply crazy, he supposed. Probably that was why she slept with him. He examined his face, and wiped a hand across his unruly hair and combed his fingers through the tight, curly tangles of his beard.

She was as obsessed as he was, if not more so—more conspiracy-minded, more focused in her methods, better organized, more *professional*. It was likely, he thought, that she would find Hayden before he did.

He ran some water into the basin of the sink and patted it onto his cheeks.

And she *was* very attractive. Quite out of his league in a lot of ways, he supposed. He thought again of that photo she had shown him, the picture of Hayden and Rachel Barrie, that hollow sensation in the pit of his stomach as he looked at their happy faces, an old hurt rising up from childhood.

Why couldn't it have been me? he wondered. *Why couldn't a pretty girl fall in love with me? Why does Hayden always get everything?*

When he came out of the bathroom, Lydia Barrie was already up, already partially dressed, and she turned to look at him, wistfully.

"Good morning," she said. She was wearing a bra and a slip, and her formerly coifed hair was tousled into a tangle, like one of the witch wigs they sold back at the magic store in Cleveland. Her makeup was almost completely smudged off, and her eyes were haggard, hungover. You could tell for certain she was getting ready to enter her forties, though he didn't find that fact unappealing. In her rumpled, unpolished state, there was a vulnerability he found himself feeling tenderly toward.

"Hey," he said sheepishly, and he smiled as she put a hand shyly to her hair.

And then he saw the gun.

It was a small revolver of some sort, and she was holding it loosely in her left hand as she smoothed her right hand over her hair, and he watched as she made an attempt to unobtrusively tuck the weapon into her attaché. For a second, she acted as if she hoped he hadn't noticed.

"Holy shit," Miles said.

He took a step back.

Actually, he guessed that he had never seen a gun in real life, though he had probably viewed hundreds of people with guns on television and in movies and video games. He had watched many people get killed; he knew what it was supposed to look like: the small circular hole in the chest or the belly, the blood spreading out in a Rorschach across the shirt.

"Jesus," he said. "Lydia."

Her expression wavered. At first, she seemed to hope that she could play innocent—she widened her eyes, as if she were preparing to say: *What? What are you talking about?* And then she appeared to realize that such a tactic was fruitless, and a cool, defiant look crossed her face before, at last, she shrugged. She smiled at him ruefully.

"What?" she said.

"You have a gun," he said. "Why do you have a gun?"

He was standing there in his underwear, still a bit groggy, still a bit dazzled by the fact that he'd had sex for the first time in two years, still circling through the conversations they'd had the night before, and the picture of Hayden and Rachel, and the sadness he'd felt. Lydia Barrie raised her eyebrows.

"You don't have any idea what it's like to be a woman," she said. "I know you don't think your brother is dangerous, but be realistic. Put yourself in my shoes. I need some security, Miles."

"Oh," Miles said. They stood there, facing each other, and Lydia laid the gun on the bed and held up her hands as if it were Miles who had the weapon.

"It's just a little mousegun," she said. "A little .25-caliber Beretta.

I've carried it for years," she said. "They're not particularly deadly, as guns go—I would call it more of a deterrent than anything else."

"I see," Miles said, though he wasn't quite sure he did. He was standing there in his boxer shorts with their ridiculous hot pepper print, and he crossed his hands uncertainly over his chest. A wobbly shudder ran through his bare legs, and he wondered, briefly, if he ought to make a dash for the door.

"Are you going to kill my brother?" he said at last, and Lydia widened her eyes at him as if astonished.

"Of course not," she said, and he stood there as she pulled her skirt on up over her thighs and zipped up the back, and then she gave him a pinched smile. "Miles," she said. "Dear heart, I asked you last night if you had a plan, and you told me that you more or less expected to improvise, once you located your brother. Well, I'm not going to improvise. When I was fired from Oglesby and Rosenberg, one of the first things I did in my 'free time' was acquire private investigator and bail enforcement agent licenses from the state of New York. Which was an enormous help, as I was looking for— Hayden." She slipped her arms decisively into the sleeves of her blouse. "And the first thing I did when I arrived in Canada was hire Mr. Joe Itigaituk, who is a licensed Canadian private investigator, so that when we take your brother into custody, I won't be interfering with the sovereignty of a foreign power."

Miles watched as Lydia fastened the buttons down the center of her blouse, from the neck to the belly, her fingers moving in a deft sign language as she talked.

He glanced at the door, which led to the hallway, and his leg shuddered again.

"I'm not a murderer, Miles," Lydia said, and they stood there, looking at each other, and her expression softened as she looked him up and down.

"Why don't you put your clothes on," she said. "Mr. Itigaituk and I are flying to Banks Island in a couple of hours, and I thought you'd like to come along with us. That way you can be absolutely sure that no one will hurt him. If you're there, he may come along with us peacefully."

It was Lydia's belief that Hayden was currently occupying an abandoned meteorological station located on the northern tip of Banks Island, not far from the limit of permanent ice.

"Though the limit of permanent ice is not as stable as it used to be," she said as they rode in the taxi. "Global warming and so forth."

Miles was reticent. He leaned his head against the window, peering out at the treeless streets, a row of brightly colored townhouses—turquoise, sunflower-yellow, cardinal-red—linked together like children's building blocks. The dirt along the roads was the color of charcoal, and the sky was cloudless, and he could see the melting tundra just beyond the line of houses and storage facilities. It was green out there, even spotted with wildflowers, though it seemed to him that the landscape wouldn't truly be itself until it was covered again in ice.

Lydia had not given him the full details of how she had traced Hayden to this particular spot, just as Miles had not fully explained his own, less rational methods—the intuition or presentiment or idiocy that sent him driving for days upon days, four thousand miles. But Lydia was fairly confident. "The fact that we're both here in Inuvik seems like a good sign, doesn't it? I feel very encouraged, actually. Don't you?"

"I guess so," Miles said, though now that the prospect of Hayden's capture was looming, he felt a sense of apprehension branching through him, taking root. He was thinking of the way Hayden had screamed when he was put in restraints at the mental hospital. It was one of the most awful things that Miles had ever heard—his brother, eighteen years old, a grown man, bellowing out these dreadful crowlike shrieks, his arms flapping as the orderlies descended on him. It was a few days after the new year, and it was snowing in Cleveland, and Miles and his mother stood there in their winter coats, dandelion fluff snowflakes melting in their hair as Hayden was pressed to the floor, his back arching, legs jerking as he tried to kick free, his eyes wide as he tried to bite. "Miles!" he was crying. "Miles, don't let them take me. They're hurting me, Miles. Save me, save me—"

Which Miles had not.

"You're quiet," Lydia Barrie said, and she reached over and brushed his forearm, as if there were a crumb or a speck of dust. "Worried?"

"A little," he said. "I'm just thinking about how he's going to react. I don't know, it's just—I don't want him to get hurt."

Lydia Barrie sighed. "You're a sweet person," she said. "You have a kind heart, and that's a wonderful quality to have. But you know what, Miles? He's running out of options."

Miles nodded, and looked down to where Lydia had lightly pressed the pads of her fingertips against the back of his hand, just below his wrist.

"He's found himself in a corner," Lydia said. "And I would venture to guess that there are some extremely bad people who are closing in on him. People much more dangerous than I am."

He had suspected as much himself, when he'd gotten that letter from Hayden. *I have been in deep hiding, very deep, but every day I thought about how much I missed you. It was only my fear for your own safety that kept me from contact. . . .*

"Yes," Miles said. "I think you're probably right."

He couldn't help but think again of that photo of Hayden and Rachel, together on the couch at Christmas. He hoped they were still together—that Rachel would be there in the meteorological station with him. He could imagine the moment, when he and Lydia opened the door and Hayden and Rachel stood there in the tiny shacklike room, haggard and startled, and probably thin. What, after all, had they been eating up there in that abandoned place? Fish? Canned goods? Had they been able to shower? Would they be wild-haired like hermits?

Undoubtedly they would panic at first. They would be expecting a looming thug or a swift, efficient assassin—

And then, they would see that it was just Miles. Just Miles and Lydia, a brother and a sister. And wouldn't they, after that first shudder of recognition, be grateful? It would be a reunion of sorts. He and Lydia had come to save them, and they would understand that there was nowhere else to run, that they had reached the end.

And at least it was someone they loved who had found them.

The taxi had arrived at the airfield, where Mr. Itigaituk was waiting for them. The taxi dropped them off, and Lydia paid the driver, and then she turned to wave as Mr. Itigaituk approached. He was a short mustachioed middle-aged Inuit man in a corduroy jacket, jeans, and cowboy boots, and to Miles he looked more like a high school math teacher than a private eye.

The man frowned when he saw Miles, but he didn't say anything. Miles watched as he and Lydia Barrie shook hands, and he stood a short distance away as they spoke together in low voices, as Mr. Itigaituk eyed Miles skeptically and then nodded, his dark eyes resting coolly on Miles's face.

The airfield was about fifteen kilometers outside of town, and he was aware again of the endless sunlight, the green, flat expanse of tundra rolling away from them in all directions, the glint of muddy bogs and melt ponds in the distance.

Just beyond, at rest on the tarmac, was the small six-seater Cessna that was waiting to take them to Banks Island, to Aulavik.

21

Ryan looked up and there was a figure standing in the doorway.

He was almost asleep, bent over his computer, his hands curled into position, his fingertips aligned on *asdf jkl;* and his chin had grown heavy until at last his neck drooped and elbows grew slack and his forehead began a slow descent toward the surface of the table.

It was a particular dream state. After a few beers, a few bong hits; after a long time traveling, crossing time zones—passing from pacific to mountain to central to eastern—after calming his drunk, possibly 'shrooming father who was stumbling around with a gun; after getting him into bed and gently sliding the gun out of his limp hand and putting it away and then sitting in front of the computer screen with his eyes closed.

Dutifully, he had made reservations for them both to fly to Quito, Ecuador, under the names Max Wimberley and Darren Loftus, and the confirmation was still there on the screen, a box floating on the surface of the monitor like a leaf in a pond, and Ryan was thinking, *I should go to bed. I can't believe how exhausted I am.* And he rolled his dry, sticky tongue inside his mouth and peeled open his eyelids.

He'd had dreams like this before.

A man was standing there, silhouetted behind the mesh of the screen door. He stood under the porch light, where moths were circling and bumping groggily against the surface of the ceiling, and there was a revolving shadow-lantern effect above the man's head. Ryan let his eyes close again.

He had been having these small hallucinations for a while now, imagining that he saw people he knew, these flickers that he knew were nothing but the detritus of exhaustion and stress and lingering guilty feelings, too much beer and pot, too much time alone with Jay, no one else to talk with; too much time sitting in front of a computer screen, which sometimes appeared to pulse with a rapid millisecond strobe, like those old subliminal advertising messages he'd read about.

It reminded him of this one time at Northwestern. He and Walcott had been partying all weekend and he was sitting at the window of his fourth-floor dorm room, smoking a joint. His arm was extended out into the open air to keep the smoke from stinking up the room, and he was trying to blow rings out into the foggy spring night, looking down at the empty sidewalk and the streetlamps that were made to look like old-fashioned gaslights, and there was no traffic, and suddenly someone reached up and touched his wrist.

He felt this very distinctly. It was impossible, he knew. His arm was extended four stories above the ground, but nevertheless someone reached up and clutched it for just a second. It was as if he were trailing his arm out of a boat instead of a fourth-floor window, as if his fingers were brushing the surface of a lake when a hand, a drowning person, had reached out of the water to grasp his wrist.

He'd let out a cry, and the joint had fallen out from between his fingers, and he saw the orange light of the lit end tumbling down through dark space as he yanked his hand back quickly into the room. "Holy shit!" he said, and Walcott had looked up from his laptop, regarding Ryan sleepily.

"Huh?" Walcott said, and Ryan just sat there, holding his wrist as if it had been burned. What could he say? *A ghostly hand just swam up four stories and tried to grab me. Someone tried to pull me out of the window.*

"Something bit me," he said at last, calmly. "I just dropped my joint."

All of this came back to him vividly—more like time travel than memory—and he gave his head a shake, the typical gesture of the daydreamer, as if you could rattle your brain back into place.

He squinched his eyes shut, thinking maybe this would wipe the blackboard clean, but when he opened them, the figure in the doorway had actually become more distinct.

The man had come closer. He was in the room now, stepping toward Ryan, a tall man in a black suit, the shiny cloth glinting.

"Is Jay home?" the man said, and Ryan's body jerked as he lifted up into full consciousness. "I'm a friend of Jay's," the man said. Real. Not a dream.

The man was holding a black plastic object, which looked at first like it might be an electric razor. Something that could be plugged into a computer? A communication device, like a cell phone or a receiver, with a pair of metal tongs extending from the end of it?

The man stepped forward quickly with the thing held out, as if offering it to Ryan, and Ryan actually reached out his hand for a second, right before the man pressed it up against his neck.

It was a Taser, Ryan realized.

He felt the electricity pass through him. He and his muscles contracted painfully, and he was aware of the spasms of his arms and legs flailing, his tongue hardening in his mouth, a thick strip of meat as he made a gurgling sound in his throat. His lips shook out spittle.

And then he was becoming unconscious.

It wasn't a hallucination. It wasn't anything except blankness, thick, fuzzy black spots that began to swell over his line of vision. Like mold spreading in a petri dish. Like the film cells of a movie melting.

And then: voices.

Jay—his father—nervous, sidling.

Then a calm reply. A voice from a relaxation tape?

I'm looking for Jay. Can you

help me out with that?

Ouch, Jay said, a little shrilly.

I don't know, I don't

Is the name Jay Kozelek familiar to you?

I . . .

Where is he?

. . . don't know

All I need is an address. We can make this very easy on you.

Honestly

Anything you might be able to tell me will be a big help right now.

Honest to God, I swear

I don't

Ryan's head lifted, but his neck felt like a limp stalk. He was sitting in a chair, and he could feel the pressure of the duct tape that held him—his forearms, his chest, his waist, his calves, his ankles—and when he tried experimentally to flex, he was aware that he was held fast. His eyes slit open and he could see that he and Jay were sitting at the kitchen table across from each other. He could see that a trickle of blood was running from Jay's hair, across his temple and his left eye and along the edge of his nose and into his mouth. Jay made a sound as if he were snuffling, as if he had a cold, and a few droplets of blood spattered out and speckled the tabletop.

"Look," Jay was saying to the man, humbly. "You know what this business is like. People are slippery. I hardly even know the guy," he said, very eager, very helpful, still trying to find a fingerhold on his old charming Jay self. "You probably know more about him than I do."

And the guy standing over him mused on this.

"Oh, really," the guy said, and he stood there looking down at Jay.

It was the guy who had shocked Ryan with the Taser, and for the first time Ryan got a good look at him. He was a big guy, late twenties, narrow shoulders and wide hips, about six foot one or two, and he was wearing a shiny black Italian suit that a mafioso might wear—though he didn't look much like a gangster. He had a boyish, Midwestern, potato-shaped head, a shock of straw-colored blond hair, and he reminded Ryan of no one so much as the graduate student who had been a TA in his computer science class back at Northwestern.

"You know what," the guy said, "I don't believe you."

He lifted his fist and clouted Jay in the face. Hard. Hard enough that Jay tilted back and more blood droplets flew out of his mouth, and Jay let out a high, surprised yelp.

"It's a mistake!" Jay said. "Listen, you've just got the wrong guy, that's all. I don't know what you want me to say. Tell me what you want me to say!"

Ryan was trying to keep himself as small and soundless as possible. He could hear movement—some general thumping and crashing in the next room, and through the doorway he could see men wearing black pants and shirts, two men, he thought, though possibly more, unplugging the hard drives from the rows of computers on the tables and tossing the monitors and keyboards and other extraneous hardware onto the floor, sometimes hitting things with long curved pieces of metal, crowbars, and one of them picked up Jay's Ouija board from the coffee table and looked at it curiously, front and back, as if it were some form of technology he'd never encountered before. Then he paused, maybe sensing that Ryan was looking at him, and Ryan quickly closed his eyes.

"I'm, like, thinking about torturing you," the Taser man said to Jay at last. He had a soft, reasonable, almost monotone voice, reminiscent of a DJ on a college radio station. "Listen to me. It's actually one of the fantasies that kept me going all these years. Thinking about torturing Jay Kozelek is one of the few things that made me happy all the time I was in prison, so don't fuck with me. I tracked him here. I know he's here somewhere. And if you don't tell me where Jay is, I'm going to torture you and your little buddy here until you puke blood. Okay?"

Ryan's lips parted, but nothing came out. No sound, not even a breath.

This was a situation Ryan had never thought too much about. In all the time he and Jay had been engaged in criminal activity, even when he was getting those IMs in Russian, even when he ran from those guys in Las Vegas, he had never pictured himself tied to a chair in a cabin in the deep woods of Michigan with a man who said *I've been thinking about torturing you.*

He was surprised at how useless his mind was. He had always imagined that in some desperate situation, his brain would sharpen—his thoughts would begin to race—his epinephrine would kick in—his instinct to survive would suddenly rise to the surface—but instead he felt a dull, pulsing blankness, a numb heartbeat, like the quick breath of some trapped rodent. He thought of a rabbit, a small animal in the wild, how it will sink into a motionless state as if it is pretending it is invisible. He thought of Jay's meditation tapes: *Picture a circle of energy near the base of your spine. This energy is strong. It connects you to the earth. . . .*

And sitting there, it was as if he was nothing but earth. A sack of dirt.

Meanwhile, the man had his hand in Jay's long hair, and as he was talking, he curled a lock of Jay's hair around each finger, a tangle that he pulled tighter even as his voice grew softer.

"I was in prison for three years," the man was saying. "*Prison.* You may not realize this, dude, but prison has a tendency to make you kind of mean. And you know what? Every single day of every single month, the one thing that made me happy was imagining ways that I could hurt your friend Jay. I thought about that a lot. Sometimes I would just close my eyes and I would ask myself: what should be done with Jay? I would think of his face, and what he would look like when he was tied to a chair, and I would think: What would be the worst thing? What would make him suffer the most?"

The man paused thoughtfully, with a fistful of Jay's hair entwined between his fingers, growing taut.

"And so you see," the man said, "The fact that I don't *have* Jay is really pissing me off."

By this point, Ryan had begun to find their conversation surreal, incomprehensible, but it was hard to focus on anything except the expression on his father's face, Jay's gritted teeth, his blank, trapped eyes.

Ryan guessed that the man had been planning to pull a hank of Jay's hair out by the roots, but this required more force than he initially expected. "Ow!" Jay screamed, but the hair remained stubbornly attached to his scalp, and after a brief struggle the man realized that it would require more leverage, or more muscle, than he wanted—or was able—to expend.

"God damn it," the man said, and instead he gave Jay's head a vigorous shaking, the way a dog might whip a rag with its teeth, and Jay's face jittered rapidly before the man gave up and loosed Jay's hair with a flourish.

He hadn't yanked the hair out, but it had hurt enough that Jay was now whimpering and cringing.

"I haven't seen him in years," Jay said. "I don't have any idea where he is, I swear."

Jay was crying a little, a faint childlike snuffling, a quivering of the shoulders, and this gave the man pause: torturing someone was more work than it had been in his fantasy.

"The last time I saw him, he was planning to go to Latvia. To Rēzekne," Jay said earnestly, and drew in a wet breath through his nose. "He's been out of the picture for a long time, a very long time."

But this wasn't what the man wanted to hear, and Ryan himself had no idea who they were talking about. Was there a different Jay?

"You didn't understand me, did you?" the man said. "You think you can just feed me another line of bullshit, don't you?" And he let out a stiff, theatrical chuckle. "But ve have vays of making you talk," he said, in an imitation of a German or Russian accent.

Ryan watched as the man felt in the pocket of his jacket, the way someone might grope for a lucky coin, and when he touched the object in his pocket, his eyes focused again, his resolve began to return, and his expression settled into a small, private smile.

From his pocket he withdrew a coil of thin silver wire, and he regarded it as if he were recalling some pleasant long-ago memory.

Jay didn't say anything. He just hung his head, and his long hair made a tent around his face, his shoulders rising and falling as he breathed. A droplet fell out of his nose and onto the front of his shirt.

But the man didn't notice. He had turned his attention away from Jay and now looked over at Ryan.

"So," he said. "Who do we have here?"

Ryan could feel the man's eyes fall on him. The brief sense of invisibility lifted away, and he watched as the man unwound the length of wire, a simple rubber handle at either end. The man tilted his head.

"What's your name, man?" the guy said. He gestured casually, stretching the wire out until it was taut, until it quivered like a guitar string.

"Ryan."

And the man nodded. "Good," he said. "You know how to answer a question."

And Ryan wasn't sure what to say to that. He was staring across the table, hoping that Jay would lift his head, that Jay would look at him, would give him a signal, some sense of what to do.

But Jay didn't look up, and the man bent his attention toward Ryan.

"You're Kasimir Czernewski, I guess?" the man said.

Ryan was staring down at the tabletop, on which water stains had spread into a map—a continent, surrounded by tiny islands.

He could feel his skin shuddering—the involuntary physical response he associated with being wet and cold, but this, this was actual fear, this was what being terrified felt like.

"We've been keeping an eye on you, too, you know," the man said. "I think you're going to be surprised to find how many of your bullshit bank accounts are not solvent anymore."

Ryan could hear the words the man was saying, he could process them, he knew what they meant—but at the same time they didn't feel like real sentences. They sunk into his consciousness like a weighted fishing line cast into a pond, and he felt the ripples circle out across his body.

What did he want from Jay right then? What does a son want from a father in such a situation?

To begin with, there is the fantasy of heroic action. The father who might give you a confident, reassuring wink—a little *chk, chk* at the edge of his mouth, and suddenly he breaks free of his bonds and produces a gun that was strapped to his ankle and the bullets enter the back of the torturer's head and he freezes midstep and falls face-forward and your dad gives you a shy grin as he rips the tape from his legs and swings around, gun aloft, aiming for the henchmen—

And then there is the father of steely determination. The father who shows you his gritted teeth: *Stay firm! We'll face this together! We'll be okay!*

Or the father of regret—eyes brimming with tenderness and sorrow, eyes that say: *I am with you. If you suffer, I will suffer tenfold. I send you all my love and my strength . . .*

And then there was Jay. Blood had been running out of his hair into his face, and tears had made pathways through some of the dried blood, and when their eyes met, they barely recognized each other.

For the first time in a long time Ryan thought of Owen. His other father. His former father—the father he had known all his life, who had raised him, the father who thought he was dead. At this very minute, Owen might be waking in Iowa to let the dog out, standing in the yard in his pajamas and watching as the dog sniffed and circled, looking out at the streetlights that were beginning to go dim as the sun came up, bending down to pick up the newspaper from the grass.

For a moment, Ryan was almost there. He might have been sitting like a bird in the old bur oak in front of the house, peering tenderly from above as Owen unwrapped *The Daily Nonpareil* to look at the headlines; as Owen snapped his fingers and whistled and the dog came running, pleased with herself; as Owen glanced up, as if he could sense Ryan somewhere above him, leaning down, a brush of air across the top of Owen's uncombed, sleepy head.

"Dad," Ryan said. "Dad, please, Dad."

And he saw Jay wince. Jay didn't look at him, he didn't lift his head, but a shudder ran through him, and the man in the suit straightened with interest.

"Oh my goodness," he said. "This is an unexpected development."

Ryan lowered his head.

"Ryan," the man said, "is this your father?"

"No," Ryan whispered.

He let his eyes fall back to the cloud-shaped water stain on the table. A continent, he thought again. An island, like Greenland, an imaginary country, and he let his eyes trace along the coastlines, the bays and archipelagos, and he could almost hear the voice of the meditation tape.

Imagine a place, the voice said. *Notice first the light. Is it bright, natural, or dim? Also notice the temperature level. Hot, warm, or cool? Be aware of the colors that surround you. Allow yourself to simply exist. . . .*

A hiding place, he thought, and for a second he could picture the tents that he used to construct when he was a little boy, the kitchen chairs draped with a big quilt, the dark space in the middle where he would pile pillows and stuffed animals, his own underground nest, which he pictured extending outward into soft, dim, winding corridors made of feathers and blankets.

"I'm going to start with the left hand," the man said. "And then the left foot. And then the right hand, and so on."

The man reached down and touched the freckled skin of Ryan's forearm, very lightly.

"We're going to put a tourniquet here," he murmured. "Which is going to be tight. But that way you won't bleed out quite so fast when I cut your hand off."

For some reason, Ryan was almost distracted. He was thinking of Owen. He was thinking of that ghostly hand that had risen up and grasped his wrist, back when he was a student in a dorm room. He was thinking of his cave under the bedspread.

The man said: "Above the wrist? Or below the wrist?"

And Ryan hardly knew what was being asked until he felt the

wire encircling just above his hand, just above the joint of his thumb. He was shaking so badly that the wire quivered, too, as the man tightened it.

"Please don't," Ryan whispered, but he wasn't sure whether any sound had come from his mouth, after all.

"Now, Ryan," the man said, "I want you to tell your father to be reasonable."

Jay had been watching all of this with a stricken, glassy look, and his eyes widened as he watched the man wrap the thin wire around Ryan's wrist.

"I'm Jay," he cried hoarsely, and the sound was like the call of a crow on a branch. "I'm Jay, I'm Jay, I'm the person you're looking for, my name is Jay Kozelek, I'm the one you want. . . ."

But the man only let out a thick, disgusted sound.

"You must think I'm an idiot," the man rasped. "I *know* Jay Kozelek. He was my *roommate.* I know what he looks like. We used to sit around and talk and watch movies together and all that shit, and I thought he was my friend. That's the worst thing. I actually felt personally close to him, so I know exactly what his face looks like. Do you get that? I know what his face looks like. Do you honestly think you can scam me, after all this time? Do you think I'm a moron? Do you think I'm kidding around here . . ."

None of this made sense to Ryan, but he couldn't think properly in any case.

The man had already begun to tighten the grip on the handles of the cutter, and Ryan let out a scream.

It actually took a very short time.

Astonishingly short.

The wire was sharp, and it sank deeply into the flesh until it reached the radiocarpal joint. It hitched just below the radius and

ulna, slipping along the edge of bone until it found the softer gris-
tle, and the man tightened his fists around the handles and pulled
tighter, pumping his arms in a quick sawing motion, and the hand
came off abruptly. Cleanly.

Ukh, the man said.

There was that memory,

   a ghost reaching up out of the air to touch his wrist and

Not really conscious.

Not looking, not looking at his hand, but there was a hard
voice—*Jesus fucking Christ, what are you doing?*—and Ryan's eyes
opened and he could see the man standing there, looking down at
the floor, blinking. The wire still held loosely in his hands, but he
had gone pale and there was a wet sheen over his face. A pinched
look, as if he'd taken a drink of something he should have spit out.

There was another man there, too, now—one of the ones Ryan
had thought of as a "henchman"—saying, *oh my god Dylan are you insane you said you weren't really going to do it,* and Ryan shuddering and
woozy as the two figures blurred into silhouettes and then sharpened against a flare of light reflected against the kitchen window,
one of them holding a kitchen towel and bending toward Ryan

and Jay's voice—

"He's going to bleed to death, you guys, it's not his fault, please
don't let him bleed to death—"

And then the man, Dylan, staring at Ryan with a wide-eyed, hor-
rified revulsion. The rumpled black gangster suit hung on him like
a costume someone had dressed him in while he slept, and he
stood there, dazed, uncertain, like a sleepwalker who had awakened into a room that he thought he'd only been dreaming about.

"Oh, jeez," Dylan whispered.

Then he bent over to throw up.

22

It was three and a half hours from Denver to New York on JetBlue Airways, time enough to swing from panic to acceptance and back again several times, and Lucy sat upright in her chair in a state of uneasy, pendulous suspension, her hands folded tightly in her lap.

She had never been on an airplane before—though she couldn't bring herself to admit this embarrassing fact to George Orson.

David Fremden. Dad.

She had been trying to wrap her head around the fact that actually there was no such person as George Orson.

It wasn't simply that everything she knew about him had been invented, or borrowed, or exaggerated—it wasn't simply that he had lied. It was larger than that, an uncanny feeling that opened up in her mind whenever she tried to think calmly and logically about the situation.

He didn't exist anymore.

It made her think of the days after her parents died, the laundry basket still full of their unwashed clothes, the refrigerator stocked with food her mother had planned to cook that weekend, her father's cell phone filling up with calls from customers who wanted to know why he had missed his appointments. At first they would leave behind a few empty spaces in the world—customers who relied on her father, patients who were waiting for her mother to nurse them at the hospital, friends and coworkers and acquaintances who would miss them, for a time—but these were very minor rips and tears in the fabric of things, easily repaired, and the thing that shocked her the most was how quickly such absences began to close. Even after a few weeks you could see how soon her parents would be forgotten, how their presence became an absence, and then—what? What did you call an absence that ceased to become an absence, what do you call a hole that has been filled in?

Oh, she kept thinking. *They'll never come back.* As if the idea were supernatural, science-fictional. How could you believe that such a thing was possible?

That was the thought she had, in bed beside him the night he'd told her the truth, as she traced her fingers across the arm, which was not George Orson's arm. *I'll never talk to George Orson again,* she thought, and she drew her hand back.

He was right there, the same physical body she had been with for so long now, but she couldn't help but feel lonely.

Oh, George, she thought. *I miss you.*

And now she thought it again as she sat in her seat next to David Fremden on the airplane and tried to compose her thoughts.

She missed George Orson. She would never talk to him again.

She had never been on a plane before and she was aware of the terrible, unfathomable distance between herself and the ground. She could sense the air quivering beneath her feet, a shudder of empty space, and she tried to avoid looking out the window. It wasn't so bad to look out and see the thick meringue contours of clouds, but it was harder when the earth began to appear through. The topography. You could see the geometric spread of human habitation, the tiny pencil lines of fields and roads and the boxy spatter of towns, and it was hard not to think of how it would be to fall—how long you would have to plunge before you finally landed.

She'd never have told this to George Orson, anyway. She'd have hated to seem so unsophisticated, for George Orson to see her as some silly rube of a girl, atingle with ignorant dread over the idea of air travel, pressing her nails into the upholstery of the seat arms as if somehow that could anchor her.

David Fremden, meanwhile, looked entirely composed. He was watching the miniature television screen that was embedded into the headrest of the seat in front of him, pausing over a program on pyramids on the History Channel, passing quickly by the news and the weather, smiling nostalgically at an episode of an old 1980s sitcom. He didn't look at her, but he let his hand rest on her forearm.

"You still love me, don't you?" he had asked her—and the question pulsed, as if she could feel it through the whorls of his fingertips.

But there were other things she had to bear in mind, as well. Events were moving fairly fast now. The world continued on, and she had to make some decisions, even without reliable information. There was, purportedly, 4.3 million dollars, in a bank in the Ivory Coast, Africa. There was, at least, more than a hundred thousand dollars currently in their possession.

Their carry-on baggage was in the overhead compartment, right there above them, and that was fine so far, though that, too, was a source of unease.

They had spent their last night in the Lighthouse Motel, side by side in the library, each with a cylinder of cellophane tape, each with a stack of hundred-dollar bills.

David Fremden had a big old atlas, 25 x 20, and Lucy had a dictionary and a Dickens novel, and they sat there, affixing bills to the pages.

"Are you sure this will work?" Lucy had said. She was flipping her way through *Bleak House,* fragments of text rising up as she laid a bill on the page and pinned it down. *"The fog is very dense, indeed!" said I.* And she pressed Ben Franklin over the line of words, and then flipped a couple of pages forward. *"It's disgraceful," she said. "You know it is. The whole house is disgraceful."* And she covered it again, though once again some grain of the book rose up: *We found Miss Jellyby trying to warm herself at the fire . . .*

"It's not a problem," David Fremden said. He himself was working more rapidly than she, lining a row of three hundreds down the center of Ireland, pressing a tongue of adhesive tape along the edge of the bills with his thumb. "I've done this before," he said.

"Okay," she said.

"The universe," he observed, "makes rather an indifferent parent, I am afraid."

"But isn't there an X-ray machine?" she said. "Won't they be able to see through the covers of the books?"

. . . is the portrait of the present Lady Dedlock. It is considered a perfect likeness, and . . .

"Look," David Fremden said, and he sighed. "You'll just have to trust me on this. I know how these security systems work. I really do know what I'm doing."

And so far, yes, he had been right, though she had been dreadfully nervous. Her body had felt almost mystically visible when they came to the front of the security line, as if her skin were giving off an aura of light. She was shocked that people weren't staring at her, but no one seemed to notice. She put her satchel—which contained a few toiletries and a T-shirt and the books—into a gray plastic tub, and she couldn't help but think of the swollen pages of *Bleak House,* stuffed full of money, even as she bent down to remove her shoes, even as the conveyor belt carried her bag through the tunnel of the X-ray machine.

"Okay," said the security guard, and motioned her forward through the doorway-shaped metal detector, a thick, blank-eyed, weight lifter guy, perhaps not much older than she was, beckoning her through, and there were no alarms, no hesitation as her bag passed through, no second glance at her wretchedly dyed hair, nothing.

David Fremden put his hand on her elbow.

"Good job," he murmured.

And so now the plane was on the tarmac in New York. They were sitting in their seats, waiting for the captain to turn off the FASTEN SEAT BELTS sign, though some of the passengers around them were already impatiently stirring in their seats. Lucy herself was still trying to recover her equilibrium from the experience of landing, the grinding sounds the wheels made as they unfolded, the sudden, quivering bump as the plane touched the landing strip, the way her ears had filled up with a plug of viscous air. She tried to be stern with herself. *You're such an idiot, Lucy. Such a white trash hillbilly, what are you scared of? What are you scared of?*

But the truth was that her leg had developed a tic, she could feel one of the muscles giving a small involuntary twitch and when she put her hand on her thigh she could hear another voice in her head, a small, sad tremor.

I don't want to do this. I think I've made a mistake.

It was like butterflies had begun to alight on her, hundreds of butterflies, and they were each one of them made of lead. It wasn't long before she was covered with them.

There was a soft, deep bell tone, and en masse the rest of the passengers began to sigh and rise, converging into the aisles and opening the overhead compartments and leaning close to the person in front of them, not disorderly, not exactly, but almost like a school of fish or migrating birds, and she looked up as David Fremden stood to join them.

"Brooke," he said. He reached down and took her hand in his and gave it a tight squeeze. "Come on, sweetheart," he whispered. "Don't fail me now."

It was easy enough to get onto her feet. It was easy enough to shuffle down the narrow aisle of the airplane, following behind David— her father—

He handed over her backpack with one of those gently teasing smiles that reminded her so much of George Orson. That grin that had so impressed her back when she was a student in his AP history class, back when he told her he thought she was sui generis. "People like you and me, we invent ourselves," he had said, though there was no way to know back then that he meant it literally.

She missed George Orson.

But she took a breath and fell into the shuffling queue of travelers. It was easy enough. Easy enough to put her head down and trudge through the tight rows of seats. Easy enough to walk past the stewardess, who stood at the front of the plane nodding like a priest, peace be with you, peace be with you, ushering them into the accordion tunnel that led up into the terminal.

"You look peaked," David said. "Are you feeling all right?"

"I'm fine," Lucy said.

"Why don't we get a cup of coffee," he said. "Or a soda? A little something to eat?"

"No, thanks," Lucy said.

They had turned into the rambling avenue that ran past the various gates—counters and podiums surrounded by clusters of anchored chairs, pods full of waiting people, and as far as she could tell, no one was looking at them. No one gave them a second glance, no one wondered if they were father and daughter, or lovers, or teacher and student. Whatever. Back in Pompey, Ohio, the two of them might have caused a stir of curiosity, but here they hardly registered.

Lucy gazed at a trio of women in burkas, blue, faceless, nunlike figures, chatting amiably in their native tongue, and a tall, balding man swept past them, speed-walking, swearing joyfully into his cell phone, and then an old woman in a wheelchair, wearing a full-length fur coat, pushed along by a black man in gray coveralls—

Lucy could feel the weight of her backpack. *Bleak House* and *Webster's Dictionary* and *Marjorie Morningstar*, which between them contained perhaps fifty thousand dollars.

She adjusted the strap on her shoulder, then tugged at the hated butterfly T-shirt as it inched up, exposing her belly. She was aware of how much she would have disliked Brooke Fremden, back in the day. If Brooke Fremden had come traipsing down the halls of Pompey High School, with her cutesy mall-girl clothes and her juvenile, perky backpack, Lucy would have been repulsed.

But when David Fremden looked over his shoulder at her, his look was mild and fatherly and distracted. She was just a girl, just a teenage girl. This was what they looked like; it didn't matter to him as long as she was keeping pace.

He didn't miss Lucy, she thought.

"You've done this before," she said. "I'm not the first."

This was on the night before their trip. They were still in the house above the Lighthouse Motel, and they sat there on the couch in the television room, side by side, their bags packed and the rooms hushed in the way of places that are about to be abandoned.

The books were taped full of money, and they should have just gone to bed, but instead they were sitting there watching the opening monologue of some late-night talk show host, and his face, David's face, was entirely blank, that flat television-watching expression, and at last she repeated herself.

"You've been other people before," she said, and at last he looked away from the TV and glanced at her warily.

"That's a complicated question," he said.

"Don't you think it's fair to be honest with me?" she said. "We're . . ."

Together?

She thought about it.

Maybe it was better to say nothing. It was weird—all this time she'd spent in this musty television room, all the hours she'd spent alone with nothing but old videos for company, *Rebecca* and *Mrs. Miniver* and *Double Indemnity* and *How Green Was My Valley* and *My Fair Lady* and *Mildred Pierce*. Sipping diet soda and glancing out at the raggedy Japanese garden and waiting for the chance to get back into the Maserati and drive away to someplace wonderful.

He had been "a lot of different people." He admitted as much.

So—it was probably logical to think that there had also been other girls, other Lucys, sitting on this same couch and watching the same old movies and listening to the same stillness as the Light-house Motel brooded over its dusty swathe of empty lake bed.

"I just want to know—" she said. "I want to know about the others. How many have there been—in your life. In all this."

And he looked up. He pulled his gaze away from the TV and met her eyes and his expression wavered.

"There's never been anyone else," he said. "That's what you don't understand. I've been looking—I've been looking for a long time. But there's never been anyone like you."

So.

No, she didn't believe him, though maybe he had managed to convince himself. Perhaps he truly thought that it didn't matter if she was Lucy or Brooke or whatever other name she would take on. Perhaps he imagined she would remain the same person on the in-side, no matter what name or persona she adopted.

But that wasn't true, she thought.

More and more, she was aware that Lucy Lattimore had left the earth. Already there was hardly anything left of her—a few scraps of documents, birth certificate and social security card in her mother's drawer back in the old house, her high school transcript resident on some outdated computer, the memories of her sister, Patricia, the vague recollections of her classmates and teachers, already fading.

The truth was, she had killed herself months ago. Now she was next to nothing: a nameless physical form that could be exchanged and exchanged and exchanged until nothing remained but molecules.

The stuff of stars—that's what George Orson once said when he was holding forth to their history class. *Hydrogen and carbon and all the primordial particles that existed from the very beginning of time, that's what you're made up of,* he told them.

As if that were a comfort.

They would be flying to Brussels, first. Seven hours, twenty-five minutes, on a Boeing 767, and then from there another six hours and forty-five minutes to Abidjan. They had already made it through the most difficult passage, David Fremden said. The customs exercises in Belgium and Ivory Coast were negligible. "We can actually relax now and think about the future."

4.3 million dollars.

"I don't want to stay in Africa for very long," he said. "I just want to get the money situation settled, and then we can go wherever we want.

"I've never been to Rome," he said. "I'd love to spend some time in Italy. Naples, Tuscany, Florence. I think that would be a wonderful, growing experience for you. I think it would be exciting, actually. Like Henry James," he said. "Like E. M. Forster," he said. "Lucy

Honeychurch," he said, and chuckled as if this were a bit of levity she would appreciate—

But she had no idea what he was talking about.

Back in the day, back when he was George Orson and she was his student, she half enjoyed his high-handed trivia, the bits of Ivy League education he would drop into conversation. She used to roll her eyes and pretend to be exasperated by his pretentiousness, the way he raised his eyebrows in that gently reproachful way—as if she'd expressed some lack of knowledge that surprised him. "Who's Spinoza?" Or: "What's sodium pentothal?" And he might have a complicated and even interesting answer.

But that was not who they were anymore, they were not Lucy and George Orson, and so she sat there wordlessly, she looked down at her ticket, New York to Brussels, and

Who's Lucy Honeychurch? Who's E. M. Forster?

It didn't matter. It wasn't important, though she couldn't help but think again of the question she'd asked George Orson the night before: what happened to the other ones, the ones before me?

She could imagine this Lucy Honeychurch—a blond girl, no doubt, a person who wore thrift store sweaters and vintage eyeglasses, a girl who probably thought she was more clever than she actually was. Had he taken her to the Lighthouse Motel? Had they walked together through the ruins of the drowned village? Had he dressed her up in someone else's clothes and hurried her to an airport with a fake passport in her purse, off to another city, another state, some foreign place?

Where was the girl now? Lucy wondered, as people began to stand, as the plane for Brussels announced the beginnings of boarding.

Where was the girl now? Lucy thought. What had happened to her?

23

Here was Banks Island, Aulavik National Park. A polar desert, Mr. Itigaituk told them dryly, in his genial, affectless voice. As they flew, he pointed out landmarks as if they were on a tour: there was a pingo, a conical volcano-shaped hill, filled with ice rather than lava; here was Sachs Harbour, a cluster of houses on a barren, muddy shore; and here were the small interlocking ponds of the dry valleys, and—look!—a herd of musk oxen!

But now, as they walked across the tundra toward the place where the old research station was supposed to be, as the waiting Cessna plane grew smaller and smaller behind them, Mr. Itigaituk was taciturn. Every twenty minutes or so, he stopped to regard his compass, to press his binoculars to his eyes and scan the gray expanse of pebbles and rocks.

Miles had been given a pair of rubber boots, and a jacket, and he took a nervous glance over his shoulder as he trudged along through the damp gravel and puddles and the chill, faintly misty air.

Lydia Barrie, meanwhile, was striding along with remarkable poise, particularly for someone who was surely, Miles thought, colossally hungover. But it didn't show in her face, and when Mr. It-igaituk pointed out a bowl-like depression of gray-white fur—the corpse of a fox, which a goose had made a nest out of—Lydia regarded it with dispassionate interest.

"Gross," Miles said, staring down at the fox's head, the skin tight over the skull, the shriveled eye sockets, the teeth bared and freck-led with goose dung. Two eggs lay in the rounded impression of rot-ten hair.

"Well said," Lydia murmured.

It had been a few miles since they'd said anything to each other. There was, naturally, a certain amount of awkwardness, given what had happened between them the night before, a certain post-intimacy reticence—which wasn't made any easier by the ambient disquiet that had settled over him. A hum in his ear that wouldn't go away.

This was crazy, he thought.

Was it probable that Hayden had come to this place, was it likely that he was actually living here in this tundra flatland, the pinprick of the Cessna still visible, many kilometers behind them?

Perhaps he had been on more futile chases than she had, per-haps he had grown fatalistic. But this didn't look very promising.

"How much farther do you think we have to go?" he said, glanc-ing tactfully toward Mr. Itigaituk, who was by now about ten yards ahead of them. "Are we sure we're going in the right direction?"

Lydia Barrie adjusted the fingers of her glove, her eyes still on the fox, the bones and fur that had made some goose such a com-fortable resting place.

"I'm feeling fairly confident," she said, and they looked at each other.

Miles nodded wordlessly.

———

For a while, he had been telling her about Cleveland.

About Hayden, naturally, but also about their childhood, and their father, and even his life today, his job in the old novelty shop, Mrs. Matalov and her granddaughter—

"And yet here you are," Lydia said. "It sounds as if you could have been happy, Miles, and yet here you are, on an island in the Arctic Ocean. It's a shame."

"I guess," Miles said. He shrugged, a little flustered. "I don't know. 'Happy' is a strong word."

" 'Happy' is a strong word?" she repeated mildly, in the way a therapist might. She raised her eyebrows. "What an odd thing to say."

And Miles shrugged again. "I don't know," he said. "I just meant—I wasn't *that* happy in Cleveland."

"I see," she said.

"Just—neutral. I mean, I was working at a catalog company, basically. It wasn't anything special. You know. Spending my nights in an empty apartment most of the time, watching TV."

"Yes," she said, and straightened the collar of her coat as wind blew across them.

It wasn't cold, exactly. Miles estimated that the temperature was somewhere around fifty degrees Fahrenheit, and the endless daylight beamed down upon them. The sky had a glassy, silvery sharpness—more like the reflection of a sky in a pair of mirrored sunglasses. That eerie phosphorescent blue the earth has, when seen from space.

"So," Lydia said at last. "If we find him, do you think you'll be happy then?"

"I don't know," Miles said.

It was a lame answer, no doubt, but honestly he wasn't sure how he would feel. To have things resolved, finally, after all these years? He couldn't quite imagine.

And she seemed to understand that, too. She inclined her head as their feet made soft hushing sounds through the gravel, which was piled in wrinkled ridges like the pebbles in the bed of a stream. Left that way, Miles guessed, by the accumulation and melt of snow.

"And if we don't find him?" Lydia said, after they had trudged in silence for a while. "What then? You'll just get back into your car and drive home to Cleveland?"

"I suppose so."

He shrugged again, and this time she laughed, a surprisingly lighthearted, even affectionate sound.

"Oh, Miles," she said. "I can't believe that you *drove* all the way to Inuvik. That just astounds me." She glanced up ahead at Mr. Itigaituk, who was a dozen or more yards ahead of them, leading determinedly onward.

"You're a very odd person, Miles Cheshire," she said, and regarded him thoughtfully. "I wish—"

But she didn't complete her sentence. She let it drift off, and Miles guessed that she had thought better of what she was going to say.

He was trying to think about the future.

The longer they walked, the more it became clear to Miles that this was yet another one of Hayden's elaborate practical jokes, another maze that he had created, that they were winding their way through.

He *would* go back, he guessed. Back to Cleveland, back to Matalov Novelties, where the old lady was waiting impatiently for him to return to work; and he would return to his corner of the cluttered store, sitting at his computer under the framed black-and-white photos of old vaudevillians, sometimes contemplating the photo of his own father, his dad, dressed in a cape and tuxedo, holding a wand with a flourish.

As for Miles, he was not a magician, nor would he ever be, but he could picture himself becoming a respected figure among them. Their shopkeeper. Already, he had a good eye for the inventory and expenses at Matalov, already he had straightened the disordered shelves and updated the website to make shopping more user-friendly, doing something *useful* at least, making a small pathway through his life that his father might have respected.

Wasn't that enough? Wasn't there the possibility that he could settle in, that he could become happy or at least content? Wasn't there the chance that—after this one last time, the shadow of Hayden would begin to draw away from his thoughts and he could finally, finally escape at last?

Was that so difficult? So improbable?

And then he glanced up as Mr. Itigaituk turned and called back to them.

"I see it," Mr. Itigaituk said. "It's just up ahead!"

Lydia adjusted her sunglasses and craned her neck, and Miles shaded his eyes against the gleaming sky and the wind, squinting toward the horizon.

They all stood there, uncertainly.

"So," Miles said at last. "What do we do now?"

Mr. Itigaituk and Lydia Barrie exchanged a look.

"I mean," Miles said, "do we just walk up to the door and knock? Or what?"

And Lydia regarded him, her sunglasses an unreadable blankness.

"Do you have another suggestion?" she said.

The research station was like a beachfront house. A stilt house, Miles thought, except that there was no water or shoreline in sight, no sense that there would ever be flooding here.

The building itself was little more than three linked mobile homes, propped up on piles, about four or five feet off the ground. It had the white corrugated metal siding he'd seen so much of back in Inuvik, and on the flat roof was a small orchard of metal antennae and satellite dishes and other transmitting instruments. Along the side of the building was a large capsule-shaped tank, such as holds natural gas, and a few metal barrels, also raised on stilts, probably for petroleum. Some wires ran from the main building to a small wooden shack, the size of an outhouse.

"Are you sure this is . . . ," Miles said, and Mr. Itigaituk turned to glare at him with a brisk hunterlike focus.

"Shhhhhhh," Mr. Itigaituk said.

The place was obviously abandoned, Miles thought. The windows—four on each side—were not windows you could look out of. They had a gray opaque film over them, probably a form of insulation. A weathervane, an aluminum wind spinner, was creaking in the tranquil thicket of metal poles on the roof of the building.

As Mr. Itigaituk crept forward, a raven lifted up from the ramshackle outhouse structure and sailed off.

"He's not here," Miles whispered, more to himself than to Lydia.

He had never believed in any of Hayden's paranormal nonsense, though over the years he had played along with various of Hayden's obsessions: past lives and geodesy, numerology and Ouija boards, telepathy and out-of-body travel.

But he did believe in *something*.

He did believe that when he finally found Hayden, when he finally came within striking distance, he would be able to tell. There would be some extrasensory "twin" radar, he thought. An alarm would be triggered and he would sense it in his body. It would go off in his chest like a cell phone set to vibrate. If Hayden was inside this building, Miles would know it.

"This isn't the place," he murmured.

But Lydia only turned to him, blankly. She put out her gloved hand and rested it on Miles's shoulder.

Hush.

She was watching with an ardent, almost quivering attention. He thought of a gambler, that prayerful second of held breath as the roulette wheel slows and the silver ball settles into its place at last.

She looked so certain and focused that he couldn't help but doubt his own instincts.

Maybe. Maybe it was possible?

She seemed to know things that he did not, after all, she seemed to have done her research.

What if Hayden really was there? What would they do?

Miles and Lydia stood at a distance from the building as Mr. Itigaituk came to the set of wooden stairs that led up to the door.

They watched as Mr. Itigaituk crouched to creep up each step. Together they watched; they caught their breath as he placed his hand on the knob of the door.

Not locked.

Miles closed his eyes. *Okay,* he thought.

Okay. Yes. This is it.

The place was empty.

The door opened unsteadily, and Mr. Itigaituk stood for what seemed like a long while, peering in. Then he turned and looked at them.

"Uninhabited," Mr. Itigaituk said, and finally the spell broke. Miles and Lydia both realized that they'd been standing at a distance, as if waiting for Mr. Itigaituk to defuse a bomb.

"Nothing," Mr. Itigaituk said critically, and gave them both a mild, accusatory look. "Nobody here for a long time."

A *very* long time, Miles realized. Perhaps a year, maybe more. He could tell from the mushroomlike cellar smell of the air as they stepped inside.

The front room, about the size and shape of a semi truck trailer, was gray-carpeted and entirely devoid of furniture. Some pieces of paper were pinned to the corkboard that lined the walls, and they set up a flutter of henhouse anxiety when the wind came in.

"Hello?" Lydia called, but her voice was small and wan. "Rachel?" she said, and stepped hesitantly toward the open doorway that led toward the back rooms. "Hello? Rachel?"

It was darker in the back rooms.

Not pitch-black, but dim, like a hotel room with the shades pulled, and the resourceful Mr. Itigaituk took a small flashlight from his pocket and clicked it on.

"God damn it," Lydia Barrie said, and Miles said nothing.

Here, in this next room, the walls were lined with folding tables, such as you might find in a high school cafeteria. And there was some unplaceable equipment—a large boxy thing, with jagged picket-fence teeth; smaller weathervanes and pinwheel-like wands; a file cabinet with the drawers removed, folders scattered on the floor.

The musky old-clothes smell was stronger now, and Mr. Itigaituk ran the line of his flashlight into a side room that Miles saw was a kitchen and pantry area. Dirty dishes were piled high in the sink, and empty cans and candy bar wrappers lined the counter space, beneath cupboards that were open and mostly empty.

A box of Cap'n Crunch cereal, almost unrecognizably faded, was sitting on the table, next to a bowl and a spoon and a can of condensed milk.

Mr. Itigaituk solemnly turned to look at Lydia, and his expression confirmed what Miles had been thinking. The place had been abandoned for—years, Miles guessed. It wasn't even a close call.

"Fuck," Lydia Barrie said, under her breath, and at last she took a flask from her bag and sipped from it. Her face was drawn, tired, and her hand had a tremor as she offered the flask to Miles.

"I was feeling so confident," she said as Miles took the flask. He considered it, but didn't drink.

"Yes," Miles said. "He's good at this. Fooling people. I guess you could say that it's his life's work."

He held the flask out to her, and she took it, putting it to her lips again.

"I'm sorry," Miles said.

He had been doing this for so long now that this was a familiar feeling—the urgency and anticipation, the swell of emotion. And then disappointment. Anticlimax, which, in its own way, was like sorrow. It was not unlike having your heart broken, he imagined.

And then they both looked up as Mr. Itigaituk cleared his throat. He was standing a few yards away, near the dark entrance to the back rooms.

"Ms. Barrie," he said. "You may want to look at this."

It was a bedroom.

They stood in the doorway, staring in, and it was from here that the smell of old earth and musty cloth emanated most strongly. It was a narrow room, with barely enough space for a bed and some shelves, but it had been decorated extravagantly.

Decorated? Was that the right term?

It reminded him of the stuff they'd talked about in one of the art classes he took at Ohio University. Art Brut, the teacher called it. Outsider Art: and he'd thought then of the dioramas and statues that Hayden used to make when they were kids.

This "decoration" was along those lines, though much more elaborate, filling the entire room. There were mobiles that had been strung from the ceiling, origami fish, origami swans and peacocks, origami nautilus shells and pinwheels; clouds made from cotton batting, wind chimes made of small stones and microscope slides. The shelves were filled with knickknacks that Hayden had made out of rocks and bones, nails, bits of wood and soup cans, plastic wrap, strips of cloth, some feathers, some fur, computer parts, all kinds of unrecognizable junk.

Some of these creations had been arranged into a tableau—and Miles had worked in the magic shop long enough to recognize scenes from the tarot cards. Here was the Four of Swords: a tiny figure made out of clay or mud or flour rested on a cardboard bed, covered in a tiny blanket cut from a piece of corduroy, and above the bed were three nails, pointing downward. Here was the tower—a conical structure made from pebbles, with two miniature paper clip stick people hurling themselves from the turret.

Beneath these objects, clothes had been arranged on the bed. Side by side: a white blouse and a white T-shirt, arms outstretched. Two pairs of jeans. Two pairs of socks. As if they had been sleeping there next to each other and then had simply evaporated, leaving nothing but their empty clothes.

And all around these figures were various flowers: lilies made from goose feathers, roses made out of the pages of books, baby's breath made from wire and bits of insulation. Flecks of mica glinted as Mr. Itigaituk passed his flashlight over the—

Shrine, Miles supposed you would call it.

It was like one of those memorials that one sees along the side of the highway, the jumble of crosses and plastic bouquets and stuffed animals and handmade signs that marked the place where someone had been killed in a car wreck.

Above the empty clothes, some large flat rocks had been arranged in an arch, and on each rock a rune had been etched.

Runes: it was the old game, the old alphabet that they'd invented back when they were twelve, "letters" that were somewhere between Phoenician and Tolkien, which they'd pretended was an ancient language.

He could read the letters well enough. He still remembered.

R-A-C-H-E-L,   it said.   H-A-Y-D-E-N.

And then below that, in smaller letters, it said:

e-a-d-e-m   m-u-t-a-t-a   r-e-s-u-r-g-o

He guessed it was like a grave of some kind.

The three of them stood there mutely, and they could all see what this exhibit was meant to convey, they could all tell that they were in the presence of a memorial, or a tomb. There must have been a breeze coming in from the front door, because the mobiles had begun to stir lightly, casting slowly turning shadows on the wall as Mr. Itigaituk's flashlight caught them. The wind chimes made an uncertain, rattling whisper.

"I guess those must be Rachel's clothes," Lydia said at last, hoarsely, and Miles shrugged.

"I'm not sure," he said.

"What is it?" Lydia said. "Is it a message?"

Miles shook his head. He was thinking about the oddly stacked figures of rocks and branches that Hayden used to make in the backyard of their old house, after their father died. He was thinking of the tattered copy of *Frankenstein*, which he'd received in the mail not long after his trip to North Dakota, the passage in the final chapter that had been highlighted:

Follow me; I seek the everlasting ices of the north, where you will feel the misery of cold and frost to which I am impassive. . . . Come on, my enemy.

"I think it means that they're both dead," Miles said finally, and then he paused.

Did he really think that? Or did he just wish that it were true?

Lydia was shuddering a little, but her face remained still. He didn't know what she was feeling. Rage? Despair? Grief? Or was it merely a version of the numb, blank, wordless hollowness that had settled over him as he remembered the letter that Hayden had sent him: *Do you remember the Great Tower of Kallupilluk? That may be my final resting place, Miles. You may never hear from me again.*

"He left this stuff for me," Miles said quietly. "I guess he thought I would understand what it meant."

Knowing Hayden, Miles assumed that every single object in the room was a message, every sculpture and diorama was supposed to tell a story. Knowing Hayden, each object was built as if it would be given the attention that an archaeologist would give to a set of long-lost scrolls.

And—Miles supposed that he did understand the gist of it. Or at least he could interpret—in the way that fortune-tellers found a story in the random lines of a person's palm or the sticks of the *I Ching;* the way mystics found secret communications everywhere, converting letters to numbers and numbers to letters, magical numerals nestled in the verses of the Bible, incantatory words to be discovered in the endless string of digits that made up pi.

Would it be a lie to say there was a narrative to be found in this jumble of dioramas and statues and mobiles? Would it be dishonest? Would it be any different than a therapist who takes the stuff of dreams, the landscapes and objects and random surreal events, and weaves them into some meaning?

"It's a suicide note," Miles said at last, very gently, and he pointed toward the stack of stones, with the paper clip people throwing themselves from the summit.

"That's the Great Tower of Kallupilluk," he said. "It's . . . a story we made up when we were kids. It's a lighthouse at the very edge of the world, and that's where the immortal ones go, when they are ready to leave this life. They sail off from the shore beyond the lighthouse, and into the sky."

He gazed intently at these objects that Hayden had left for him, as if each one were a hieroglyph, each one a still frame like the fresco cycles of ancient times.

Yes. You could say that there was a story here.

———

In Miles's version of things, he imagined that they had come here in the fall.

Hayden and Rachel. They had been in love, like they were in that photograph that Lydia had shown him. This was a place that they thought they could hide, just for a short time, just until Hayden got things back on track.

They hadn't planned to stay long, but winter came faster than they expected, and they were trapped before they knew it. And Rachel—you could see her in that mobile, there, with the down feathers and bits of colored glass—had gotten sick. She had gone out to look at the aurora borealis. She was a romantic girl, an impractical girl, an amateur photographer—you could see the rolls of film in that diorama, perhaps they could be developed—perhaps they'd contain the pictures she took in her last days—

But she didn't realize. She didn't understand that in this country, even a few minutes of exposure to the elements could be terribly dangerous. You could see her there, delirious in her bed, under those nails—

And by that time, the food had begun to run out, and Hayden didn't know how long the generator would last. And so he'd made a sled for Rachel, and he'd wrapped her in blankets and coats and furs, and he set out. He planned to try to walk to the southern part of the island. It was their only hope.

"No," Mr. Itigaituk said, and shook his head cynically. "That's ridiculous. They would never make it. It would have been impossible."

"He knew that," Miles said. "That's what those stones mean, there. He understood that it was hopeless, but he wanted to try anyway."

Miles looked at Lydia, who had been standing there, listening blankly as he'd talked. As he *interpreted*.

"No," she said. "That doesn't make sense. How could they have been dead for so long? How could—we both have letters from him, recent letters—"

Letters that might have been left with someone, perhaps. Please send these out if I don't come back in a year. Here's a hundred dollars, two hundred dollars for your trouble.

"Maybe you're right," Miles said. "Maybe they're still alive somewhere."

But Lydia had fallen into her own thoughts. Not convinced, but. Even so.

It probably wasn't true, but wouldn't it be nice to believe?

It would be such a relief, Miles thought, such a comfort to think that they'd finally come to the end of the story. Wasn't that the gift that Hayden was giving to them, with this display? Wasn't this Hayden's version of kindness?

A present for you, Miles. A present for you, too, Lydia. You've come at last to the edge of the earth, and now your journey is finished. An ending for you, if you want it.

If only you'll accept it.

24

Ryan had been living in Ecuador for almost a year now, and he had begun to get used to the idea that he would probably never see Jay again.

He was getting used to a lot of things.

He was living in the Old Town part of Quito—Centro Histórico—in a small apartment on Calle Espejo, which was a fairly busy pedestrian boulevard, and he had become inured to the sound of the city, its early waking. There was a magazine stand just below his window, so he didn't need an alarm clock. Before daylight, he would hear the metal clatter as Señor Gamboa Pulido set up his racks and arranged his newspapers, and shortly thereafter voices began to weave their way up into his half consciousness. For a long while, the sound of Spanish sentences was little more than burbling music, but that had begun to change, too. It had not taken as long as he'd expected before the syllables had begun to solidify into words, before he realized that he himself had begun to think in Spanish.

He was still limited, obviously. Still recognizably American, but he could get by in the market or on the street, he could absorb the patter of the disc jockeys on the radio, he could watch television and understand the news, the plots and dialogue of the soap operas, he could exchange friendly conversation at the coffee shops or Internet cafés, he was aware when people were talking about him—watching curiously as he bent over the keyboard, impressed by how quickly he could type with one hand.

He was becoming accustomed to that, as well.

Sometimes in the morning there were occasionally odd twinges. The ghost of his hand would ache, the palm would itch, the fingers would appear to be flexing. But he was no longer surprised to open his eyes and find that it was gone. He had stopped waking up with the certainty that the hand had come back to him, that it had somehow rematerialized in the middle of the night, sprouted and regenerated from the stump of his wrist.

The keen sense of loss had faded, and these days he found that he stumbled less and less over that absence. He could dress and even tie his shoes without much trouble. He could make toast and coffee, crack an egg into a skillet, all one-handed, and some days he wouldn't even bother to wear his prosthesis.

"Eggs" was one of the words that he sometimes stumbled over. *Huevos? Huecos? Huesos?* Eggs, holes, bones.

For the time being, he was using a myoelectric hook, which fit like a gauntlet over his stump. He could open and close the prongs simply by flexing the muscles in his forearm, and he was actually pretty adept at using it. Nevertheless, there were days when it was easier—less conspicuous—to simply button a cuff over the bare empty wrist. He didn't like the interest that the hook aroused in people, the startled glances, the fear from women and children. It was enough to be a gringo, a Yankee, without the added attention.

In the beginning, as he made his way through the Plaza de la Independencia, in the promenade around the winged victory statue, he would find that it attracted notice, despite himself. He remembered Walcott's admonition: *Never look at people directly in the face!* But nevertheless he found that shoe-shining street urchins would dash behind him, making their shrill incomprehensible cries, and the old country women, in their gray braids and anaco caps, would deepen their frowns as he passed. Quito was a city full of a surprising number of clowns and mimes, and these, too, were drawn to him. A ragged, red-nosed skeleton on stilts; a white-faced zombie in a dusty black suit, walking like a mechanical toy through a crosswalk; an elderly man, with lipstick and green eye shadow and a pink turban, holding up a fistful of tarot cards, calling after him, "*Fortuna! Fortuna!*"

Sometimes it would be a college kid, with a backpack and sandals, army surplus clothes. "Hey, dude! Are you American?"

This happened to him less frequently now. He passed through the plaza without much incident. The old fortune-teller merely lifted his head as Ryan passed, the brothel makeup worn down by perspiration, sad eyes following as Ryan made his way toward the Presidential Palace, the white colonnaded façade, the old eighteenth-century jail cells that had once lined the foot of the palace now opened and transformed into barber shops and clothing stores and fast-food joints.

Above the city, on the mountaintops, a Calvary of antennae and satellite dishes gazed down. And through the gaps in buildings he could occasionally see the great statue on Panecillo Hill, the Virgin of the Apocalypse in her dancing pose, hovering over the valley.

———

Financially, he was doing okay. Despite the setbacks, he still had a few bank accounts that had not been discovered, and he had begun, very cautiously, to transfer monies from one to the next— a little trickle that was keeping him comfortable. He had set up some trusts that were, in fact, producing dividends, and in the meantime he had managed to find a new name that he had settled into. David Angel Verdugo Cubrero, an Ecuadorian national—with a passport and everything—and when people would look at him oddly, he would shrug. "My mother was an American," he told them, and he set up a savings account and got David a couple of credit cards, and it seemed to be fine. He appeared to have escaped.

The men who had attacked them, the men who had cut off his hand, had apparently lost his trail.

He guessed that Jay had not been so lucky.

Whatever had happened that night was still blurry in his mind. He still didn't know what the men had been after, or why they had insisted that Jay wasn't Jay, or why they had left in such a panic, or how Jay had managed to get free from the chair he was taped to. No matter how many times he tried to put it together in his mind, the events remained stubbornly illogical, random, fragmentary.

By the time they reached the hospital, Ryan had lost a lot of blood, and the color had washed out of his vision. He could remember— he thought he remembered—the automatic sliding doors opening as they stumbled into the entrance of the emergency room. He could remember the surprised, quivering nurse in her balloon-patterned smock, puzzled as Jay thrust the beer cooler at her. "It's his hand," Jay said. "You can put it back on, right? You can fix it, right?"

He could remember Jay kissing his hair, whispering thickly, "You're not going to die; I love you, Son; you're the only one who has ever been there for me; I'm not going to let anything bad happen to you; you're going to be fine—"

"Yes," Ryan said. "Okay," he said, and when he closed his eyes, he could hear Jay telling someone, "He fell off a ladder. And his hand—caught on a piece of wire. It happened so quickly."

Why is he lying? Ryan thought dreamily.

And then, the next thing he could recall he was in a hospital bed, the stump of his wrist mummy-wrapped and the ghost of his hand throbbing dully, and the young doctor, Doctor Ali, with his black hair pulled back in a ponytail and his weary brown eyes, telling him that there was some unfortunate news, about his hand, the doctor said they had been unable to reattach the extremity; too much time had passed, and as a small hospital they were not equipped—

"Where is it?" Ryan said. That was his first thought. What had they done with his hand?

And the doctor had glanced at the tiny blond nurse who was standing off to the side. "Unfortunately," the doctor said ruefully, "it's gone."

"Where's my father?" Ryan had asked then. He was comprehending things all right, but nothing was sinking in. His brain felt flat, two-dimensional, and he gazed uncertainly at the door to his hospital room. He could hear the *clip, clip* of someone's hard-soled shoes against the floor of the hallway outside.

"Where's my dad?" he said, and again the doctor and nurse exchanged solemn looks.

"Mr. Wimberley," the doctor said, "do you have a phone number where your father can be reached? Is there someone else that you'd like us to call?"

It wasn't until Ryan had finally looked in his wallet that he had found the note. The wallet—still with his Max Wimberley driver's license—was stuffed with money. Fifteen one-hundred-dollar bills, some twenties, some ones, and there was also a small folded piece of paper, Jay's neat, tiny block-letter handwriting:

R—Leave the country ASAP. I will meet you in Quito, will contact you when I am able. Hurry!

Love always, Jay.

When he'd first arrived in Quito, he kept expecting that Jay would arrive any day. He would scope through the pedestrians on the plaza and the cobblestone sidewalks, he would peer into the narrow cluttered shops, he would sit in various Internet cafés and type Jay's names into search engines, all the names that he could re-member Jay ever using. He'd check through every email account he'd ever had, and then he'd double-check.

He didn't want to think that Jay was dead, though maybe it was easier than imagining that Jay just wasn't coming.

That Jay had abandoned him.

That Jay wasn't even Jay, but just some—what?—another avatar?

In those first few months, he would stand at the balcony of his second-floor apartment, listening to the peddler girls who stood outside the Teatro Bolivar, just down the block. Beautiful, sorrowful Otavaleñas, sisters perhaps, twins, with their black braided hair and white peasant blouses and red shawls, holding their baskets of strawberries or lima beans or flowers, chanting "One dollar, one dollar, one dollar, one dollar." At first he'd thought the girls were singing. Their voices were so sweet and musical and yearning, twined together in counterpoint, sometimes harmonizing: "One dollar, one dollar, one dollar." As if their hearts had been broken.

Now almost a year had passed, and he didn't think of Jay quite so much. Not quite so often.

In the afternoon, he'd walk down to Calle Flores to an Internet café that he liked. It was just past the coral-colored stucco walls of the Hotel Viena Internacional, where the American and European students could stay for cheap, and the Ecuadorian businessmen could spend a few hours with a prostitute. Just down the hill, where the narrow side street opened abruptly into a panorama view of the eastern mountains, the stacks and stacks of houses were set in corn-row circles beneath the thin blue sky.

Here. Just an open doorway with a hand-painted sign: INTERNET, and a set of steep, crooked stairs. A cramped back room with rows of ancient, dirty computers.

The proprietor was an old American. Raines Davis, he was called, perhaps seventy years old, who sat behind the counter, slowly filling an ashtray with cigarette butts. His thick white hair had a yellowish tinge, as if stained with smoke.

Often the place was full of students, all hunched over their keyboards, eyes fixed on the box of the monitor, but sometimes in the late afternoon it was more or less empty, and that was Ryan's favorite time, very tranquil, very private, the thin cirrus of cigarette smoke hanging just below the ceiling. Yes, sometimes he would type in "Ryan Schuyler," just to see if anything came up; he would look at satellite photos of Council Bluffs, it was so sophisticated these days that you could see his house, you could see Stacey's car in the driveway, pulling out, on her way to work, he guessed.

He had even wondered what would happen if he contacted them, if he let them know he was alive after all. Would that be kind or cruel, he wondered. Would you really want the dead to come back to life again, after you'd spent so much energy trying to put the world back in order? He wasn't sure—didn't know who to ask—though he could imagine bringing the question up to Mr. Davis someday, when they knew each other better.

Mr. Davis wasn't a talkative person, but they would converse from time to time. He was an old military man, Mr. Davis. A true expatriate. He had grown up in Idaho, but had lived in Quito for thirty years now, and he didn't expect to ever return to America again. He didn't even think about it anymore, he said.

And Ryan had nodded.

He imagined there must be a point when you stopped being a

visitor. After the tourists had flown off, after the exchange students had stopped playing native, after the idea of "back home" had started to feel fictional.

How far away, the child he'd been to Stacey and Owen Schuyler. How distant, the gawky, eager boyfriend he'd been to Pixie, the roommate he'd been to Walcott, the son he'd been to Jay.

Was this any less real than the small, transient selves he'd discarded? Kasimir Czernewski, Matthew Blurton, Max Wimberley.

At a certain point, you must be able to slip loose. At a certain point, you found that you had been set free.

You could be anyone, he thought.

You could be anyone.

25

George Orson was losing his cool.

He'd wake up in the middle of the night with a thrashing cry, and then he would sit with his knees pulled up, with the bedside lamp on and the television going. "I'm having bad dreams again," he said, and Lucy sat there uncomfortably beside him as he emanated a long, barren silence.

It was their second day in Africa, holed up in a fifteenth-floor room at the Hotel Ivoire, and George Orson would go out and come back, go out and come back, and each time he returned, he looked more flushed and unnerved.

Meanwhile, Lucy had been sitting there in their room, high in the spire of a skyscraper hotel, bored and pretty freaked out herself, delicately un-taping currency from the pages of books, staring down at the stream of traffic on the highway below. Six lanes of cars, running the circumference of the Ébrié Lagoon—which was not the azure brochure blue she had expected, but just ordinary grayish water, not much different from Lake Erie. At least there were palm trees.

She heard him at the door, rattling the knob, muttering to himself, and when he finally burst in, he threw his key card onto the carpet, his teeth bared.

"Motherfucker," he said, and hurled his briefcase onto the bed. "God-fucking-damn it," he said, and Lucy stood there, holding a hundred-dollar bill, blinking at him, alarmed. She had never heard him swear before.

"What's wrong?" she said, and she watched as he stomped over to the minibar and yanked it open.

Empty.

"Fucking piece-of-shit hotel," he said. "This is supposed to be four stars?"

"What's wrong?" she said again, but he merely shook his head at her, irritably, passing his fingers across his scalp, his hair standing up in dry, grassy tufts.

"We're going to get new passports," he said. "We need to get rid of David and Brooke as quickly as possible."

"Fine with me," she said, and she watched as he went to the phone on the desk and lifted the receiver from its cradle with a flourish of controlled fury.

"*Allô, allô ?*" he said. He took a breath, and it was uncanny, she thought. His face actually seemed to change as he adopted his deep, exaggerated French accent. His eyelids drooped a bit, and his mouth turned down and he lifted his chin.

"*Service des chambres?*" he said. "*S'il vous plaît, je voudrais une bouteille de whiskey. Oui. Jameson, s'il vous plaît.*"

"George," she said—forgetting herself again, forgetting that he was "Dad." "Is there a problem?" she said, but he only held up one finger: *Hush.*

"*Oui,*" he said into the phone. "*Chambre quinze quarante-et-un,*" he said, and then, only after he had set the phone down, did he turn to look at her.

"What's going on?" she said. "Is there a problem?"

"I need a drink; that's the main problem," he said, and he sat down on the bed and took off his shoe. "But if you want to know the truth, I'm feeling just a touch worried, and I'd like to get us some new names. Tomorrow."

"Okay," she said. She set *Bleak House* down on the coffee table and discreetly put the hundred-dollar bill into the front pocket of her jeans. "But that doesn't answer my question. What's going on?"

"Everything's fine," he said, shortly. "I'm just being paranoid," he said, and dropped his other shoe onto the floor. One of those men's slip-on loafers, with leather tassels where the laces should be.

"I want you to go down to the salon downstairs tomorrow morning," he said. "See if they can make you a blonde. And get it cut," he said—and she imagined that there was just a slight edge of distaste in his voice. "Something sophisticated. They should be able to manage that."

Lucy put her hand to her hair. She hadn't yet undone her Brooke Fremden braids, though she hated them. Too childish, she'd said. "Am I supposed to be sixteen? Or eight?" she'd said, though ultimately she had let herself be talked into it, when George Orson insisted.

I never wanted this hair in the first place. That's what she wanted to remind him, but it probably didn't matter. He had taken his palm-size notebook from the pocket of his suit jacket, writing in his fussy, tiny block letters.

"So you'll get your hair done first thing in the morning," he was saying. "We'll get the pictures taken before noon, and we can hopefully have the new passports done for us by Wednesday morning. We'll move to a new hotel by Wednesday afternoon. It would be good if we could get out of the country as soon as possible. I'd like to be in Rome by Saturday, at the latest."

She nodded, staring down at the carpet, which was spotted with the indentations of small black cigarette burns. The remnant of an old piece of gum, worn as flat as a coin. Unremovable, apparently.

"Okay," she said, though now she was feeling nervous as well.

She had not been out of the hotel room without George Orson, and the idea of the hair salon was suddenly daunting. *I'm just being paranoid,* he'd said, but she was sure he was anxious for a good reason, even if he wouldn't admit it.

It would be scary, she thought, going out into the public areas of the hotel, all by herself.

Everyone was black, that was one thing. She would be conscious of being a white girl, she would be visible in a way that she wasn't used to, there would be no crowd to vanish into, and she thought of the times that she and her family had driven through the black parts of Youngstown, how it had felt like the people on the street, the people waiting at the bus stops, had lifted their eyes to stare. As if their old four-door sedan were trailing an aura of Caucasian-ness, as if it were lit with phosphorescence. She remembered how her mother would press the automatic lock buttons on the car door, testing and retesting them.

"This is a bad neighborhood, girls," their mother said, and Lucy had rolled her eyes. *How racist,* she thought, and made a point of lifting the lock on her own door.

This, of course, was different. It was Africa. It was a third world country, a place of coup attempts and armed uprisings and child soldiers, and she had read the State Department advisory: *Americans should avoid crowds and demonstrations, be aware of their surroundings, and use common sense to avoid situations and locations that could be dangerous. Given the strong anti-French sentiment, people of non-African appearance may be specifically targeted for violence.*

But she didn't want to be a coward, either, and so she simply stood, watching as George Orson took off his socks and massaged the ball of his bare foot with his thumb.

"Will they speak English?" she said at last, hesitantly. "At the hair salon? What if they don't speak English?"

And George Orson looked up at her sternly. "I'm sure they'll have someone there who speaks English," he said. "Besides which— Darling, you've had three years of high school French, which should be quite sufficient. Do you need me to write some phrases down for you?"

"No," Lucy said, and she shrugged. "No—I guess I'm . . . I'm fine," she said.

But George Orson exhaled irritably. "Listen," he said. "Lucy," he said, and she could tell that he was using her true name deliberately, to make a point. "You're not a kid. You're an adult. And you're a very smart person, I've always told you that. I saw that about Lucy right away; she was a remarkable young woman.

"And now," he said. "Now you just need to be a little more assertive. Are you going to spend the rest of your life waiting for someone to tell you what to do, every step of the way? I mean, Jesus Christ, Lucy! You go down to the lobby, you speak English, or you patch together some pidgin French, or you communicate through sign language, and I'll bet you can manage to get your hair done without someone holding your hand through the process."

He put up his arms and fell back onto the bed with a private sotto voce huff of frustration, as if there were an audience out there watching them, as if there were someone else he was commiserating with. *Can you believe I have to deal with this?*

She wished she could think of some icy, cutting retort.

But she couldn't think of anything. Speechless: to be talked to in this way, after all of his lies and evasions, after all that time she spent in the Lighthouse Motel, waiting patiently and faithfully, to hear now that she wasn't "assertive"?

"I need a drink," George Orson murmured moodily, and Lucy just stood there, gazing down at him. Then, at last, she turned back to her book, to *Bleak House,* sitting down as with a sweater she was knitting and slowly unfastening the taped bills, observing as the transparent adhesive pulled the letters off of the old pages.

So she would be assertive, she thought.

She was a world traveler, after all. In the past week, she had been to two continents—albeit only a few hours in Europe, in Brussels—but soon she would be living in Rome. She was going to be *cosmopolitan,* wasn't that what George Orson had told her, all those months ago, as they drove away from Pompey, Ohio? Wasn't that what she had dreamed of?

This was not exactly Monaco or the Bahamas or one of the Mexican resorts on the Riviera Maya she used to swoon over on the Internet. But he was right, she thought. It was an opportunity for her to be an adult.

So when he left that morning, promising that he'd be back before noon, she'd steeled herself.

She dressed in a black T-shirt and jeans, an outfit that, while not exactly mature, was at least neutral. She brushed out her hair, and found the tube of lipstick she'd bought back when they were driving cross-country in the Maserati. There it was, barely used, still in a zippered pocket of her purse.

She put five hundred dollars into her purse as well, and the rest of the money she wrapped in a dirty T-shirt at the bottom of the cheap, girly Brooke Fremden backpack George Orson had bought her back in Nebraska.

Okay, she thought. She was doing this.

And she boarded the elevator, coolly and confidently, and when a man entered on the next floor—a soldier, in camouflage and a blue beret, red epaulets on his shoulders—she kept her face entirely expressionless, as if she hadn't even noticed, as if she weren't aware that he was gazing at her with steadfast disapproval and there was a pistol holstered at his waist.

She rode down all the rest of the way, alone with him in silence, and when he held the elevator door and made a gentlemanly gesture—*ladies first*—she murmured *"Merci,"* and stepped into the lobby.

She was really doing this, she thought.

———

It took a long time to get her hair done, but it was actually easier than she'd thought. She was frightened when she first went into the salon, which was empty except for the two employees—a thin, haughty, Mediterranean-looking woman, who looked as if she were examining Lucy's T-shirt and jeans with revulsion; and an African woman who regarded her more mildly.

"*Excusez-moi,*" Lucy said, stiffly. "*Parlez-vous anglais?*"

She was aware of how clumsy she sounded, even though she enunciated as best she could. She remembered how, back in high school French, Mme Fournier would grimace with pity as Lucy tried to bumble her way through a conversational prompt. "Oh!" Mme Fournier would say. "*Ça fait mal aux oreilles!*"

But Lucy could say a simple phrase, couldn't she? It wasn't that hard, was it? She could make herself understood.

And it was okay. The African woman nodded at her politely. "Yes, mademoiselle," she said. "I speak English."

The woman was actually quite friendly. Though she tsked over the dye in Lucy's hair—"terrible," she murmured—she nevertheless believed she could do something with it. "I will do my best for you," she told Lucy.

The woman's name was Stephanie, and she was from Ghana, she said, though she had lived in Côte d'Ivoire for many years now. "Ghana is an English-speaking country. That is my native language," Stephanie said. "So it's pleasant to speak English sometimes. That's one characteristic with the Ivorians I don't understand. They turn to laugh at a foreigner who makes a mistake in French, so even when they know a little English, they refuse to speak. Why? Because they think the Anglophones will laugh at them in turn!" And she lowered her voice as she began to work her rubber-gloved fingers through Lucy's hair. "That is the problem with Zaina. My coworker. She has a good heart, but she is a Lebanese, and they are very proud. All the time, they are worried about their dignity."

"Yes," Lucy said, and she closed her eyes. How long it had been since she had talked to anyone besides George Orson! It had been—what?—months and months, and she almost hadn't realized until just now how lonely she had been. She'd never had many friends, she'd never particularly liked the company of other girls at her high school, but now, as Stephanie's fingernails drew soft lines across her scalp, she saw that this had been a mistake. She had been like Zaina—too proud, too concerned with her own dignity.

"I'm so happy to see that tourists are coming back to Abidjan," Stephanie was telling her. "After the war, after all the French fled, the other countries would all say, 'Do not travel to Côte d'Ivoire, it is too dangerous,' and it made me sad. Once, Abidjan was known as the Paris of West Africa. Did you know that? This hotel, if you could have seen it fifteen years ago, when I first came to this country! There was a casino. An ice-skating rink, the only one in West Africa! The hotel was a jewel, and then it began to fall into disrepair. Did you see that once there was a pool that surrounded the whole building, a beautiful pool, but now there is no water in it. For a while, I would come to work and there were so few guests that I imagined that I was in an old, empty castle, in some cold country.

"But things are getting better again," Stephanie said, and her voice was mild and hopeful. "Since the peace accord, we are returning to our old selves, and it makes me happy. To meet a young woman such as you in this hotel, that's a good sign. I will tell you a secret. I love the art of coiffure. And it is an art, I think. I feel that it is, and if you like what I do with your hair, you should tell your friends: 'Go to Abidjan, go to the Hotel Ivoire, visit Stephanie!' "

Later, when she tried to tell George Orson the story of Stephanie, she found it difficult to explain.

"You look remarkable," George Orson said. "That's a fantastic haircut," he said, and it was. The blond was surprisingly natural-looking, not the fluorescent peroxide color she had feared; it hung straight, cut blunt above her shoulder, with just a little wave to it.

But it was more than that, though she wasn't sure how to articulate it. That dreamy sense of transformation; the intense sisterly intimacy as Stephanie had leaned over her, serenely talking, telling her stories. It was what it must feel like to be hypnotized, she thought. Or like being baptized, maybe.

Not that she could say this to George Orson. It would be too overwrought, too extreme. And so she just shrugged, and showed him the clothes she'd bought at the boutique in the hotel mall.

A simple black dress with thin straps. A dark blue silk blouse, lower cut than she'd usually buy for herself, and white pants, and a colorful African-print scarf.

"I spent a lot of money," she said, but George Orson only smiled—that private, conspiratorial smile he used to give her when they first left Ohio, which she hadn't seen in a long time.

"As long as it's not more than three or four million," he said, and it was such a relief to hear him joke again that she laughed even though it wasn't very funny, and she posed flirtatiously, standing up against the bare off-white wall as he took her picture for the new passport.

He thought he could get them new passports within twenty-four hours.

He was drinking more, and it made her uncomfortable. More than likely he had been a drinker all along, sequestered in his study in the old house above the Lighthouse Motel, slipping heavily into bed beside her in the middle of the night, smelling of mouthwash and soap and cologne.

But this was different. Now that they were sharing a single room, she was more aware of it. She watched him as he sat at the narrow hotel room writing desk, scrutinizing the screen of his laptop, typing and surfing, typing and surfing, taking gulps from his tumbler. The bottle of Jameson whiskey he'd gotten from room service was almost empty, after only two days.

Meanwhile, she lay in bed, watching American movies that had been dubbed into French, or reading through *Marjorie Morningstar*, which had survived the removal of the taped bills better than *Bleak House* had.

They'd had a moment, when he'd seen her new haircut and clothes, a brief return to the couple she'd imagined they were, but it lasted only a few hours. Now he was distant again.

"George?" she said. And then when he didn't answer: "Dad . . . ?"

This made him wince.

Drunk.

"Poor Ryan," he said cryptically, and he lifted his glass to his lips, shaking his head. "I'm not going to screw up this time, Lucy," he said. "Trust me. I know what I'm doing."

Did she trust him?

Even now, after everything, did she believe that he knew what he was doing?

These were still difficult questions to answer, though it helped to know that she was carrying around a backpack that contained almost a hundred and fifty thousand dollars.

It helped that they were no longer in Nebraska, that she was no longer a virtual prisoner in the Lighthouse Motel. When he left the next morning on one of his errands, she was free to wander if she wished, she could ride the elevator down to the lobby of the hotel. She carried the backpack with her, strolling through the corridors and shopping boutiques in her new clothes, trying to think. Trying to imagine herself forward just a few days. Rome. 4.3 million dollars. A new name, a new life, maybe the one that she'd been expecting.

The hotel was a massive complex, but surprisingly quiet. She had expected the lobby to be crowded with people, like the throngs that had rushed along the terminals of the airports in Denver and New York and Brussels, but instead it was more like a museum.

She moved dreamily through a long lobby. Here on the wall was a stylized long-faced African mask—a gazelle, she guessed—with the horns curving down like a woman's hair. She saw two African women, in bright orange and green batik, strolling peaceably; and a hotel employee gently shepherding a bit of litter into his long-handled dustpan; and then she passed outside into an open-air promenade, with tropical gardens along one side, and graceful botanically shaped abstract statues, and a colorful obelisk, decorated with shapes and figures almost like a totem pole; and then the promenade opened up, and there was a cement bridge that led across turquoise pools to a small green island, from which you could look across the lagoon toward the skyscrapers of Abidjan.

Wondrous. She was standing on a path lined with globed street-lamps, under a cloudless sky, and this was probably the most surreal thing that had ever happened to her.

Who, back in Ohio, would have ever believed that Lucy Lattimore would one day be standing on a different continent, at the edge of such a beautiful hotel? In Africa. With an elegant haircut and expensive shoes and a light, fashionable white pleated dress, with the hem lightly moving in the breeze.

If only her mother could see her. Or that horrible, sneering Todd-zilla.

If only someone would come along to take her photograph.

At last, she turned and walked back through the gardens again, back toward the center of the hotel. She found her boutique, and bought another dress—emerald green, this time, batik-printed like the outfits of the women she'd seen in the hallway—and then with her shopping bag she found her way to a restaurant.

Le Pavillion was a long, simple room that opened into a patio, almost entirely empty. It was past lunchtime, she supposed, though there were still a few patrons lingering, and as the maître d' led her to her place, a trio of white men in flowered Hawaiian shirts looked up as she was led past.

"Beautiful girl," said one of them, bald, arching his eyebrows. "Hey, girl," he said. "I like you. I want to be your friend." And then he spoke to his cohorts in Russian or whatever, and they all laughed.

She ignored them. She wasn't going to let them ruin her afternoon, though they continued to talk raucously even as she held her menu up like a mask.

"I am good lover," called the one with spiked dyed orange hair. "Baby. We should meet us."

Assholes. She gazed at the words on the menu—which were, she realized, entirely in French.

When she came back to the room, George Orson was waiting for her.

"Where the fuck have you been?" he said as she opened the door.

Furious.

She stood there, with the backpack full of their money, and a tote bag from the boutique, and he winged a projectile at her—a little booklet, which she deflected with an upraised hand. It hit her palm, and bounced harmlessly to the floor.

"There's your new passport," he said bitterly, and she stared at him for a long time before she bent to pick it up.

"Where have you been?" he said as she stoically opened the passport and looked inside. Here was the photo he'd taken yesterday— with her brand-new hairdo—and a new name: Kelli Gavin, age twenty-four, of Easthampton, Massachusetts.

She didn't say anything.

"I thought you were ... kidnapped or something," George Orson said. "I was sitting here, thinking: *What am I going to do now?* Jesus, Lucy, I thought you left me here."

"I was having lunch," Lucy said. "I just went downstairs for a minute. I mean, weren't you just complaining that I wasn't assertive enough? I was just—"

He cleared his throat, and for a second she thought he might be about to cry. His hands were shaking, and he had a bleak look on his face.

"God!" he said. "Why do I always do this to myself? All I ever wanted was to have one person, just one person, and it's never right. It's never right."

Lucy stood there looking at him, her heart quickening, watching uncertainly as he lowered himself into a chair. "What are you talking about?" she said, and she supposed that she should speak to him gently, apologetically, soothingly. She should go over to him and hug him or kiss his forehead or stroke his hair. But instead she just regarded him as he hunched there like a moody thirteen-year-old boy. She tucked her new passport into her purse.

She was the one who should be frightened, after all. She was the one who ought to need comfort and reassurance. She was the one who had been tricked into falling in love with a person who wasn't even real.

"What are you talking about?" she said again. "Did you get the money?"

He peered down at his hands, which were still quivering, making spasms against his knees. He shook his head.

"We're having negotiating problems," George Orson said, and his voice was smaller, the mumbling agitated whisper he'd get when he woke up with his nightmares.

Not like George Orson at all.

"We may have to give up a much larger cut than I expected," he said. "Much larger. That's the problem, it's all corruption, everywhere you go in the world, that's the worst part of it—"

He lifted his head, and there was hardly a trace of the handsome, charming teacher she'd once known.

"I just want one person I can trust," he said, and his eyes rested on her accusingly, as if somehow *she* had betrayed *him*. As if *she* were the liar.

"Pack your bags," he said coldly. "We need to move to a new

hotel right away, and I've been sitting here for a fucking hour waiting for you. You're lucky I didn't leave."

As she waited down in the lobby, Lucy didn't know whether to be angry or hurt. Or frightened.

At least she had the backpack with their money. He wasn't likely to leave her without that, but still—the way he had talked to her, the way he had transformed in the last few days. Did she know him at all? Did she have any idea what he was really thinking?

Besides which, she couldn't stop thinking about what he had said about the money. *Negotiating problems,* he'd said. *We may have to give up a much larger cut.* Which upset her. She had been counting on that money, maybe even more than she had been counting on George Orson, and she found herself touching the lumps in her backpack, feeling through the canvas to the stacks of bills that she'd arranged beneath some folded Brooke Fremden T-shirts.

It was late afternoon, and people were arriving at the Hotel Ivoire at a greater pace than they had the day before. There were a number of Africans, some in suits, others in more traditional dress. A few soldiers, a pair of Arab men in embroidered kurtas, a Frenchwoman in sunglasses and a wide-brimmed hat, arguing on a cell phone. Liveried hotel agents were trailing along behind various guests.

She should not have come down to the lobby alone, though at the time it had felt like an act of defiant dignity. She had packed her bag angrily as George Orson spoke in rapid, incomprehensible French on the phone, and when she finished with her suitcase, she stood there, trying to piece together what he was saying—until he had glanced up sharply, covering the receiver with his palm.

"Go ahead on down to the lobby," he said. "I have to finish this phone call and I'll be down in five minutes, so don't wander off."

But now it had been more like fifteen minutes, and still he hadn't appeared.

Was it possible that he would ditch her?

She felt her backpack again, as if somehow the money might be spirited away, as if it weren't entirely solid—and she was tempted to unzip the backpack and double-check, just to be positive. Just to look at it.

She scoped again through the expanse of lobby, the cathedral ceilings and the chandelier and the long decorative boxes full of tropical plants. The Frenchwoman had lit a cigarette and stood gently tapping the toe of her high-heeled shoe. Lucy observed as the woman glanced at her watch, and after a hesitation Lucy walked over.

"Excusez-moi," she said, and made an attempt to imitate the accent that once upon a time Mme Fournier had tried to inculcate in her students. *"Quelle,"* Lucy said. *"Quelle . . . heure est-il?"*

The woman looked at her with a surprising benevolence. Their eyes met and the woman took the cell phone away from her ear as she examined Lucy, up and down, with a soft, motherly look. With pity, Lucy thought.

"It is three o'clock, my dear," the woman replied, in English, and she gave Lucy a questioning smile.

"Are you quite all right?" the woman asked, and Lucy nodded.

"Merci," Lucy said, thickly.

She had been waiting for him for almost a half hour now, and she turned and walked toward the elevators, her wheeled suitcase trailing crookedly behind her, the beautiful open-toed sandals she had bought for herself clicking against the glowing marble tile, the people seeming to part for her, the African and Middle Eastern and European faces regarding her with the same wary concern that the Frenchwoman had, the way people look at a young girl who has been a fool, a girl who knows at last that she has been cast aside. *You're lucky I didn't leave without you,* she thought, and when the elevator doors slid open with a deep musical chime, Lucy could feel the swell of panic inside her. The numbness in her fingers, the sense of insects crawling in her hair, a tightness in her throat.

No. He wouldn't abandon her, he wouldn't really abandon her, not after all of this, all the distance they had come together.

She was aware of the elevator beginning to rise, and it was as if the gravity were lifting up out of her body like a spirit, it was as if she could open up like a milkweed pod, a hundred floating seeds spilling out of her, floating off, irretrievable.

She thought of that moment when the policemen stood on their porch, her opening the door to their stony faces; that moment when she called the admissions office of Harvard, that sense of sundering, that sense of her future self, the molecules of her imagined life, unmoored, breaking into smaller and smaller pieces, scattering outward and outward and outward like the universe itself.

For a second, when the elevator came at last to the fifteenth floor, she thought that the doors were not going to open, and she pressed the button with the "open door" symbol on it. She pressed the button again and ran the heel of her hand along the creased line where the elevator doors were sealed together, her fingers shaking, "Oh," she was saying, "Oh," she was saying, until abruptly the doors parted, slid open, and she almost stumbled out into the hallway.

Later, she was glad that she didn't call out his name.

Her voice had left her, and she paused outside the elevator, just breathing, the air filling her lungs in soft, irregular hitches, and her hands scrabbled against the canvas of her backpack, feeling for the solid bundles of currency the way a person in a plunging airplane might clutch for their oxygen mask, and then when she felt the certainty of those stacks of bills, she fumbled in her new purse and found her passport, Kelli Gavin's passport. That was safe, too, and there was the confirmation number for her flight to Rome, and she . . . she . . .

The velocity of her fall seemed to slow.

Yes, this was what it felt like to lose yourself. Again. To let go of your future and let it rise up and up until finally you couldn't see it anymore, and you knew that you had to start over.

Later, she realized that she was lucky.

She was lucky, she supposed, that she was trying to be unobtrusive, trying to get a grip on herself, lucky that she'd stopped outside the elevator door to check her bag once again, lucky because that chill calm had swept down and clutched her in its talons.

Lucky that she didn't call attention to herself, because when she turned the corner, there was a man standing in front of the door to their hotel room.

Posted there, in the doorway of 1541, in the tower of the Hotel Ivoire.

Waiting for her? Or merely blocking George Orson's escape?

It was one of those Russian men she had seen in the restaurant, the one with the spiked orange hair, the one who had called to her: *I am good lover.*

He was standing with his back against the door, his arms folded, and she froze there at the edge of the corridor. She could see the gun, the revolver he was holding loosely, almost sleepily in his left hand.

He didn't look dangerous, exactly, though she knew he was. He would probably kill her if he saw her and made the connection, but he didn't look her way. It was as if she were invisible, and he was smiling to himself as if at a pleasant memory, gazing up at the ceiling, at the light fixture, where a white moth was circling. Mesmerized.

The other two men, she assumed, were in the room already, in the room with George Orson.

26

"We are on our way to the hospital," he told Ryan. "Listen to me, Son. You are not going to bleed to death." He kept repeating it and repeating it, long after Ryan had lapsed into unconsciousness again, just mumbling it to himself the way he used to tell himself stories in that attic room when he was a kid, he could remember that feeling, rocking back and forth and running through the same lines again and again until he'd finally put himself to sleep.

"I promise you are going to be all right," he said, as the head-lights illuminated the tangle of branches that overhung the long back roads. "I promise you are going to be all right. We are on our way to the hospital. I promise you are going to be all right."

Of course, he'd said the same thing to Rachel, back when they were in Inuvik, pretending to be scientists, and that hadn't turned out so well.

———

This time, though, he was able to keep his word.

Ryan was in the emergency room, and though there would no doubt be many hours of surgery and blood transfusions and so forth, it would almost certainly turn out okay.

It was nearly six in the morning, a Thursday morning in early May, still before sunrise, and he sat in the fluorescent-lit waiting area in a plastic chair next to the vending machines, still holding Ryan's blood-spattered hoodie, and Ryan's wallet, with the newest driver's license. Max Wimberley. He took the folded stash of currency from his jacket pocket and tucked a few hundreds into the sleeve of Ryan's billfold.

Jesus, he thought, and he put his face down into his palms for a while—not crying, not crying—before at last he found a scrap of paper and began to write a note.

It was probably for the best.

He was sitting in the parking lot, in an old Chrysler he'd found unlocked, and he was weeping a little now, distractedly, as he removed the ignition cover at the bottom of the steering column.

He had been a good father, he told himself. He and Ryan had made a nice life together while things lasted; they had been close in a way that was important, they had made a connection, a deep connection, and even though it had ended sooner—and more tragically—than he'd expected, he had been a better dad than the real Jay ever would have been.

Thinking of Jay, he felt a little twinge of—what?—not exactly regret. All that time they'd spent together, back before he went to Missouri, all that time, he'd done nothing but encourage Jay to contact his son. "It's important," he kept telling Jay. "Family is important; he ought to know who his real father is; he's living a lie otherwise," and Jay giving him that wry stoner stare he had, as if to say: *Are you joking?*

But the fact was, Jay could never bring himself to do it because he was lazy. Because he didn't want to expend the emotional energy, he didn't want to take on the responsibility of truly caring for another person, and that was the reason he wasn't a particularly good con man, either. Hayden had done his best to teach him, but ultimately Jay wasn't all that competent. He made so many errors, so many errors—God! Ryan was so much better suited to the ruin lifestyle than his father ever was—

But with Jay it was just mistake after mistake, even with a perfect avatar like Brandon Orson, even with everything all set up in Latvia and China and Côte d'Ivoire. And so when Jay hadn't returned from that ill-advised trip to Rēzekne, Hayden hadn't been surprised.

Though he had felt sorry that Jay's poor son would never know the truth, he had felt—what?—curious about that son, even during that period when he was living as Miles Spady, back at the University of Missouri, even when he and Rachel were stuck in that godforsaken research station, bickering and getting depressed, even then he'd find himself thinking about Jay Kozelek's long-lost son, and when things went wrong with Rachel and he finally got back to the U.S. and he was sitting in a motel room in North Dakota, he thought—

What if I contacted Jay's son, in his place? What if I did for Jay what he couldn't do for himself? Wouldn't that be a kind of favor, wouldn't that be an honor to his memory?

Well.

Well, as Miles would say.

He sat there in the emergency room parking lot, in the unlocked Chrysler, thinking of this, and then at last he bent down to examine the wires that ran into the steering wheel cylinder, sorting through the tangle of them until he found the red one. It was usually the red one that would provide the power, and the brown one that would handle the starter, and he hunched in the front seat, trying to concentrate. He wiped the back of his hand across his eyes again, and dried the wetness on the front of his shirt.

It would have had to end eventually, anyway. It was amazing he'd been able to convince Ryan in the first place, and certainly over time suspicions would have arisen, questions he wouldn't be able to answer. Probably Ryan would have eventually wanted to move on, maybe even reconnect with his parents, which was fine, which was natural, you couldn't expect these kinds of things to last forever.

Yes. He took out his pocket knife, and carefully stripped away the plastic casing around the wires. A very delicate procedure. You didn't want to get shocked; you didn't want to touch the live current.

He frowned, focusing his attention, and there was a tiny spark as the car shuddered awake. A new life.

"Could anything be more miraculous than an actual authentic ghost?"

He was traveling south down I-75, just past Flint, when this came to him.

A quotation.

He had come across it a long time ago, back in that terrible semester he'd spent at Yale. Thomas Carlyle, the nineteenth-century Scottish essayist, fierce and craggy and bearded, not even someone he'd particularly admired, but he'd memorized the passage anyway because it seemed so beautiful and true and so beyond the rest of the students in the class.

The English Johnson longed, all his life, to see a ghost, Carlyle had written. "But could not, though he went to Cock Lane, and thence to the church-vaults, and tapped on coffins. Foolish Doctor! Did he never, with the mind's eye as well as with the body's, look round him into that full tide of human Life he so loved; did he never so much as look into Himself? The good Doctor was a Ghost, as actual and authentic as heart could wish; well-nigh a million of Ghosts were travelling the streets by his side. Once more I say, sweep away the illusion of Time; compress the threescore years into three minutes; what else was he, what else are we? Are we not Spirits, shaped into a body, into an Appearance; and that fade away again into air and Invisibility?"

He was passing under a bridge, reciting this aloud, and he wasn't really crying though his eyes were leaking a little, the glare of headlights behind him and the glowing reflective circles of markers at the edge of the road and a green interstate sign that said

TO COLUMBUS FOLLOW

"Are we not all of us Spirits?"

He wondered what Miles would have to say about that idea.

He hadn't talked to Miles in a while now, not since the thing with Rachel had gone bad, not since that unfortunate trip to North Dakota, and he wondered. Maybe he could just write Miles a letter, maybe he could send Miles up to the final memorial he had made for himself on Banks Island. *Eadem mutata resurgo:* "Although changed, I shall arise the same." Which maybe Miles would understand. Maybe Miles could move on, Miles could transform himself, too. Live his own life.

Of course, he would have to get Miles up to Canada somehow, but with Miles that wasn't so very difficult. Poor Miles: so obsessive and determined.

He had been reading recently about something called "Vanishing Twin Syndrome," which Miles would surely be interested in. According to an article that he'd read, one in eight people start in life as a twin, but only one in seventy are actually born as twins. Most of the time, the vanishing twin spontaneously aborts, or it is absorbed by the other sibling, or the placenta, or the mother herself.

He was crying again as he passed from Michigan into Ohio, thinking of Ryan, he supposed, though he knew he shouldn't.

He had produced an unusually large harvest of lives, that was what he had been told—and he'd passed from death to death, over centuries, he'd passed from Cleveland to Los Angeles to Houston; from Rolla, Missouri, to Banks Island, NWT; from North Dakota to Michigan, and each time he'd been a different person.

His hands were shaking, and at last he had to pull over to a rest area, he had to curl up in the backseat without a blanket or a pillow, his palms tight against his skull, and outside, the rain had turned into sleet, ticking steadily against the surface of the stolen car.

What if he just settled into a new life and stayed there? Maybe that was the answer. He had failed as a father, and yet he had the soul of a teacher, he thought, and that idea appealed to him, made him calmer, the notion that he could still touch a young life in some way.

What if he became something ordinary, maybe just a simple high school teacher, he thought, and all the students would like him, and he would exert an influence that would extend beyond himself. He would live on through them. Maybe that was corny and stupid, but it didn't seem like such a bad plan for the present, and he pressed himself against the cold upholstery, squeezing his eyes shut hard.

He would never again think of Ryan, he promised himself.

He would never again think of Jay or Rachel.

He would never again think of Miles.

Are we not all of us Spirits? A voice whispered.

But he would never think of that again, either.

Acknowledgments

My wife, the writer Sheila Schwartz, died after a long battle with ovarian cancer shortly after I completed this book. We were married for twenty years. Sheila was my teacher when I was an undergraduate student, and we fell in love, and over the years that we were together, she was my mentor, my best critic, my dearest friend, my soul mate. I spent the last weeks of copyediting looking at the notes that Sheila had written on the manuscript, and it's impossible to express how grateful I am for her wise advice, and how terribly I will miss her.

I have been lucky to inherit a patient, thoughtful, and brilliant editor, Anika Streitfeld, who walked me through this book from conception to completion, and who has been an amazing, supportive, and wise presence throughout. I have also deeply appreciated the help and enthusiasm of the staff at Ballantine during my long tenure there, who have taken such good care of my books. I am grateful to Libby McGuire and Gina Centrello for their long-standing patience and goodwill.

Other people who are dear to me have contributed significantly during the process of writing: my wonderful agent, Noah Lukeman, who has always been a great supporter and friend; my best buddies, Tom Barbash and John Martin; my sons, Philip and Paul Chaon; my sister and brother, Sheri and Jed, who have been reading fragments of this for a long while and offering advice; my writing group, Eric Anderson, Erin Gadd, Steven Hayward, Cynthia Larson, Jason Mullin, and Lisa Srisuco; and all my students at Oberlin College who have, over the years, been an inspiration to me.

This book pays homage, and owes a great deal, to many fantastic and better writers who inspired me, both in childhood and beyond, including Robert Arthur, Robert Bloch, Ray Bradbury, Daphne du Maurier, John Fowles, Patricia Highsmith, Shirley Jackson, Stephen King, Ira Levin, C. S. Lewis, H. P. Lovecraft, Vladimir Nabokov, Joyce Carol Oates, Mary Shelley, Robert Louis Stevenson, Peter Straub, J.R.R. Tolkien, Thomas Tryon, and a number of others. One of the fun things about writing this book was making gestures and winks toward these writers that I've adored, and I hope that they—living and dead—will forgive my incursions.

Support during the writing of this book came in the form of grants from the Ohio Arts Council and the Oberlin College Research Grant Program. I am deeply thankful for their help.

AWAIT YOUR REPLY

DAN CHAON

A Reader's Guide

A Conversation with Dan Chaon

Random House Reader's Circle: How did you come up with the concept for *Await Your Reply*?

Dan Chaon: I actually didn't start out with a concept.

All of my work starts out in very small pieces. Usually I begin with an image or a scene, and in this case a few of the sequences were there from the beginning: the severed hand in the ice bucket, the lighthouse on the prairie, the man driving toward the midnight sun with the pine-tree air freshener turning in the wind of the defroster, the great pyramids standing on the plains of North Dakota in a blizzard, the hypnotist having a heart attack in the middle of a performance. They were like postcards that had been mailed to me by strangers.

I was aware that all of these weird images were part of the same world, but I had no idea how they were connected. I began to work on each of these moments in turn, creating scenes and characters and slowly beginning to expand outward, so that I was figuring out how the people got into these situations. Slowly I found that there were three basic narratives. I then had to figure out how they were connected.

A lot of my process relies on instinct and guesswork, especially in the beginning. I like puzzles, and for me a novel is like a jigsaw, the pieces of which you are creating as you go along, hoping that it will all fit together in the end. I have heard of some writers who work with an outline, but I don't. Nearly all of the surprises in the novel were actually surprises to me, the author, as well, which was exciting. Slowly I figured out why Jay and Ryan and Lucy and George Orson and Miles and Hayden all belonged in the same book, and that was a lot of fun, although nerve-racking too.

The thematic and plot connections emerged as I got deeper into the characters and their individual situations. I was lucky with this book that it all eventually seemed to come together.

RHRC: How much of the novel was inspired by the advent of the Internet in our daily lives, from online banking to social networking sites like Facebook?

DC: This was the first book I wrote primarily on the computer, rather than working out in longhand first. It was also the first time I'd written with an Internet browser directly at hand, and so I think it was a huge influence. There was a lot of Internet surfing that went on as I wrote. I looked at YouTube videos of Inuvik, Northwest Territories, and I had my tarot read by an online fortune-telling program so I could use some of those details, and I used MapQuest to plot out the routes my characters were taking across the country. Almost all of my research, such as it was, occurred on the World Wide Web.

With this being the case, I suppose it's no surprise that the Internet became a kind of character in the book. But it was difficult to manage, as well—so much technology had changed from the time that I began the book to the time it was finally finished, and I kept most of the specifics vague for that reason.

RHRC: You were adopted, and much of your fiction touches on that topic, either explicitly, as with your previous novel *You Remind Me of Me* and Ryan's narrative in *Await Your Reply,* or implicitly, with your thematic interests in identity and fate. Can you talk about this a little? Are there autobiographical seeds to this novel?

DC: I think there are autobiographic seeds to every novel. Otherwise, how could a writer relate to the characters and the situations? That being said, I've never been interested in writing memoir, even under the veil of fiction. The thing I love about short stories and novels is the wonderful freedom they give a writer to take some small experience and transform it, rethink it, unravel it. I suppose that, in that way, I'm a little like Hayden, and perhaps you shouldn't trust anything I tell you about my "real life."

But since you asked about adoption—I *do* think that aspect of my background has been very influential on my thinking. For the most part I am pro-adoption, but for better or worse it's definitely a form of identity theft, at least as it was practiced during the time I was born. My birth certificate has the names of my adoptive parents, and my original, "real" birth certificate is weirdly, permanently classified. When I apply for a passport, for example, the state of Nebraska must act as an intermediary for me—and in that way, I'm a little less real than a nonadopted person. The bureaucracy that surrounds closed adoptions has the effect of creating this secret, ghost life that I trail along behind me, even though I have actually met my biological parents. Nevertheless, I will go to my grave with no official right to this basic information about myself. It's just one of those odd things.

Maybe it was because I was adopted, but I thought a lot about alternate lives when I was growing up—although I suspect that it's a kind of thinking that every kid engages in. Why am I here, in this place, in this town, with this family? Do I really belong here? I was the first person in my family to go to college, and when I went to Northwestern on a Pell Grant with all these well-to-do, polished kids, I have to admit that I did a lot of confabulation. There was a great sense of cognitive dissonance for me, between the life I was leading at Northwestern and the life I had left behind.

Then, later, I fell in love with and married a woman who was my college teacher, twelve years older than me, and Jewish. (Back in Nebraska, I'd never met a Jew.) Well, that was another major transformation. I felt as if I'd entered a whole new life once again.

There's a particular passage from one of my stories, "Big Me," from *Among the Missing*, which I think applies here as well: "There are so many people we could become, and we leave such a trail of bodies through our teens and twenties that it's hard to tell which one is us. How many versions do we abandon over the years? How many end up nearly forgotten, mumbling and gasping for air in some tenement room of our consciousness?"

So, yeah. I may have a peculiar attachment to this concept, but I don't think it's unique to me. I suspect that most of us have that experience—that sense that we have become a different person, either by design or by accident.

RHRC: How did you organize the structure of the book, which is so complicated? Did you write it in the order that it's read?

DC: When I started out, I didn't have any idea how the three threads were connected. I just knew that they *were*—somehow.

The first hundred pages of the book took me about two years to write. I revised and revised again, fiddled around with the personalities of the characters, added and deleted subplots and minor characters—basically trying to frame out the farmland that I was going to be working with, cutting brush and taking rocks out of the soil and so forth.

The second hundred pages took about nine months. This was when I began to use cliff-hangers at the end of each chapter, leaving each thread with an unanswered question that I had to figure out, and that pushed things forward for me more quickly. At this point, I was showing the book chapter by chapter to my editor, Anika Streitfeld, and to my wife, the writer Sheila Schwartz. They would each give me a little feedback and I'd float various plot concepts—which Anika or Sheila, or both of them, would frequently and kindly shoot down or talk me through.

The last hundred pages was written in a little less than two months, but it really wasn't until the final few chapters that I truly had everything figured out. The last bit of plot clicked into place the way a difficult math problem sometimes does. Bing! Suddenly it seemed so obvious! And I remember emailing Anika at about four in the morning: "Does this sound crazy?"

I had to go back and do some adjusting and revising—but it was actually quite surprising to me to discover how much of the plot was already there, embedded in the narrative without my noticing. It didn't actually require a lot of rewriting.

My wife, Sheila, died of cancer not long after I'd finished the final revisions, and it's both difficult and comforting now to look at this book, since there is so much of her in it—chapter by chapter, her advice and thoughts and spirit. She wrote in pencil on the last page of the last chapter: "You did it, honey!" But really we did it together.

RHRC: In your acknowledgments, you write that *Await Your Reply* pays homage to various writers you've loved, from Ray Bradbury to Shirley Jackson to Stephen King, among others. What was the extent of your "gestures and winks" toward their works? Is this your own playful version of writerly identity theft?

DC: One of my early jobs when I was first out of undergrad was as a DJ. This was back in the late eighties, when the concepts of the "mash-up" and sampling were still in their infancy. But there was something about those concepts that I really, really liked—the way the songs seemed to be having a conversation with one another, and, by being combined, actually transformed into something new.

I'd like to think that there's some of that going on here, too. Many of the "samples" are tucked into the imagery, like Easter eggs: for example, readers of Lovecraft's *At the Mountains of Madness* and Poe's *Narrative of Arthur Gordon Pym* will recognize those birds that are circling Miles in the Arctic, with their cry of "tekeli-li!"; people who have seen Takashi Miike's movie *The Audition* will recognize that horrific piano wire in chapter 2; people who have read Shirley Jackson's *The Haunting of Hill House* will notice echoes of poor

Eleanor Vance's final thoughts, and—well, let's just say that there are a few dozen of these throughout the book, which some people might enjoy finding themselves.

But my intent wasn't merely to create a bunch of cute in-jokes, either. To a larger extent, I was using these little touchstones to draw forth a particular texture and mood. For me, it was almost an invocation, a séance. That Ouija board is in Jay's house for a reason!

As a writer, I feel like I'm always in conversation with the books that I've read. Occasionally, an interviewer will ask, "Who are you writing for? Who is your audience?" In many ways the answer is that I'm writing for those authors I've loved, and the books I've loved. If you're an avid reader, and a book gets under your skin, it can affect you as intensely as a real human relationship. It lingers with you for your whole life, and there is always this desire to re-experience that amazing sense of connection you get from "your" books. I understand completely why people want to write fan fiction. To me, I guess, all fiction is fan fiction at a certain level, just as it always has an element of identity theft.

RHRC: There are so many settings in the book, from the abandoned lighthouse motel in Nebraska, to the Las Vegas Strip, to the Northwest Territories of Canada, and so on. Was this an intentional impulse on your part, to set the book in so many disparate locations? How much of these settings is imagined? How did you manage to capture these places so vividly on the page?

DC: I started out my writing career thinking of myself as something of a regionalist writer, focused on the Great Plains area and with a particular attachment to the lives of working-class people. Recently, however, as my work has begun to reach a larger national and international audience, and as I've worked with translators and traveled abroad to literary festivals, I've been increasingly inspired to broaden the canvas of my worldview. I've been interested in finding ways in which I can expand and recontextualize my fictional world without losing the essential grounding that I find in the lives of ordinary midwestern Americans.

In *You Remind Me of Me*, the main character, Jonah, believes himself utterly alienated from the larger world: "He had no connection to the major world of human endeavor—no relationship to politics, or sociology, or economics, or the great movements of his time. The stuff that would be remembered. What could he say but that his people were the detritus of various empires." In contrast, *Await Your Reply* begins to imagine the ways in which even people like Jonah are connected to the larger world, and especially the ways in which globalism and the age of mass communication have begun to touch the lives of the marginalized characters that have been my particular interest over the past few books.

In any case, the geography of the book is a mixture of the real and the imagined. The lake is based on Nebraska's Lake McConaughy, where I used to vacation when I was a kid. Lake McConaughy really is drying up, and there really was a motel with a lighthouse theme in the area. The image of the lighthouse on the edge of an empty lake was one of the early inspirations.

A lot of the Cleveland locations are taken directly from my observations, as I have lived here now for more than twenty years. Matalov Novelties is, of course, invented, but Parnell's Pub is quite real. You can usually find me there on Monday night.

Some of the other locations were inspired by my travels. I wrote a good portion of that Las Vegas chapter (chapter 14) while staying at the Mandalay Bay Hotel as a guest of the University of Nevada, Las Vegas. And I wrote parts of chapter 24 when I was visiting Quito, Ecuador, with my son, Philip.

Still more of the places here are completely invented. I patched together my version of Inuvik from YouTube videos and travel brochures that were kindly sent to me by the town of Inuvik; similarly, I researched Abidjan via the Internet and through books I borrowed from my excellent public library.

And luckily, I'm a fiction writer. When I didn't know something—or when some geographic detail didn't quite fit with my plot—I just made it up.

RHRC: This is an incredibly (and delightfully) plot-driven novel, though it also maintains careful attention to prose and character. How did you strike that balance between spinning a good yarn and delving deeply within your protagonists' psyches?

DC: For me, prose and characters come first. Not because I'm an artiste or something, but because that's the way that I discover the world of the story.

I wish I could think about plot more deliberately, but I just find that I can't. It seems that for me as a writer, "plot" has to emerge once I've gotten a firm grip on the characters, and I have to actually spend some time with them before I know what they are going to do next.

In the case of this particular novel, I was very deep into the perspectives of the primary characters, and the plot developed as Lucy became suspicious of George Orson, as Ryan began to feel that he couldn't rely on Jay, as Miles fretted and fretted over the mysteries of Hayden. Those were the driving forces for me, and I honestly didn't know how things were going to turn out when I was writing.

Looking back, it seems that I must have known how things would come together from the beginning, but when I re-read my notes, there are all sorts of ridiculous possible plot points that I considered along the way. At one point, I had a grand conspiracy that involved the Catholic Church, Yale University's Skull and Bones, the investment banking industry, and past-life regression. Which obviously didn't work out. I'm really grateful that this seems like "a good yarn," but (I suppose I shouldn't admit this) I didn't know it was a good yarn until I was finished with the book.

RHRC: Aside from the criminal identity theft in the book, there are other shades of it, such as Miles and Hayden's dad's professional guises as clown and magician, and Ryan's mother, Stacey, saying that Jay "turned himself into a loser," as if our identities can be switched at will, depending on the situation. In this regard, the book feels both playful and very dark. Was this your intention, or did these themes come up on their own?

DC: Does a human life, a "personality," exist as a single thread that can be followed through time? Is the "me" of twenty years ago the same "me" that exists now? Will I still be "me" in twenty years?

I find myself drawn to these questions, and the more I think about them, the more they feel uncomfortable and difficult to answer. I've been reading a lot about the problem of memory, and I'm fascinated by the work of researchers like Elizabeth Loftus, which suggests that memory and our sense of our own life stories are more fictional than we'd like to believe.

None of this would bother me, of course, if I were a nihilist. I think that I keep turning back to this material because I'm romantic and naïve and I still want to believe that there is something we call a soul. To be a novelist, you have to believe in this, I guess. You have to hope that what we do on this earth matters, you have to believe that there is a true self, as opposed to a false self. But I don't accept those assumptions as a priori true. I feel like I'm always in a struggle to try to convince myself that the soul exists, that it counts in the scheme of things.

The quote from Thomas Carlyle that comes at the end of the book is actually something that I've often thought about since I first read it back in grad school twenty years ago: "Are we not Spirits, that are shaped into a body, into an Appearance? And that fade away again into air and Invisibility? . . . We start out of Nothingness, take figure, and are Apparitions; round us, as round the veriest spectre, is Eternity; and to Eternity minutes are as years and aeons."

336 | A Reader's Guide

I'm an American, and I have faith in the possibility of transformation, the do-it-yourself hope that you can become whoever you want to be, but there must be a little bit of the gloomy Scot still lingering in my blood. I find that it creeps into nearly everything that I write about.

I hope that the fates of the various characters—Ryan, Lucy, Miles—leave enough open to interpretation so that the reader can still come down on either side. I'd personally like to believe that at least one or two of them will be okay—that not all of them are lost souls.

RHRC: You've written one other novel, *You Remind Me of Me*, and two collections of short stories. How is writing a novel different from writing a short story? How is reading a story different from reading a novel?

DC: That's a hard question to answer, because it feels like the demands of an individual piece are different each time. I made one transition when I was writing *You Remind Me of Me*, my first novel, and when I started work on *Await Your Reply* I felt as if it required a new set of skills that I had to learn as I went along.

With both *You Remind Me of Me* and *Await Your Reply*, I think you can tell that I started out as a short story writer, and that my thinking as a writer is influenced by the short form. Both books are really focused on the chapter as a unit of construction, and as I was writing I tended to think of the individual chapters as self-contained entities. Also, both books use groups of characters whose stories eventually connect, rather than focus on a single narrative line.

But there's a different feeling that comes with working on a novel. I always say it's like the difference between dating and getting married. It's not just that you're committing to the characters and the subject matter for a much longer time, it's also that you've taken on a world that is both larger and more finite.

I know that sounds vague. But think about what happens when

you get married. You've made a choice—presumably a lifelong choice—and so your future is circumscribed in one way, but it also means that you can imagine it in more complex detail; you can begin to see the contours of the map more fully. Of course, it doesn't always work out the way that you'd like, but nevertheless the map is definitely more visible.

To put it another way: The novel, as a form, seems like it is about world-building. You are creating an atlas that your characters inhabit, and the expanse of the world is as important as the individual moments. With stories, on the other hand, the larger expanse of world isn't as important. They are all about moments in time. The world of the short story exists in a state of suspended animation. The future lives of their characters, more often than not, are shrouded. I would go so far as to say that in some ways, short stories are about the mystery of time—of the present moment, the unknowability of the future—while novels are about the attempt to encapsulate time.

A few readers have expressed frustration about the last Lucy chapter in *Await Your Reply*. They'd like to know what happens to her afterward, and I understand that desire, although I ultimately decided that I was happier ending with Lucy on the verge, at a crossroads—which, I think, is the urge of a short story writer rather than a novelist. Old habits are hard to break.

Questions and Topics for Discussion

1. The structure of this novel is unconventional and complex, and each storyline echoes, intertwines with, and plays off the others. How did the novel's nonlinear and fragmentary nature affect your understanding of the plot? How did its complicated, pixilated nature reflect the themes of identity?

2. Before they go looking for Hayden and Rachel, Lydia Barrie says to Miles, "What kind of person decides that they can throw everything away and—*reinvent* themselves? As if you could discard the parts of your life that you didn't want anymore" (page 197). What do you think is the appeal of reinvention for Ryan, Lucy, and Hayden? What motivates each character to shed their original selves? Do you think it's possible for people to "discard" unwanted aspects of themselves?

3. The novel continually circles around the notion of a soul, from Lucy's assuming that George Orson has one, "though she still didn't know the soul's real name" (page 223), to the Vladimir Nabokov epigraph at the beginning of part two: "The soul is but a manner of being . . . any soul may be yours, if you find and follow its undulations" (page 93). What do you make of these two conflicting ideas? In the world of the novel, where identities are constantly shifting and dissolving, do souls remain unscathed and whole? Why do we rely on this concept of the soul? How does it help us to understand ourselves and others?

4. During Ryan's tenure with Jay, he muses on how the identities he inhabits are like "shells . . . hollow skins that you stepped into and that began to solidify over time. . . . They began to

take on a life of their own, developed substance" (page 103). How do we see this come true in the novel? What makes the characters in the novel real or unreal? Is it true that "you could be anyone," as Ryan later tells himself (page 297)?

5. In chapter 10, the narrative addresses the reader: "You are aware of your life as a continuous thread, a dependable unfolding story that you tell yourself. . . . You are still you, after all, through all of these hours and days; you are still whole" (pages 88–89). Is this how you conceive of yourself? Has this book affected how you perceive yourself and your identity? How did you interpret this chapter?

6. While Miles never changes his identity, he does attempt to reinvent himself to some degree when he moves back to Cleveland. Why do you think Miles is unable to continue with this new, stable life? What propels his obsession with Hayden? Do you think, at the end of the novel, Miles is truly finished with his journey—has he accepted the "ending" Hayden has offered him?

7. Do you think anyone in the novel is able to connect with another person? Is there a real connection between Lucy and George Orson, for instance, despite his lack of a real identity? What about between Hayden and Miles? Ryan and Jay? Are authenticity and honesty requirements for human intimacy?

8. Dan Chaon once said, "I have always thought of myself as a kind of ghost-story/horror writer, though most of the time the supernatural never actually appears on stage." Does this ring true for *Await Your Reply*? The novel is billed as literary fiction with the suspense of a thriller and the echoes of horror and gothic fiction. Did you notice a playfulness with genre? If so, where? Did it remind you of anything you've read in the past?

9. *Eadem mutata resurgo:* "Although changed, I shall arise the same." This is the Latin phrase that Hayden includes in his memorial at Banks Island, and which he reflects on in the last chapter. What do you think this phrase ultimately says about Hayden and his actions?

10. At what point were you able to put these storylines together, to understand what had happened? How did your understanding of the events shift as you read further? Did you believe something early on that did or didn't come to fruition?

Hayden (first-person version)

I wake up along the side of the road where, in a ditch, there is a patch of mossy clover like a pillow. An old farmer drives by in a pickup and gives me a ride in it.

In the dream, my dead mother was calling me on the phone. It was all very normal and undreamlike. I was surprised because I hadn't heard her voice in years and years.

"I'm very concerned about you, Hayden," my mother said. "Have you been taking your medication?"

I said, "My God, Mom, I can't believe it! Are you really alive? How are you?"

"I'm fine," she said. Her voice was businesslike but not unkind. "I think the real question is, how are you? What are you doing to yourself? You're a mess."

"Well," I said. I was a bit taken aback. She sounded so judgmental, and all I wanted to do was talk. "It's complicated, really," I said. "I'm going through some changes."

"I know," she said.

"It's not as bad as it might sound," I said.

I was almost awake by that time, and I heard myself speaking the words aloud, and I opened my eyes and stared at the weeds and gravel near my face. I couldn't even recall what state I was in. It might have been Kansas.

I say to the old man, "Are the crops good in Kansas this year?" and he moves his fingers lightly along the curve of the pickup's giant steering wheel. He doesn't look at me.

"I wouldn't know," he says. "I've never been there."

"Ah." The rhythm of the tires over the dirt road made my eyes heavy again, in the old man's silence and the warmth and smell of the defroster. I felt my mind open and close like a camera shutter, my chin bumping my chest and then rising up again. I say, "Would you mind if I slept for a while? I'm real tired."

He says, "Go right ahead."

It would be nice to get back to that conversation I was having with my mom, but of course it never works that way. I close my eyes and put my balled hands against my belly. I always do this. I've tried to go to sleep in other positions, but I can't. I once had the thought that I must have had my fists curled up against my stomach when I was in the womb.

What happens when you start to dream? I've read a lot about the functions of the brain, but I find the theories hard to believe. Chemicals control it, they say. Little flashes of energy traveling from nerve to nerve, ultimately nothing more than dull test-tube physics, as if you could put electrodes into a potato and it would begin to have nightmares. But ultimately no one really believes that thoughts are chemicals, not even the neurologists and drug-peddling psychiatrists.

When I was a child, I used to imagine that thoughts floated out of us, like a web trailing behind a spider. I pictured feathery, invisible threads unraveling from our heads as we walked. A dream starts out as a thought and then it begins to loosen and finally drifts away, unmoored, floating upward like an angel. If you were in a room full of sleeping people, these things would fill the air like the downy seeds of cottonwood trees. I used to feel heavy with all the thoughts I tried to keep a hold of.

I can hear the low, warm vibration of the truck in my dream, and I am vaguely aware of the soft smell of exhaust fumes, which makes my head feel slightly larger, as if I am growing a cap. But I am not inside a truck.

In another life I might have once been some sort of small, heavy mammal, the kind with a thick pelt and short, nearly useless legs. You see these types of creatures sometimes in your yard late at night, when your mother and stepfather and brother are asleep and you step onto the back porch for a joint—opossums or raccoons, startled as the porch light comes on, their eyes glinting as they lope-jiggle-scurry into the bushes, like people on thorazine trying to escape a mental hospital. Their bodies are too slow and casual to express terror. They seem both comic and arrogant as they waddle into the shadows, but they are actually quite desperate. This is a part of the dream I'm having. For a while, on the medication, I was nothing but an animal and they could have kept me like that forever if I'd let them.

I had taken the precaution of shaving off my hair before I abandoned the car, which altered my appearance considerably. For a while I was sure that everyone would make the connection between my disappearance and the car that I stole from the parking lot of the mall. I don't know whether they did or not.

But in any case a few days later I was in another state, and I went into a bar. It was the type of bar I expected it to be: a local place, very rough, full of drunken workers. I might have once been nervous. But I was thinking of my idea when I walked into the dark and smoke. A television mounted up above the bar was showing *Entertainment Tonight,* and I felt my cheek twitch in the way it does sometimes, half of my face pulling up an involuntary smile, when I'm being looked at. It was a little crowded. Almost everyone was a man—laborers with thick boots and flannel shirts and hard, sad eyes. They were aware of me.

In retrospect, I wonder how I must have looked to them. The group of young toughs whom I approached seemed to draw back as

I came near to them, and one could see their confused, boyish earnestness beneath their loud talk and flushed, beery grins. I had to take it easy, I thought, coming toward them in the attitude of someone walking up to a stranger's dog.

"Hi, fellows," I said, and not one of them answered. So I simply plunged in. "I need to get my nose broken," I said. I reached in my pocket and withdrew a crumpled bill. "I'll give fifty dollars to whoever will help me out."

They looked at one another. There were four of them, probably all in their early to mid-twenties, house painters from the look of their clothes and skin. They all had shaggy hair flecked with white paint—a few strands here and there gummed together and stiff—and their hands and foreheads were freckled with it.

I smiled—gently and, I thought, sanely. "I realize it's a strange request," I said. "What if I made it a hundred dollars?"

"Are you some kind of fucking freak?" said one, a heavyset blond whose looks were somewhat reminiscent of those first-grade reader pictures of Dutch boys walking among windmills and tulips in wooden shoes. He glowered at me.

"Let's say four hundred dollars then," I said. "I can't go any higher than that."

Another, with a pocked face beneath a straggly beard, said, "Why don't you break your own dang nose?"

"I would," I said. "But I'm not sure how to go about it."

The five of us gathered in the alley behind the bar and I stood up against the wall with my jacket behind my head as a cushion. I had bought them several rounds of shots in addition to offering the four hundred dollars, but they were still doubtful. I hinted to them that I was being pursued by some criminals. The liquor, and my vagueness, seemed to fire their imaginations.

"Are you sure you want to do this, man?" said the bearded guy, who had wrapped his handkerchief around his knuckles.

I closed my eyes. "Yes," I said. I imagined I was asleep on an airplane, buoying above the rush of air and velocity. "Yes," I said. "Do it."

And I waited peacefully for what seemed like a very long time, so that I almost believed they'd left me and I almost opened my eyes when a fist connected. I was surprised—not by the pain, which I expected, but by the very vivid, lightninglike, glowing tree that branched through my brain at the moment of impact, and which still remained hovering in front of me when I opened my eyes—the way a ghostly circle of light will bob in front of you if you look at the sun. There was a great deal of blood, and the boy who had hit me kept saying, "Oh, man, oh, man, that hurt, Jesus!" and another one of them untucked his shirt, ripped off a piece, and gave it to me to stanch the blood.

This reminded me of a time after my dad died when my brother and I were trying to fly a kite in the park and a young man who had been watching us from a distance came over and explained that a kite needed to have a tail, which I had forgotten. We searched around for a while, looking along the edges of the field for a bit of rag, and after a minute or two the young guy said, "Oh, what the hell," and cut off a long strip from the bottom of his T-shirt—just like that—with a pocketknife. I recall feeling a little shocked. "You didn't have to do that," I said, but he just shrugged, and we knelt down, the three of us in the grass, to work on the kite. I remember being impressed because I honestly had never realized that if I wanted I could rip my shirt on purpose and there would be no repercussions. Maybe that's where the whole thing started. Later I dropped a glass on the floor for no reason except that there was a certain type of feeling; then another time it was a wooden kitchen chair that broke amazingly easily into pieces until I was holding nothing but two twigs and shaking them against the floor; and one night in the garage I went after the hood of my stepfather's car with a hammer, maybe five or six times, as hard as I could. I felt a little flushed, and I remember later that same night I stood over my mother and my stepfather as they slept in their bedroom, still holding my hammer, and I felt as if I had a message for them, something that I needed to tell them urgently, and then my mother rose up suddenly with a start.

The old man wakes me up when we get to the interstate and he lets me off at a truck stop.

"This is as far as I can take you," he says. He doesn't say anything else, but he looks at me for a long moment, and I touch the bandage on my face, smoothing the adhesive against my skin. I smile.

And though he doesn't smile back, though he doesn't look at me kindly or even curiously, I touch his hand—just for a moment. It strikes me suddenly that he has taken an unexplainable risk. My clothes are beginning to smell bad, and my nose is still swollen grotesquely. What would possess him to pick up a person such as me, I wonder; does he think of himself as taking a chance?

"Thank you," I say, and his eyes hold me, grim old eyes with a flicker behind them. Like me, he has had many lives.

"Take care," he says.

PHOTO: © PHILIP CHAON

DAN CHAON is the acclaimed author of *You Remind Me of Me,* which was named one of the best books of the year by *The Washington Post, Chicago Tribune, San Francisco Chronicle, The Christian Science Monitor,* and *Entertainment Weekly,* among other publications. Ballantine has also published two collections of his short stories: *Fitting Ends* and *Among the Missing,* which was a finalist for the 2001 National Book Award.

Chaon's work has appeared in many journals and anthologies including Best American Short Stories of 1996 and 2003, the Pushcart Prize 2000, 2002, and 2003, and the O. Henry Prize Stories, 2001. His fiction has been a finalist for the National Magazine Award in Fiction in 2002 and 2007. He was the recipient of the 2006 Academy Award in Literature from the American Academy of Arts and Letters.

Chaon lives in Cleveland Heights, Ohio, and teaches at Oberlin College.

Join the Random House Reader's Circle to enhance your book club or personal reading experience.

Our FREE monthly e-newsletter gives you:

• Sneak-peek excerpts from our newest titles

• Exclusive interviews with your favorite authors

• Special offers and promotions giving you access to advance copies of books, our free "Book Club Companion" quarterly magazine, and much more

• Fun ideas to spice up your book club meetings: creative activities, outings, and discussion topics

• Opportunities to invite an author to your next book club meeting

• Anecdotes and pearls of wisdom from other book group members . . . and the opportunity to share your own!

To sign up, visit our website at
www.randomhousereaderscircle.com

When you see this seal on the outside, there's a great book club read inside.